THE PRINCIPAL PROBLEM

A BLUE RIDGE NOVEL
BOOK 1

SIENNA MILLS

Cover Illustration: Chloe Quinn, Astound
Developmental Editor: Terri Rose, @editsbyterrirose

CONTENTS

DEDICATION

For anyone who thinks their past defines their future.
It doesn't.

CONTENT WARNING

To check content warnings for this book, scan the QR code below or visit www.siennamillsromance.com/content-warnings

CHAPTER 1

BRIE

BUZZ.

My eyes dart to my phone.

"Don't look at it," I chastise myself as I park my car in the near-empty lot.

Buzz.

My hand twitches.

Buzz.

I sigh and reach for my phone.

It's exactly what I knew it would be. The parents of Everett Academy are waking up and continuing the conversation where they left off, as if I can't see what they're saying about me.

As if I didn't create the damn group chat myself.

> Well I say good riddance to her.

Buzz.

> Teachers are a dime a dozen.

Buzz.

Never heard of anything so trashy.

Buzz buzz buzz.

"I'll show you *trashy*," I snarl, chucking my phone in the passenger seat before I can do something stupid. Like tell all those judgy parents to go to hell.

I remind myself Christopher had me fooled, too.

My phone buzzes again, but I squeeze my eyes shut and slump back in my seat.

With a full-body shake, I blow out a raspberry, forcing all the negativity out of my system. This is fine. Good, even.

I left all those busybodies behind, and this is a fresh start. Two states away.

My eyes skate over the mountains as the sun's rays bathe it in golden morning light. It makes me want to puke.

Buzz.

Unable to help myself, I reach for my phone.

She probably wasn't even qualified to teach. Got her job the old fashioned way. On her knees!

My face twists. "Gross!"

I mute the chat and slump back again.

All this nasty gossip behind my back—in front of my back?—should reassure me. It should tell me I was right to quit my prestigious private school job one day into the second semester. That driving here overnight was a great choice.

But it doesn't. I feel crazy. I'm nervous. And agitated.

It's entirely possible I am completely out of my mind.

"That's it." I scrub a hand down my face. "I'm out of my mind."

I up and *left* my entire *life* in order to, what? Be a *substitute teacher*? Back in *Blue Ridge*?

Even my internal monologue goes shrill at the name of my hometown.

When I left fourteen years ago, I thought it was for good. But I can't afford to go the rest of the school year without work, and apparently Blue Ridge is the only place in the universe that'll hire me. There's literally nowhere else to go.

And now that I'm here, I wonder what *these* people will say about me. I know all too well Blue Ridge is no safe haven, just as gossip-hungry as the parents of Everett Academy.

Especially when it comes to my family.

My stomach is in knots. What am I going to tell the principal here about why I left Everett Academy? I can just picture the news spreading like wildfire. *Did you hear? Brie Casey is back with her tail between her legs.*

Rubbing my palms into my eyes, I groan. Maybe it won't be so bad. Blue Ridge looked different as I drove through the sleepy streets to get here. Revitalized and shiny.

I open the visor to check myself in the mirror.

Greasy hair, circles under my eyes, and chapped lips. *Cool cool cool.*

But there's no way I can unearth my toiletries bag without being late. Not with the contents of my entire apartment stuffed into my car.

Turning off the car, I brace myself against the cold and march to the double doors.

My feet already know the way to the main office. So

much so that I barely pay attention as I trudge down the linoleum and cinderblock halls.

So much so that I *almost* don't register the nameplate outside the inner office as I knock on the open door.

No.

Every muscle in my body tightens. My heart plummets through the ground, into the depths of the earth—no—*hell*.

I really thought being back in Blue Ridge was the worst thing to happen to me.

But there he is, staring right at me, sitting behind the principal's desk like it's the Iron Throne.

Sawyer Strong.

The Prince of Blue Ridge, and the bane of my entire childhood.

I'm numb.

And he's even better looking than the last time I saw him fourteen years ago.

Sawyer was always big, the way high school jocks are, but now he's broad. Solid.

And those deep blue eyes bore straight into my skull.

His thick hair is styled back except for one careless strand that falls forward over his temple. His face is serious and familiar, but undeniably manly now with dense stubble that does nothing to hide his severe jawline.

This has to be a nightmare. Maybe I fell asleep on the drive down, crashed, and am blissfully in a hospital bed somewhere in Kentucky.

Please let me be in a coma.

I bite my lip hard enough to make it sting, like an idiot who watches too much TV.

Nope. Definitely conscious.

How did I not know Sawyer Strong was the principal?

I dart a quick, panicked glance behind me, toward the hallway.

This was a terrible idea.

I *feel* it when his gaze slowly drags down my body, and then back up, an inscrutable expression on his face.

When our eyes connect, my stomach does a flip. *Nerves.*

"Brie Queso." He says it quietly, almost to himself.

But I hear it as loud and clear as when he christened the nickname in first grade.

My nails dig into my palms as memories of *Who cut the cheese? Must have been Brie Queso* pierce their way into my mind.

It would be funny if it wasn't just one of a thousand examples of his incessant torture. For thirteen years—kindergarten through twelfth grade—Sawyer and his lackeys were the absolute worst. I don't count those few months senior year when he fooled me into believing he might have a heart. In the end, he proved he didn't.

His body tenses as he shoves to his feet. Judging by the way his jaw is clenched, he doesn't want me here either.

He rounds the desk, revealing navy slacks, a baby blue button up, and a patterned tie. I have to tilt my head back to meet his eyes. Leave it to Sawyer to keep growing past high school.

Suddenly, he's inches from me and the fine hairs on the back of my neck stand up. A shiver works its way through me before I remind myself I'm here for a *job*, and I swallow all the words I used to dream of screaming at him one day.

Of course, in those fantasies, he's hunched, balding, and has a beer belly. Also, crying.

He clears his throat. "Brie Casey." His voice, deep and throaty, scrapes all the way down my spine. "Didn't think I'd ever see you again."

I bet you didn't.

"Likewise, Principal Strong."

He frowns. "Don't be ridiculous. Call me Sawyer."

Being called *ridiculous* by Sawyer Strong makes my hackles rise. I'm off to a fantastic fucking start here in gorgeous Blue Ridge, Tennessee, where I've shown up homeless and my new boss is the reason I used to cry myself to sleep at night.

He offers me his hand. I clench my jaw and stare at it, waiting for the punch line. The *trick*.

Sawyer's eyebrows furrow at my hesitation. He watches me, waiting.

Be professional. Polite, and professional.

I slide my sweaty palm into his dry one. His eyes are too sharp. I pull my hand back and rub it on my pant leg.

He follows the movement, mouth tightening. "When the school board told me yesterday they'd found me a third grade sub, I didn't know it would be *you*."

Asshole.

I set my jaw. "Well, I'm here and ready to work." I can be polite and professional while also sending him a message: I'm not Sawyer's plaything. Today's Brie Casey has a backbone.

My remark is met by that familiar toothy grin—a smirk, really. An evil one that says he's ready to play.

Bring it on.

The corner of his mouth lifts, like he's amused by my new attitude. It doesn't matter that it makes my skin itch, I won't run and hide.

This isn't prom.

"Do you have a problem with that, *Principal* Strong?" I emphasize his title and give him a cloying smile.

The grin drops from his lips. He schools his face back into neutrality as he leans back against his desk.

He clears his throat. "It's unusual for us to have a long-term substitute. Can you tell me a little about your experience with third grade?"

I spit out the truth without thinking. "Kids this age are so open and vulnerable. What they learn now can shape them for the rest of their lives, which I know from personal —" I choke off the words when I remember exactly who I'm with.

Sawyer's eyes flare subtly. Does he remember tormenting me when we were both students at this school?

Sawyer was the universally-adored loudmouth who singled me out and made me question myself on a daily basis. No matter how much I tried to avoid him, he was always *there*.

Choosing the seat next to me on the first day of school to maximize his annoyance all year. Picking me to be on his team in PE just so he could justify throwing balls at my face. Heckling me any time it was my turn to speak in class.

I can't read his expression. My fists tighten as I wait him out.

After a moment, he says, "I saw you were working at Everett Academy for the last few years. Why the move mid-academic-year?"

There it is.

The question that makes me want to sink into the ground.

Parents in the group chat are probably rejoicing in my departure as we speak, and I don't believe for one second Sawyer Strong will see my side.

No, I can see it in his eyes. Sawyer just wants ammo

against me. Some *reason* to trigger Blue Ridge into running me out of town with pitch forks.

I can already picture them egging my car as I drive past, shouting "Shame!"

How the hell did I think coming back here was ever going to work?

My nerves prickle, but I force a polite smile because I *need* a semester's worth of paychecks to, you know, live. "It became clear a change would do me good."

Sweat beads on my upper lip as I meet his eyes, hoping he won't ask me anything else about why I quit. A drop rolls languidly between my breasts, and I resist the urge to squirm. My armpits are starting to feel a little ripe, but I stay still.

The minute draws out and I swear I hear the tick of every second from the clock on the wall.

Abruptly, Sawyer pushes off the desk and says, "We better get a move on it before the bell rings."

My shoulders drop and I visibly wilt in relief for a second before I catch myself and straighten up to follow him out of his office.

MY HEART HAMMERS in my chest as Sawyer leads me down the hall to my classroom for the next five months. At any second he could pick up right where he left off in his office and grill me about Everett Academy.

I wipe all the worry from my face. Sawyer is nothing if not astute, and he knew exactly what buttons to push when we were kids. If I was self-conscious about a haircut, Sawyer was loudly and insincerely complimenting me for it that day in the cafeteria.

If he picks up on *any* hint I don't want to discuss my past employment, he'll use that knowledge to ruin me.

So far though, Sawyer hasn't pulled the rug out from under me. He's playing the part of the consummate professional.

Probably he's biding his time. There's nothing stopping him from calling Everett Academy and asking for the story, then treating me like a hostile witness in a murder trial. Or worse, telling the entire town what a failure I turned out to be, to no one's surprise.

Maybe I'd be smart to get ahead of it, control the

narrative. Still, however he hears about it, I come off looking bad, and Christopher comes off looking sympathetic.

"Brie?!"

I jump a little as the familiar voice interrupts my thoughts. I whirl around, and my mouth drops open. This isn't how I want either of my sisters to see me—greasy, without a good explanation, and under Sawyer's thumb.

Mara, my little sister, is already striding toward me, an abandoned cart piled high with computers behind her. My heart squeezes as I look up at her heart-shaped face, swallowing the guilt that threatens to rise in my throat, along with the painful, urgent need to keep her safe. I haven't seen her in person in months.

"Brie! What are you doing here?" She tugs me into her and I breathe in her warm softness, a shock after dealing with Sawyer's attitude.

My eyes dart toward him, and I pull away from my sister. I don't want to lie to her, but I can't tell her the whole truth. I can't tell anyone. "Substituting."

"*Here?* For how long?" Mara raises her eyebrows, but not at me. At *Sawyer*. Her gaze is pointed, and Sawyer quickly looks away.

Before I can wonder about it, I focus my attention on her. "Just for the semester. What're you doing here?" Last time we spoke, she was still working her private cybersecurity job.

"I asked her to help secure the student laptops with age-appropriate apps," Sawyer says tersely, looking back at Mara with narrowed eyes.

Mara's lips curve into a smile, oddly playful in nature. "Yup. Ran into him last week. It was very . . . *therapeutic.*"

Now I *know* something's up. Again, I glance at Sawyer,

wondering what he's hiding. Does he have a secret too? A muscle ticks in his jaw.

"We'll let you get back to it, Mara," he huffs, something like warning in his voice. He grabs a computer off her cart. "I need to issue Brie a login before I show her to her classroom."

I stand there, looking between my sister and my enemy, wondering why a bully like Sawyer seems to be at Mara's mercy.

"Shall we?" Sawyer's clipped words are more order than suggestion.

He doesn't touch me, but his hand hovers over the small of my back, guiding me toward the computer lab. I jerk toward the room just to create more space between us, even if part of me wants to dig my heels in and elbow him in the ribs.

"I'll call you," I say over my shoulder to Mara.

"Kids'll be arriving soon," Sawyer snarls, close enough that his warm breath tickles my neck.

I stand awkwardly as he opens the computer and leans over it on a desk. As his long fingers move deftly over the keyboard, he brings me up to speed on day-to-day expectations for the third grade class. The muscles of his forearms, on display with his rolled-up sleeves, pop as he types. His eyes are focused on the screen, but his jaw is tight as he speaks, like he's barely tolerating my existence.

While he explains the different applications I have access to, a light pitter patter of feet down the hall begins, gradually turning into a stampede.

Then I hear a sweet little gasp outside the door. "Aunt Brie?"

Sawyer pauses his monologue as tiny arms wrap around my torso.

"Hey, Dizzy Lizzie!" I hug my niece back tightly as warmth oozes through my chest.

How did this girl even recognize me? I haven't seen her in person since last summer, when I joined her and my sisters for a Lake Michigan beach weekend. The love in her big green eyes, so similar to her mom's, fills me with a painful kind of affection.

"Aunt Mara told me to come here for a surprise! What're you doing here?" Her sweet little voice is filled with hope and wonder.

I don't look at Sawyer despite his heavy, impatient attention on me.

"I moved here," I say, keeping my tone light. "At least, for a little while."

"Why?" she asks in that overly-familiar way kids have.

Thinking fast, I scrunch my nose and say, "Too cold in Indianapolis, so I'm substituting for the third grade class!"

She frowns. "I wish I was in third grade already."

I boop her nose. "Next year, you will be."

Her face lights up. "Will you have dinner with us?"

My face freezes in a tight smile. "Probably!"

Heavy guilt sinks into my stomach. I didn't think any of this through, just drove all night like a maniac and showed up here.

She audibly gasps. "Will you *live* with us?! We can have dinner every night!"

"I'm not sure!" It comes out a tad shrill.

I wish Sawyer were anywhere else right now, but looking into Lizzie's big hopeful eyes is like a breath of fresh air.

Smoothing her hair, I say, "I have to talk to your mom, but I'm getting tacos with a friend tomorrow, so I don't know about dinner *every* night."

She nods like she's negotiating a business deal. "We can have dinner *most* nights."

With a deep inhalation, I say, "Let me talk to your mom first. Now go to class, I'll see you later. Love you." I give her one last squeeze.

"Love you!" She turns to Sawyer. I gape as he lifts his hand up just out of her reach, and she jumps up to slap it. "Bye, Principal Strong!"

"Later, Lizzie."

She runs out the door, giant mermaid backpack bouncing on her back. She smacks into a kid and screeches "Sorry!" before running at full speed again.

"She's klutzy like her aunt," I sing under my breath before I can filter myself.

When I glance over, Sawyer's face is tense and red climbs up his neck. Probably the effort to not insult me within earshot of a bunch of kids is causing his insides to melt.

As he bends to hover over the computer again, I notice the pattern on his tie for the first time as it dangles in front of him. Little rubber ducks.

What?

Shutting the laptop, he gestures for me to follow him out of the computer lab, and points in the direction we came from. "In case you forgot, the gym and cafeteria are back that way."

He leads me toward the junction where all the colorful hallways meet. Red for Pre-K through first, blue for second and third, and yellow for fourth and fifth. As we approach, I tense up, remembering what else is here.

Pointing, he says, "Of course, you recall the library."

"Yup. I remember."

CHAPTER 3

FIFTH GRADE

"YOU HAVE to put your sleeping bag next to mine," Dev said. His chest was puffed up, spine straighter than normal.

I guess I'd been walking with better posture, too. All the fifth graders probably were that Saturday afternoon. We all felt older, more mature. Like we were finally being taken seriously by the world.

Sleeping over at the school library was a rite of passage for anyone who lived in town from even before my mom was a fifth grader. I was three when Gia did it, and I still remembered how her and Mom's gleeful energy radiated throughout the house—getting Gia the new *Aladdin* sleeping bag, a fresh pair of pajamas that were so bright they could have been Lisa Frank, and even a fluffy pair of slippers.

Gia had protested when Mom came home with the bags of brand new goods, but Mom gave her a look that brokered no argument. This is exactly why she worked so hard mopping floors and scrubbing toilets, she'd told her. The fifth grade sleepover was an inauguration of sorts, and Gia was going to have everything for it.

It was a core memory of mine.

And now that it was my turn, I was thrumming with anticipation. Even if I did have Gia's ratty old sleeping bag. Her stained pajamas. Slippers that had worn through on the bottom in several spots.

None of that mattered, though. This made me feel closer to Mom than I had in a long time. Like if I could do this thing that had made her so alive with excitement before, it might feel like she were . . . simply alive again.

I shook away the thought. I wasn't a baby. I knew how death worked. She wasn't coming back, no matter how bad things were getting. In the years since Mom died, Dad had sunk lower and lower. I was old enough in fifth grade to be embarrassed by it, to understand that when adults whispered to one another as I passed them in town, they were talking about me. Old enough to notice the word *trash* was tossed around an awful lot when I was around the rich kids.

It wasn't until I was older that I realized Gia must have shielded Mara and me from the worst of it—taking us to the library after school, setting up playdates that I later suspected were babysitting gigs. Then, it would be my turn to shield Mara.

But in those moments, I was gleeful as my best friend Dev and I made our way to school.

Turning to Dev, I said, "You have to promise not to play any tricks on me."

Dev had a habit of hiding behind the dumpster on the corner of our bus stop and scaring the bejeezus out of me. I had to hand it to him, though—he never played tricks like that at school. He always had my back.

"I would never," he said. "But you have to promise not to snore."

"I don't snore!"

"Sure you do, I bet it sounds like this." His breath sawed in and out in loud, rumbling, old-man sounds, and we both doubled over in laughter.

Inside the school library, we were instructed to lay out our sleeping bags before heading to the cafeteria for an early dinner. Dev had a blanket he folded over in lieu of a bag, and I dutifully set out my *Aladdin* hand-me-down next to it as Dev headed across the library to peruse the books in the big kid section.

"Oh my god," I heard behind me, and froze. "Is that an *Aladdin* sleeping bag? What are you, three?"

I ignored the taunts and reached into my backpack with shaking hands to lay out my folded pajamas neatly inside the sleeping bag.

I'd already unfurled my thin pillow, trying to block out their snickering laughter. Just one thing was left. The stuffy I'd slept with as long as I could remember. The bulbous pink mouse Mom had given me as a baby for her Brie Cheese.

Squeakers was my ride or die, even as a fifth grader. Dev always gave her a pat on the head whenever he came over, accepting her like a third in our friendship. It never even occurred to me to leave her at home, not since that scary night when Dad threw everything that reminded him of Mom out onto the street.

But as I took Squeakers out, laying her lovingly on my pillow, the hushed whispers made my hands clammy. I knew right then, without a shadow of a doubt, pulling her out of my backpack had been a mistake. I wished Dev hadn't left me to go look at books while I set up my stuff alone.

"Wow." I recognized Ethan's voice behind me, exaggerating his volume because what he was about to say to his friends was really for my ears. "It makes total sense that Brie Queso's stuffy would be a rat. I mean, rats love cheese *and* trash."

The sounds of Sawyer's and Rich's cackling laughter followed. I still hadn't turned around. My blood had turned to ice in my veins. If I opened my mouth, I didn't know if I'd scream or cry. All I could do was wish I hadn't brought Squeakers with me, wish I could somehow turn back time or cast a spell to make this all okay. I was still at the age when wishing for magic was a logical response.

Someone made gnawing sounds behind me.

I *hated* them. Of all the kids in my class, they were the meanest. Sawyer was the leader since his dad was mayor. His friends lobbed cruel insults at me like it was a game, trying to gain favor with their king while Sawyer sat back and watched, amused by my suffering.

It made me so mad. On the nights it kept me up, I'd be so angry I'd end up punching my pillow, whisper-screaming all the things I'd wished I'd said back to them, but never would.

"You know what?" Rich said from behind me.

Anger took hold of me. I stood and spun around. They were still wearing their coats, backpacks slung over their shoulders.

"*What.*" I said, jaw jutting out.

Rich glanced at the adults at the far end of the library before turning to me, eyes gleaming with feigned concern. "Hey, no need to get so upset. All I was going to say is the rat looks hungry."

Ethan's eyes widened in understanding before he played along. "Yeah, he does. You must not be feeding him enough."

I wasn't about to tell Ethan he'd misgendered my

mouse, but that pissed me off almost the most. Maybe if I hadn't been distracted by it, I would have caught onto their plan earlier, been able to prevent it.

"You do it," Rich whispered, nudging Sawyer. "You won't get in trouble."

Ethan nodded fervidly. "Yeah, Sawyer, do it."

Without realizing it, we'd shifted. The three of them had circled around me, closer to the head of my sleeping bag than I was now.

Closer to Squeakers.

Sawyer's eyes narrowed with determination as he looked at me, then at the teachers, far away and focused on other students, then back at me. His quick and jerky movements reminded me of how a real rat would behave.

His hand closed on Squeakers, and my heart tightened. I still didn't know what was happening, what his plan was for her.

He hurried with her to the large trash can in the corner, glancing over his shoulder at me once. His back shielded his movements from anyone watching, and when he turned around, he wasn't holding Squeakers anymore. The snickers from his friends said it all. She was in the trash. Where she belonged. Just like me.

Part of me believed it. Everyone and their mother—literally—said as much.

A stinging sensation started at the back of my throat, spreading up to my eyes.

I will not cry, I thought to myself. *I'll rescue her when they walk away.*

The thought hadn't even settled in my mind when Sawyer unwrapped the garbage bag from around the can. All I could do was watch, frozen, as he tied off the end and started walking toward the main entrance of the library.

As Rich and Ethan followed, one of them jostled my shoulder and roused me. I stumbled forward, trying to catch up.

"Hi, Sawyer," the librarian said sweetly to her prince. "We have people to do that, you know."

"I know, ma'am," he said politely. "But something in here kind of stinks, so I thought I'd take it out to the dumpster myself before it ruined our night."

She looked at him like the sun rose and set on Sawyer, and let him go.

There was nothing I could do.

Sawyer could talk his way out of everything and anything. No adult ever distrusted him. He wielded power no one but his father and older brother had.

As I blinked back tears, I could feel Dev hurry to my side.

"What was in there?" He asked, smart enough to already know the gist of what happened.

The concern and love in his voice steeled me. "Squeakers." My voice held a lofty determination. I was going to get her back. I'd jump in that dumpster and find her myself, even if I was labeled the Trash Queen for the rest of my life.

He inhaled a sharp breath. He knew what Squeakers meant to me.

"You can't, Brie," he said, hurrying after me. "You'll get in trouble. You'll never hear the end of it."

I marched after Sawyer.

"Brie Casey." The librarian's voice was harsh with warning, and when I turned, her glare made my heart sink. I felt so small.

That's all it took. I turned and trudged back to Dev, tears in my eyes.

I cried myself to sleep every night for weeks after that.

Why couldn't I just ignore them? I kept asking myself.

I let them see how angry they made me. They saw how much Squeakers meant, so they pushed. If only I hid how important she was to me, nothing bad would've happened.

It was all my fault.

CHAPTER 4
SAWYER

AFTER DEPOSITING Brie at her classroom, I march back to my office on high alert. I don't know what the hell Brie's doing in my school, but seeing her again after all these years reignites all the savage instincts I thought I grew out of.

I've got to get a grip on myself.

CHAPTER 5

BRIE

MY BREATH FOGS out in front of me as I trudge out to my car.

It's been a long day. A long thirty-six hours. A long few months, really.

The kids in my class are all sweet, but I could tell their feelings are hurt. A teacher they loved basically ghosted them. I'm not complaining since that's why I have a job, but it's going to take some time for them to trust me.

That, along with the knowledge that Sawyer's my new boss, not to mention the fact I'm in Blue Ridge in the first place . . . basically my life is imploding.

Halfway to my car, a voice to my left says, "Brie Casey, is that you?"

I stop, turn, and take in the short, stout woman before me. She has a few more grays and a couple extra worry lines, but her eyes are still as sharp as a hawk's, and her lips just as permanently pursed as they were when she was terrorizing my class with irregular Spanish verbs.

"Señora Martinez?"

"No, it's Eva Longoria. Come here."

I'm a head taller than her, but before I can even process that she tells jokes now, my face is pressed tight against her chest.

Señora Martinez was one of the only adults who treated all her students the same, regardless of who our parents were or what neighborhood we lived in.

"I work in the front office now. I heard you're our new substitute." Her voice is laced with excitement, belying the stern expression she's always worn.

Delicately, I extricate myself from her arms.

"Yeah, that's me," I say, pulling my coat tighter around me.

She takes me by the shoulders and holds me out for inspection, like a piece of fruit at the grocery store. "You're thin."

I flutter my eyelashes. "Thank you."

"It wasn't a compliment. You look bad." She cups my chin, angling my head this way and that. "And you look like you didn't sleep last night." She doesn't give me the chance to tell her it's because I didn't. "No matter, I'm so glad you've come home." *Not home.* "And lucky for us because we need you. Is it true you can stay all semester?"

"Um . . ."

I don't know how to answer this question. I wouldn't have come down here without that assurance. But Sawyer didn't say anything about it, and I assume it's technically up to him, even if the district is who called me.

For the hundredth time, I think, *I need this job.*

Señora Martinez seems to have retained the ability to read people's minds because she leans forward and whispers, "That's a *yes.*"

Despite the cold, warmth blooms in my chest. "Yes."

"Good. Now get going, it's cold out here. See you

tomorrow." She winks before turning toward a luxury SUV and hoisting herself into the drivers seat.

I give her a wave as I head toward my car, a little surprised by the smile forming on my face.

As I reach for the door handle, lost in thought, a deep voice cuts through the chill.

"Brie!"

There goes that smile.

Sawyer hurries toward me, tie gone and the collar of his shirt open beneath his jacket, even though it's in the thirties.

I pause. *He's going to fire me. Tell me he'd rather be a teacher short than have me here.*

Give me self-esteem issues again.

Folding my arms over my chest, I wait for him to approach, my stomach knotting.

His long legs cross the distance in no time. As he stalks closer, I notice how brooding he looks, scowling down at me.

And it clicks something into place.

No, it pisses me the fuck off.

Yeah, I need this job. Yeah, Sawyer's my new boss. Yeah, I fled from one scandal right back to the hometown I swore up and down I'd never return to.

But I won't let Sawyer Strong fuck with me the way he used to.

I'm stronger than that.

"I wanted to check in with you before you left," he says. "How was your first day? Do you have any questions or need anything?"

Wait, what? This isn't what I expected, nor is it exactly a chase-after-me-in-the-freezing-parking-lot kind of conversation.

Don't let down your guard.

"My day went well," I answer with my *fuck off* smile.

His eyes sweep over the windows of my car, stuffed full of my belongings I'd thrown in the night before. I step to the side, blocking his view as I straighten my spine, daring him to say a word.

The corners of his mouth tilt down. "Do you want to talk about anything?"

The intensity in his eyes has my stomach fizzing like a bottle of champagne. My heart beats fast, and I don't understand it.

"Nope. I pretty much remember how the school works," I reply. "I was only a student here for six years."

His jaw relaxes and his throat works in a swallow. "Right."

He rubs the back of his neck, looking lost for a moment. He glances at the school, then back at me. Suddenly, his brows dip and he steps closer, stealing my breath.

"Is everything okay, Brie?" His voice is so deep, so low, so husky. When did his voice get so husky? I feel it between my legs. His voice is the *last* voice I want to feel between my legs.

I step back and raise my chin to look at him.

"Why are you really here?" His voice is quiet, like he's asking me a secret. Like I should trust him. Like he's my *friend.*

But I don't.

And he isn't.

All at once, I understand exactly what he's asking. The reason he followed me out here in the first place. He wants to know about my past, for me to fess up about Christopher and being pushed out of Everett Academy.

Sawyer Strong, the man, is crafty and patient in a way

the boy wasn't. I'd caught a glimpse of that our senior year. He knows how to play the long game.

I ought to remember that.

All the frustration, desperation, and anger I've swallowed down since yesterday rise to the surface. Without permission, my face screws up into what my little sister Mara calls my Angry Badger Face.

I push off my car and step into Sawyer's space, my chest brushing his. The sharp intake of breath tells me he wasn't expecting me to stand up for myself.

Surprise, mother fucker.

Pointing at the school, I say, "In there, I'll be polite and professional. Teacher-like. My only comfort is knowing you have to do the same. But school's out, and I don't have to answer any of your questions. I don't even have to talk to you. In fact—" I cut myself off and let my actions speak for themselves.

Spinning on my heel, I bump Sawyer out of my way with my hip, almost tipping over in the process, and get in my car.

As I pull out, any satisfaction I might have felt grows hollow when I glance at Sawyer in my mirror. He's still mostly stoic, but one side of his mouth ticks up, partway to his evil, playful smirk.

Like I played right into his hand.

THE SOUND of brad nails punching into the subfloor echoes off the vaulted ceiling. I don't waste time looking up at Will's progress as I grab another panel of plywood, taking care to lay it perfectly in place before picking up my nailgun and methodically driving nails around the perimeter.

I'm gonna beat him this ti—

"Done!" Will calls out from his side of the room.

"Shit!" I say, firing the last two nails and sitting back on my boots. I wipe my brow with my sleeve. "How are you so much better at this than I am? I'm bigger—"

He holds his thumb and index finger half an inch apart. "Only a little."

"Stronger—"

"Debatable."

"The better athlete—"

"Possibly." My brother smirks. "Brawn isn't everything, little brother. I'm smarter—"

I fold my arms over my chest. "False."

"The wiser strategist—"

"Definitely inaccurate." A huge part of being a SEAL was strategy, and I was damn good at it.

"And better looking—"

"Slander!"

He ignores me. "It follows that I'd be better at this manly stuff than you." He takes a look around. "Subfloor for the whole house is done now. Must feel good."

I follow his gaze.

"Would've taken me at least twice as long alone. Thanks, man."

I'm fortunate to have a brother like Will who likes me enough to help with manual labor. This cabin might be the first thing I'm really proud of. It's something I truly wanted, not to prove a point to anyone, but because I wanted it for myself.

Since snatching it up from old Mr. Collins last summer, I've devoted every spare moment to fixing it up. Compared to the open concept living space we finished a few weeks ago, this back area with the bedrooms is cake.

And spending this time with my older brother is a nice byproduct. We might always have the kind of relationship that thrives more on companionable silence than gushy feelings, but it's more than I expected when we were younger and nearly a decade's difference in age made a relationship with him seem impossible.

Will claps me on the shoulder. "That's what brothers are for. Even if it does get me on the old man's bad side," he adds.

Our dad tolerated it when I rented an apartment after the Navy, but he wasn't too happy when I bought the place way out here.

Strongs don't live east of town, he said.

He should have known by then I don't care about his rules.

"What's next for tomorrow?" Will asks. "Wanna get a head start on the underlayment, or work on plumbing?"

For no discernible reason, Brie's angry face in the parking lot this afternoon claws its way to the forefront of my mind for the thousandth time.

She'd clearly been running on no sleep. Judging by the stuff in her car, I'd bet good money she drove all night to come back home.

But why?

"Earth to Sawyer." By Will's tone, it's not the first time he's said it.

"Yeah?"

"What's on the agenda for tomorrow?"

I shove my hands in my pockets and clear my throat. "Night off tomorrow."

Will's eyebrows shoot up to his hairline.

"Rich is in town. Might see if he and Ethan wanna get some tacos."

Will's eyes flash in understanding, and he looks too sanctimonious for my taste. "This wouldn't have anything to do with Brie Casey being back in town would it?"

I don't take the bait. "I keep giving the guys the brushoff. It's no way to be a friend."

My brother folds his arms, waiting me out.

I keep my face neutral but ask, "How do you even know she's back?"

Will levels me with a bored expression. "You have to ask that when Luce works at your front office, and her sister works at mine?"

"Good point." Despite being her boss, hearing Señora Martinez referred to by her first name still unsettles me.

"So?" he prompts.

"What?" I busy myself with putting away my tools.

"The girl you tormented is back" —I suppress a sneer at the accurate characterization— "and you're suddenly interested in going out to a bar for the first time in years." He leans against a wall stud. "Aren't you supposed to be setting a *good* example, Principal Strong?"

"Alright, Mr. Mayor," I drawl. "Rich doesn't come back to Blue Ridge all that often these days, and it's been too long." This is actually true. Besides my buddy Jake, with whom I maintain a mostly text-based friendship, Rich is probably my best friend. "You wanna come out tomorrow or not?"

He pushes off the wall and walks across the room. "Nah, I'm too old for that shit. You shouldn't either. If you know what's good for you, you'll leave that girl alone." He opens the exterior door and stops to face me.

I brace myself for more.

"But if you do go, at least *look* like the principal you are and shave. You look like a bear."

CHAPTER 7

BRIE

"I'LL BE out of your hair for dinner tomorrow," I say as I load the dishwasher as my older sister, Gia, packs up the leftovers from dinner.

Mara and her new firefighter boyfriend, Tucker, are in the living room, playing a game with Lizzie.

Gia hums her acknowledgment. The thing about Gia is . . . I can't read her. She's my own sister, and I don't know what she's thinking, ever.

While I was working the school pick-up line this afternoon, she appeared out of nowhere, leaned up to kiss my cheek, and said, "A spare bedroom's ready for you. We eat at 5:30."

I was too stunned, too *baffled*, to even respond before she was driving away with a gaggle of kids in her bubblegum pink car.

Not that I'm complaining. I had no plan when I drove down here, and I could do worse. *Way* worse.

If someone told me that I'd one day be staying in a house in the neighborhood of Belmont, I'd assume it was because I was a live-in maid, *not* because my sister lives in a six-bedroom home with her daughter here.

Gia does data entry for a living, and Mara's pretty sure she doesn't get child support from her ex. No matter how curious I am, I won't ask her about it.

Dishes clink in the sink, and I bring myself back to the conversation. "We're meeting at a place called Jolly Jalapeño," I say.

"Is that how you pronounce it?" Gia asks, messy bun flopping to one side as she tilts her head. "I know it's a *J*, but in my head, I've been calling it Holly Jalapeño. You know, two *H* sounds. Alliteration and all."

Frowning, I say, "I have no idea. I only read it in a text."

I reach for my phone in my back pocket to check the text Dev sent me. A deluge of notifications from the group chat I muted earlier greets me, and I scan them from where I left off.

> Poor kiddo keeps asking what bad things her teacher did.

> Just say she fucked around and found out!!

> Life lesson, kids: don't be a slut LOL

Bile rises in my throat. My hands shake as I remove myself from the group chat—something I should've done yesterday—and shove my phone into my pocket again, glancing at Gia to make sure she hasn't noticed.

I rewind the conversation and try to keep my tone even. "How do you not know how the restaurant is pronounced?"

She shrugs. "I don't get out much. But they have great food. We order from there sometimes."

Even though I'm nodding, I can't get those messages from the Everett Academy parents out of my head. Dirty little secrets I'd never want anyone to know about, least of all Gia.

I couldn't stomach her disappointment in me if I told her why I'm here. That I'd been too flattered, too naive, too desperate to feel seen by someone like Christopher. That I'd mistaken attention for affection, mistook manipulation for intimacy.

Long story short, I dated the older, tenured teacher for five underwhelming weeks. *Five!* I believed him when he said he was separated, in the middle of divorcing his estranged wife. Instead, his very much in-the-picture wife was trying to patch things up with Christopher while he was taking me to dinners across town. And in a fun twist, it turns out she's one of the more powerful members of the Everett Academy school board.

I became the villain in a story I didn't want any part of, and in the months that followed, I was painted as a jezebel, some young hussy who seduced a good man and tried to destroy his marriage.

Rumors spread. Whispers that I'd done the same with other men in the community. Administrators, teachers, fathers.

Eventually, the board called a meeting. A witch hunt, really. With raised brows and tight smiles, they asked loaded questions, implying I was some kind of sexual opportunist.

The men at the meeting might as well have pinned a scarlet *A* onto my blouse.

I tried to defend myself, to explain I'd thought it was real, I didn't know the truth. That I hadn't set out to hurt anyone. But none of it mattered, their minds were made up.

He kept his job. I was labeled as unprofessional, dramatic, and unstable. A liability.

My contract at Everett Academy wouldn't be renewed.

And the worst part? Over the holidays, the rumors somehow compounded. Yesterday, the first day after break, parents greeted me with *How dare you*s and *You should be ashamed of yourself*s. Even my students snuck horrible notes on the whiteboard, in my lunch, on my chair.

It's why I was so desperate to leave.

Gia hands me the dutch oven to wash, and I clear my throat. "This was delicious, by the way. Thanks again for having me."

She pops a top onto the Tupperware. "Don't thank me, it'll get old fast. We're happy to have you, Lizzie was already complaining about you not eating with us tomorrow. I think she's secretly hoping you'll bring her with you."

I smile at that. "I'm not sure she'd want to come, it kind of sounds depressing. Tomorrow's Woeful Wednesday? Or, no, Wistful Wednesday."

"Never been," she says. "I think their most popular night of the week is Taco and Trivia Tursday."

"*Tur*sday?"

"Yeah. I've never been to that either. For obvious reasons."

My eyebrows shoot to my hairline, eager for this little nugget of information from my big sis. "What reasons?"

She stops what she's doing and turns to look at me, ticking the reasons off her fingers. "I have a kid. Anyone I loosely keep in touch with also has kids. I'd have to leave the house after 7pm. I'd have to get dressed" —she gestures to her sweats— "and, most compelling of all, they call it Taco *Tur*sday."

"None of those are good reasons," I say.

She hums her acknowledgment again, though this time it's laced with disagreement.

I won't let her off that easy. "Now you have a built-in babysitter." I point at myself with one hand as I tick my retorts off on the other. "Your friends can also get a babysitter, *or* you can make new, childless friends since it's one of, like, three bars here. Wearing actual clothes and leaving the house after 7pm is good for you sometimes. And 'Taco Tursday' is a hilarious name."

"Agree to disagree," she says flatly.

Through a yawn, I say, "Maybe I should have planned for next week." At this point, I've been awake for thirty-six hours, and I'm pretty sure I could sleep for a week straight.

"You could reschedule," she suggests.

"It's tempting, but I'm really excited to see Dev."

"Dev! You guys were the sweetest friends growing up."

"You could come," I say. "I'm sure Mara would babysit, and you can wear pants without a drawstring."

"No." She says it like it's its own sentence. After a beat, she adds, "Though I am mildly intrigued by the idea of a forty year old hanging out with kids in their early thirties. Ripe for comedy."

"Excuse me, first *you're* in your thirties. You aren't forty for another year. And second" —I stop what I'm doing now to look at her— "*kids?!*"

She grins, knowing she hit her mark.

"Ugh, you are so annoying," I say, though I'm grinning when she hands me the last pan to wash.

So Gia has a sense of humor.

She glances casually at me. "I saw Dev at Maddy's a few weeks ago. He's filled out prett-*y* nicely," she says. "And that *voice*. Hearing him talk is like swimming in the darkest molasses, silky and smooth."

I lift my eyebrows. "When did you get so poetic?"

She shrugs. "It's prose, not poetry."

"Okay, when'd you get so prosaic?"

"That's insulting."

Chuckling, I think about Dev again. Time and distance have reduced our friendship to the kind where we might not speak for months, then randomly text each other every day for a week. In fact, a meme popped up from him as I was getting gas outside Louisville early this morning. It felt like a lifeline, so I let it spill that I was on my way to Blue Ridge.

Tomorrow will be the first time we'll be in the same room in years. But growing up, I considered him my best friend. He never asked too many questions, and he was always smiling, always in a good mood.

And he was always good-looking. The selfies he's sent me over the years tell me Gia's right—he's only gotten better with age.

Suddenly, going out tomorrow night sounds much better than catching up on sleep.

THE NEXT DAY, when I walk into Jolly Jalapeño, I scan the place for my friends. I nearly talked myself out of coming, Will's warning echoing in my mind.

It doesn't help that I found myself wandering down the Blue Hall and stopping at Brie's classroom no fewer than eight times today.

On my last visit, her eyes met mine. She smiled at the class, gave them a quick task, and stepped out into the hallway.

Through gritted teeth, she said, "If you're going to micromanage me, do it already. You popping up every forty minutes is disruptive."

I nearly cracked a molar as I walked away. I didn't return for the rest of the day, which I take as a win. Even if the final bell rang fifteen minutes later.

Still, I already told Ethan and Rich I'd meet them, so here I am.

Jolly Jalapeño is a Korean-Mexican restaurant that's only a few years old, but it feels like it's been the heart of this town forever. Each weeknight features a different draw for the crowds, and it has a particular ambiance that would be tacky anywhere else.

A long, sunburnt orange bar takes up the back wall facing the front door. To my right is a short narrow stage beneath the large front window. All the rest of the available wall space is adorned with traditional Korean artwork and lined by booths.

The open space in the center is inelegantly furnished with mismatched plastic card tables and folding chairs, which were supposed to be temporary, but when the regulars got wind of the change there was small-town mayhem. People, apparently, love how easily they can be rearranged or moved out of the way.

So there they remain in their cheap plastic glory.

Colorful paper picado banners flutter from the ceiling, and string lights glow softly overhead, casting the acrylic cactus on the corner of the stage in a golden hue.

It's cheesy and perfect for this town.

The guys are late as usual. I roll up the sleeves of my flannel shirt, take a seat at the bar, order a beer, and question my life up til now. Fourteen years of being a functional, normal person. Then Brie Casey comes stumbling back to Blue Ridge, and I'm reduced to the same instincts I had when we were kids.

A firm hand cuffs my shoulder.

"Che ajab!"

"You cursing at me in Farsi again?" I ask Ethan. He looks like he just left a GQ photoshoot in slacks and a button-down.

He feigns offense as he takes a seat on my left. "I would never. Just saying it's a nice change to meet you out. I'm tired of Shane and James," he says, referring to his other two best friends.

"You texting Ethan and me wouldn't have anything to do with a certain someone being back in town, would it?" Rich takes the stool on my right.

I take it back, *Rich* looks like he came out of a GQ photoshoot in his expensive tailored suit.

My hand stops halfway to reaching for my beer. I want to ask how Rich of all people knows about Brie, but instead I tip my head up at the speakers where 90s grunge blares mournfully. "I came for the nostalgia."

"I hear Brie's working at the school," Ethan says. "Did she know you were the principal when she agreed to that?"

"How long are you in town?" I ask Rich, ignoring the question.

He rubs his hands together and grins over at Ethan. "No way she knew Sawyer'd be her boss."

Since when is everyone obsessed with Brie?

Sighing, I say, "She didn't know. The district does all the hires, even subs, so we were both surprised." Leave it to Blue Ridge to run schools differently than literally anywhere else.

Ethan's smile falters. "And when she found out?"

I take a sip of my beer. "She called me *Principal Strong*."

Rich grins. "Ice cold." He tilts his head at something past me and Ethan. "Dev's here."

I turn to look, and my pulse kicks up a notch when I spot him. That's confirmation enough Brie's on her way.

This was a bad idea.

Dev Shah was the only person Brie might have called a friend. She ate lunch with him, took the same electives as he did. I hardly ever saw one of them around town without the other.

The worst part is, Dev was a really nice guy. Even on

the occasions he'd push his way between us like her knight, I knew it.

And he's got one hell of a beard. I rub my own clean-shaven jaw, wondering why I listened to Will.

"Aaaand there she is," Rich says.

My body tenses instinctively.

I turn just in time to see Brie step into the restaurant, a look of uncertainty as she scans the booths. When she finally spots Dev at the far end of the bar, her face lights up.

I grimace.

He waves, and she runs to him, jumping into his open arms. He catches her, swinging her side to side as they hug.

Dev whispers something in her ear. They're too far away, and the bar's too loud, but I put every ounce of futile effort into hearing what they say.

Is Brie here for Dev? Have they been together all this time, long distance?

Nah. I would've heard. Right?

Rich whistles. "Not as bad as I expected."

Ethan shrugs, "Abbi and I were looking back at our yearbooks the other day. Brie was really pretty. How come we never noticed?"

Right. *We.*

"Don't pop your jaw," Rich says cheerfully, slapping me on the back.

"Thanks," I grit out.

Dev rubs Brie's back beneath her jacket.

Rich lowers his voice. "I don't think she's noticed we're here yet." He nudges me. "What're you gonna say to her?"

Ethan's tone is grave. "Don't you think we're too old for this shit? Time to leave her alone? I mean, hell, you're her boss now."

I hardly hear him, eyes still fixed on the longest hug in

history. Dev arches his back, taking her with him so that her feet dangle. Her giggle travels across the bar.

"Yeah, but they're not at work," Rich points out. "Besides, who's gonna believe her over Sawyer?"

"Woah there," Ethan says, peeling my fingers off the glass I've been clutching. Out of the corner of my eye, I can see him watching me, head tilted. "Ho-*ly* shit."

"What," I say, about ready to combust.

"Dev needs to take her to his car if he's going to keep that up," Rich says.

Ethan's gaze is still heavy on me as he tells Rich, "Dude, you're gonna want to shut your mouth."

"What?" Rich asks. "It's just Brie Queso."

Ethan shakes his head as he reaches for his beer. "Fine, but when Sawyer clocks you one, don't say I didn't warn you."

"Why would he?" Rich asks.

"You're an idiot," Ethan says. "No. We've both been idiots."

Finally, the hug ends and I tear my gaze away from the scene. "What are you two going on about?"

Rich shows me his palms. "Don't look at me, I'm as lost as you are."

Ethan says, "How long have you had a thing for Brie?"

I roll my eyes. "You're projecting, man. You've had hearts in your eyes since you and Abbi got together."

"Uh-uh," Ethan insists. "There's something there."

Rich looks between us. "Seriously? You've got a hard-on for Brie *Queso*?"

My teeth grind, wishing they'd both stop talking.

"Have some respect," Ethan says to Rich.

"*He* should have some *self*-respect," Rich bites back.

"This was a bad idea." I shove my drink away and move to stand.

Ethan puts his hand on my shoulder, keeping me in my seat. "We're sorry." He looks pointedly at Rich.

"Yeah. *Sorry*." Rich looks anything but.

"I shouldn't have brought it up," Ethan says. "You're right, I'm happy as hell and probably projecting. Don't go, stay and hang out."

"It's fine," I mutter. "I'll finish my beer."

Before I can stop myself, my eyes find her again just as Dev offers her a shot of something honey-colored. They clink glasses. Her wet tongue darts out from between her lips to lap at the salt on the back of her hand.

"So, how long have you wanted to get in her pants?" Rich asks, grinning.

I shoot him a sharp look. "You don't know what you're talking about."

How he hasn't grown an ounce since high school, I don't know. The man is literally one of the most important tech geniuses in the country—so much so that I don't know how he has the time to be here right now—but he has the emotional intelligence of a toddler.

Ethan says, "Dude, if you don't behave yourself, we're not letting you out anymore."

Rich frowns, but zips his lips, and Ethan changes the subject to some consulting he's doing for Rich's company.

My gaze flicks back to Brie. Her hand flattens against Dev's chest and stays there while she says something that, apparently, requires him to lean in. I count to twelve before they break apart.

"Dude, you look like a lovesick puppy," Rich snorts.

Ethan leans behind me and smacks him on the head.

"You don't have to talk about it," Ethan says patiently,

"but let me remind you that Abbi and I also have a storied past. She thought I was a player."

Rich shakes his head like he's clearing it before turning to Ethan. "Abbi always liked you. You were forbidden fruit, her best friends' older brother. Besides, Abbi was always chill. Brie is nauseating. And even if she weren't, she *hates* Sawyer. Always has."

I raise my eyes to the ceiling, willing it to collapse in on us.

"There's a fine line between love and hate," Ethan replies. "Both get the heart pumping the same."

"But Brie *seriously* hates Sawyer."

My gaze automatically moves past Ethan again.

She isn't there. I turn to look behind me. Brie *and* Dev are nowhere to be seen.

Thank fucking god and good riddance, I think as I will my pulse to calm down.

"You okay, man?" Rich asks.

"Just tired of hearing about Brie Casey." I drain the rest of my beer and stand up.

"You aren't leaving," he says. "I flew out from Silicon Valley for this."

It's like a punch to the gut, and I slump back on my stool. "Seriously?"

He tilts his head side to side. "Well, I might have had a meeting with Layla this morning."

Layla, Ethan's little sister, has a cybersecurity business. The same one Mara, Brie's little sister, works for.

And that explains how Rich knew about Brie.

"But I stayed 'cause of you," Rich hastens to add.

I shake my head. He might be a jackass on the surface, but the man's loyal.

"Let him go," Ethan says to Rich. "Dude needs some

time alone with his feelings."

I shoot Ethan a dirty look. He's turning into a bigger jackass than Rich.

"Alright, alright," Rich says. "I'll be back in a few weeks for another meeting." He points a stern finger at me. "And you better come out when I'm here."

I stand again, grateful to get out of here, and not sure why I came in the first place. "We'll do this for real when you're back in town."

We say our goodbyes, and I head toward the hallway that leads to the back entrance. When I round the corner, someone small barrels into me. I catch her by the hips, steadying her.

The faint smell of pear and citrus runs an electric shock through me.

I know that smell, know who it belongs to before my brain can process.

"*You!*" Brie says, looking furiously up at me.

Her hands press against my chest. For a moment I think she'll shove me, push me against the wall. Make me atone for my sins.

But she doesn't.

Before I can say something stupid, I let go of her hips and step back, breaking all contact. "I was just leaving."

Her jaw is set. "I don't have to talk to you." The anger in her voice is offset by the slight slur.

How many shots did she have?

"No, you don't," I agree.

She looks so much like she used to. Same full lips and high cheekbones. But her wavy brown hair is shorter, just brushing her shoulders. And her big brown eyes are different too. Furtive innocence replaced with fire and vinegar.

She looks like she wants a fight, and I'd happily be her punching bag.

Come at me, I silently dare.

As if hearing my thoughts, her chin tilts up, eyes blazing threateningly. "I don't have to answer any of your questions either."

For the first time all day, I want to laugh. "I didn't ask any." *But I've got plenty*.

"Because we're not in school," she continues, emphasizing each word with a sharp pointer finger to my sternum.

I shove my hands in my pockets. "But in school you'll be polite and professional," I echo her words from the parking lot.

My tone isn't meant to come out teasing, but I know it does when she makes the same face from yesterday afternoon, baring her teeth and narrowing her eyes.

It's cute.

"We're not in school now," she repeats.

She takes another minuscule step toward me, and my blood pressure rises. I want to tell her to stay back, that she's playing a dangerous game.

"So I don't have to be either of those things," she adds as she takes another step.

My body moves of its own accord, spinning us around, crowding her in the hallway, taunting her with our size difference.

"Fuck polite and professional," I say before I can choke back the words. "Those standards shouldn't apply to you."

Her mouth falls open as she stares up at me, like she's doing complicated math. Her chest rises and falls in a heavy rhythm. The pink in her cheeks is slight, probably from the drinks she's had.

But I want to turn her cheeks crimson.

Wait. My brain replays everything up to the present moment, finally catching up.

What the hell did I just say?

And to a substitute at my school.

To *Brie*.

I shut my eyes from the sight of her. She's always been able to burrow her way under my skin, infecting me like a bad rash, itching until I have no choice but to scratch.

But we aren't kids anymore.

For the first time, I realize how fucked up it is on a professional level that I'm even here, talking to her this way. She wants nothing to do with me, and I'm her *boss*.

She opens her mouth to respond, but I cut her off.

"Goodnight," I say, and shove through the back exit.

CHAPTER 9

TWELFTH GRADE
BRIE

I ALMOST ALWAYS WALKED home after working at The Square, the ancient diner located, *that's right*, on the town square.

As I was counting my tips, making sure I could cover the overdue electric bill, I kept glancing out the windows. Rain was coming down in sheets. The rumble of thunder was getting closer, occasional lightning splitting the sky as the night wore on.

Temperatures were hovering just above freezing—too warm for snow, but absolutely cold enough to dread walking home.

The streets were already flooded.

All shift, I hoped Gia would stop in near closing. Why anyone would choose to live in Blue Ridge after college was beyond me. Hell, if it weren't for Mara, I wouldn't live here *now*.

I wasn't complaining, though. Gia picked me up sometimes after I clocked out.

But tonight, when I turned the *Open* sign to *Closed*, my heart sank. I stood inside the door of the diner, peering out at the empty street. The pouring rain still hadn't let up. No Gia.

I steeled myself for the cold and did my best to pull my hood over my head.

Five months.

The familiar mantra was pavlovian at this point. Something doesn't go my way? Repeat the mantra.

Only five months until I graduated. Then I could be out of Blue Ridge forever.

I felt guilty leaving Mara behind, but Gia promised she'd have a two-bedroom by then. Mara wouldn't have to live with our dad, and I knew she already was doing alright at school because there was no Sawyer in her class. She'd be alright.

My feet were already soaked by the time I walked the half block to Main Street. A gust of wind blew my hood off, freezing rain pelting my face. I swiped the hair out of my eyes as lightning flashed over head, cracking so loud it rattled my jaw.

All I could do was walk a little faster, water squelching in my shoes as I squinted to see past the next street lamp.

Headlights appeared behind me, illuminating my miserable path. I braced myself for a splash of water from its tires, but it didn't come.

As the car slowed, a rock sank in the pit of my stomach.

Shit shit shit. Nothing good could come of a car slowing down for me in the middle of the night. I kept my head straight ahead.

"Hey!"

The word was almost drowned out by the rumbling thunder. I walked faster, but the car kept pace with me.

"Brie!"

My head snapped to my left at the familiar voice, deep and throaty. I squinted through my wet lashes.

Shit.

Sawyer.

Knowing it was him was both a comfort and a bane. Sure, I wasn't about to be murdered by the mayor's son, but that didn't mean he wasn't about to be cruel.

My body tensed as I faced forward again, navigating the freezing rain. That splash of water would probably come any second.

"It's a fucking downpour!" he shouted. "What the hell are you doing out there?"

"Thought I'd do a polar plunge," I yelled back without looking.

Five months.

"Very funny, get in!"

"Leave me alone, Sawyer." I couldn't begin to guess what he'd do if I actually did what he asked, but I wasn't about to find out.

"I'm serious, Brie."

"So am I. Go fuck yourself." Despite being soaked to the bone, that felt good.

"Get in the damn truck, Brie!" His voice held none of his usual haughtiness. It was a frustrated growl, and I relished it.

A fresh gust of wind blew a veritable ocean at my face. Icy water dripped down my neck and into my sweater.

The sound of his engine revving caught me by surprise, and for a split second, I thought maybe he *would* murder me, run me over right here. A moment later he was blocking half the sidewalk with his truck, cutting the engine, and storming out like a bull.

Sawyer strode through the rain and began walking next

to me, matching my pace step for step as I bypassed his truck.

"What the hell are you doing?" I demanded.

"If you won't let me drive you, I'm walking with you."

I turned to face him, not believing my luck. The stubborn son of a bitch. The spoiled brat. The absolute gall of him.

Sawyer wasn't used to being told no.

"And why would you do that?" I spat.

He heard me, I knew he did, but he didn't say anything.

"You're getting soaked," I informed him, speeding up.

"So are you," he countered.

Thunder boomed directly overhead. My scream didn't even register in my own ears as the thunder rolled on for seconds, heart galloping in my chest.

"Come on, it's miserable out here." He still had to shout to be heard, but his voice was softer.

More freezing rain trickled down the inside of my sweater.

I looked back at his truck just as lightning lit up the sky behind it. I could let him drive me for ten minutes, or I could walk through the storm for forty. And he really would walk with me the whole way, Sawyer was nothing if not tenacious.

"Fine," I hissed. "Let's get this over with."

A minute later, the car was on, and he was cranking the heat. The stark temperature difference had me shivering, teeth clacking together. He clicked a button, and delicious warmth began to emanate from beneath me like nothing I'd ever felt.

Of course he'd have buttery leather seats that heated your ass.

It was *heaven*.

It felt so good after being on my feet for hours and then trudging through the cold and rain even for just a few blocks, I moaned as I sank deeper into the seat.

Startled, I looked over to see if he'd heard.

He was watching me, face half-illuminated by the streetlight. His eyes were dark, but not in the mean way his friends always looked at me.

It was in that way I sometimes caught him looking at me when they weren't around. The way that made my stomach pinch.

I faced forward again, shivering despite the heat. We were still parked, and I watched as a crackling burst of light zigzagged down the sky, illuminating the truck for a brief moment.

"Here." He reached for my jacket, and I flinched away. With a huff of frustration, he snarled, "I'm just trying to help. Your jacket is soaked through, take it off."

He was right. This time when he reached over, I let him slip the sodden sleeves off my arms. After hanging it up on the back of his headrest, he turned to me.

Wet hair was stuck to my face, I was shaking from the cold. I must have looked like a pathetic stray dog.

Leaning over to reach for something behind my seat, he came back with his letterman jacket. With a stern look—a warning not to freak out—he gently draped it over my front.

Even though I didn't know where this version of Sawyer came from, I wanted to trust it. None of the usual alarm bells were ringing in my mind to stop it.

I pulled the jacket up over me, letting the collar cover the bottom of my face. I got a big whiff as I did so. Chlorine and boy smell.

It . . . didn't make me gag.

He was still watching me. "Fuck, you look awful."

I was used to his insults, but something about him uttering it in the quiet empty cab, without an audience, stung more than normal.

He turned his whole body toward me, one hand on the dash, the other on the back of my seat, and frowned down at me. "Why were you walking home in the rain at this time of night?"

I looked at him over the top of his jacket. Part of me wanted to tell him to fuck off again, that it was none of his business. But something stopped me. I was in his truck, after all, covered in his jacket.

If he could play nice, so could I.

I said, "I do it all the time," but it came out muffled.

Eyes still narrowed, the look in them shifted from frustration to amusement. The corner of his mouth lifted into a half-cocked smile.

He raised his hand and lowered the collar down, tucking it below my chin. "What was that?"

I ignored the backflip my stomach did. "I do it all the time. I work at The Square."

"You know, you could get sick walking home in weather like this."

I rolled my eyes without heat. It was exactly the kind of thing a privileged guy like Sawyer would say. As if I didn't know the risks I took.

"Don't have much choice," I muttered.

"What?"

"I don't have a rich daddy to buy me a truck," I snapped.

"So yours lets you walk home in the freezing rain?"

I snorted. "Haven't you heard? Daddy's probably got his head on the bar at AA right now." Altitude Adjustment, distastefully known as AA, was the dive bar on the outskirts of town Dad frequented to gamble and drink.

All the heat gone in my voice, I added, "I'll be lucky if I don't have to bail him out in the morning." Any shame I should have felt at the admission wasn't there. Maybe I was just too exhausted to feel it tonight.

He glanced at me, eyes disbelieving. "He makes you bail him out?"

I sniffed. "Gia won't do it anymore. Says he'll never change."

There was a comfort in speaking it out loud, even to Sawyer. Dev and I danced around the subject of my dad. Gia refused to talk about him. And I tried to protect Mara from as much of it as I could. That meant it was always bottled up.

Now that it was just *out there*, it was a small relief.

That is, until he looked at me, disgusted. "Shit, Brie."

I braced for the usual cutting remarks. Worse, probably, with the ammunition I just handed him.

Instead, almost as an afterthought, he put the truck into gear and started steering confidently through the torrents of rain. The storm didn't seem to bother him, but with the looks he kept sliding my way, I knew I sure did.

Well, the feeling was mutual.

Tonight didn't change anything: I hated Sawyer Strong.

I shivered. Straightening in my seat, I threaded my arms through the sleeves of his jacket.

"Five months," I murmured.

"What's that?" he asked.

Our eyes connected. His were guileless.

"Five months," I said. "Then I can get the hell out of Blue Ridge for good."

His jaw tightened. "Blue Ridge isn't that bad."

I couldn't help the loud scoff. "Yeah, I'm sure it's great for you, the Prince of Blue Ridge. But for me? It's a little different," I said, voice dripping in sarcasm. "Besides, the town'll be glad to be rid of *trash* like me."

A muscle ticked in his jaw as I used the word he'd used about me so many times.

Why was this getting to him?

As we approached the east side of town he said, "Where do I turn?"

I gulped. "Just drop me off at the next intersection."

Everyone knew I lived in Edgewood, but the Casey residence in particular was in bad disrepair, especially since I started working at the diner a few years ago and had less time to maintain it.

I couldn't imagine seeing it through Sawyer's eyes. Peeling paint, shutters half-rotted and barely hanging on, roof sagging in places. At least it was dark out.

Sawyer made a harsh sound in the back of his throat. "Yeah, right. I'm not leaving you on the side of the road around here."

I winced at the way he said *here*. He might as well have called my neighborhood Gomorrah.

"Where's your house?" It was an order.

I eyed the door handle. Could I pull off a tuck-and-roll?

Reading my mind, he locked the doors and sped up. "I'll just keep driving until you tell me. I'll go all night."

I crossed my arms and slumped in my seat. He *would* easily waste gas like that. Burn money without a thought.

The last thing I wanted was to be stuck with Sawyer longer than necessary.

"Take a right up ahead. Third house on the left."

A minute later, we were parked in front of my house. He bent, looking through the windshield and past the wipers scraping futilely at the rain.

He blinked. "This . . . is your house." His voice was

almost monotone, and his expression was equally blank. Almost like it was too much for him to process. He'd never fathomed anyone might live in a dumpshack like this.

I swallowed, even as I lifted my chin. "Yeah."

A boom of thunder struck, a comedic exclamation point on the tragedy that was my life.

When he didn't say anything else, I said, "Alright," and reached for the door handle.

"Wait!"

I turned to look at him, wary. But his expression was almost pained.

After a second's confusion, I wrenched out, "Thank you for the ride."

"Is your dad home?" he blurted.

My mouth opened and closed before answering. "I don't know yet."

"If your dad calls you tonight . . . to" —his throat bobbed on a swallow— "to bail him out. Will you call me? I'll pick you up, take you to the station."

My jaw dropped in a perfect imitation of a largemouth bass. "You're joking."

"No." He shook his head emphatically. "I want you to call me. Not just tonight. Any night. Whenever it happens, call me. Maybe I could even, I don't know, help."

"How?" I scoffed. "Get Mayor Daddy out of bed and beg him to handle it?"

I knew I wasn't being nice, that I was *trying* to make him mad so he'd drop the subject and leave. I was playing with fire. If I upset him too much, he might retaliate against me at school.

That didn't scare me, though.

Five months.

I could handle anything for five more months.

But when I met his eyes, he didn't look angry like I expected. His brow knitted, and he dipped his head.

"I know what you think of me, Brie, but I'm not like the others. My dad's the last person I'd go to for help. And I wouldn't tell anyone, I swear."

My heart started an incessant pounding against my ribcage. *I think he's being sincere.*

He reached for my hand and squeezed it. An electric current passed between us. Heat rushed through me, a sensation I'd only ever heard my peers giggle about. I didn't have the luxury of experiencing it myself. Crushes were for girls with free time. Girls who didn't have secrets to hide, a sister to keep safe.

But I couldn't help the way my breath stuttered when I saw his large hand wrapped around mine. There was something protective about it. It made me want to believe he *could* help if I just asked.

No.

I wouldn't let my first crush ever be *Sawyer*. Because he was nice to me *once*.

How pathetic could I get?

I pulled myself together and snatched my hand back like he'd burned it, bitterness swirling in me even as my stomach clenched.

"You are *exactly* like the others," I bit out. "In fact, you're the worst of them because they all look up to you. Even if you don't start it, you stand by while they treat me like the trash they think I am."

Swinging the door open, I hopped out and turned toward him one last time.

"Don't do me any more favors." I slammed the door shut and raced across the mud to my door, not feeling the rain.

I shoved my key into the lock and was inside my house

in half a second, heart thumping, listening for him to leave. My breaths were coming out fast as I leaned back against the front door, allowing my eyes to adjust to the darkness inside. The faint scent of old cigarettes and booze greeted me as always.

Finally, I heard his truck pulling off the curb and driving away.

He was gone.

For some reason, *that* hurt more than anything else.

I sucked in a breath and lifted my arm to brush the wet hair from my face. When I felt the soft leather on my cheek, a sob escaped.

My hand was still swallowed by the sleeve of his letterman jacket.

Lifting the lapel, I buried my face in it and took a big whiff, letting his scent envelop me and drive away the stale cigarette smell. Chlorine and Sawyer.

Suddenly, my chest felt too small, squeezing around itself.

I couldn't help feeling like something had been lost tonight.

Something that was almost in my grasp.

Then the tears came.

CHAPTER 10

BRIE

THE FOLLOWING WEEK, I can't stop agonizing over that night I ran into Sawyer at the bar. Every time I catch myself thinking about it, I sternly remind myself I don't care. Then my mind promptly replays the whole thing over again, bringing into focus a new detail.

Like the way the sleeves of his flannel, a surprising choice for him, were rolled up to reveal strong forearms. Or the way his firm hands caught me by the hips when I bounced into him. Or the way he smelled liked chlorine and toasty beer.

Why did I even notice those details?

Now, I watch Sawyer run his hand casually through his hair as he stands on the gym floor in his form-fitting slacks and button-down, waiting for kids to clamber over one another for the perfect seat on the bleachers.

His tie looks like one long hotdog with mustard on it.

I sit at the end of the row of teachers for the school-wide assembly. When all the kids have settled down, Sawyer turns on the microphone to greet everyone. His voice is deep and even, but that night at the bar, it was deeper. Raspier. Like tires crunching over gravel.

Fuck polite and professional. Those standards shouldn't apply to you.

What does that even mean? If it's an insult, I've heard better. Or, worse?

Immediately after Sawyer said those words and left, I found Dev in the corner booth and got absolutely plastered, barely tasting my food and desperately trying to forget I'm stuck in this town for the next five months and *Sawyer Strong* is my boss.

It didn't work.

"We haven't met yet," whispers the young woman next to me. "Are you the third grade sub?"

I glance at her as Sawyer's voice continues to blare out. She looks as though she stepped out of a fairytale. A perfectly curved blond ponytail, large blue eyes, and a matching blue dress that fans out over her folding chair. And she's tall. Even sitting, she towers over me.

With a tight smile, I whisper, "Yeah, Brie Casey," and turn pointedly forward again.

Sawyer's clothes are borderline obscene, stretching over his muscles as he paces in front of the students and gestures to keep them engaged.

Fuck polite and professional. Those standards shouldn't apply to you.

I give my head a discreet shake. All Sawyer's doing is trying to get into my head. Be confusing on purpose.

This is what he *does*.

Just like after that night he picked me up in the rain senior year.

"Oh my gosh!" The teacher beside me reaches for my

hand and clasps it tight, clearly in response to something Sawyer said. "He didn't!"

I focus on his words just in time, delicately trying to extricate my hand from this stranger's death grip.

"That's right." The corner of his mouth twitches as he waits for something to dawn on his audience.

You could hear a butterfly's wings flutter in the silence. Even the youngest kids are holding their breaths, eyes huge and unblinking, eager anticipation written on their faces.

Sawyer continues, "The BRES Jamboree *will* have a petting zoo this year!"

Everyone in the gym loses their fucking mind. The smallest kids are screeching at the tops of their lungs, the older kids are hugging one another, and even the teachers are whooping and hollering.

Clapping maniacally, the Disney princess next to me leans over and says, "Sawyer's been working on this for *months*! He personally met with business owners and farmers around town to help fund it and pull it all together."

"Really?" My incredulity tumbles out as I turn my attention back to Sawyer.

He watches the gleeful kids patiently. There still isn't a smile on his face, but there's a tint of pink on his cheeks that wasn't there before, visible only because he's clean-shaven today.

Like he was that night at the bar.

I've barely seen him since then. I keep expecting him to show up at my classroom like he did my first couple days of working here, to micromanage me or embarrass me in front of the students or *something*. But he hasn't. It's been radio silence. He's kept his distance.

Just like I want.

"Ms. Casey," Sawyer's voice booms out, startling me.

"Ooh," the princess coos. "That's you!"

"I'm sure many of you have seen her around the halls by now," he continues. "We want her to stay here at BRES, so let's make sure she feels welcome by all of us."

The kids all clap politely. I catch Lizzie, beaming in the third row, and return the smile with a little wave.

From next to me, the blond claps with more enthusiasm than a cheerleader on her third latte. "Yay!"

After Sawyer gives his closing reminders and dismisses everyone, I hold my finger up to my class, indicating they need to wait patiently before we can leave.

I was locked out of the computer this morning and, though I'm loathe to do so, I need to ask Sawyer about it.

My new best friend is chatting my ear off while I wait. "PreK nap overlaps with third grade lunch. Want to meet in the teachers' lounge? My teacher's aide handles nap so I usually eat my lunch at that time anyway, so it's perfect. Can you believe our official lunchtime is 10:15? *In the morning?*"

I hold my hand up, signaling for her to stop, and give her a polite smile. "What's your name again?"

"Tess!"

"It's really nice to meet you—"

"Milo," she trills serenely as she shuffles toward a little red-haired boy, "hands are not for hitting!" She smiles over her shoulder at me and says, "See you at lunch!" before chasing her class out the gym.

That's one way to make plans.

One lunch won't kill me, I decide. Besides, I get the feeling Tess will do most of the talking.

I turn, scanning the gym for Sawyer. For a moment, I think I missed him, that he's already left. But then I see him down on one knee in front of a little boy, a kindergartener by my guess.

Edging closer, I hear him tell Sawyer why he plans to bring his stuffed giraffe to show-and-tell instead of his pet cat.

Sawyer gives the boy his undivided attention. His face is serious and he's nodding along like there's nothing more important to him as the boy stumbles through his reasons.

Watching the exchange does funny, annoying things to my insides.

Mercifully, an older teacher calls to the boy. He runs off, comes to a squeaky stop on the gym floor, then runs back for a jumping high-five with Sawyer before running toward his teacher again.

Sawyer stands, planting his hands on his hips as he surveys the students filing out the doors. His eyes land on me as I step toward him. A flash of surprise and something I can't read crosses his face.

Then, like turning the page of a book, his expression turns bland.

"Can I help you, Ms. Casey?"

I hesitate at his curt tone. It's not just professional, but cold.

Swallowing, I say, "I think the login you gave me for the computer expired. I'm locked out."

He looks up at the ceiling. "And that's why I usually stay away from the computers." His gaze lands on me for a nanosecond before darting away again. "I'll send Señora Martinez to your classroom."

Before I can say *thanks* he turns on his heel and leaves me in the middle of the gym to pick my jaw up off the floor.

Sure, I might have said something about being polite

and professional at school, but I never said anything about treating me like a complete stranger.

A burst of anger surges through me as I remind myself *again* that this is what he does. It's psychological warfare. He intentionally tries to mess with my head. Even after fourteen years, he's still the same person. He's still the mayor's son who blithely walks all over everyone else.

But I'm not that girl from the wrong side of town anymore, no matter what he or the rest of Blue Ridge thinks.

My phone buzzes in my pocket, and I take a quick peek before turning to my class. It's from Dev. I've been so embarrassed about how drunk I got that night, all I've texted him since then is cat memes.

> Still wanna come on that date to
> Angelica's? It's happening this Saturday.

A date. With *Dev*.

I take in a sharp breath and motion for my class to follow me out of the gym.

Dev couldn't be more different from Sawyer. With Dev, I know exactly what to expect. Easy. Reliable. Friendly.

The way he worded the message was a little weird, but that's Dev. Not concerned by much, and definitely not the kind of person who reads over his texts before hitting *send*.

I grin. Of course I want to grab dinner. Of course I want to go on a *date*.

Dev and I get along so well—always have. He doesn't ask a lot of questions, and neither do I. Our friendship has always rested on a firm respect for boundaries. An escapist friendship, in a way. He knew I wouldn't ask him about his parents' expectations or school. I knew he wouldn't ask about my dad or money.

We could be great together.

That's the dream, isn't it? To be married to your best friend?

And Gia was right, he went from a lanky kid with too-big facial features to a man with movie-star looks, and his voice *is* like drowning in silky molasses, or whatever she said.

Before stuffing my phone into my back pocket, I glance at the text once more, arching an eyebrow at the last line.

It's happening this Saturday.

It's commanding and dominant.

Maybe that's what Dev is like in bed.

My nose scrunches at the thought of Dev in bed.

Why is my nose scrunching at the thought of Dev in bed?

It's because I'm at school, I tell myself. Salacious thoughts are inappropriate, and my body knows that.

At that logical reasoning, my enthusiasm for our date returns, and I walk my kids back to the classroom as I draft a reply in my head.

CHAPTER 11

BRIE

MY LUNCH BEEPS, and I pull the sleeves of my sweater over my hands to take the hot container out and walk to the empty table a few feet away, rather than taking it back to my empty classroom like normal.

There's a trio of older teachers at the table near the door. I don't ask to sit with them and they don't offer.

"Hey!" Tess says as I fan my mouth from the molten cheese I just shoved in it. "Want me to blow in your mouth?" she asks.

I nearly choke as I shake my head hard enough to dislodge my brain.

"Kidding." She grins as she takes a seat opposite me and unpacks a sandwich. "This is nice! I usually eat lunch by myself, which you'd think would be great after all the 'Ms. Brooks' this and 'Ms. Brooks' that, but I need some adult interaction, you know?"

Not really. I like my solitude, but I say, "It must be hard teaching a bunch of four and five year olds. Second is the youngest grade I've taught." Something tugs at my memory as I blow on another bite of Gia's delicious chicken parm from last night. "Wait, did you say Brooks?"

She nods.

"I think your brother was a year ahead of me in high school. Super competitive? Famously cross-examined the principal when he tightened up the dress code? Nash Brooks?"

Tess looks too young to have overlapped with us, but they have the same eyes.

Her smile is incandescent. "That's my brother! It'll come as no surprise he's a fancy lawyer now." She takes a bite of her sandwich. Her blue eyes—not deep blue like Sawyer's, but bright like the sky—study me for a moment. "So you're from Blue Ridge. Are you *so* glad to be back?"

"It's changed a lot," I hedge.

"Isn't it great?" Tess asks dreamily. "I fell in love with Blue Ridge when we moved here in elementary school, but it just keeps getting better and better."

My face stays neutral as I nod, but she sounds bananas.

"I can't imagine living anywhere else," she goes on. "I went to school in Knoxville, but it was too Big City for me. Blue Ridge is more my speed. Everyone knows one another, Maddy's Bakery has her apple cider cake donuts, the Book Nook always has the newest Jackie Pine romance. Blue Ridge has everything you need."

She looks at me expectantly, so I say, "What about Jolly Jalapeño? That place seems popular. You ever go there with friends?" Remembering what Gia said, I add, "I hear it's the place to go if you're young and childless."

Tess's reaction stops me mid-chuckle. She's suddenly very interested in her sandwich bag as her smile grows rigid. "I don't go out much. Teachers are early risers, right?" Then she shrugs so nonchalantly it comes back around to being very *un*-nonchalant. Chalant.

It's clear Tess wants to move on, and I feel bad for mentioning it, so I change the subject. "Do you hang out with Nash a lot?"

Her face lights up, but it doesn't meet her eyes. "Not as often as I'd like. He lives in Chattanooga."

My brows drop. "That's, what, an hour and a half away?"

"An hour fifteen," she corrects. "But he's so busy. Especially right now with the Kelly case."

"Who's Kelly?" I ask.

She shrugs, "No idea, but every time I call, he has to go a few minutes later because he's 'swamped with the Kelly case.'" A thought seems to occur to Tess. "If you were in school with my brother, you must have already known Sawyer."

Shit. Didn't think it through when I brought Nash up. I focus on my lunch.

She tilts her head. "So . . . were you friends with Sawyer in high school?"

"Not exactly." It wasn't supposed to come out so terse.

Her expression changes into an open-mouthed grin, eager for a good story. I'm used to this.

She moves her sandwich to the side and plops her elbows on the table. "Tell me."

With a forkful of chicken parm in my mouth, I mumble, "There's nothing to tell."

"Then why does your face do that weird thing when I say his name?" she asks.

"Hm?"

"Sawyer," she says. "There!"

I put on a blank face and think detached thoughts. I am the epitome of unaffected.

"Sawyer," Tess tries again, then giggles as I feel my face twist. "Sawyer. Sawyer. Sawyer!" She leans in more, nearly halfway over the table now, ready for me to spill the tea. "Did you guys date?"

"Oh my god, no. Definitely not."

Sitting back, she eyes me. "I heard he was totally different in high school. Nash thought I was joking when I told him who the new principal was."

"New?" I can't help asking.

"Principal Brown retired at the end of last year."

"Principal *Brown*?" I ask. "As in *Sadge* Brown?"

She grins. "The very same. Working for him really wasn't all that different from being a student under him."

I laugh imagining it.

"So . . ." she starts again. "Sawyer?"

My nails dig into my palms. If I don't tell her something, she'll probably just ask Nash. He was only a year older than us. What happened at prom probably got back to him through people he was still friends with after he left for college.

All she has to do is tell Nash I started working here. I'm sure the first thing out of his mouth would be *And the place didn't crumble into dust?*

Tess must see something in my expression, because she holds up her hands. "Sorry! I just met you, I shouldn't have asked. Everyone has a right to privacy."

My phone pings with a reminder. Five minutes before I retrieve my class from the cafeteria.

I could tell her *something*. It's not like Sawyer's treatment of me is even a secret, how could it be in this town? A fresh start was never realistic for me here.

And it's all temporary anyway. I'm out at the end of the semester. By then, schools will have hired for next year.

I take one more look at Tess. The way she looks at me is different than anyone from Everett Academy, the pack of hyenas that tried to rip me apart. Their questions were laced with vindictiveness, hungry for any drama they could get their hands on and regurgitate to others.

But Tess seems nice. Innocent, even. She has no idea who Sawyer was to me in school. She probably thinks she was merely asking a normal get-to-know-you question.

Softening, I say, "It's okay, I just don't like gossip. Sawyer wasn't the nicest to me when we were younger."

Tess's eyebrows shoot together, eyes big. "Really?"

I shrug like it's no big deal. "Mostly teasing. Loud-mouth stuff."

For the first time, the smile disappears from Tess's face as she presses her lips together and takes one of my hands in both of hers.

It surprises me, but it grounds me, too. Reminds me I'm in the here-and-now. School is way in the past.

"I get the sense there's more to it," she says, "and I'm sorry that happened to you." She hesitates, like she's debating what to say next. "I know what it's like to be treated poorly."

Titling my head, I wonder what kind of monster would treat this woman poorly.

She squeezes my hand, her face earnest. "I know this is going to be hard to believe," she says. "I mean, everyone changes, but most people don't change who they really are *inside*, you know? But Sawyer—"

My phone alarm goes off, jarring us both out of the moment.

Tess releases my hands, and bites her lip. "Sorry if that was too much or weird."

Laughter bubbles up my throat as I gather my things and stand. "It *was* weird. And maybe too much. But I didn't mind it," I say, surprised to find it's true.

She mimes wiping sweat off her brow. "Phew!"

"Have a good rest of the day," I say as I gather my things.

"See you tomorrow at lunch!" she calls out after me.

I chuckle as I leave the lounge, feeling lighter somehow. Controlling the narrative has its merits. Maybe she won't even find out what Sawyer did to me at prom.

CHAPTER 12
SENIOR PROM
BRIE

DEV LET OUT A LOUD, piercing whistle when I stepped out of Gia's car. She'd insisted on driving me to his house even though it was only a few blocks away.

Gia winked at me over the dented roof of her beat-up sedan. "I hope you're ready for everyone to stare at you at Senior Prom. You look great." She tilted her head at the front window. "They all seem to think so, too."

All of Dev's younger siblings had their noses to the glass, watching. I gave them a finger-wave.

Dev, clad in formal attire that was a little too baggy on him, grinned at me. He had a fantastic smile. Lips that formed the perfect crescent moon shape, gleaming white teeth, and dimples that gave him a boyish charm.

"Brie, you look fantastic. So hot."

I couldn't hide my smile. Dev always knew what to say, even if I was wearing Gia's old dress. I was taller and naturally curvier than Gia had been at my age. Garments that draped modestly over her chest or ass hugged mine, making me feel exposed and self-conscious.

"Thanks," I said. "You look really good, too."

"Mind if I take some pictures?" Gia asked.

I rolled my eyes, but secretly loved it. I wondered if this is what Mom would have been like at big moments like these.

"You know Dev and I are just going as friends, right?" I told her.

Dev was wickedly handsome. He'd grown from a wide-eyed grinning boy to someone whose picture would look right at home on a teenage girl's wall next to posters of boy bands.

"Yeah," Dev said with his usual easygoing smile, "we're just friends."

"Even better," Gia said coolly, "I just want to memorialize this. You'll be happy to have it when you're older."

Despite the lack of butterflies in my stomach, I was having probably the most fun I ever had. Dev and I danced with our loose group of friends. Four girls and three boys. They were misfits like Dev and me, but we rarely hung out with them on the weekends. We mostly found ourselves at the same table during lunch. Still, we all agreed there was safety in numbers, and the seven of us decided to stick together.

Our odd number wasn't a problem until the rap song we were dancing to faded into something slow and soft, the opening notes to my newest favorite song. I knew Dev had a thing for one of the girls, so I didn't begrudge him when they coupled up. But when I looked, the others were already paired up, too.

Disappointment sank low in my belly. I really liked this song.

I turned to exit the dance floor, but stopped short. My breath caught as Sawyer stood before me. His tux fit him like a glove, eyes intense as they scanned my face, then my body. It felt like a caress, and I shivered.

He held his hand out to me, and I lifted my eyes to his.

My last real interaction with him had been months ago, on that stormy night. Since then, he'd given me a wide berth in the hallways.

The first month, I feared he had something horrible planned for me. But as days wore on, I grew comfortable. Even his goons left me alone. I'd stopped searching for them when turning a corner or entering the cafeteria. And before long, I'd even caught myself letting my eyes wander to Sawyer in class, curious about him.

Sometimes I caught his eyes wandering back. More often, they were already on me, causing my stomach to do those flips I was getting so used to.

The aversion I'd felt about Sawyer being my first crush dissolved. It didn't matter if I was averse to it, it was happening.

It had happened.

Still, I didn't take his hand when he offered it now.

He must have sensed my hesitation, because Sawyer's deep voice, low enough for just me to hear, said, "Will you dance with me, Brie?"

This was different from the lingering glances at school. There were people around, they'd see everything. Alarm bells sounded in the back of my mind, but they were faint compared to the colorful confetti scattering in my chest.

With bated breath, I slipped my hand in his. My heart pounded as he drew me closer, his gaze on me the whole time.

I didn't think this was what Gia meant when she said everyone would be staring at me, but she was right all the same. I felt everyone's eyes as Sawyer guided my hands up to his neck before placing his own on my hips, a foot of space between our bodies.

Whispers had me wishing I could hide. I shifted closer to Sawyer. I felt him let out a shuddering breath as he drew me into his body.

Again, I was reminded of that night in the rain. His hand around mine, larger than mine, protective.

Now it was his larger body shielding me from the rest of the dancers.

With my cheek pressed to his chest, the sound of his heartbeat drowned out the whispers, or maybe they'd stopped. I relaxed into him more. Beneath the expensive cologne, chlorine still clung to him along with that particular shade of *boy* I knew was Sawyer's unique scent.

The letterman jacket beneath my bed still smelled of him. The most illicit thing I ever did was bury my face in it every so often, thinking about Sawyer at night. My dirtiest guilty pleasure.

Without meaning to, I sunk further into his embrace and inhaled deeply.

Sawyer's hands clenched around my hips, pulling me more firmly into him. He felt so good, so solid.

"You're so pretty." I felt more than heard the murmured words against my temple.

I swallowed a lump in my throat. I couldn't believe it. Couldn't believe those words were meant for me. *From him.*

Without even realizing I was doing it, my hands ran up his neck. My fingertips played with his soft hair, and he shivered against me.

I did that.

Pulling back, I looked into his eyes. They were dark, but not in the way I'd seen in the past. Not mean. There was something like supplication there. And desire.

For the first time, I felt wanted. And I was eager to give it to him, whatever it was.

I ran my fingernails lightly over the back of his neck. A rumble vibrated through his chest as he let out what sounded like a groan. Everything inside me tightened.

My breath caught when his hands started to move, too, gently caressing up and down my bare back, leaving a trail of fire in his wake.

In a shaky whisper, I said, "That feels good," and pressed closer, wanting more.

Suddenly, Sawyer's body went stiff. His hands jerked to my hips, and he shoved me back.

I looked up at him, dazed. *What just happened?*

The whispers were audible again, even louder than before.

Sawyer reached up to remove my hands from his neck. I hadn't realized I was still clinging to him.

Embarrassment and hurt lanced through me as he dropped my hands, and I rubbed them on the thighs of my dress.

I glanced around.

Oh god.

Everyone was looking at us. The entire gym. Some looked over slyly while others shamelessly stared with upturned lips and sparkling eyes, looking at me in that cruel way teenagers had that was both pitying and hungry for drama.

Sawyer noticed at the same time I did. His eyes widened, a flush blooming on his cheeks, before he looked back at me. He raked his gaze over me as I wore what I'm sure was a horrified expression.

A flash of anguish crossed his face and he stepped

toward me, reaching for me like he might pull me to him, shield me with his body again.

And I wanted him to, I wanted him to so bad. Anything to hide from the stares.

"No way, Sawyer." Rich's voice, loud and disbelieving rang through the crowd. "You don't seriously have the hots for Brie Queso."

A few people snickered as I shut my eyes against that stupid nickname.

Sawyer's face turned tomato-red. He glanced at me one more time before the look in his eyes hardened, all worry wiped clean.

I knew that look. Even before he said it, I knew what was coming.

"I thought I'd give her a taste of the good life," Sawyer said. "It's all downhill from here for trash like her."

I turned to get out of there. Someone flinched like literal garbage was coming their way. I looked up to find Rich pretending to recoil away from me.

"Don't try to hang on to me next, I've got a date," he half-shouted.

People around him roared with laughter, and my humiliation was complete. I had never been so low in my life.

Every step I took off the dance floor, another comment like that followed.

My eyes stung.

How could I have been so stupid?

I hadn't just become more comfortable at school since that night in the rain. I'd grown complacent. How could I have let my guard down after so little time?

My entire life, Sawyer was cruel to me. I knew what kind of person he was, the kind who thought he could do whatever he wanted, take whatever he wanted. Three months of basic human decency, and he had me for free.

I was in the hall before I realized Dev had followed me out.

By Monday morning, the entire town had heard what happened, and they were talking. Whispers about how I'd tried to cling onto Sawyer Strong, the Prince of Blue Ridge, but he wouldn't have me. Exaggerated rumors of me throwing myself at him, begging for his attention.

Pitying looks from some, pious looks from others.

One more week.

CHAPTER 13

BRIE

IT'S SATURDAY EVENING, I borrowed what my little sister Mara calls her "booby shirt," and I watched a tutorial on how to do a soft smoky eye.

When I sashay downstairs, Gia is reading on the couch in the living room while Lizzie is spread out at the table in the kitchen painting runny watercolor hearts.

Lizzie looks up, mouth open wide. "You look *beautiful,* Aunt Brie."

"You *are* beautiful," I tell her, smoothing my hand over her hair and kissing the top of her head. "And smart, and curious, and creative, and very hard working."

She grins. "Do you have a date?"

I hesitate, glancing at Gia before I answer. Is Lizzie even aware what a date is, or has she just heard the term around school? At her age, it could go either way, and as far as I know, Gia doesn't date.

Unless that's why Lizzie asked in the first place. Maybe Gia goes on dates all the time.

I look at my big sister.

She shrugs in that *kids be crazy* way she does sometimes, even though Lizzie is the farthest thing from crazy.

"Yes," I finally answer, "I have a date. With Dev."

Even though the memory of him mentioning Angelica's when we were out together is fuzzy, I've reread Dev's text so many times I have it memorized. He used the word explicitly. *Date.*

I keep waffling between surprise that my oldest friend so brazenly asked me out, and confidence that this is a great idea.

My top priority is to avoid a repeat of the Christopher situation, which would never happen with Dev. We don't work together, and I trust him.

"Are you going to get dessert?" Lizzie asks hopefully.

"Maybe," I say. "Maybe tiramisu." It was always my favorite of theirs.

Gia stands up and lays her book down on the sofa arm. The colorful illustrated cover catches me by surprise.

So no-nonsense Gia likes romance books.

"Angelica's," she says, walking over. "Great first-date spot."

"Not a lot to choose from." I take my keys from the hook by the door.

Though, to be fair, it is the right choice. The Square is no good for a first date, and Celine's is too fancy.

Angelica's is the perfect in-between. It's the kind of place that has vinyl red checkered tablecloths, but also candles and fresh flowers on every table. They make their pasta in-house, but their menus are laminated.

Ignoring my small-town jab, my big sister looks me up and down. Her expression says, *I know what shirt that is.*

"I bet Dev loves *dessert*," she says.

A bubble of laughter climbs out of my throat. "I'll find out," I say as I open the door. "Don't wait up."

"I won't," she says as she walks to the stove.

"Where did all these people come from?" I mutter to myself.

Since Dev lives walking distance to the restaurant, I volunteered to meet him there. But now, I can't find any parking around downtown.

Then again, if I lived here for good, I'd do anything I could to get out of the house on a Saturday night, too.

At last, I find a spot all the way in front of Madam's Hardware, its florescent internal lights flooding the sidewalk.

It was Adam's Hardware when I was little, but Adam lost it in the divorce. Ms. Agnes kept it out of spite and tacked on an *M* to the front. The whole town supported her when it came out Adam cheated with a girl from the community college, and she's been doing great business ever since. Even the old loafers who walk down everyday just to sit in front of the wood stove sipping their coke with peanuts never missed a beat.

I park my car behind a red truck. It reminds me of a bigger, fancier red truck I got a ride home in once. Thank fuck it's not the same. The last person I want to run into is its owner.

When I step out, two of the regular loafers, Gus and Walter, shuffle out of Madam's Hardware, ready to go home to their respective wives.

"You're back," Gus grumbles at me.

I'm not back. The words are right there, already in my

mouth, but I swallow them down. Wouldn't want to give old Gus good news.

Instead, I give him a cloying smile. "Thanks, Gus."

He bats his hand in the air, muttering to himself as he walks past.

With a genuine smile, I pull out my phone as I walk toward the town square. An early February breeze pebbles my skin, and I realize I left my coat in the car.

As I spin around to go back for it, my eyes are glued to my screen, texting Dev I'm here.

I jolt as I slam into a hard body, forcing me to stumble backward.

Then I freeze, and not from the chill in the air.

Sawyer's eyes widen in horror. I'm no happier to see him.

He's wearing another flannel shirt beneath his unzipped jacket. It's unbuttoned at the top, revealing tan skin beneath, a smattering of dark hair peeking out from the edges.

Aside from his terse reply after the assembly, he hasn't spoken to me since that night at the bar, when I ran into him just like this. Every time we cross paths in the hallways at school, he gives me a curt nod and looks straight ahead.

Even though it's my best case scenario, having Sawyer avoid *me* for a change, something about it eats at me.

And of course it's just my luck to run into him *now*. It's like this town is actively trying to get me to leave it. Just when I think I might have a decent night, it throws Sawyer into my path, reminding me I don't belong here.

Irritation brews in my stomach, and I *very maturely, thank you very much,* ignore him as I start to walk around him. At the same time, he tries to do the same, but miscalculates and steps right in front of me. We do this dance two more times before I stop.

I glare up at him.

His body is tense. The strong muscles in his neck are taut. His Adam's apple bobs as he swallows. Thick, dark stubble has grown in since the assembly a few days ago.

That assembly. The way he said *can I help you, Ms. Casey?* in that robotic monotone replays in my mind.

And suddenly, I'm not cold anymore.

Indignation heats me.

I glance down at the box of screws in his hand. So this is what the Prince of Blue Ridge is doing on a Saturday night?

And *I* have a date.

Well well well, how the turntables, Michael Scott's voice in my head says.

"Fun night planned?" I try keeping my tone light, but when his eyes narrow, and the corner of his mouth quirks halfway to his evil playful smirk, I know I've failed.

This is the Sawyer I remember, not the frosty principal at school.

My pulse ratchets up.

"Ran out of hardware," he says, unapologetic. His eyes drop, running over me. When they land on my booby shirt, his smirk widens, showing off his perfect teeth. "Who're you trying to impress?"

The fucking nerve of this man.

I step toward him, squaring my shoulders, thrusting the assets my shirt is so good at showing off and only wishing a little they were as good as Mara's. "I'm not *trying* to impress anyone."

He lowers his eyes again, not even bothering to hide what he's looking at. Red stains his cheeks.

Eat your fucking heart out, Sawyer. You will never *have this.* I jut my chest out even more.

Just as I register the intense burning in his eyes, the lights at Madam's Hardware flicker off, casting the right side of Sawyer's face in shadow.

"Not trying to impress anyone?" he chides, suddenly close enough for me to feel the heat radiating off him. "It's the middle of winter and you don't even have on a coat."

The gravel in his voice leaves me suddenly parched. I lick my lips, and his eyes track the movement.

"It was sixty degrees today," I say, as if I wasn't on my way to grab my coat just a minute ago.

He leans in, almost crowding me. "And you used to wear a jacket anytime it dipped below seventy." His eyes flicker down again. "It's forty now."

That explains why my nipples have pebbled into hard peaks. Definitely the cold.

"You need a coat," he says in that cocksure tone of his.

I take a step forward and glower up at him. "You aren't the boss of me." It's out of my mouth before I realize . . . he is indeed the boss of me.

His eyes glint and that familiar smirk is back. "You sure about that?"

Gesturing to the sidewalk, I add, "You're not the principal of the sidewalk."

Weak, Brie.

He leans in until his mouth is by my ear, and I forget about details and arguments. All I can do is hold my breath.

"Where are you going, looking like that?"

His breath trails over the shell of my ear. I shiver. Goosebumps erupt down my neck. All the air vacuums out of my lungs as time stands still.

My eyes dart down. His chest hair looks soft, but the

muscle beneath looks firm. And it's so warm here, inside Sawyer's personal space.

Sawyer.

I blink, coming back to my senses.

The fucking audacity of Sawyer Strong. I hold back from shoving him away and telling him it's none of his business.

Instead, I give my shoulders a little shimmy. "I have a date."

His smirk dies, replaced by drawn lips and narrowed eyes.

Ha! I raise my chin, daring him to take his next shot. It's a goddamn thrill being the one to throw Sawyer off for a change.

He opens his mouth to respond. My eyes are immediately drawn to his lips. It's in this moment that I realize our faces are inches apart. We're toe to toe. Breathing the same air. Sharing body heat.

On an inhalation, I smell him. Chlorine. Spicy soap. *Him.*

"Brie!" a voice calls from behind him.

I startle, stumbling away from Sawyer as I trip on my own feet, arms reaching for something solid.

Sawyer grabs my waist, steadying me against his body.

I clutch at his arm with one hand, the other pressed against his chest, the muscle just as firm as I predicted. His heart beats in a quick staccato.

"Brie?" Dev's voice cuts in again, this time closer and less sure.

I jerk out of Sawyer's arms. I'm instantly cold. Dev comes into view behind him, and my face brightens.

My date.

He's bundled in a bright green puffer jacket, an

authentic smile on his face. One gloved hand waves as . . . *wait*. Whose hand is he holding?

Sawyer shifts, and I see her, a woman I don't recognize.

She wears a patchwork jacket, and bangs peek just below a purple cloche hat. Thick cat-eye glasses accentuate her dramatic eye makeup. Her red lips are perfectly lined.

I'm struck stupid by how insanely cool she looks. Then by the fact that they look like a couple. On a date.

What's Dev doing with someone else when we're *going on a date?*

I feel Sawyer's eyes on me. I don't look. His smugness would only add to my rapidly growing mortification as my confusion takes a backseat.

Dev gets closer. The moment he registers Sawyer, his expression turns bewildered, almost concerned.

They shake hands.

"Hey, man." Dev's usual affability is layered with caution as he keeps his attention on me.

That is, until he introduces us to Harvest, who lives over the mountain in Seneca Falls.

Harvest.

Her name is *Harvest*.

Oh hell. The name triggers a fuzzy memory from Jolly Jalapeño of Dev mentioning dinner at Angelica's . . . and now I remember Dev mentioning something about a harvest in the same sentence.

My tipsy ass skipped over it and shouted, "I'd love to go with you!"

My eyes dart around as panic climbs up my chest. My skin itches.

I invited myself on Dev's date tonight. It was never supposed to be him and me.

I visibly cringe.

Is there a manhole I can crawl into? I would happily live the rest of my days with giant sewer rats if I could escape this moment right now.

"You're having dinner with us?" Dev asks Sawyer judiciously.

The words *absolutely fucking not* are in my throat when Sawyer says, "Yeah, I am." He lifts up the box of screws. "Let me just take this to my truck."

Oh, hell no.

I follow him to the red truck, barely registering that I misidentified it before.

He opens the door, and I step close to him.

"What are you doing?" I hiss. "No way you're—"

His hand comes up, cupping my chin, effectively shutting me up.

Sawyer's voice is a deep rasp with no hint of teasing. "I'm going to eat dinner with my old buddy, Dev." His eyes drop to my lips for a second before rising. "I'm starving."

When I regain my voice, I blurt out, "You had plans, though." I point dumbly at his box of screws. "Or what about friends, you could go out with friends tonight. You have lots of those." I swallow. "Or your dad. Be a good son, go to dinner with him."

Any idiot could piece together that what I thought was a date between me and Dev is actually very much a date between Dev and Harvest, with a side of Brie. And Sawyer's no idiot.

I'm already busy coming up with excuses to leave Dev to his date. I don't have the energy to worry about whatever Sawyer has up his sleeve, too.

His eyes dim, and he drops his hand. "These are for tomorrow." He tosses the screws onto the passenger seat. "I don't have plans with any friends. And dinner with my dad is the last thing I want."

A fist squeezes in my stomach. I don't want him to come. My embarrassment is already heavy, but with Sawyer there, it'll only get worse. He'll do something to make me wish I could find a cannon that'll shoot me into space.

He gently tugs me out of the way and shuts his door, underscoring the end of this discussion.

"I remembered your truck being bigger," I say, resigned to my fate.

His brows knit together. "It's not the same truck."

Before I can process that information, Dev calls, "You guys coming?"

Sawyer calls back, "Coming," and puts his hand on the small of my back to guide me back to the sidewalk.

There's no way I come out of this with my dignity intact.

CHAPTER 14

SAWYER

I AM SO FUCKING STUPID.

That night at the bar, I caught myself just in time. And since then, I've maintained my distance, kept a professional tone. Filtered all Brie-related thoughts.

Now, though? I've lost my fucking mind to her. Whatever remaining brain cells I have do the polka to the tune of Brie's breathing.

What have I done? I don't even know what this is. A double date?

Yeah, right.

But seeing Brie out on the town, dressed like *that*, hit me like a sledgehammer. I lost all sense of reason. I mean, what was I doing, cupping her chin like that? Touching her like she's mine?

I pinch the bridge of my nose because, even as I mentally kick my own ass, I know I'd do it all over again if given the chance.

The look on her face when she saw Dev walk up with another girl nearly gutted me, a feat considering I was already flayed when Brie told me she was going on a date.

I can't say I'm upset she isn't going out with Certified Nice Guy Dev Shah right now, but I never want to see that mix of mortification and devastation on her face again. I saw enough of it when we were kids.

At least this time it wasn't my fault.

Speaking of Dev, what kind of idiot *doesn't* date Brie when given the chance? His fucking loss.

Not your fucking gain, I remind myself, and I deserve the pain that comes with knowing that.

As we cross the street and head toward Angelica's on the corner, we split into twos, but not the way I want. Harvest and I walk ahead while Dev and Brie trail behind. I nod as Harvest tells me this is her first time visiting Blue Ridge, and focus instead on the conversation behind me.

Dev murmurs, "Barely a month working under him and you're dry humping downtown?"

I stifle a chuckle, picturing Brie's bared teeth and narrowed eyes.

Brie shushes him and speaks too low for me to hear. My brain fills in all the contemptible things she's within her rights to say about me.

Truth be told, being here right now against her wishes proves I'm still an ass. But I left her humiliated and upset too many times in the past. I couldn't do it again.

Inside the restaurant, Mrs. Muzzarelli comes out from around the bar saying, "Oh my goodness gracious! Brie Casey, I heard you were back in town."

Brie leans awkwardly into the hug, looking a little shell shocked, almost as if she's surprised Mrs. Muzzarelli remembers her. Everyone remembers everyone in this town. Doesn't she know that?

"Good to see you all here." Mrs. Muzzarelli offers me a

teasing wink as she adds, "Especially the Prince of Blue Ridge himself."

I stifle a groan. Most people haven't called me that since I started teaching and it was clear I'll never follow in Dad's footsteps. Still, Mrs. Muzzarelli is a good woman and means well.

Kissing her cheek, I say, "It's good to be here."

She hands us off to the hostess, who shows us to a booth near the back. Harvest and Dev slide in on one side and Brie hesitates for just a second before moving to sit across from them. She trips over her feet, not for the first time tonight, and ends up on all fours on the bench.

I have to stuff my hands in my pockets to keep them to myself while she awkwardly makes her way into a seated position.

When I slide in, her scent wafts over me. Pear and citrus and *Brie*.

My pants grow tight, and I make the mistake of looking down at her. *Holy hell* the red shirt she's wearing is a godsend from this angle.

Stop acting like a teenager.

"Why did that woman call you the Prince of Blue Ridge?" Harvest asks, but I barely hear her.

My entire focus is on Brie. I'm fully hard now and burning up. I pull off one sleeve of my jacket, leaning toward her as I do. I make the critical mistake of inhaling deeply. I quickly tug off the other sleeve and drape the jacket over my lap.

"Sawyer comes from a long line of mayors," Dev explains.

"Wow, *so* impressive," Harvest says, but my eyes are on Brie, who rolls her eyes infinitesimally, and somehow that's hot, too.

Our waiter, a high school kid I recognize, comes by to fill water glasses. I drain it as he tells us the specials and asks for our drink orders.

"I'll have a Peroni," Dev says when no one chimes in.

Harvest smiles, "Same."

Dev smiles across at us. "Should we get a pitcher?"

Brie's eyes dart between them across the table and the menu in her hands.

This is so familiar, I know exactly what she's thinking. She has no interest in a cold pint right now. For such an old friend, Dev does a shit job reading her.

Throwing my arm across the back of the booth, I look up at our waiter, "Two glasses of your cheapest red, Doug."

Brie shoots me a sharp look. "Of course you'd think I like the cheap stuff."

I look at her, stunned. "I can't tell the difference, that's why I ordered it." I look at Doug. "Two glasses of your most expensive red, please."

Glaring at me, she tells Doug, "Bring the cheap stuff, and keep it coming."

He nods and leaves.

As Harvest says something quietly to Dev, Brie turns to me. Instinctively, I lean to meet her.

"I can order for myself," she mutters.

"And you did. Turns out we have the same taste." I wink.

She shuts her eyes like she's counting to ten and licks her lips. *That mouth.* It starred in so many of my teenage fantasies. Her eyes flit across the table, like she doesn't want to bring down the mood for Dev.

"I mean," she says, voice so low I have to move closer to hear, "I can answer for myself."

"Like how you answered for yourself at Ravi Engel's

birthday party?" It's meant to be a gentle tease, but her expression turns scornful.

"I was twelve." Her chest heaves as she stares up at me, eyes flashing.

I bite back a smile as I stare right back. This verbal sparring is the hottest foreplay I've had in a while.

"So, uh, how's work been?"

Dev's question has us blinking across the table. His arm is around Harvest's shoulders, which somehow makes his voice less annoying than usual.

"It's going well." Brie's voice softens, the hard edges of her expression smoothing out. "I love third grade. The kids have been really engaged and fun."

It's clear from the way she talked that first day in my office that she's passionate about teaching. I'm not surprised. She always poured herself into her favorite subjects at school with an almost singular focus.

Doug drops off our drinks and a basket of bread, and takes our orders.

"Where did you move from?" Harvest asks.

"Indianapolis." Brie lifts her glass to her lips. Her throat bobs as she swallows, and her tongue darts out to lick her bottom lip.

Harvest asks, "Why did you move in the middle of the school year?"

"Yeah," Dev says. "Is it a good story?"

Ignoring how fucking elated I am that Dev doesn't know the reason, I notice the way Brie stiffens next to me. Her hand forms a ball in her lap.

I want to know why she left her old school in a hurry. Obviously, Brie isn't in Blue Ridge because she was suddenly nostalgic for the small town she was so eager to leave. I still remember the rawness in her voice that night in front of her house. *Five months. Then I can get the hell out of Blue Ridge for good.*

Something had to have driven her here. Or driven her *out* of where she was before.

The impulse to find out what happened and what I can do to fix it is strong. But I want to learn the truth because she decides to tell me, not because her asshole friend pressures her for a good story.

Asshole, nice guy—sometimes there isn't a big difference.

"Who cares?" I intervene.

Brie gives me the stink eye.

"She saved my ass," I continue. "Our third grade teacher, Ms. Cook, eloped with someone she met over winter break and never came back. No notice or anything. I could've kissed Brie when she showed up."

Pink crawls up her neck. My entire body is begging me to bury my face there and take a juicy bite.

"Wait, *you* work at the elementary school?" Harvest asks, nose scrunched in dismay.

Out of the corner of my eye, Brie shifts, stink eye transferring to Harvest. Her shoulders square and she leans forward, as if to hear every word. If I didn't know better, I'd describe her pose as defensive.

"I do," I say as Doug drops off our entrees.

"I thought you were the mayor," Harvest says, voice lilting up even though it isn't a question.

"He's the *principal*," Brie spits, planting her hands on the table. "Between student teaching and actual teaching jobs, I've worked at more than a few different elementary schools, including two nationally-ranked private institutions. Sawyer runs his school better than any I've seen, and he's universally beloved by everyone there. The teachers all speak highly of him, and kids go out of their way just to high-five him. He'd be wasted as mayor."

All I can do is stare as her face turns from impassioned to . . . shocked. I'd bet good money Brie didn't mean to say those things about me, but the words are out there now.

There are pieces of her I've never understood, like how feisty-and-independent Brie always quietly accepted my public torments without a fight. But this? This makes sense to me. Brie might not be chatty, but when she does open her mouth, she only says what she means. It's what's always drawn me to her.

"Wow," Harvest says, fixing her eyes on me like Brie suddenly doesn't exist. They're warm, *too* warm, as they trace over me. "That's *sooo* impressive," she drawls.

"I forgot how good the mushroom gnudi is," Brie says a little too jaggedly, eyes shooting invisible lasers at Harvest, who's all but ignoring her actual date.

"You've been here before?" Dev asks her.

I start to laugh. Of course Brie's eaten here before, it's one of the few restaurants in town. But Brie ducks her head, color tinting her cheeks.

Dev explains to Harvest, "Brie and I didn't eat out much growing up."

"Remember?" Brie answers quietly, eyeing Dev's plate of seafood linguini. I fork some of my own seafood linguini onto her plate as she says, "I worked here over summers because The Square wouldn't let me do doubles."

Doubles? I knew from that night in the rain that, while I cruised around town with friends and our parents' credit cards, Brie worked for her allowance, which she sometimes had to use on her pathetic father. But two jobs over summer break? And beyond that, it's unfathomable her job here was the only reason she ever ate the food here.

"Aren't you a little young to be principal?" Harvest asks, picking the conversation back up where she was last included. I wonder if her voice sounded this nasally all along. "You must have worked yourself to the *bone* to get where you are."

Brie chokes on her pasta. My eyes cut to Harvest. She flutters her eyelashes at me.

Unruffled, Dev leans back in their booth with a placid smile, but I notice his arm is no longer draped behind her.

"The man works hard," he says like the wingman I don't want. "I heard you earned your masters while teaching. Before that, you got your degree *while* you were on active duty? You were a SEAL, right?"

Brie's head snaps to me. "You enlisted?"

"Wait." Harvest shifts her gaze to Brie, a wide grin pulling at her mouth. "How do you not know? I assumed you guys were dating," she nods toward my plate. "Sharing food—"

Brie's gaze snaps between our plates, eyebrows knitting. For a second, I wonder if she'll hurl the linguini back at me.

I don't know what compels me to do it, but I cover her hand with mine in her lap. She tenses for one strained moment before determination takes hold of her, and she brings our hands up to rest on the table. A message to Harvest. I know she's doing this for Dev, I know she probably hates to see him snubbed by his own date, but I'll take it.

For his part, Dev looks as happily sedate as ever.

"—holding hands," Harvest finishes with an arched eyebrow. "I thought you two were together."

Brie tightens her hold and scoots closer to me. Our thighs press together. Her smell wafts toward me. I'm simultaneously the most content I've ever been, and so keyed up I could flip over a car.

Brie smiles at Harvest. It's so saccharine it comes around to being venomous. When she rests her head on my shoulder, I make the mistake of peering down. Her shirt looks stretchy. I shift uncomfortably as my jeans try to strangle my dick.

"We didn't keep in touch while I was away," Brie replies. "But we made quick work once I came back."

Dev laughs, completely obtuse. "Brie hated Sawyer in school."

Brie and I stiffen, but he doesn't seem to notice. How was I ever jealous of this guy? He's a complete bonehead.

"Seriously?" Harvest breathes, hungry for drama. "Why?"

I grind my molars. There are things I did that I'm not proud of, behavior I've had to work through with my therapist to understand they were all in response to my own demons. Sometimes it's hard for me to believe I'm not that guy anymore.

When neither of us answers, Dev does. "Lots of reasons." He turns to Brie, guffawing. "Remember when you wore heels in ninth grade?"

Brie's spine goes ramrod straight. She tries to pull her hand away, but my hold is strong.

"What happened?" Harvest prods.

"Halloween, Brie was dressed as some twenties flapper—"

"Holly Golightly," I correct. "From *Breakfast at Tiffany's*." Fuck if I know why I'm helping Dev tell the story.

"Right. I wasn't there," Dev continues, "but Brie walks into math class—"

"Art," Brie and I say tensely together.

"Sure," Dev says, giving zero shits about veracity. "So she walks into art class, and Sawyer throws a bunch of marbles at her feet." He bursts out laughing. Before I can cut in, he adds, "So there she is, in front of everyone, swinging her arms around, trying to stay upright. Like a giraffe on roller skates or something!"

Brie's body tightens even more beside me, which I didn't think was possible. "Colored pencils," she says, trying so hard to keep her voice steady it's almost monotone.

"I didn't *throw* them at you," I mumble weakly.

She twists her hand out of mine, truce over. "I loved that dress. I found it with what was left of my mom's things, and I'd never felt so elegant walking into school that day. Like Audrey Hepburn." She shakes her head, and almost to herself adds, "I was so stupid." Her eyes harden when they find me again. "And of course, you proved exactly how stupid. It took you just a split second to ruin something I was excited for all week."

My stomach lurches.

I remember it all perfectly, but it didn't happen in a split second like she thinks.

The day prior, Brie had come into my family's bookstore to sell some old bodice rippers. I was the only one in. Without anyone around, I was able to just be myself. It was the best interaction we'd had, maybe ever, even if it was a little awkward. I gave her a good deal, and she gave me a tentative smile.

But Dad walked in from the back entrance just in time to see her leave out the front. He gave me more than a hard time that night for not just doing business with a Casey but giving her more than she deserved.

I was still stewing the next morning when Brie walked

in not dressed like a ghoul for Halloween, but looking even prettier than normal. If I let myself soak in the memory, I can still feel the bitter rage take hold of me.

I could *never* have Brie, even though she was right *there*.

Looking back, it's lucky all I did was knock over some pencils. I don't know if I meant for Brie to be the target. I still don't know if I wanted to see her suffer, like I was suffering, or if she was just collateral damage.

But Brie was always clumsy, susceptible to accidents anyway. That day, she didn't stand a chance. It happened in slow motion. There was nothing I could do but watch, slack jawed, as her arms windmilled out as she skidded along the floor.

Everyone in the class roared with laughter, some cheering for me.

"I landed on my ass, right on my tailbone," she adds, still ignoring me. "For six months I couldn't sit without the reminder."

I wince. I didn't know that.

"But it was an accident," Harvest says helpfully. "Right, Sawyer?" She winks at me, and I want to throw up.

Brie looks at me with all the contempt I deserve. "Just like prom was an *accident*? Or heckling me at every presentation? Or, let's go to a classic, laughing the loudest when I tripped in first grade and knocked out my top two baby teeth?"

"I was in first grade," I grit out. "I saw someone fall, I laughed. The second I saw blood, I ran to you. I took you to the nurse's office!"

She leans in, doubling down on her indignation. "You did not! Dev did!" she all but spits.

"It was *me*," I say.

My dad was so angry that evening, at his son for taking a

hurt kid to the nurse's office just because of who her father was. No matter what I said, he believed I was secretly friends with Brie, deliberately disobeying his orders to stay away from her.

Brie and I are nose-to-nose. She's ready to gouge me.

All I want is to kiss sense into her.

Out of the corner of my eye, Dev holds his finger up, about to speak, but Doug's hesitant voice cuts through instead. "Can I get you all anything else?"

Still glaring at me, Brie says, "Check, please."

WHEN I GET BACK to Gia's, a light glows below my sister's door. Without thinking, I knock.

"Come in."

Gia is sitting up in bed. She takes her reading glasses off and lays a book down on her bedside table. It's a different pastel-colored illustrated cover than she was reading earlier.

"How was your date?" she asks.

I make a face.

She pulls down the duvet and pats the bed next to her.

For a moment, all I can do is stand there. I don't have a *get in bed and cuddle* relationship with anyone, including my sisters.

But now that she's offered, I really *really* want to. Gia found me my first day in Blue Ridge and practically ordered me back to her home. She's folded me into her little family as if it's the most natural thing in the world. I've tried to do my share and help out around the house, but she's never even insinuated she wants anything back while she feeds me and asks what I want to watch on TV.

It's not until this moment that I realize how bad I want to cuddle with someone who loves me.

I shuffle over. As I climb in, her arm opens up in a classic mom move. I hesitate only for a second before leaning into her.

"It wasn't a date," I say. "At least, not with Dev."

Maybe it's the lull of her breathing, or the orange blossom scent that reminds me of Mom, but I spill, starting with the scene outside Madam's Hardware.

Gia is an amazing listener. Mostly, she hums her acknowledgement every so often to let me know she's listening.

"Up until you asked for the check," she says, "you and Sawyer were still holding hands? And this all happened after you guys dry humped on the sidewalk—"

"Those were Dev's words. There was no . . . *grinding*."

She says nothing, and I can't take the silence.

"There was no genital-to-genital touching!"

Gia's laugh bubbles out, and it vibrates happily against my back. "Too bad, that's the best kind of touching."

"Not when Sawyer's involved."

"Do you need to see Dr. Levine?" she asks, referring to the optometrist in town. "*Especially* when Sawyer is involved."

Ew.

I say, "Ew."

She twists to meet my eyes. "Those Strong boys might have their heads up their asses, but there's no *ew* when it comes to how they look." Relaxing back again, she adds, "Besides, Lizzie loves him, and she has great judgment."

Kids usually do. *Kids go out of their way just to high-five him.* In summarizing my night to Gia, I conveniently left out how, without meaning to, I let my guard down when

Harvest attacked him for "working at the elementary school" and lost it on her. But that had nothing to do with Sawyer in particular. I hate when people look down on educators in general, as if we aren't critically important to the success of future generations.

I feel Gia shrug behind me. "He's the best of all of them as far as I can tell."

He's definitely the lesser of two evils when the ex-mayor is concerned. Sawyer's dad was a piece of work, a real snake of a politician.

"Will doesn't seem so bad," I say. I never really inter-acted with Sawyer's older brother much, but by all appearances he *seems* okay. For a Strong.

Gia scoffs, and it's the most emotion she's ever displayed. "You ever see *Hamilton?*"

"Uh, yeah," not sure where she's going with this.

"Will is Aaron Burr. He doesn't let anyone know what he's against or what he's for. He'll play any angle as long as it gets him what he wants."

This sounds oddly personal.

"Anyway," she says, "we're getting off-topic. After you and Sawyer *didn't* dry hump, but *did* hold hands, you blew up on each other over a trip down memory lane."

I didn't go into the specifics of the colored pencils inci-dent with Gia. She has no idea how bad things were for me after she left for college, and I never want her to feel guilty for leaving. But she was a witness to some of the more minor teasing I endured at the hands of Sawyer and his friends.

"Pretty much," I say. "It just reminded me of all the reasons I can't trust him. Basically all my bad memories from school are because of him."

"You know, Sawyer *was* the one who took you to the nurse that day," she says.

I pivot to see if she's serious, mouth agape. I still remember her picking me up after school, two baby teeth clutched in my palm.

"And," she continues before I can process or ask questions, "it sounds like he didn't do anything wrong tonight."

What! I'm speechless.

"If anything," she says, "he saved you from embarrassment. For all Dev knows, you intended tonight to be a double date all along."

I pout and lean back against her again.

"Think about it," she urges. "From what you told me, anything bad from tonight was purely some miscommunication from your past."

That's sugarcoating it.

"As far as I can tell, he didn't do anything wrong tonight," she repeats.

I scramble for a retort, something he did tonight to intentionally hurt me. Even after he invited himself along, he didn't expose me for thinking I was going out with Dev. He didn't engage in Harvest's flirting. But he did argue with me about our shared memories.

Wait. I look up at the ceiling, trying to remember the conversation. *Harvest* was the one who called the colored pencils an accident. Sawyer only argued about being the one to take me to the nurse in first grade, which, according to Gia, was true.

In hindsight, the worst thing he did *tonight* was order wine for me. Which I *did* want.

My chest feels suddenly hollow. I don't know what to do with this information, my brain hurts just thinking about it. It's like finding out the alphabet was in the wrong order this whole time.

"Maybe you're right," I say grudgingly. "Maybe nothing

bad happened tonight, but it still *feels* like a bad night. That's what matters, right? How someone makes you feel."

I ignore the memory of the heat of him in front of the hardware store, how my body lit up when Sawyer threaded his fingers through mine, the solid feel of his thigh pressed against mine beneath the table.

Gia's inhalation lifts me with her, and I gently come back down as she exhales.

"Yeah," she finally says. "How someone makes you feel is really important."

I CAN'T STOP THINKING about my conversation with Gia. *How someone makes you feel is really important.*

It makes sense, like something that should be true. But I felt good about Christopher in the beginning, and look where that landed me.

"Landed me in this podunk town with a serious lack of parking," I mutter to myself as I turn back onto Main.

At least the Christopher situation left me wiser. Does it really matter if Sawyer was decent at Angelica's? *One night?*

No.

None of it matters, I remind myself. I'm gone at the end of the semester anyway, and all this is temporary. At least one of my applications to a school in a real city is sure to pan out, and I'll be gone by the start of summer.

Finally, I spot a car leaving from in front of the library, and turn my blinker on.

I'm meeting Tess at Jolly Jalapeño. She was different at lunch today. Lighter and more buoyant. It made me realize she'd slowly been deflating since I first met her. So when she suggested we go out, I thought, *Why not?*

As I step onto the sidewalk the windchill cuts straight through my coat and whips my hair around wildly. It's not dark yet, but the old fashioned street lamps are on. If I forget where I am completely, I can admit they give downtown a certain charm.

I lower my head against the wind as I pass the library, followed by a handful of colorful houses that have mostly been converted into shops. An antique store in a purple craftsman, the window basement sporting a neon sign advertising tarot reading, a green bungalow with a sign that reads COFFEE + PLANTS, and a shockingly pink two-story used as a coworking space, which is itself shocking in a town like this. I lift my head to sniff the air as I get closer to the sweet doughy smells hovering around Maddy's Bakery, even after it's long been closed for the day.

On the corner is the stately blue Victorian that houses Book Nook on its bottom floor, a staple of Blue Ridge owned by the Strongs. Although it was usually Sawyer's older brother Will at the register, any chance of seeing Sawyer when I didn't have to made my insides crawl. I never went in there if I could help it.

Now, I stop to look at the eye-catching display in the window. My gaze falls on a book with an illustrated cover similar to the ones I've seen Gia reading. Lavender with little gold stars in the background, an outline of a small town not unlike Blue Ridge, and two characters in the foreground with folded arms glaring at each other.

I've never heard of the author, Jackie Pine, but there's a good chance Gia has based on the books I've seen her reading. I glance at the sign over the display: *Local New Releases.* She probably doesn't have this one yet.

Mind made up, I step onto the wooden staircase, sure that whatever teenager working tonight won't recognize me. I'm halfway up when the internal lights flick off and a shadow approaches the glass front door.

My insides turn to ice as Sawyer comes into view through the glass. I freeze, like maybe if I stand perfectly still he won't notice I'm here. He reaches for the *Open* sign.

Our eyes lock.

Busted.

My heart picks up speed. I turn stiffly back to the sidewalk and walk as rapidly as I can without looking unbalanced.

Behind me, I hear the door open and keys jangle. Then thumping footsteps down the stairs.

Don't come this way, don't come thi—

"Why're you running away?"

I pretend I don't hear him.

"I can open back up for you if you need a book."

I peek at him. "No, thanks."

"Then why were you coming up the stairs?"

"I wasn't. I was stretching my legs."

"Ah, right right right. Makes sense." When I don't say anything, he says, "Where're we going now?"

We? I look at him sidelong. If he were anyone else, I'd think he was flirting. Or, maybe, if *I* were anyone else.

"Nowhere," I say.

For an entire block, we walk in tense silence. I take him in through the corner of my eye. Again with the open jacket and collar. His flannel is a dark green this time, and his jeans are snug enough that when he turns to push the pedestrian call button on the lamppost, my gaze has no choice but to drop to his ass.

I tear my eyes away and jaywalk across the empty intersection.

He follows me.

When we reach the other side of the street, I pause, waiting for him to go on his way.

He stops, too.

I finally face him and flap my arms. "Well?! Which way are you going?"

He mimics my arm-flap, looking like an overgrown child. "It's a secret."

He didn't do anything to hurt me that night at dinner, I remind myself.

Biting the inside of my cheek, I look past him, wishing traffic was worse so I could push him into it.

"You wish it were rush hour right now, don't you."

I'm stunned into honesty. "Yes."

It's his grin that does it, has me laughing incredulously. His eyes shine when I do. It brightens his whole face. He's always handsome, but the pleasure in his expression takes it to another level, makes him almost too beautiful to look at. His full lips, glimmering kind eyes, and ticklish-looking beard are almost too much.

The wind blows, and my hair flies everywhere, but I'm not cold.

"You know how insufferable you're being," I say without heat.

His eyes dim a fraction. "What do you want?"

"Just leave me alone," I say on a shrug.

The mischief fades from his expression. "Okay, Brie. I'll leave you alone."

There's a tug on my heart I can't explain, a pull at the gentle way he says my name.

He reaches out, and tucks my windswept hair behind

my ear. The nerves there light up, then trail a path down my body, sparking every inch to life along the way.

I'm in suspended animation, waiting for *something*.

Suddenly, he blinks. He pulls his hand back, and stuffs it into his pocket.

He says, "Have a good night," not bothering to meet my gaze.

Why do I feel like I just lost something? Confusion swirls through me as I grope for mental purchase. Is *this* his game? To act decent, get me worked up just for the fun of it, before turning icy?

Wait, no! The denial echoes through me.

I was not *worked up*.

The lingering heat between my legs whispers otherwise, but I ignore it. Sawyer Strong will not get to me. The game has changed, but the player is the same, and I refuse to be duped this time.

When he starts walking in the direction I'm going, I can only follow. I catch up when he stops at the next intersection.

"Are you following me?" His tone is teasing, but there's a dolor to it.

"Not intentionally . . . Where are you going?" The question is futile. There's only one place he could be headed, unless he's going on a tour of the fire department.

The *Walk* sign illuminates and we cross together.

"Jolly's. I'm meeting Ethan and Rich."

Dread swirls in my gut. It's just my luck he's going where I'm headed. And meeting up with his minions.

"I guess I am following you," I say tersely. "I'm meeting Tess."

His eyebrows shoot up, his iciness forgotten. "Good for her. I don't think she gets out a lot."

I bite my lip. That's the feeling I had, too. Even though she's from here, I've never heard Tess talk about friends. It's hard reconciling that with the easy friendship she's offered me.

As we approach the restaurant, the din inside becomes more audible.

Sawyer exhales raggedly, like he's dreading what he's about to do.

Then he reaches for the door.

"Tess and I were just coming for the tacos," I say dumbly as I stare across the restaurant.

Apparently, Blue Ridge does not mess around for Taco and Trivia Tursday.

It's a madhouse, it looks nothing like when I met Dev here my first week in town. The restaurant is absolutely *crammed*. Tables are pushed together, more seats than they can accommodate shoved into the mix, and they're all filled by trivia-goers who might as well be holding pitchforks for all the viciousness with which they jeer at one another.

As I stare, a hand appears beneath the sea of tables and grips my thigh. I shriek as a woman's face appears at my knees. She thanks me as she uses me for leverage to crawl out before heading toward the bathrooms.

People I recognize wave or nod at Sawyer, throwing uncertain glances at me. My insides crawl with anxiety as he acknowledges them all like it's just another Tuesday.

This is not what I had in mind when I agreed to meet Tess out.

If this were literally *any* city, there'd be another place for tacos around the corner, one across the street, maybe another a few blocks down. In any other city, I could text Tess to meet me somewhere—*anywhere*—else. But we're in Blue Ridge, and I don't want to let her down, so here I am, sitting at the last available table next to Sawyer.

Then my eyes widen and my pulse quickens as I notice Ethan Darvish walking over from the bar. Even though Sawyer was very clear about meeting his friends here, I feel like I'm in an episode of *The Twilight Zone*.

Be a fucking grownup, the voice in my head urges. *It's been fourteen years for shit's sake.* But something about being back in this town, with the same people who made my life a living hell, has me relapsing to the same emotional state I was in last time I was here, like I never left.

When Ethan sees me with Sawyer, there isn't even a fleeting look of surprise on his face. Instead, a giant grin breaks through his features.

"Brie," he says, leaning over and . . . *hugging me?*

My arms remain glued to my sides.

"Um, hi?" It comes out as a question.

Ethan looks at me—I mean *really* looks at me—with eyes full of intense meaning. "I'm really glad you're here."

"Thanks," I say, heart inflating a fraction.

See? the smug voice says.

The last time I saw Ethan Darvish, he was in a tux standing behind Sawyer, laughing at me with the whole school. He'd never been as cruel as Rich, but he'd still been their accomplice. And yet, looking at him now, with his open smile and kind words, he seems like a completely different person.

Maybe he is.

I glance up at Sawyer, who nods at Ethan conspiratorially.

Or maybe he isn't. It's a tiny pinprick to my heart, deflating it.

"Margarita okay with you, Brie?" Ethan asks, relieving a frizzy-haired server of a pitcher. "I already ordered a bunch of food."

"Sure," I say, trying to smile.

You're just being paranoid. We're adults now. Not everyone is out to get me. Maybe Ethan really has grown. And if Ethan's grown, maybe—

"Brie Queso!"

I wince, then raise my eyes to Richard B. Whitmore III. The most successful person I've ever been near.

Also, the biggest ass.

Maybe I'm in an episode of *American Horror Story* instead.

"Dude!" Rich's elated eyes travel between Sawyer and me before he claps him on the back. "You did it, man!"

Oh god. What did Sawyer do?

Am I part of some kind of bet? Am I the butt of some joke? *Again?* Is this why Ethan wasn't surprised to see me here?

I haven't felt this particular fight or flight response in years. I thought I felt it when I spotted Sawyer in his office that first day, but it wasn't this. Blood gushes in my ears, my heart beating like a hummingbird's.

"Rich," Sawyer grits out, eyes hard. "You remember Brie *Casey*. She'll be joining us with a friend."

Tess. I glance at the door, then the time. She's only a few minutes late, but the adrenaline already coursing through my system ramps up.

"I might not be staying," I say to my hands.

Understatement of the century. The second Tess gets here, we're leaving. We'll go to The Square for burgers, or grab a pizza from Angelica's and eat it in my car if we have to.

Ignoring me, Rich snorts, "What friend? *Dev?*"

The way he says his name, with casual derision, has my fingernails digging into my thighs.

"A friend from work," Sawyer says evenly, like he's speaking to one of the kindergarteners.

Rich snorts. "Didn't know Brie Queso had other friends."

His taunts are disturbingly familiar. Rich certainly hasn't grown in fourteen years.

And Sawyer still hangs out with him.

"Rich." Sawyer's voice is low and patient, but dripping with severity.

As an adult who's lived in the real world, away from Blue Ridge, I would view what's happening here as some idiot (Rich) who doesn't know how to keep his mouth shut, and a nice guy (Sawyer) who's putting him in his place.

But as the person who grew up here, around these exact men when they used to torment me, my paranoia only rises. Rich was never sly like Sawyer, always openly derisive. But they were always on the same page with one another. My body is tense, bracing for the inevitable.

Ethan changes the subject. "How was your meeting, *Richard?*"

"Productive," Rich answers carelessly, wedging his chair between Ethan and me. He turns, crowding me. "I hear you're a substitute teacher." Somehow he makes my job sound dirty.

I force myself to meet his eyes. There's nothing there, not even the malice I expect. Just a wall. "Yup."

His eyes may be blank, but his grin is like the devil's. "You're chatty."

The same server drops off some chips and appetizers. Sawyer reaches for the leg of my chair and drags me toward him until it's flush against his. Our thighs touch. His shoulders are so broad he has no choice but to extend his arm over the back of my chair. I look up at him, but he's staring at Rich, jaw clenched. The muscles in his neck protrude. And I get a whiff of—

I'm transported back in time and even though it shouldn't, my heart pounds a little faster.

"Do you still swim?" The quiet words are out of my mouth before I can stop them.

He looks down at me, surprised. "Most mornings, after I work out." His voice is low, for me only. "Why?"

Heat crawls up my neck. "Chlorine."

I *swear* the pulse in his throat stutters, but he presses his mouth into a straight line and nods once before returning his gaze to Rich.

"So where're you staying?" Rich asks me before crunching loudly into a chip.

My eyes cut to his. "Emerson Avenue."

He whistles, brows raised. "You shackin' up with some—"

Sawyer is on his feet, finger in Rich's face. "That's enough." People in nearby seats nudge one another, and I consider crawling under the island of tables.

I hate that Rich's words hit their mark, but they're the perfect imitation of what I heard at Everett Academy, pressing on a bruise that hasn't healed yet. Somehow, the worst of both my worlds have melded. *Trash, meet slut.*

Rich looks at Sawyer. "Seriously? She's been back in town for, like, a second. I've been by your side for years, and you treat me like this?"

In answer, Sawyer falls into his chair, arm snaking over my shoulders, lighting my skin on fire beneath my clothes.

Rich scoffs. "Dude. It's Brie *Ques*—"

"Nope." Ethan grabs the collar of Rich's neatly pressed button-down, ignoring his protests, and drags him toward the back hallway where the bathrooms are.

Sawyer's arm drops from my shoulders, and I'm suddenly cold even as I try to process what just happened.

"Listen," he says, "I'm sorry. Rich has no sense. No empathy. He's a complete nitwit. If he crosses the line again, I will personally evict him." He licks his lips, and I can't help tracking the movement. "But if you want to leave right now, I get it. I'll order some tacos to go and bring them to you. You won't have to see him again."

My heart beats slow and heavy in my chest. I should take him up on his offer. Leave right now. I know I should.

So why don't I?

Sawyer's thigh brushes mine. That unique-to-him smell wraps around me. I watch the fist in his lap grow tighter with every passing second.

Then I remember something Rich said.

"What did he mean when he said 'you did it'?"

Sawyer's throat works on a nervous swallow. He leans over for two of the glasses Ethan poured ages ago, and I wonder if he'll answer.

"Came out to Tursdays," he says dismissively, handing me a marg without meeting my eyes.

I'm sure he's hiding something, but I don't push him. What's the point? He'll never confess to it. But it's all the evidence I need that he's not the good guy he's been pretending to be. There's a comfort to Rich's open loathing. With him, I know where he stands. But Sawyer's made a fool of me too many times to fall for his act again.

"Fifteen minutes to trivia time!" the emcee announces, and the bar erupts in cheers and jeers, piercing my thoughts.

"We've been here for half an hour?" I ask, alarmed.

My eyes flick to the door. Then the time. Worry pulses dully in the back of my mind. Tess doesn't strike me as a flake. But people are different outside of work. Maybe she *is* the type to run perpetually thirty minutes behind in her social life.

No. Instinctively, I know that's not her.

I shoot her a quick text letting her know I'm here. I stare at my phone for a few seconds, waiting for the three dots to show up.

"She's a big girl," Sawyer says coolly. "She's probably just looking for parking."

I relax a little. Parking was a nightmare, and has probably only gotten worse.

When Ethan's back with a chastened Rich, and another ten minutes passes, I still haven't heard from her. Even the Korean fried cauliflower taco that Sawyer practically shoved at me, and subsequently had me black out in ecstasy, isn't enough to assuage my worries.

It's this town. It puts me on edge, in a constant state of fight or flight. What do I even know about Tess, anyway? She's a work colleague. And a grown woman. Maybe she changed her mind about coming. Or took a nap and just, *poof,* forgot.

I take in a deep breath then exhale slowly, letting all my paranoia and suspicions drain out of me, and focus on the conversation.

"Where's Abbi tonight?" Sawyer asks Ethan.

"Girls' night with my sisters," he says.

To me, Sawyer explains, "Ethan's with Abbi, James

Baret's little sister. She was a freshman when we were seniors."

I vaguely remember her, best friends with Ethan's twin sisters of the same year.

Rich laughs. "I still can't believe you settled down, man. You were such a player!"

"Hey," Ethan protests, "she was with someone else for *ten years*. What was I supposed to do? Join a convent?"

Sawyer sputters into his drink, and I know he's imagining the same thing as me: Ethan in a nun's habit.

"Monastery," he corrects.

Rich smirks. "Joining a monastery wouldn't help, kings have huge harems."

"Monarchy," I say, biting back a smile.

Rich tilts his head, puzzled. "You're talking nonsense."

"Malarkey," Sawyer and I say together.

"You lost me," Rich says.

Sawyer and I grin at each other, warmth washing over me.

This is okay. This is fine. This isn't high school. I don't have to trust these people to enjoy myself tonight.

Then the door to the restaurant opens, and a wild-eyed Tess stumbles in.

CHAPTER 17
SAWYER

I WATCH Brie tow Tess to the bathroom as people around us thump their fists on the table in sync to their chants of "TACO TURSDAY" like a bad SNL skit.

There was something clearly off about Tess, like she was giving off uncanny valley vibes. Her demeanor was *almost* perfectly put together. Her eyes were *almost* perfectly bright. Her lips pulled up in *almost* a perfect smile. But none of it was quite right.

For half a second I consider following them, seeing if I can help somehow, but I don't want to get in the way, make Tess uncomfortable.

I look past Rich to Ethan. "What do you think was going on?" I ask, tipping my head toward the hallway Brie disappeared into with Tess.

"No idea," he says. "Maybe family trouble?" Ethan just met Tess tonight, so he wouldn't know her only real family is Nash.

I shake my head. "Doubtful."

"Alright alright alright," the emcee's voice blares as he shuffles papers in his hand and the restaurant quiets. "Let's make sure everyone's here. When I call your team's name, give me a little shout." He calls out names like *Trivia Newton John*, *Pen-Fifteen*, and *Insufferable Pedants* to responding cheers from the corresponding team.

Rich pops forward and says, "She's probably just on her period."

"You're disgusting," I sneer.

He gives me a smug better-than-thou look. "Tell that to a woman. It's completely natural. Apparently."

"Periods aren't disgusting," I say. "*You* are. Tess didn't come in here like that because she's on her period."

The emcee calls, "And finally, *Anyone Up For A Game of Naked Twister After This?*"

Rich stands up and shouts, "Offer's open, ladies!" over a chorus of boos from the other teams.

Ethan has a look of mild disgust on his face as he forces Rich into his seat by the shoulder. "I told you to stop naming the team without us."

"You guys weren't paying attention," Rich shrugs.

Frustration boils over in my chest. Everything was going fine with Brie before Rich sat down. I could see it in her eyes when Ethan greeted her. She was relaxing. Things are never going to be how I really want them, I know I don't deserve the forgiveness I dream of or the desire I fantasize about, but Brie and I were at the same table and she wasn't looking for the fastest escape route.

For a brief moment, she was even smiling.

Then Rich showed up.

Next to me, Rich whisper-yells, "Sawyer! How many brains does an octopus have? One, right? It's a trick question?"

"Nine." I reply automatically.

"*Nine?!*"

In one swift move, I take Tess's abandoned seat next to him and yank the pencil out of his hand as he writes in the answer. He looks up, and his eyes widen.

"Richard," I say, keeping my tone even and clear so he doesn't miss a word. "If you ever treat anyone like that again in my presence, our friendship is over. If you so much as breathe in a way that makes Brie uncomfortable, our friendship is over. That means insulting Dev, too."

Rich guffaws. "*Dev?*"

"Yeah. *Dev*. That goes along with treating *anyone* like shit."

"Dude, I woulda thought getting in Brie's pants would loosen you u—"

I'm on my feet, knuckles white as I fist Rich's collar. Vaguely, I'm aware of how eerily quiet it is around us, how Ethan scrubs his face with both his hands and looks up at the ceiling, but my focus is on Rich, the person I've called a friend my entire life. Was I ever as bad as him? Did he get worse? How did I ever tolerate him or myself, or any of it?

"One. More. Word," I dare. "Try it out. One more word."

"Bu—"

Ethan clasps his hand over Rich's mouth. "Dude, you have *got* to shut up. What's the matter with you? Who do you spend time with when you're in California?"

Rich's company is worth billions of dollars. I'm certain he's not used to this treatment. He lives in California, where he's surrounded by people whose salaries are paid by him. They have every incentive to put up with his bullshit.

His expression goes from bewildered to indignant as he slaps Ethan's hand away. "Dude, *you* guys are who I hang out with. Why do you think I'm back here all the time?" He stands up, chair scraping against the floor. His eyes harden as he closes the distance between us. "But I've got better places to be if you'd rather hang out with trash."

Red bleeds into my vision, but I force myself to not react as we face off for what feels like ages.

Rich is my oldest friend. Ethan had a happy family, other friends, was always popular, but Rich always felt like another me. Even as a kid, I recognized his parents were just as shitty as my dad, that when Rich and I were together, it was an escape for us both.

My therapist helped me see that my hurtful behavior was a mask, something that helped me avoid looking in the mirror and seeing how much I was really hurting. It was self-preservation. I always assumed the same was true for Rich, the other me.

But I was wrong about him. I could justify our behavior at eight, twelve, eighteen. But now that we're both in our thirties? The red fades from my vision, replaced by pity.

This is just who Rich is.

He must register my resignation, because he huffs, "Fuck off." He balls the paper from the trivia game in his fist and chucks it at me as he walks away, calling out, "If anyone's up for a game of naked twister, I'm leaving now."

A trio of girls who look like they probably attend the college just outside town scramble out after him.

I fall into my seat, feeling like I aged decades in the last three minutes.

"When he calms down, we'll talk to him," Ethan says.

"When'll that be?" Rich can hold a grudge.

He shrugs. "A couple months, at least."

With a weary sigh, I nod. "Sounds about right."

After several moments, Ethan picks the conversation back up where we left it before we gave Blue Ridge something new to talk about. "Is Tess dating someone?"

Glancing toward the bathrooms, I say, "I don't really know. We're friendly at work. Well, she's friendly with everyone. But it's superficial, she keeps to herself. I was surprised when Brie said she was meeting her tonight."

Ethan hesitates before asking, "How are things going with Brie?"

I shove my hand into my hair, and I must still be agitated because of Rich because I blurt, "She's driving me up the fucking wall. She doesn't trust me, you should see the look in her eyes when I'm around. It's like she's just waiting for me to ruin her life."

And the worst part is, I know I deserve it. Every mistrusting look, every sneer.

I add, "I know it's impossible, but I wish we could just start at zero."

"Have you talked to her? Like, *really* talked to her?" Ethan asks. "I mean, sat down and had a conversation, shown her you're different?"

Ethan doesn't know my whole story, doesn't even know about the years of therapy, but there's solace in knowing at least he can see I'm not the same as I used to be. It gives me hope that, if she'd just look, Brie might see it too.

But he doesn't know what all's involved in having a conversation like that with her. There's too much history to trudge through, too much baggage, and she'll probably hate me more afterward. It's better to spare her.

I shake my head. "Honestly, I didn't think it'd be like this." When I saw her that first day, I thought she'd be a sub, and I'd be her boss, and we'd be cordial. Let the past stay in the past, act like strangers who work together. "I didn't expect to keep bumping into each other." *Or to still have feelings for her.*

Ethan grins sardonically. "In *Blue Ridge*, you didn't think you'd bump into her?"

"Besides," I add, ignoring him, "it'd be unprofessional to dig into it all, right? I'm her boss."

Ethan raises his eyebrows. "Unprofessional, like tugging her chair toward you in a crowded restaurant? Or putting your arm over her shoulders like you're claiming her? Or nearly getting into an altercat—"

"I got it," I interrupt, rubbing the back of my neck and laughing ruefully.

I am so fucked. I've got to start acting like an adult when I'm around her.

CHAPTER 18

BRIE

I STEP INTO THE BATHROOM, Tess stumbling in behind me as chants of "TACO TURSDAY" swell from the restaurant. She goes straight to the sink, gripping the edges as she stares at herself in the mirror. I try to catch her eye, but she won't look at me.

"What's going on with you?" I ask.

She breathes in, and as she exhales, I see her face transform in the mirror. Her eyes brighten, a soft smile appears with a glimpse of white teeth, and her shoulders straighten.

My eyes narrow. I had that exact move perfected by the end of my last semester at Everett Academy.

Now, she turns to me, and in an oddly soothing voice says, "Nothing, I'm fine."

I take a step toward her. "No, you're not. Tell me what happened." *Or I swear I'll shake it out of you.* Not really. I wouldn't resort to violence. But man, do I want to.

Her smile falters. "Really, it's nothing."

"Good. I like nothing."

She swallows, and I see the cracks start to form. Her shoulders drop and her eyes start to water.

Oh god. I pushed too hard. I'm no good at this, too rough around the edges. I don't know how to be comforting to someone else.

My hands rise uncertainly. "Tess?"

A sob wrenches out of her, and she tumbles into my arms. I pat her awkwardly at first, trying to say soothing things, but almost everything comes out as gibberish. How do I comfort someone when I have no idea what's wrong?

She's taller than me by several inches, but she seems so small in this moment. I hug her tighter, telling her I'm here, it'll be okay, whatever it is, we'll fix it.

When the crying turns into soft hiccups, I draw my head back and look at her.

The mask is gone. Her sad blue eyes make my heart ache. I wipe away the final tears with my thumbs and tuck her hair behind her ears.

"Talk to me."

She shakes her head. "It's embarrassing."

"I'll be the judge of that."

With a watery laugh, she nods and takes a fortifying breath. "It's my ex, CJ. He's having a hard time understanding we're not together anymore." She smiles, almost like nothing's wrong. "But it's just words, and words can't hurt me."

I want to take her by the shoulders and shout *What do you mean they can't hurt you? Did you see yourself a second ago?!*

A memory swims forward of the first time we had lunch together. *I know what it's like to be treated poorly.* Protectiveness worms through me.

I ask, "What happened?"

She looks up at the ceiling and blinks rapidly. "We dated for years. He was never a great boyfriend, but he'd fallen in with a bad crowd a year or so ago, and I watched him turn into a bad *person*. I gave him an ultimatum. When nothing changed by New Year's, I broke up with him. But then the calls started. When he called a couple days ago, I told him off. It felt really good. I thought that was the end of it." That's why she was in such a good mood when she invited me out. "But tonight, he was at my door when I opened it to leave. He kind of forced his way through." When she sees my face, she's quick to add, "He never laid a hand on me, but he . . . he kind of walked forward, which made me walk backward, and we ended up in my apartment with the door locked."

"Tess!" I practically shout. "He might not have put a hand on you, but that's *physical*. Like, kidnapping or false imprisonment or something. I mean, it can't be legal!"

She shakes her head. "It was my fault. If I hadn't walked backward, he wouldn't have come inside."

That's three times now. Three times I've wanted to shake her. "It was not your fault," is all I say through gritted teeth.

She doesn't hear me. "He begged me for another chance. He used all the predictable tactics. I've talked about it with my therapist. Weaponizing love, she calls it. I knew what he was doing, but it still affected me—"

"Of course it did."

"—and I finally got him to leave when I told him I'd think about getting back together."

My jaw drops, and I hastily bring it back up. I don't want her to think I blame her.

"It's what he wanted, it was the only way to get rid of him," she says.

And guarantees he'll be back. But I don't tell her that. She surely already knows. And what choice did she have?

"Tess, this isn't normal. People don't act like this."

"I know," she says. "He's having trouble letting go."

I'm shaking with frustration and fury. What kind of monster would act like this? And to *Tess*, of all people?

And here, I thought my problems were so important. Even the thing with Christopher pales compared to this. The mind games Sawyer plays? Just that: little games.

I wish there was something I could do for her.

"Does anyone else know about this?"

She shakes her head. "Not really. There was nothing to tell before tonight."

"What about Nash?" From the little I remember about her brother, I'd bet money if he already knew, this guy wouldn't dare mess with Tess.

"I wouldn't want to bother him, he's got his own life."

That's the fourth time.

My fingernails dig into my palms so hard, I expect to draw blood. "Do you have anyone you can stay with?"

She half-laughs, half-sobs. "I haven't done a good job keeping up with my friends."

Of course she doesn't. Her asshole ex would have isolated her as much as possible.

I give her a reassuring smile.

She says, "Is that supposed to be a smile?"

A disbelieving, single syllable resembling a laugh escapes my throat. "It was supposed to be. Come home with me tonight. Gia would kill me if I let you stay anywhere else."

"No." She says it with so much fortitude, I draw back a little. "Tonight's done, he won't be back."

"But—"

"I mean it, Brie. He won't be back for a while. I won't let this disrupt my life anymore, let alone anyone else's."

"But we're friends, it's not a disruption. I *want*—"

"We are friends. Thank you." She stoops to hug me, seeming entirely too much like her usual self.

When she pulls back, I don't let go. I won't. I have to do something. I rack my brain.

"Promise me something," I say. "Tell someone else. Tell Nash."

She sucks in a sharp breath. She really believes she's a burden to her big brother.

"Tell him," I urge, "and let him know I know."

She presses her lips together in a tight line, but she finally nods.

I don't loosen my hold on her. "And memorize Gia's address: two Emerson Avenue. In Belmont."

"Okay," she says.

"Say it."

"Two Emerson Ave."

I give her one more squeeze. Someone enters the bathroom, and sounds from the bar echo in with her. Pink crawls up Tess's cheeks as I break the hug.

"Wanna go to The Square and get a milkshake?" I ask. "The diner will be quiet on a *Tursday*." I roll my eyes at the word.

She smiles, sniffling. "I'd like that."

"I'll go get our stuff. Meet you back here."

I leave the bathroom, walk down the hallway, and round the corner back into the restaurant. Sawyer's right where I left him.

Laughing.

Having a great time as Ethan grins back.

No sign of Rich, though. With any luck, the earth opened up beneath him and swallowed him back to the depths of hell where he belongs.

For a little while, I forgot how awful they are. All of them. I was almost pulled in by Sawyer's charm, Ethan's hospitality. The way they dealt with Rich. I let it distract me from my worry over Tess. She was late and I *knew* there was something wrong, but when Sawyer said it was probably parking trouble, I let myself believe him. She could've been hurt—or worse!—while I was bantering about harems and royalty with that chlorinated asshole who doesn't give a shit about anyone but himself.

Sawyer looks up as I approach. He shoots to his feet, fake concern painting his face.

"How's Tess? Where is she?"

"She's waiting for me in the bathroom." I grab my jacket and Tess's purse, and drop some cash on the table.

"You're leaving?"

"We're leaving."

My phone vibrates in my back pocket. I reach for it in case it's Tess calling from the bathroom.

It's a text from Dev.

Guess what

I ignore it, but before I can pocket my phone again, it vibrates in my hand.

Harvest dumped me for Sawyer.

I read it two more times, trying to process. As I do, a prickling sensation climbs up my spine, and pure unadulterated rage lodges its ugly claws into me.

It's official. Everyone sucks. Tess's toxic waste of an ex-boyfriend treating her like garbage. Nash *not* making it clear to his little sister that she's important enough to tell things to.

And Sawyer.

How did he do it? Did he get Harvest's number while we were all there? Did he even wait until the next day to call her, or did he have her over that very night? She was eager enough.

Sawyer steps close, his voice low. "What can I do? Is Tess okay?"

I pause to look at him.

"How do you do that?"

He blinks. "Do what?"

"How do you make your face so sincere? Your voice so full of concern?"

His brow dips. "I *am* concerned."

"Right," I scoff. "Tess and I are leaving, and I'm positive neither of us wants to see another man again."

I want to clap at the hurt that flashes across his face.

The man deserves an Oscar.

CHAPTER 19
SAWYER

THE NEXT MORNING, I walk into work feeling like the undead, circles under my eyes and beard unruly. My mind is still on Tess and Brie, exactly where it's been all night. Okay, if I'm honest, it's been sixty-percent Brie.

Eighty-five, tops.

That's not to say I don't care about Tess—I do. But based on what Brie said about neither of them wanting to see another man again, I assume Tess just needs some time to realize she's better off without whatever loser she was dating.

Brie, though? I can't figure her out. One minute, we're fine, for us at least, and the next, she's epically pissed off. Specifically, pissed off at me.

She accused me of faking my concern, but that couldn't be further from the truth. I wish I could understand where her sudden glacial attitude came from.

For hours, I work on autopilot. I chat with children's parents, answer emails, have a phone call with the school district. By lunchtime, gun to my head, I couldn't tell you which parents I spoke to, what the emails were about, or why the district called.

Glancing at the clock for the thousandth time, I notice third grade lunch is starting. When Brie has a standing date with Tess at the teachers' lounge.

Defiantly, I take my book out of my bag and sit at my desk with my lunch like I've done a hundred times. I unscrew my thermos, take a leisurely bite of my chili, lean back in my chair, and open my book to the dog-eared page.

My eyes glaze over the words as I consider storming down the hall, locking Brie in a closet with me, and having a real conversation like Ethan suggested. I'd ask her *very nicely* to explain what I did last night to make her so angry. I want to know if she can ever see who I am, instead of who I was.

And, since this is a fantasy, I'd kiss the hell out of her.

No. She'd kiss the hell out of me.

But I can't do that, especially the last bit. Not at school, at least. *Polite and professional*. Those were Brie's words, and they're good ones.

I glance at the clock. It's already five minutes into third grade lunch.

Five minutes I could've spent with her.

Scratching my jaw, I rise deliberately to my feet and pick up my thermos and water bottle, as if intentional movements will convince myself I'm being rational when I know with absolute certainty I'm behaving like a junkie. I *just* gave myself a pep talk about polite and professional, yet all I can think about is getting answers.

As I draw near the teachers' lounge, I brace myself for whatever I'm about to walk into. More hostility from Brie? A teary-eyed Tess? The inaugural meeting of their new man-haters' club?

I push through the door, and several teachers pass me, leaving just Tess and Brie inside.

A heavy rock lands in my gut as I take them in. Tess's head is tipped back while she blinks up at the ceiling. Brie has her head in her hands, shoulders shaking.

I take swift strides toward them. Before I can ask what's wrong, Tess pulls herself together enough to say, "And I haven't had a pickle since!"

Brie cackles like a banshee.

I huff out a relieved laugh.

They glance over, and their laughter fizzles. Brie turns her gaze pointedly away. It stings, but I ignore it and plunk my thermos and water bottle on the table. If I did something wrong, she's going to have to explain.

I drop into a chair at the small round table. Brie's looking everywhere but me.

Tess meets my eyes. Her lips press together in an embarrassed smile.

"You good?" I ask her.

She nods. "Yeah. Sor—"

I interrupt, "No apologies. And you don't have to tell me anything. But I hope you know you always can."

And there it is, a genuine smile as she nods. I've always liked Tess. We started teaching here the same year, and even though I'm not particularly close to her, she's kind of like the annoyingly chipper little sister I never had. I hate to think someone broke her heart.

She shifts, and a flash of something conspiratorial crosses her face as she glances at Brie then back at me with playful mischief in her eyes. Even though I don't know what it's about, I can't help feeling like Tess and I have an alliance.

"So, Sawyer," Tess starts, voice suspiciously nonchalant, "I hear you're dating someone new."

My first instinct is to deny it, but with the expectant way Tess is looking at me, I decide to play out whatever game this is. "It's possible. What of it?"

Brie's eyes snap up, finally focusing on me. She looks murderous. Is it still because of whatever she was mad about last night, or is it the prospect of me dating someone? Hope rises in my chest that Brie might be jealous of some imaginary other woman.

"Well," Tess continues, "I heard that you went to dinner with Brie and Dev."

That hope expands in my chest knowing Brie's been talking about me with Tess.

I reply, "That was weeks ago."

"*And*," Tess goes on, "Dev had a date."

This stumps me for a moment, and I almost blurt out, "He did?" But of course he had a date. It's why I went to dinner in the first place, the crestfallen look on Brie's face when she saw Dev with someone else had me jumping into action before I could think better of it.

"*Aaand*," Tess says, "now you have a thing with Harvest."

"Harvest?" At first, I think she's talking about the garden I'm planning after my cabin's built.

Tess frowns and looks at Brie. "Isn't that her name? Harvest?"

It hits me. *Harvest*. Dev's date.

Then I hear her words anew and I choke on my bite of chili. So much for Tess and me in an alliance. She's trying to bury me, I'm completely on my own here. Why would she think I have a thing for *Harvest*?

I gulp my water and bang my fist into my chest before I answer. "Where did you hear that?" I cough out.

Tess's mouth is agape and she doesn't answer, but Brie's eyes narrow on me, like I'm some scheming criminal.

I'm tired of guessing at what's in her head. Of not knowing why she's mad at me, or what she blames me for. Ever since she's been back, I've been nothing but chivalrous to her. Except for the lack of professionalism on my part. And maybe barging in on her not-real-date with Dev. And arguing about what really happened in first grade.

But none of that warrants *this*.

Fed up, I return her expression, narrowing my own eyes at her. I'm acting more like a kid on the playground than the principal, but Brie does this to me. She drives me to the brink of insanity, forcing the worst out of me until I almost break.

She rolls her eyes.

And then I *do* break.

"Use your words, Brie." I say it with condescension I wouldn't even use on a student.

She scoffs. "I have no words for you, Sawyer." Then a humorless smile spreads across her lips. "Or, maybe I can think of two."

I lean one elbow on the table, meeting her grin with my own maniacal one. "Don't be shy. Go ahead and say it, honey." I place my other elbow on the table. "And while you're at it, tell me what all you told Tess about our date that night."

"It wasn't a date," she sneers.

Smirking, I say, "But you gossiped with your friend like it was." It's more wishful thinking than anything else. I want it to be true.

"Only to tell her how much of a jerk you were," she hisses.

Tess raises a finger. "Actually—"

Brie cuts her off with a death glare, and Tess leans back in her chair, wide eyes ping-ponging between us.

When I chuckle, her death glare transfers to me.

I plant my hands on the table and stand up. "What *exactly* is your problem with me, Brie? Please, share with the class. Because I can never tell."

Her eyes widen, shocked I'm calling her out. "God forbid someone not like the Prince of Blue Ridge! But that's all there is to it, it's as simple as me not liking you. You have no respect for anyone else, no regard for anyone's feelings. You think you can just do whatever you want, *take* whatever you want."

I made a sound like *pfft*. If that were at all true, Brie and I would have a very different relationship.

"What am I supposed to have taken?" I ask indulgently.

She lurches to her feet, indignant I even have to ask. "Oh, I don't know. How about *Harvest*?"

My eyes cut to Tess—I completely forgot she brought her up earlier. But I'm still not following. "Harvest?"

"Dev told me," she snarls.

At this point, I'm pretty sure I've connected the dots. She's not jealous of some imaginary woman. She's protective of Dev. But if she's accusing me of something, I need her to spell it out, every inconceivable detail. "Dev told you what?"

She rolls her eyes. Not just her eyes. Her entire torso rolls in one exasperated halo. "Harvest dumped him. For *you*."

"And why would she do that?"

A flicker of uncertainty crosses her face, but she leans closer and doubles down. "Because you *took her*."

I can't help the snort of laughter that escapes. "You're talking about a human person."

"Fine, it takes two, and she made her choice," she says primly, "but don't deny your part."

"My part in *what*?"

She flaps her hands in the air. "In breaking Dev's heart!"

Dev wasn't exactly smitten that night. "I doubt it."

Coming around the table, she points her finger at my chest. "So you admit it!"

I turn my body toward her. "Admit I broke Dev's heart?"

"That you're with Harvest!"

I step closer. "I don't admit that."

Her arms cross, pushing up her pretty tits. "Why not?"

My hands shove into my pockets. "Because it isn't true."

She bares her teeth, making that same angry face I love so much. "So it's all a game? You proved you could take her from Dev, then dumped her?"

It's impressive. This mental gymnastics. All to keep thinking the worst of me.

"I was never with her. Never talked to her, saw her, or thought of her for a second after that night until this conversation. And" —I pause, staring at Brie for one loaded moment— "I wouldn't have her."

Brie frowns, like *this* is the most confusing part of all, before hardening her face again. "Because she's not good enough for you? Figures."

Hands still in my pockets, I tilt toward her and enunciate so she doesn't miss a word. "Because I'm not interested in her."

She inhales sharply. Her pupils dilate and that plump lower lip juts out. It would be so easy to capture between my teeth. I have to tighten every muscle in my body to stop myself.

"So!" Tess claps her hands once.

Brie and I jerk away from each other. We blink back into reality, and after one more loaded look, we fall into our seats.

"I like your tie," Tess says.

I look down. Bluey stares back.

"Thanks."

This is my favorite tie because kids go crazy for *Bluey*, I get at least triple the high-fives when I wear it. I wear these goofy ties to appear more approachable to the kids. I dole out high-fives like candy, I show up to a gym class at least once a week to challenge the class to a race against me, and I have a special secret box for kids to leave messages for me if they're ever too scared to talk. Once, a kindergartener left a drawing that prompted us to learn his older step-brother was bullying him.

The point is, I take this job seriously. But I haven't been acting like it lately.

I look around. We're still the only teachers in the lounge, and I heave out a shuttering sigh.

Fuck. I can't keep doing this. I got carried away. Again. Completely unprofessional in a professional setting. I shouldn't have even allowed myself to come down here.

Brie is back to dutifully ignoring me, which is for the best.

"Next week's spirit week," Tess says, completely oblivious to my internal scolding. "Do you have any intel on when Funny Bunny will make an appearance?"

When the BRES mascot makes his appearance during

spirit week is a surprise to everyone except the person in the suit.

Spoiler: it's me. I'm Funny Bunny.

"Nice try," I tell her, screwing the top on my thermos and standing up. "It's a surprise."

CHAPTER 20

SAWYER

"YOU LOOK LIKE SHIT," Will says when I climb out of my truck.

"Feel like it too." I glance up at the large Colonial I grew up in.

My brother pats my shoulder. "It won't be so bad. Last month, things were civil. It's getting better."

I look down as we walk up the stone pathway to the front door, not bothering to argue. The truth is, can things really be considered civil if I dissociate the whole time? Sure, it means there are no arguments that way, but *civil*? Not likely.

"It's fine," I tell him. "The way I look and feel, for once, doesn't have anything to do with this dinner."

Will's hand stops halfway to the doorbell. "What is it, then?"

Scratching my jaw, I look up at the magnolia tree I used to get yelled at for climbing as a kid because it might have affected the landscaping.

Out of the corner of my eye, I see Will fold his arms over his chest. We may not have seen a lot of each other growing up with our age difference, but Will and I have become close since I moved back to Blue Ridge. He can read me too well.

"It's the Casey girl, isn't it."

"What is this, a period drama? Her name is Brie."

He gives me a flat look. "Fine. It's *Brie,* isn't it."

"What've you heard?" My eyes are back on the shiny green leaves. Aside from his first warning weeks ago, Will and I have managed to avoid talking about her.

"I heard you guys went out a couple weeks ago to Angelica's . . . And that she was with you at trivia night."

Thank fuck he doesn't know how I acted in the teacher's lounge this morning.

Despite feeling like shit, my lips quirk. "You mean on Tuesday?"

"I'm not saying that."

I chuckle, but he levels me with a serious expression.

"Look," he says, "I don't know what happened between you two when you were kids, I only heard the rumors. But tormenting Brie Casey—"

The door swings open, and Dear Old Dad stands in the doorway, his Mayor Mask perfectly in place to greet his two sons. I look at my watch, 6:31.

How much did he hear?

"You're late," he grumbles.

His eyes skate over us. He notes Will's tailored shirt and pressed slacks with a slight nod before moving to me. I'm in chinos and a button-up, sleeves rolled to my elbows. It's more of an effort than he deserves, but I do it for Will. And it still doesn't matter because Dad's lips curl with disappointment, giving me a twisted sense of satisfaction.

He turns to walk back through the foyer, his dress shoes

clicking on the marble floor as he calls over his shoulder, "Food's ready."

Of course it's ready, he gets it catered.

Will squeezes my shoulder, sensing my irritation. "We'll talk more later," he says under his breath as we follow.

Dad insists on us using the formal dining room for these dinners, even though it seats sixteen and it's only ever the three of us.

"You were talking about the Casey girls," he says genially when we've all filled our plates.

I freeze. Will visibly winces, and I almost feel bad for him. He doesn't even ask for us to be one big happy family. All he's ever wanted is for the three of us to tolerate one another. But it's complicated. How my big brother endured the pressure of being the mayor's first-born is baffling. I couldn't do it.

When neither Will nor I answers, he goes on with a toothy smile. "Heard the middle one came back. I thought we were rid of her, down one, two to go. But now we have to start all over again." He studies me through his glasses. "You going to run her out of town again, Son?"

Bile rises in my throat. He's talking about Brie and her sisters like they're a family of rabid animals in this town. Is this what he was like when he was actual Mayor? Treating whole families in his constituency like vermin?

And Brie thinks I'm just like him, I think bitterly. *The Prince of Blue Ridge.*

"Not if I can help it," I grind out.

"Well, why not?" he asks with mock surprise. "I was never prouder of you than when you ran her out the first time."

Will clears his throat. "Dad, he didn't run her off. Brie

and Sawyer were seniors. Lots of kids move after graduation."

I know our dad is silently adding to Will's statement. *Lots of kids go to college.* It's just one item on a mile-long list that Dad can never forgive me for. Giving up a spot at his elite alma mater I was destined for in order to forge my own way. The degrees I got online are worthless in his eyes.

"Yes, well, that middle one stayed away, didn't she? Until recently."

I roll back my shoulders, my blood spinning in my skull.

Be civil. Don't engage.

His sharp eyes bore into me as he sneers. "The whole town knew what you did to her during your prom. That's why she stayed away."

"We don't know that, Dad," Will says.

Dad looks like a predator. *No.* Worse. He looks like a scavenger. A vulture.

"Oh, but I do. You know how I know?" He doesn't wait for an answer. "Because I know *people.* You don't stay mayor of a town like Blue Ridge for decades without understanding how people work. Their desires, their dreams. More importantly, their fears." He turns to Will. "You'd do well to remember that if you want to keep your position, Son."

I shake my head. "You sound like a comic book villain right now."

"Ridiculous," he announces with a sweep of his hand. "You're a Strong. We're the heroes in this town. It's in your blood. You lost your way, but you'll find it again. All you have to do is tap into that person before you left. The one who knew people like I do. You knew how to work that girl like a puppet, didn't you." His chuckle is cold.

"Are you listening to yourself right now?" I push my

chair away from the table and toss my cloth napkin onto my untouched food. "This is something you're proud of me for? Being an asshole to a teenage girl?" I lean forward, meeting his eyes. "The worst parts of me are all your doing."

"Watch your tone."

I laugh, standing up. "Or what? You'll cut me off? Deny me my inheritance? *Disown* me? You've played all your cards. You have nothing left."

"Sawyer," Will says as I round the table.

"Sorry, Brother."

When I leave, I don't give my dad the satisfaction of hearing me slam the door.

CHAPTER 21

BRIE

ALRIGHT. Fine. I might have accused Sawyer of something he didn't do. Jumped to a conclusion. Treated him *very slightly* unfairly because of it.

But how was I supposed to know this was the first time ever when he wasn't the asshole?

Dev confirmed Harvest asked him for Sawyer's number. Not the other way around.

(Which is, by the way, extremely rude and insensitive. How she had the tits to ask a guy she's dating for another guy's number, I don't know. But Dev has a heart of gold and when I asked him why he gave it to her, his white teeth appeared in his thick beard and he said, "Who am I to stand in the way of love?")

However! I can say with a hundred percent confidence that Sawyer is still an irritating ass.

He's in a bunny costume right now, talking to my students in a stupid voice, completely ignoring me.

And *yes*, I know how that sounds. But he is absolutely one-hundred-percent, no-doubt-about-it ignoring me.

When I offered to offload the box of fidget toys from

him, he turned his head away from me, and proceeded to fumble them in his bunny paws instead of accepting my help. I couldn't see his eyes, but I just *know* he was looking at me when I offered—I could sense it.

What's more, when he asked if anyone had any questions, and none of my students raised their hands, I spoke up and asked one to get the ball rolling. Like a *nice supportive teacher* would. And *once again*, he looked at me with those vacant bunny eyes before turning back to the students without answering the damn question.

It's fucking infuriating!

I'm fuming by the time the Funny Bunny presentation is over and the final bell rings.

My rage fuels me as I wave the kids off at the pickup line, Funny Bunny doling out hugs at the far end.

And I am apoplectic as I trail through the empty school, smiling stiffly as the last teachers wave their goodbyes. Even the promise of meeting Tess at Jolly's for a drink isn't enough to cool me down.

So when I return to my classroom only to find him there, still in the stupid costume, gathering the props he left behind, I turn rabid.

"Hey!" I call out.

He freezes, just for a second. But it's enough. I have him. He can't pretend he didn't hear me this time. I see him take a deep breath through the suit as he turns around to face me in the empty classroom.

Voice muffled, he says, "How can I help you, Ms. Casey?"

For one horrible moment, I think I have it all wrong. What if it isn't Sawyer in that costume?

But one look at those broad shoulders, the way he tries to stuff his paws into non-existent pockets, then pulls the paws off and rubs the back of his furry neck, and I know it's him.

Marching up to him, I shut the classroom door and say, "Why are you avoiding me?"

"I'm just being professional here," he says, resigned.

"Professional, my ass!" I hiss. "You're acting like I don't exist!"

"I don't know what you're—"

Before he can finish, I yank the bunny head off. Sawyer's face is startled and sweaty. His cheeks are red and his eyes, dark and brooding, hold mine with startling intensity.

"Trust me," he says, voice husky but clear as day, "I know you exist."

His gaze drops. To my lips. My neck. My breasts. Lower. It singes my skin before his eyes rise to meet mine again. Desire lances through me, almost painful in its severity.

For one insane moment, I forget where we are. Forget we're in a classroom. In the school. In *Blue Ridge*. I forget who he is. All I want is to grab him by the fur and drag his lips to mine. I want him to touch me. Claim me. Do things to me I've never wanted from anyone before.

Then his eyes cut away, and it's like being plunged into an ice bath.

I want him to claim *me? What the actual fuck?*

Suddenly, I'm angry all over again. At myself, but mostly at him. And he's *still* ignoring me. Even now.

"Why are you ignoring me." I force the words through gritted teeth, practically spitting them.

"I'm not—"

Lifting the bunny head up, I wallop him over the head

with it. In the back of my mind, I'm utterly grateful the school's empty in my moment of madness.

"Ow!" He steps back and rubs his head, but I feel no remorse.

"Why are you like this?" I stomp forward and thwack him with it again.

His back meets the wall. "Would you stop doing that?"

"Would you be honest with me?" I hold the bunny head up threateningly.

He closes his fingers around my wrist and yanks the head from my grasp. He tosses it on a desk. I reach for it, grazing the ear with my fingertips, but he spins us around pinning me against the cinderblock wall.

His eyes bore holes in my skull as his warm palms press against mine. "How would you even know if I was ignoring you through the mask?"

I square my shoulders, trying to hide the way my heart thrashes against my ribcage. His eyes follow the movement.

"It couldn't be more obvious," I sneer.

His hips press flush against mine, pinning me. A voice inside me begs for more.

Shut up, you hornball. What is wrong with me?

Sweat beads at his temple. "And you're so good at reading people."

Lifting my chin, I say, "You aren't exactly shrouded in mystery."

He rocks his hips into me. The pleasure hisses through my body, and I stifle a gasp. Without permission, I grind back. His eyes darken.

His mouth hovers over the crook of my neck, breaths coming out hot and heavy. "And you could never be wrong."

A full-body shudder vibrates down my spine.

His responding chuckle, haughty and insufferable,

knocks something back into place. I huff out a frustrated breath.

Sawyer tormented me my entire life. Never let me have any peace. Taunted me, picked on me, embarrassed me every chance he could. Even as an adult, he can't help playing these mind games with me.

I'm tired of it.

"You know what, Sawyer?" I say through my teeth. "I don't even care anymore."

Sawyer's heavy body shoves up against me, taking my weight, pushing me to the tips of my toes. He's hard everywhere, and I hate how good it feels. Hate that it makes me want him. Hate that my hands plunge into his hair as my breath catches.

Intent on getting my point across, I grit out, "You can go fuck yourself."

His mouth on my ear, he says, "I'd rather fuck you."

The words go straight between my legs, making me hot and wet. My nipples pebble. I try *so hard* not to grind myself against him. But it's hard. *Everything* is hard.

"See, Brie," he says, lips against my neck, sending heat down to my core, "that's the problem." He lets out a dark chuckle that tugs on my clit. "That's always been the problem."

He pulls back just enough to meet my eyes. His are black. Like a shark's. His hands are on my hips. Every cell in my body screams for more.

His mouth travels to my other ear. "You ever think maybe" —he nips my lobe with his teeth, and I clench around nothing— "the reason I can't look at you" —his teeth graze down my neck, sucking at the very base, making me whimper— "is because I don't want a raging boner at work?" He pulls my sweater over just enough to bite my shoulder before soothing it with a kiss. I let out a low, desperate moan.

His erection presses directly onto my bundle of nerves, making me gasp in pleasure. I can't hold back anymore. I rub myself shamelessly against him, giving in to the friction I crave.

Sawyer groans. He pulses his hips just enough to make my entire body shake with need. I'm so close to release, I could come so easily with just a little more.

"Hey Brie, why—"

Sawyer and I turn to the doorway, where Tess's eyes are as large as dinner plates. They scan down to where Sawyer, in his headless bunny costume, has me pinned against the wall.

At some point, my legs must have accidentally wrapped themselves around him.

I lower my feet to the floor.

"Sorry! Just came to check on you since your car was still in the lot." She says it all like it's one word, and quickly closes the door behind her.

By the time it clicks shut, Sawyer's put a veritable ocean between us, and is blocking his crotch with the bunny head.

We look at each other, breathing hard, for a long moment, too stunned to say or do anything. Then, his eyes clear.

Voice hard with authority, he says, "That will never happen again."

His words suck all the air from my lungs. It's only when he exits into the hallway that I let myself breathe again.

CHAPTER 22

BRIE

I'M SITTING across from Tess in a booth at Jolly Jalapeño. It's early on a Tuesday, so the place isn't busy. We're both silent. I refuse to meet her eyes as I take a totally natural, super casual sip of water.

"So are you guys furries, or what?"

I spit the water right back into my glass. "No!"

Sawyer's body pressing against me barely half an hour ago, hard and eager, flits through my mind.

"Maybe."

Then the way he left hits me like a brick wall. *That will never happen again.*

"Definitely not."

Tess's laugh, a piercing shriek of delight, is loud enough for the whole bar to hear. People look over. I wave at our server in apology and turn to Tess.

"Shush! What you saw was an accident."

Her eyes glitter across the table. "I'm sure if I hadn't cockblocked you, there would have been an accidental kiss, too. Maybe some accidental groping. Your pants might have accidentally come off—"

"I *mean* it happened so fast I wasn't thinking about where we were or who he was." I drop my head into my hands. "I can't believe I dry-humped Funny Bunny in my classroom."

She lets out another giddy laugh, and bounces in her seat like she can't contain her joy.

Leaning forward, she whispers, "I knew it! I just knew you two liked each other. The sexual tension when you're together" —she fans herself with her menu— "I mean, I could cut it with a knife."

"There is no sexual tension," I say flatly.

But really? I want to scream and thrash and maybe even break something. I am *not* an overly sexual person. I have no idea where this lusty version of Brie came from, but she had to come out of hiding for *Sawyer*? Of all the men on Earth, it had to be him?

Tess's grin is wider than the Cheshire Cat's. "There's sexual tension, alright. I get second-hand horny when I'm around the two of you."

"Oh my god!" I glance around to see if anyone heard her. "What has gotten into you?"

She sips her water, cheeks high with a suppressed smile and tinged pink. "I just feel lighter since the restraining order."

I can't help beaming at her. Tess asked me to meet her Saturday morning after the Taco Tursday fiasco, and I went with her to the police station. I was so proud of her.

"I'm glad you still feel good about it."

"I do! Now I'm free." She lifts her arms up and flaps her hands in the air.

"What did Nash say when you told him about it?"

She shifts uncomfortably in her seat.

"Tess! Tell me you told your brother about the

restraining order. He has to be worried about you after what happened that night."

"Doubt it," she says, ducking her head.

And then I understand. "You never told him about that night?"

She drops her chin. "He's just so busy! I don't want to add another thing for him to worry about." Sitting up straighter, she adds, "Besides, it's all over. I have the restraining order. CJ can't bother me again."

I don't like it, but I understand her reluctance, I'm not one to spew personal details either. And all I know about her relationship with Nash is what she's told me. I don't want to overstep. Besides, she's right about the restraining order. This *should* be the end of her problems with her ex.

Still, I know that's not always realistic. I read somewhere that abused women are statistically most vulnerable after attempting to leave, or after reporting the abuse.

And I also know from my many attempts that Tess is steadfast in staying at her apartment. She won't even consider staying with Gia and me for a few weeks.

"Just promise you'll be careful. And come to me if you ever need help," I say. "With anything."

"I promise. Two Emerson Ave."

"Good."

Our server comes by to take our orders. I hope it acts as a tidy little bookend to all things ex-boyfriends and bunnies, but as soon as she's gone, Tess leans in again, eyebrows drawn up in expectation.

"Now, tell me why you're here with me instead of anywhere with Sawyer."

I huff. "I will never be anywhere with Sawyer. What you *think* you saw won't ever happen again." As I say it, my heart sinks into my stomach.

"Why not?"

"For one, Sawyer said it would never happen again . . . immediately after he jumped away from me like a celiac from a croissant."

Her head tilts to one side. "He said that?"

"Literally used those words."

"Why?"

I shrug like I'm totally unaffected. But I'm really *really* affected.

The truth is, the Funny Bunny incident was *so* inappropriate, *so* out of character for me, that I can't deny my attraction to Sawyer anymore. I've always known Sawyer is hot, just like everyone in town knows it. But I, Brie Casey, am drawn to him like a shark to blood.

No, that's not right. Something less predatory.

Maybe a fly to shit.

Either way, it's pretty damning evidence, right? Despite the headless bunny costume, he was *still* the hottest person I've ever seen. There's no getting around it. It's nonsensical. Infuriating. And, because of our past, there's no winning with him. When his attention is on me, I want to choke him. When he's ignoring me, I want him to choke me.

Wait. No. *That's not what I meant.*

But see? I'm not myself anymore. This is why a repeat of the Funny Bunny incident can never happen.

That and . . . he's my *boss*. Add that to the mile-long list of reasons why I can't stay in Blue Ridge. I can't keep working under him.

Before the stupid voice in my head can make a pun about wanting to work under him, I say, "It doesn't matter because I can't get involved with someone at school anyway. No sex with colleagues. It's my rule, and I'm sticking to it."

"Wait, why?"

My lips press tight. I won't be telling anyone here in Blue Ridge—or anywhere—everything that happened at Everett Academy, but Tess has become important to me. She's a friend, and I know she can keep a secret. I can tell her *something*.

When I lean in, she mirrors me. "There was this older teacher at my last school. Christopher."

Her eyes narrow on the name. "He sounds like a dick."

This is what friends are for.

"He was, I just didn't know it yet."

I tell her the abridged story, focusing on it being a short-lived, unsatisfying relationship and learning he was not divorcing his wife who—*surprise!*—was on the board. I leave out the gossip that spread like wildfire, turning me into a pariah, and how all the parents and staff turned on me.

She leans back in her seat. "You literally got the phone call about subbing that morning, packed up your apartment, drove all night, and then you came in to discover Sawyer is your new principal?"

"Uh-huh." I suck down the cocktail our server brought during my monologue.

I can tell she senses there's more to the story, but she doesn't ask. "That must have been one hell of a breakup."

"More than you know."

She nods, like this confirms her suspicions.

"You know what?" Tess says. "Fuck 'em. I'm glad you're here."

Her eyes are so fiercely sincere, I can't help being grateful too. "Same."

Tess settles into her seat like she's ready to pounce, and dips her head forward. "Now tell me what Sawyer did to you when ya'll were younger."

I tip my head back against the booth. "No," I groan.

"C'mon! I feel like I'm just coming back into the world. I need some hot goss!"

"This isn't 'hot goss,' it's old news."

"Not for you it's not. You're still hung up on it like a sheet on a clothesline. And not for me either because I've never heard it."

I snort out a laugh, but my skin begins to itch. The only way she'll let this go is if I make it clear I don't want to talk about it, but then it'll be a capital-T *Thing*.

"There's too much to tell," I hedge. "Sawyer was a constant bruise in my life from the first day of kindergarten."

"Give me the highlights."

My knee bounces as our server drops off another round of drinks and our food. People start to trickle into the restaurant. More than half come carrying guitar cases. Two or three sit at a table with notecards, mouthing to themselves as if prepping for a comedy set. It's Talented Tuesday, open mic night.

I turn back to Tess, who's watching me with keen eyes, and I know I have to tell her something. Prom is the first thing that comes to mind, but even after fourteen years, that memory is raw. The way I'd let myself be taken in by Sawyer months earlier, think he was a good guy after giving me a ride in the rain, only for him to make a giant fool of me in front of everyone in our class at prom.

But as I try to land on a different memory, I realize they all still sting.

Instead, I punt. "Sawyer just wasn't very nice to me."

She makes a *Go on* gesture that has my heart pounding. I wipe my hands on my pants. I've never willingly told anyone one of these stories. People *know* of course, but not from me.

Tess's eyebrows knit, and her expression turns tender, like she's about to backtrack in order to spare me. I almost hate that more.

I blurt, "Do they still do the fifth grade sleepover at the library?"

She nods, "It's a beloved tradition."

As I tell Tess about Squeakers, our food comes, but neither of us touches it.

"And then Sawyer tied off the trash bag and took her out to the dumpster." It's ridiculous, I know it is, but I'm shaking.

"I am so sorry, Brie. Kids can be so mean." Tess shakes her head. After a moment, she says, "I just can't believe Sawyer was like that. I can't picture it." She looks at me, startled at her own words. "I mean, I believe you! One hundred percent, I do. But it's hard to fit that version of Sawyer with the Sawyer I know now."

Tess is so young she never overlapped with us in school.

I hold my hands up helplessly. "I mean, you're a Brooks. The Blue Ridge I grew up in was different than the one you did. You and Nash lived in the best part of town while I had a cemetery for a backyard. Your dad's a senator. Mine was the town drunk."

"We moved here after Mom divorced my dad. But . . ." she levels me with a guilty look, "we did live in Belmont."

"And that's okay. But I bet you were never bullied. And Nash sure as hell was never teased about anything."

She dips her chin. "You're right."

Thunder booms outside, followed closely by a flash of lightning.

"The weather's been so weird," she says, and I'm grateful for the change in topic. "They said it'll snow tonight, but this feels like a summer thunderstorm."

"They predict snow?" Yesterday, the temperatures got into the high sixties. Pink and purple cherry blossoms are already starting to bud along Main Street.

"Yeah," she says. "They were even talking about closing school, but look."

She points across the street and behind me, so I have to crane my neck. The garage to the firehouse is open and men in BRFD t-shirts drag lawn chairs just outside reach of the rain to watch the storm. They don't look even a little cold.

"No way they'll close school, right? It's *March*." I think about the kids' seeds that just sprouted while we read *The Secret Garden*, and wonder how long they can go without water.

She shrugs. "It's possible. It's up to the district, and that includes the towns over and past Ormewood." Ormewood Mountain borders Blue Ridge to the north.

Another boom of thunder claps overhead. Tess and I eat as we watch the sheets of rain pour into town, and I try not to think of the last time it rained like this when I was in Blue Ridge.

CHAPTER 23

SAWYER

"SNOW DAY MY ASS," I mutter as I run to my car through the pouring rain. It's been coming down hard since yesterday. Some roads are more puddle than asphalt.

The school district is large, so when towns north of Ormewood Mountain get snow, we're off as well. Blue Ridge is usually sheltered from bad weather, but every seven years or so there's a blizzard that makes its way in. When that happens, the surrounding mountains make the storm ten times worse, acting like insulation and keeping it here until it loses steam.

I'm not surprised it didn't snow like it was predicted last night, but the temperature's plummeted all day. By late afternoon, I finally decide to play it safe and drive into town for supplies.

As I pass the elementary school, water kicks up from my tires. Some is already solid, and it finally hits me that I could be stuck at home for days just from the ice. Blue Ridge isn't prepared to salt the entire town, let alone the mountain roads leading to my place. I love the seclusion of my cabin, but that's what makes it potentially dangerous in a storm like this.

When I walk into Madam's Hardware, the pitter patter of rain follows me in. As I leave ten minutes later, the rain is gone, and big fluffy snowflakes float down from the sky. I toss the bag from the hardware store into my truck and hurry to the grocery, which takes a lot longer than it should due to all of Blue Ridge joining me.

Afterward, as I hurry to my car, I glance at Valley View Provisions across the street. I'm not usually one for fancy meats and cheese, but my legs are already walking through the slush on some weird instinct. Besides, I can check that the Clarkes, the couple who runs the shop, are prepared and can get home safely.

By the time I've run all my errands, all the shops are closing up behind me. The wind whistles, snow travels horizontally, and cars slide through the intersection even after hitting the brakes for the red light. I head home at a crawl.

Just like with the provisions store, as I drive past the elementary school, I have this inexplicable draw to it. On instinct, or maybe habit from being a SEAL, I jerk the steering wheel into the lot and do a loop around the school.

"This is a waste of time," I tell myself as I round the building.

But then my heart stops as I spot a car. *Brie's* car. It's clear no one's in it.

I squint past the snow to the window of her classroom. It's dark.

Where the fuck is Brie?

The truck creeps forward, rounding the next corner as I scan the lot. It's almost impossible to see anything. My eyes dart to the back entrance of the school, hoping she'll appear.

Movement in my periphery catches my attention.

Oh shit.

Through the haze, I see Brie at the edge of the parking lot, by the street. She's on all fours, making her way up to stand.

As fast as I dare, I speed up, anger flaring in my chest that she's out here in a goddamn blizzard dressed for a brisk day at the beach. Thin sweater, cotton pants, sneakers.

I roll down the window. "Hey! Brie!" My stomach bottoms out when she turns to me. There's a streak of something wet and red on her pants. "Is that blood?"

She's half-limping, half-running. "Fuck off, Sawyer," she manages to say.

"It's a fucking blizzard!" I yell. "What the hell are you doing out there? Your car's back that way."

"Decided to go for a refreshing run," she yells back without looking at me.

She's made it about a yard since I spotted her. "Very funny. Get in."

"Leave me alone, Sawyer."

Deja fucking vu.

She's so damn stubborn. I yank on my emergency brake and get out of the truck, knowing how this is going to go.

In a few careful strides, I'm standing in front of her, and she stops, shifting her weight to one leg because—*yup*—that's definitely blood high up her thigh, almost her hip.

Her hair and sweater are wet from the snow. How long has she been out here? She looks up at me with all the venom she can, but her teeth chatter, ruining the illusion.

"Where the hell is your jacket?" I growl.

I shrug off my coat and drape it over her shoulders. Then I step forward, closing the distance between us. She's breathing hard, blinking rapidly against the falling snow.

"What the hell are you doing?" she demands.

"This." I throw her over my shoulder, ignoring her protests, and toss her into the passenger seat. I shut the door and round the hood, part of me worried she's already out and running before I can climb in. But when I do, she's still there.

"What're you even doing here?"

"Watering my kids' seedlings," she chatters. "I didn't want them to come back to shriveled leaves."

"During a blizzard?"

She tugs my coat closed around her. "It wasn't snowing when I got here. I lost track of time reading."

"And your jacket?"

At that, she looks sheepish, ducking her head and looking out the window. "I freaked out when I saw the snow. Got out of there so fast I forgot my jacket and keys."

"And the school doors are on a timer," I finish for her.

They would have automatically locked an hour ago. That's why she was at the road. No car keys, and no way to get back indoors. She really was trying to run for it.

"Are you hurt?" I ask.

"Just my dignity."

"You could've frozen to death!" I don't mean to shout, but my body is vibrating with adrenaline.

"Running generates body heat!" she yells back.

Bracing myself on her seat, I lean toward her. "Is that why your teeth are chattering? All that body heat?"

She lifts her chin, but doesn't retort. The sound of the wipers squeaking over my windshield fills the cab. She smells like pear and citrus and snow. Her face is maybe three inches from mine. I'm so fucking grateful I found her.

I reach over to tug on her seatbelt and click it in place. I do the same with mine, then I look straight ahead and start driving.

There go my plans to stay as far away from Brie as possible.

CHAPTER 24

BRIE

BEING RESCUED by Sawyer during a storm—*again*—isn't ideal. I can forgive my eighteen-year-old self for not knowing the future, but my current self has the benefit of hindsight, and I know this won't end well.

Now that I'm out of the cold, I notice the sharp pain emanating from my hip. The back of my hip, really. Almost, but not quite, my ass.

Even if I didn't fall just as I started my mad dash to safety, there's at least a forty-percent chance my plan to run back to Gia's would have ended with me frozen to death. I would've been found a block and a half away, blue with a half-broken ass. And when they finally found me, my ghost would die all over again from embarrassment.

At least Sawyer has the heat cranked up in his truck. The first thing I'm going to do when I get back to Gia's is—

"Hey!" I chatter. "Go *right*!"

"No can do, honey." He's driving slower than I can limp. "Even if I made it to Gia's on the other side of town, I wouldn't make it back to my place."

"That's fine! Your dad's house is two blocks away!"

He lets out a loud, humorless laugh. "I'd rather freeze to death."

Without warning his truck fishtails on some ice. I scream, heart pounding in my chest. My hands shoot out, grabbing aimlessly. They land on the dash in front of me (great), and Sawyer's biceps (*holy mother of all that is large and solid*).

When we come to a skidding stop, he looks down at me. "Still want me to take you to Gia's?"

The question is rhetorical. I look past him out the window. The school is *right there*, a hazy silhouette beyond all the white. We were going at a snail's pace and we still spun out. But when I look back at him, flannel shirt open at the top, jeans hugging his thighs, hair falling carelessly over his forehead, my hand still gripping his arm, all I see is trouble.

I swallow. "Yes, please."

His dry chuckle is an irritating grate up my ribcage. "Not a chance. You're coming home with me."

I hate that he's right. Besides the ice on the road, visibility is almost nonexistent. He eases down on the gas, and we start moving again. It's the wrong direction, but I don't dare distract him by asking where "home" is. Nothing is in this direction except Mount Eden. He must be avoiding the main road, maybe there's an accident I don't know about.

Why he traded in his huge truck that had heated seats and probably four-wheel drive for this clunker, I don't know. We slip and slide all the way to the mountain road. My confusion rises when he doesn't turn back toward town, instead driving a short way up the road before turning onto a gravel drive.

The blood pumping through my veins could power a rocket ship. Pain shoots through my hip with every bump and jolt. At first, I think maybe I fractured something, but the sensation, while intense, is more surface-level.

It takes approximately one century to traverse to the cabin in the woods that I think might become my murder location. When we stop, I peer past the blanket of snow.

"Wait, you live here?"

It was hard to tell at first, but I know this place. It's old Mr. Collins's cabin. The only place I ever thought might be worth actually living in Blue Ridge for. The snow is coming down too hard for me to see if the view is as nice as I remember from the few times I hiked here.

His hand is on the back of my seat when he answers, body angled toward me. "I do. Can you walk?" I follow his gaze to my hip, and that's when I notice blood for the first time—I must have fallen on something sharp, probably ice. Embarrassment blazes through me.

"Just a flesh wound," I say in my best medieval British accent, but when I turn in my seat, I can't help wincing at the pain.

He ignores the joke and steps out, slamming his door hard. Before I can get out, he's at my side, stooping to pick me up as if I weigh nothing, and shutting the door with his hip.

"You don't have to—"

"This'll be quicker," he clips out. So much for chivalry, he's probably just cold. Then again, so am I. I'm still wearing his coat, but my sweater is wet from melted snow, chilling my skin.

I wrap my arms around his neck and settle in for the ride. His coat smells like chlorine, but he doesn't. His scent is the perfect blend of clean and spicy. It wakes up all the nerves in my body, the sensation pinballing down to between my legs.

With him focused on where he steps, I can openly study his face. His thick eyebrows are furrowed in concentration. Several days' worth of scruff covers his face, but he's shaved at the neck, giving it that soft, kissable look—

"I can feel you staring," he grunts.

Whoops.

"Plotting my murder?" he asks.

My heart is a kick drum in my chest. "I assumed that's why you brought *me* here."

"Please," he says, "if I were going to murder you, I'd do it on the other side of town, not at my house."

He's careful climbing the wooden steps, then shifts my weight to one arm while he opens his door.

CHAPTER 25

BRIE

INSIDE, he kicks off his boots and deposits me on a bench against the wall.

"Wait here." He strides away, and I distract myself from the throb in my hip by looking around.

This place is . . . cramped. The entire cabin is much smaller than I expected, just one room, like a large studio. The amount of junk jammed in here doesn't help. Dressers, a large bed, bedside tables, storage boxes stacked high in one corner. It all points to him moving from a much larger house except his couch is way too small for the space, like it came from a compact apartment. I can't understand it.

"Here," he says, hurrying back to me, carrying a first aid kit and some towels.

He kneels down in front of me and examines my hip. There's a small tear in the fabric, darkened with blood.

"I'm going to need to cut your pants down to the thigh so I can assess your cut." My jaw drops, and he hands me a towel. "Drape that over your lap if you want." His tone is steady and commanding, and he doesn't wait for an answer before he takes a pair of scissors and cuts carefully down the seam of my favorite twill pants with competent efficiency.

"These were the most comfortable pants I owned," I sigh.

He doesn't seem to hear me. He's detached almost. Like he isn't Sawyer, and I'm not Brie. There are no snide remarks or strange heated looks. Then it dawns on me, what I learned about him on our sort-of double date. This is Sawyer the Navy SEAL in action.

I've never seen this side of him before.

After my pants are slit open on the side, he looks up at me with a look that allows no argument. I lift myself off enough for him to pull them down over my thighs, gentle and careful not to hurt me. My phone tumbles out of my back pocket. He looks at it for a second, dumbfounded. I grab it to shoot a quick text to both sisters, who've blown up my messages, that I'm safe and will keep in touch.

"Can you lean over more?" he asks.

I try, but my thighs are glued together. He removes my wet shoes and socks before helping me out of my pants the rest of the way. They were useless anyway, barely keeping my pride intact by a thread.

Once I'm leaning awkwardly on the bench, weight braced against the wall, he heaves out a sigh.

"What is it?" I ask.

"Sorry about this."

Before I can ask what he's sorry about, I feel a tug at my underwear, then hear a snip. My humiliation is complete when I feel the cool air on my bare ass cheek.

"There's the problem," he says

"What is?"

"A shard of glass. I'm going to pull it out."

"Wait! Aren't you *not* supposed to do that? Like, couldn't I bleed out?"

He moves to meet my eyes. His expression is patient, voice confident. "You aren't going to bleed out. It didn't hit a major artery unless it's a much longer shard than I think. Given your—"

"But what if you're wrong?" I shriek.

Calmly, he puts his hand over mine. "Given your mobility, I'm sure it's not that deep. If it were, you'd be in a lot more pain right now." He presses his lips together then asks, "Do you trust me?"

Without hesitation, I blurt, "Yes."

It surprises me. Under any other circumstance, I'd say I don't trust Sawyer one iota. But the person with me right now isn't Regular Sawyer. He's Sawyer the SEAL.

He lets out a breath, like he's just as surprised by my answer. "Squeeze my hand," he says, reaching for tweezers with his free hand, and I do.

There's an uncomfortable pinch before he holds a piece of glass up to me. He drops it into the open lid of his first aid kit and presses a piece of gauze to my hip. "Better?"

I shift and there's a sting like with a regular cut, but the shooting pain is gone.

"Yeah." I can't keep the surprise from my voice. "All better."

Sawyer cleans and dresses my wound while keeping up a one-sided conversation. It's so impersonal, I'm sure it was part of his training, a method of distraction for the person he's treating.

"Anything else hurt? You scrape your hands?"

I hold up my palms and wriggle my legs to show I didn't twist anything when I fell. "All good."

He sits back on his heels. I see the moment he transforms from Sawyer the SEAL back to Regular Sawyer. His practiced detachment clears, and heat floods his eyes. But not the kind of heat I saw when he wore the bunny suit. He's angry.

I'm suddenly freezing again. My sweater like ice on my skin beneath his jacket.

He stands to his full height, towering over me. "Why didn't you call someone?" he all but snarls.

All I can do is shake my head. "Th-the weather. I didn't think it'd be safe—"

"*Safe?* You're talking about *safe* when you were out there without a jacket, without gloves, no car and no way to get back inside the school, stranded and bleeding?"

"I wasn't thinking about all that!" I have to admit, when he lists it all like that, it sounds bad.

He leans forward, his palms against the wall by my head, face inches from mine. "Do you have any idea how lucky I was to find you."

There's a waver in his voice, so slight I almost miss it. His eyes are wild. He's breathing hard. Just like he was after Tess caught us in the classroom.

The mortification of him telling me it would never happen again floods my senses. What makes him think he can suddenly pretend to care about me? He's hot and cold, like always, and I'm sick of being made a fool.

I shove him back, giving myself room to stand. I feel my Angry Badger Face come to life, ready to fight back.

He glances down.

This is the exact moment I realize I'm pantless. The towel that was covering me is on the floor, and half my ass is out.

It's fine. My front's covered enough, and at least I'm not wearing the gag underwear Mara sent me for Christmas.

I square my shoulders, undeterred, and take a step toward him. He takes a step back. *Coward.*

"I did what I thought was best under the circumstances."

I take another step, and so does he. *Bastard.*

"My sisters are the only ones I can count on in this town. I'd never ask them to come out in this. Not for me."

His eyes blaze, and when I take another step, he doesn't budge.

Voice low, he says, "Why didn't you call *me*."

"*You?!* Puh-*lease.*" I can't believe he has the nerve to ask that when our entire childhood is one giant red flag. I take one more step. We're toe to toe. "When have you ever come through for me?"

Hurt flashes over his face, and I falter.

The bandage on my ass for one.

Rescuing me from the blizzard for two. And both of those are just from today.

It's on the tip of my tongue to take it back, call for a truce, when his eyes narrow and he leans forward.

"Fine." His breath skates over my lips. "Good to know you feel the same way about me as you always have."

He's so close, I can see the flecks of blue in his eyes. My blood starts rushing in my ears. I'm suddenly aware of how hard I'm breathing. Both of us are. All those lusty feelings, all the desire I've been pushing back on, everything bubbles to the surface as the moment stretches taut for one breath, two. Then . . .

Snap.

CHAPTER 26

BRIE

BEFORE I CAN THINK, my hands fist his flannel, yanking him toward me. His mouth is soft and firm, his facial hair only adding to the deluge of sensations. When his hands find my hips, I bring mine up to his hair. The jacket that was draped over my shoulders falls to the floor.

I walk backward, turning us so he can sit on the bench I just vacated before straddling his lap. My mouth is level with his now, more even. I trail my fingers up the soft skin of his neck, satisfaction snaking through me when he shudders.

I shift, and he pulls his head back.

"Holy shit," he says, "your sweater. It's wet. You must be freez—"

He clamps his mouth shut when I reach for the hem and drag it over my head. His breaths come out hard. He looks at me in my cotton bra and mismatched, mangled underwear like he's never seen anything better, like I'm exactly what he wished for.

I tug on the buttons of his shirt and pry the fabric off his toned shoulders. No undershirt, *thank god*. I attack his neck, my hands exploring every inch of his torso. His warm skin, the soft hair scattered over his pecs, the hard ridges of his abs that tighten at my touch.

His fingers flex and a groan tears through him when I graze my teeth over his neck. I rock my hips, wanting more. One hand grips me tighter, his other hand careful not to touch the bandage on that side.

Then it hits me. His hands haven't moved from my hips.

He hasn't kissed me.

I'm doused in cold shame. I pull back to look at him. He gazes back through drugged eyes.

He blinks. "What's wrong?"

That's what I'd like to know. I started this, I pushed him onto the bench, I climbed on top of him. Frustration and embarrassment war inside me. But I'm already here, there's no going back from sitting on Sawyer's lap in my bra and ripped panties. How much bigger a fool could I possibly make myself by opening my mouth?

"Why won't you touch me?" I breathe.

A muscle in his jaw ticks as his chest rises and falls. "Brie, you just told me exactly what you think of me. I'm not taking the reins here and giving you something else to hate me for. I need to know you want me to touch you."

It's a good point. Sawyer drives me crazy in more ways than one. I don't trust him, his actions confuse me, and I don't understand him. But this thing between us has been building since Day One, and there's no better time to see it through than right now. We're in his secluded cabin, I'm in my underwear, and his cock is rock hard beneath me.

Heart thumping, I reach behind me and unclasp my bra. A dare.

His eyes stay fixed on mine, but the muscles in his

throat protrude. His Adam's apple moves with a heavy swallow. His hands squeeze me tight enough to bruise.

I lean forward, taking his bottom lip between my teeth, biting it hard enough to feel his groan, then sucking on it. My hands grip his shoulders as I nip at his neck, scattering wet little kisses all the way up, eliciting deep sounds from him.

My mouth presses to his ear. I don't overthink it, and I don't recognize my own throaty voice when I say, "Sawyer, I want your hands and mouth on me. Everywhere." I drag my teeth over his lobe.

He lets out a desperate whimper that makes me almost feral for him.

"*Please,*" I say.

Then he cracks. His hands skate up my ribcage, cupping my breasts from underneath as his mouth meets my clavicle, kissing along my collarbone before finding the sensitive spot where my neck and shoulder meet, making me squirm. Thumbs rub exploratory circles over my nipples, making me arch. I whimper, and he bites me lightly. He does it again and again, pulling new sounds from me, noises I've never made before.

He pulls back, eyes bouncing between my face and my chest, like he can't decide what he likes better. Then he kisses me full on. His mouth devours mine and his fingers rake over my bare thighs, up my stomach, down my arms, pulling all my nerves taut.

"Brie," he rasps against my lips.

I shiver and buck my hips, pressing flush against where he's impressively hard. He groans and hooks his fingers into the waistband of my underwear that's still intact. He pulls up, dragging it against my clit. I gasp with pleasure. His eyes flash with satisfaction.

"Tell me what you want." It's a plea, not an order.

"I want that," I say when he tugs on my panties again. They're soaked.

He plants wet kisses along my jaw, then brings his mouth against my ear, hot breath making me moan. "I need to hear you say it. I need to know you want this as badly as I do."

Heart pounding, I say, "I want you to rub my pussy. I want your fingers inside me." I swallow. "I want your tongue on me."

Before I can say more, his mouth covers mine again as a deep, tortured rumble emanates from his chest.

He breaks the kiss and watches his hand roam down my chest with hooded eyes. His finger hooks the crotch of my panties, moving them to the side.

"Fuck, Brie. You're the prettiest thing I've ever seen."

His thumb presses delicately against my clit, a button being pushed, and I make a ragged, anguished sound that no one on Earth has ever heard except Sawyer Strong.

He arches his eyebrows and looks at me as he does it again, then circles his thumb until I'm grinding into the movement.

My experience with sex up til now was always . . . basic. I could take it or leave it most of the time. It was never great, but it was rarely *bad*.

This is different. There's a need building I've never felt. I'm feral for Sawyer, reduced to my basest desires. I've never been so intimate with someone before. Never had someone play with me and study me and devour me like this.

His middle finger caresses my entrance, and he makes a disbelieving sound in the back of his throat.

"Honey, you're dripping." His other hand comes up to

cup my chin before sucking my lip into his mouth as his thumb continues to drive me crazy.

He eases one finger in, just to his first knuckle, and I whimper, fisting his hair and circling my hips. The weight of his gaze is heavy as he watches me. When he adds a second finger, shallow like the first, I weep out another whimper. Slowly, so fucking slowly, he inches deeper. Tapping, circling, rubbing me from the inside.

"Tell me when it feels good," he says.

"It feels good!"

He brings his forehead to rest against mine, chuckling. "No. Tell me when it feels *really* good."

I shake my head, not understanding. It all feels good. Almost too good. Maddeningly *good*. No one's ever made me feel *this* good.

Then he hits a spot. One magical spot that has me careening into him and gasping loudly.

"Ohmyfuckingfuck."

"Will you look at me, honey?" His voice is husky.

My eyes flick open—I didn't realize I'd squeezed them shut—and there he is. Mouth tight in concentration, eyes fervid. Somehow, through the fog of desire and pleasure and pure unadulterated *need* for this man, I realize it's *Sawyer*. My stomach flips and the sensation in my core doubles, but that realization nags at me. He's going to go cold again, I have to protect myself.

Nothing in the world could possibly give me the strength to stop what's happening now, but I have just enough in me to breathe, "Just once. We do this one time."

Eyes dimming, he nods once. "I'll take it."

Then he stands up. His fingers are still in me, other hand cradling my ass. I gasp at the change in angle and hang on for dear life.

"Where are we going?"

He walks us the few feet to his couch and lays me down, kneeling on one knee with one foot planted on the floor. He eases his fingers out. I grunt a sound of protest.

His answering smirk has me clenching around where his fingers should be. He takes his shirt off the rest of the way, and he's beautiful. Thick and muscular as he looks down at me.

"God, Brie. You're so pretty. So fucking pretty."

He kneels between my legs, delicate hands caressing the outsides of my thighs in a ticklish tease.

His fingers ghost over the bandage on my hip. "Does it hurt?"

"Not even a little." The only thing I feel right now is my ferocious need for him, the tight pulse of desire, anticipation for what's coming.

He peels off my torn panties. "If this is just once," he says, kissing the inside of my knee, moving his mouth higher with each word, "then I need to taste you." He ends the sentence with one languid lick, from slit to clit.

"*Sawyer.*" It's a slow, throaty plea.

His eyes shine, and he does it again before kissing up my lips and around my clit. He teases me with light pecks until I finally reach for his head and angle his face where I need him. He laughs against me, giving me little vibrations, and I can't help laughing back.

"I'm not going to rush this," he says.

Untangling my hands from his head, he holds my wrists with one hand on my stomach as the fingers of his other hand go back to that magical spot he discovered.

My eyes roll to the back of my head. "So good."

"I agree," he says before covering my clit with his mouth.

He climbs me higher and higher. Sucking on my clit while his fingers make wet sounds as he thrusts them over and over. When my hips grind against him, seeking more, he makes a low sound of approval. My eyes snap open to find him watching me.

"Fuck," he says against me before flattening his tongue on my clit. "You're shattering every fantasy, Brie." *Lick.* "Every." *Lick.* "Single." *Lick.* "One." *Lick.*

My knees start to wobble first. The sensation moves down to my toes, curling them. My core begins to quiver, and my walls clamp tight around his fingers. When my hips start to buck, he lets go of my hands to hold my hips down with his forearm. My fingers tangle in his hair and I arch my back as I let out a strangled cry and euphoria sweeps through me.

He keeps licking, keeps driving his fingers into me, seeing me through an orgasm that eclipses all others, extending it for long moments.

When I start to come down, his movements slow, meeting me where I am as my clit becomes too sensitive to bear anymore. My breaths are ragged. He's still pinning me down. His fingers still inside me, giving me soothing caresses. He plants one light kiss on my clit, and I think we should be done with this. On to the next thing.

But he kisses the seam of my thigh. Then up my stomach, and down to my other thigh again. His stubble adds delicious friction to my sensitive skin. His fingers pick up some power, igniting a searing heat in me all over again.

"Wha-what're you doing to me?" I moan.

His eyes shine with excited purpose. "I figure it still counts as one time" —he kisses my clit, and it isn't nearly as sensitive anymore— "as long as I don't stop." He looks down to where his fingers are buried inside me, stoking the fire in my belly, before meeting my eyes again. "You're the best thing I've ever seen, Brie."

"*This* is the best thing," I breathe.

He leans forward, taking my mouth with his. I taste myself on him, but I also taste *him*. And I can't get enough of it, I want more. When he ends the kiss, I arch my back, chasing him. The corner of his mouth ticks up, and he indulges me with another mind-bending kiss. When he retreats again, he's different. His earlier uncertainty over what I want is replaced by his usual cocksure enthusiasm, and I want this version of Sawyer too.

"You're going to give me another good one," he says. "Aren't you."

I've never come twice in a row. I've never had a partner who tried it, and I never tried to do it on my own before. I don't even know if it's possible.

But watching Sawyer's need play out on his face—not need for his own release, but a need to see me come undone again, a need for *him* to be my undoing—I know it's not just possible. It's inevitable.

I nod. "Yes."

"Tell me," he says, a smirk growing on his face. "Use your words, Brie."

Even as my pussy squeezes his fingers at his dark tone, on instinct I say, "You're the worst."

His smile broadens like this is his favorite game. "Those were the wrong words," he says, slowing his pace.

"That's not going to make me come again," I whine.

"Is that what you want?" He sucks the seam of my thigh, so close to where I need him. A promise and a threat at the same time.

"Sawyer," I say, writhing beneath him, trying to close the distance. "Sawyer, *please* make me come."

His mouth covers my clit, wrenching a moan out of me.

This time, his movements are sloppy. Frenzied. His lips mold against me as his skilled tongue remembers all the moves I like. *God*, the sounds we make together as he works me. It takes more pressure to get me there, and he delivers, watching my reactions, giving me more of everything as his hips thrust against the couch.

I'm not as quiet this time, either. I chant his name, tell him when I'm close, tell him how much I need this.

When I'm on the precipice, I breathe, "You're going to make me come. *Sawyer*. You're making me come."

He groans against me and bucks hard enough that the couch moves several inches back as I come apart, quivering and moaning. I gradually turn into a whimpering, pulsating, melted mess, breathing hard on the askew couch, unable to get a grip on reality.

When Sawyer eases his fingers out of me, a shiver, cold and unwelcome, runs through me, but I'm too beat, too defeated, too utterly and overwhelmingly fucked to do anything about it.

The adrenaline from earlier when I thought I was stranded and had to run through a blizzard, the relief when Sawyer found me, the frustration when it was clear he had to bring me *here*, then the insanity that just took place—it all culminates into absolute exhaustion. My eyelids begin to droop.

"Brie," Sawyer says softly.

Is there a hint of anxiety in his voice?

"Hm?"

"Brie, are you okay?"

"Mm-hm." I blink up at him through hooded, sleepy eyes. He's still breathing heavy, mouth wet, cheeks tinged pink. If I weren't about to be comatose, I'd need him again right now. My eyelids close on his image, too leaden to stay open.

His voice is in my ear. "Are you hungry?"

All I can do is shake my head one time. One motion from left to right.

His chuckle vibrates against my side as his arms snake beneath me. He picks me up and carries me somewhere even softer than the couch, draping a comforter over me.

He places a soft kiss on my temple. "So lucky I found you."

I SLOWLY ROUSE with my favorite scent in my nose and a perfect ass in my crotch. I tighten my hold around the soft weight in my hand.

Blinking one eye open, I freeze. It's Brie's hair in my nose. Her ass presses against my hard-as-steel cock. My hand cups her boob.

Fuck. Just the memory of eating Brie out while she moaned my name has my dick flexing in my pajama pants.

Nope. Not coming in my pants a second time in twelve hours.

I slide my body back, watching for any sign she's waking up, and slip out of bed. I started out last night sleeping on the couch, but it's the same one I bought when I moved into my first studio apartment after coming back to Blue Ridge. My feet were hanging off one side, and I woke up an hour later with a crick in my neck. I moved to the bed, figuring I could stay on my side.

So much for that plan. I stop midway to the bathroom when I look back at Brie. She's not on her side. She isn't even in the middle of the bed. She is one-hundred-percent on my side of the bed.

My heart leaps. *She* came to *me* in sleep. A slow grin plays on my face and I walk into the bathroom with a bounce in my step as I replay every hot detail from last night . . . until I remember what she said.

Just once. We do this one time.

There I was, thinking I was making her mindless, and she had the wherewithal to lay ground rules.

If I had any self-control at all, I would have stopped things before they got out of hand, and had a real conversation with her. It was the ideal opportunity, stuck in this house with nowhere to go. But I just had to taste her, didn't I.

My feelings for Brie have always made me foolish, but this takes the cake. The universe gifted me the perfect chance to set things right, and I squandered it.

I huff out a frustrated sigh as I look out the window. The snow isn't blowing horizontally anymore, but it's still coming down in big fluffy flakes. How much longer will we be held hostage together? Will she even speak to me when she gets up?

"You stupid idiot," I say to my disheveled reflection.

This entire time, all I've wanted was for Brie to see me for who I am, not what I did. But last night wasn't the way to do that. The truth is, she never would've come home with me if she had a choice. But she came because she didn't, and I threw away my Get Out of Jail Free card because I have no self-control.

A one-time deal implies just that—one time together, then she's done with me. Easily discarded, never to be thought about again.

I'm out of her system.

And, really, how can I blame her? I spent years tormenting her, the least I can do now is respect what she wants.

"Just be glad you had last night," I mutter, turning away.

I have to respect her *just one time* rule. I have to stay detached.

Even if it makes me crazy.

Even if I can still smell her.

Taste her.

Feel her.

. . . And that's how I end up jerking off in the shower.

Twice.

I LOOK up from making breakfast when I hear Brie's loud yawn. She stretches, starfishing beneath the comforter. I like her here. I want to climb into bed and make her moan my name again. See what other sounds I can coax out of her. But I have to remind myself that's not what she wants. She got what she needed, and I'm just happy I was a part of it.

It's obvious the moment she realizes where she is. She freezes, then looks down at her body beneath the cover, presumably noticing the flannel shirt I helped her sleepy self into last night. When she finds me standing at the kitchen island, she gives me a shy finger wave. It's so fucking adorable, I have to look back down at the eggs.

I ask, "Sleep well?"

"Like the dead."

A fluttering sensation enters my chest, but I tamp it down. "How's your hip?"

She looks down, like she'd forgotten until now. "Feels a little bruised, but it looks good."

Nodding, I point to the door by the headboard. "Bathroom's there. Laid a toothbrush out for you, towels in the closet. And some clothes that might fit are on the counter. Use anything you want. Holler if you can't find what you need."

She sits up and opens her mouth, then closes it, then opens it again. "You shaved."

Does she not like it?

Instinctively, I rub my jaw. "Yeah."

Her lips press together in an unreadable expression. But she doesn't say anything else as she slips out of bed and heads to the bathroom, glancing over her shoulder before shutting the door.

Twenty minutes later, I'm sitting at the kitchen island when I hear the bathroom door open. I don't look up as she pads over because I want to finish the last few stitches.

Her feet—clad in my gray wool socks, bunched at her ankles, come into view in my periphery. "Are you . . . mending my favorite pants?"

Shit. I couldn't decide if this was a nice gesture, given I was the one who ripped them, or if this was the opposite of staying detached.

"No big deal," I grunt. "Would've done it last night, but . . ." Finishing that sentence with *I licked you until you came instead* feels like a breach of her one-time only rule. Any reference to what happened last night probably is.

"I'll throw your clothes in the wash after breakfast." I tie off the thread, look up, and do a double take.

She shrugs. "The sweatpants were too big." Her hair is damp and she's wearing the flannel shirt I laid out. It comes down to mid-thigh. I can't tell if she's wearing the boxers I left for her, but if the pants were too big, those probably were, too. I wish she'd sit on my lap again so I could find out. The only other thing she's wearing are the socks.

Fuck.

I should have gone for a third round in the shower.

"Smells good," she says.

That kickstarts my brain. "You must be starving."

I stand up and put the pants on the counter, carefully placing the needle back in my sewing kit. When I look up, she's squinting at me like I'm one of those Magic Eye pictures.

Don't be curious. Don't engage. Stay detached. She doesn't want me.

"Coffee?" I ask, rounding the island.

"Yes, please." She sits at the counter while I start the kettle for the French press. An awkward beat passes when neither of us seems to know where to look.

I follow her eyes as they roam curiously around my place. The large fireplace before the too-small couch. The bedroom furniture I bought on sale a few months ago taking up too much space behind it. The small square dining table that seats four below a chandelier meant for a table at least twice as wide. And this kitchen. Right now, it's the best looking spot in here, uncluttered and spacious.

"This all looks brand new." She nods at the appliances as her hands smooth over the shiny countertop.

"That's because it is."

She nods.

I nod.

Another beat of silence that has me wondering about those boxers again.

"It's nice. I . . . I kind of love the whole style."

Don't break out into song.

"Thanks." I remember what I'm doing here, and pick up the spatula, pointing it at her as I take the lid off the warm pan. "Veggie frittata okay?"

"Sounds good."

I slide a plate toward her, and watch as she makes a bite with her fork. She pauses before eating it.

"There aren't any peppers in it," I say.

Her eyes snap up. "What?"

My hand goes to the back of my neck, rubbing. "I thought you might be wondering since you don't like them . . ."

She shakes her head, and quickly takes the bite, eyes closing momentarily. "This is really good." She says, sounding impressed, then swallows. "But, um . . . I wanted to thank you. For . . . finding me."

"Oh." My muscles relax. I didn't know I'd been tense. "I'm really glad I found you." The words are quiet.

She holds my gaze for a moment before returning to her food. Words rise and die in my throat until I finally look away and plate some breakfast for myself. We eat and sip coffee in uncomfortable silence. There's so much I want to say to her, and I sense she has something on her mind, too. The air is thick and icy as tension builds between us, but neither of us says a word as we watch the snow fall out the window.

When I collect our laundry, she follows me to the door that leads to the rest of the cabin. I look down at her. "Put on those slides," I say, nodding at a pair of sandals by the door.

I shove my socked feet into my work boots and open the door.

She walks slow, as if unsure she should even be here. But she takes in every detail of the unfinished space, poking her head into a bathroom where I just finished tiling the shower. We walk into the small laundry room, the only space back here that's completely done. She meanders out, presumably to scope out the rest of the rooms, as I throw a load in the washer.

When I'm done, I find her in the largest bedroom. Mine. She stands in front of the floor-to-ceiling windows that overlook the creek, burbling beneath sheets of ice. She looks so right standing here, and I can picture her still here once it's all finished, I've swept the dust, and the furniture is in place.

"Look," she says, pointing.

On a large patch of ice, dozens of mallards huddle together. One or two paddle around in the freezing water, dipping their head down before popping back up again.

"Looks cold."

On cue, she shivers and folds her arms. "Cozy, I think. To have everyone work together to keep one another safe."

"Maybe," I say.

She looks up. "You don't think that's what they're doing?"

"I think it's a sweet thought. But I wonder if some of those ducks would rather be on their own, not part of the group."

"They'd freeze," she says. "Besides, no one really wants to be alone."

We stand at the window for a couple more minutes.

"I thought you were some weird hoarder," she says.

I turn to her. "What?"

"Because of all the stuff." She gestures back toward the living room. "I didn't realize these rooms were back here, empty."

"Well, yeah. I'm fixing them up so I have more space for all the stacks of newspapers I plan to accumulate."

I love the surprise on her face when she laughs.

"You're fixing it up yourself?"

Is she impressed?

"Yeah. My brother helps a lot."

She gestures to the room at large, and the view outside. "This is like a dream."

Her head tilts up to watch the snow, but I watch her. All she has to do is say the word, and I would sign over the deed to this place in a heartbeat, just give it to her, no questions asked. I'd even finish it first. The words almost come out of their own volition: *Take it. It's yours.* But I swallow them down, fully aware she wants nothing from me.

Maybe I'm overcompensating, punishing myself for past behavior when I was a different person. But it's not just my feelings about myself. It's about Brie, too. I want her to be happy, want her to have everything she wants in life. Even if none of that includes me.

My throat squeezes tight before I pull myself together. I agree with her. This is like a dream.

I glance out the window. "You must have frigid dreams," I tease.

She gives a one-shouldered shrug. "I like the cold."

My brow drops as an involuntary smirk tugs on my mouth. "Didn't you say you left your old school because you didn't like the cold?"

Her eyes widen, and for a moment I think I've touched a sore spot. But then her mouth drops in mock-indignation, the edges curving upward playfully. It's *almost* a smile. For me.

"I didn't leave because I don't *like* the cold," she argues. "It's because winter was endless up there. Last year, there were flurries in *May*. May! At that point, it isn't cozy anymore, it's hell."

"Hell?" I raise my eyebrows.

"A frozen hell," she amends. "Down here, May is shorts

weather." She pauses. "Then again, there was that one asshole who wore shorts even in the snow."

"Chad Harris."

"Oh my gosh!" She shoves my arm and I flex on instinct as the ice between us begins to thaw. "Yes! Exactly like him. Where is that guy now?"

"In jail." Her eyes go wide. Keeping my tone grave, I add, "For public nudity. Eventually he thought even the shorts were too much."

She cackles, and I've never been higher.

"Come on," I say.

"Where?"

"If you like the cold so much, let's go outside."

SNOW FLOATS DELICATELY DOWN from the sky. From the way the property is perched just above town, I have a great view of Blue Ridge. The clocktower downtown, the town square, and the bowling alley near the outskirts, with its lone, unfortunately-shaped pin on the roof thrusting into the sky.

From here, it's a picture postcard of the perfect snow-covered small town surrounded by mountains. It's beautiful. But I don't fully understand what Sawyer's doing way out here instead of his rightful place in Belmont on the northwest side of town.

While I muse, I idly form a sad snowball in my Sawyer-sized gloves.

"It's pretty like this," he says behind me. "Like a snow globe."

I'm not sure what compels me to do it, maybe that I don't want to admit out loud what I think of the view, but I spin around and throw the snowball at him.

He follows its path to his chest where it breaks apart in a puff of white. "What was that for?"

I can't help laughing, he looks so put out even though he probably barely felt a thing. "For ending up with the best place in Blue Ridge. You always get—*Gah!*" I scream as he bends down to make a snowball of his own, and start running.

He's right behind me, and pelts it into my shoulder.

"That's not fair!" I yell, unable to contain my laughter. "You can move so much faster than me!"

Sawyer wears jeans, a *t-shirt*, and what some people in colder climates might classify as a windbreaker. He's dressed for agility.

I, on the other hand, am swimming in Sawyer's snow bib (insulated zip-up overalls, basically), under which I still wear his flannel shirt and rolled up boxers. Plus a hoodie. And his warmest jacket over all of it.

I am, in a word, lumbering. Like a giant running in slow motion.

He strides toward me, looking exactly like a photoshopped LL Bean model with his clean-shaven square jaw, devastating smile, and the sparkle in his eye. He reaches for the beanie on my head.

"Here," he says, donning it. "I'll make it easier on you." He tugs it down over his eyes. "I won't even throw snowballs. I'll just dodge." His cheeks are pink from the cold, but his smile is wide and gleaming.

With his eyes covered, I smile back. "Seriously?"

"Mm-hm." His throat muscles move on the sound, and I'm suddenly very hot in this getup.

Focus.

I bend down to make a clumsy snowball with my too-large gloves. They might as well be oven mitts.

"When does it end?"

He shrugs. "When you get tired of missing."

Appalled, I throw it before it's tamped down enough. It breaks apart in the air, landing mostly on his crotch.

His mouth quirks. "Cold, Casey."

Before I can tell him I didn't mean to, he reaches out with both hands and cups my shoulders. The world is reduced to a snowy swirl as he spins me where I stand. With each turn, I'm laughing harder, gasping for air by the time he's done.

"That did nothing!" I yell, but I'm already tilting to one side.

Even with his eyes covered, his arm instinctively shoots out, steadying me for just a moment.

"You good?" He asks.

"Good enough to bury you in snowballs."

His smile is incandescent before running off like a shot, zigging and zagging exaggeratedly.

Once I get my laughter under control, I realize I'm definitely all talk. There's no way I can catch up to him in my clunky gear. And without properly-fitting gloves, my snowballs are pathetic, not sticking at all.

My best options are stealth and misdirection, so I make my way quietly in the direction he ran toward. When I come across a short stick, I pick it up and hurl it at a tree several feet past him. I know he hears it when he stops in his tracks, literally says a comical "Huh?"and makes a u-turn, toward the creek.

Yessss.

I have a new mission: confuse him until he comes to me.

The next stick lands with a satisfying *clack* on a sheet of ice in the creek. He freezes, and I can practically see understanding dawn on him before he turns around again, more cautiously this time.

"Hey, Brie!" he shouts in the wrong direction. "What

do you think about some hot chocolate later? I make really great hot chocolate."

It's taking real effort not to cackle at his obvious effort to suss out where I am. This is the most fun I've had in a *long* time. No colleagues or students' parents to deal with, no job applications to fill out, and no counting down the days til I'm out of town. All I have is one singular focus: destroy Sawyer with snow.

"You like whipped cream?" he yells. "Who'm I kidding, of course you like whipped cream. I'll make some for you."

Hot chocolate with homemade whipped cream sounds amazing, but I say nothing as I look for more surfaces to fling sticks at. This part of his property is nice and open, so there aren't many options. I manage to make one more strategic pitch. He spins around, and runs straight toward me. Quickly, I gather as much snow in my giant gloves as possible, and watch.

He's four feet away.

Three.

Two.

Thump.

The snow lands on his chest, like I meant for it to, but some gets on his bare neck, melting on his skin and dripping into his shirt. His resultant yelp has me doubled over in laughter.

"I'm sorry!" I wheeze. "I didn't . . . mean . . ."

"You think that's funny?"

The belly laugh won't stop. "It wasn't . . . supposed . . ."

He cuts me off by putting the beanie over my head, covering my eyes until there's nothing but darkness and a sliver of white light where the fabric meets my cheeks.

"Your turn."

"No!" I squeal, but I run anyway. "This is *so* not fair!"

Or, I try to run. It's like trying to propel myself upstream through water, fully clothed and blanketed.

A snowball thumps softly on my back. "Should've thought of that before you stuffed snow down my shirt."

"I didn't do that! I can't even move my fingers in these stupid gloves," I say, trying to hike up my pants so I can move quicker. "Besides," I holler over my shoulder, "that's what you get for not dressing appropriately!"

"You're one to talk—" His voice is excruciatingly close, barely three feet behind me.

I'm a wounded deer being hunted by a ghost. Another snowball lands on my calf.

"—Ms. Dresses-for-sun-in-a-blizzard," he continues. "Anyway, you're wearing all my warm clothes. I had no choice. Because I'm a *gentleman*." That last word is emphasized with a snowball smacking my ass. The uninjured side.

A giggle rockets out from my throat. "Puh-*lease*. You didn't need to wear a *t-shirt*. You have, like, a thousand flannel shirts."

"Been paying attention, have you?" His voice is right at my left ear.

I let out a shrill shriek and whirl away, but my toe snags on something, which would have been fine, except I accidentally let go of my pants. The bulky insulated fabric bunches around my knees. It happens so fast. I begin tipping over, with no chance of righting myself.

Then Sawyer's heavy body tackles me, pinwheeling us in midair.

With an "Oof," he lands on his back, with me chest-to-chest on top of him, both of us shaking with laughter. Too exhausted to do anything else, I lay my head on his chest. I gasp when my lower cheek meets the cold wet fabric of his shirt.

His chuckle quakes through me.

I peel the beanie off my eyes. "Thanks for saving me. Again."

The words he'd asked in anger come back to me. *Why didn't you call* me. And my biting words back. *When have you ever come through for me?*

But Sawyer keeps saving me, doesn't he? He saved me from embarrassing myself in front of Dev by coming on that non-date. He insisted I share his table when none were left at Taco Tuesday. He found me yesterday in a blizzard, tended to my wound, *sewed my fucking pants back together*.

And landed hard on his back just now to soften my fall.

His eyes sparkle and he grins back. "I told you, I'm a gentleman."

He really is.

Playing along, I drop my mouth in mock-indignation, fighting my smile. "A gentleman who blindfolds a defense-less woman just so he can pelt her with snowballs?"

I shift to get off him, but his arm holds tight against my back.

"A gentleman who likes his fun," he says. His eyes drop to my mouth, and he wets his lip. I'm suddenly aware of how hard his body is beneath me, how powerful he is. Yet he was so careful with me during our game, tossing easy snowballs at me instead of pelting them at more tender body parts.

His arm tenses around me. I can see his pulse quick-ening in his throat, and I wonder if he can see mine doing the same. His smile fades into something more serious. Dangerous.

Every cell in my body sparks to life, begging for Sawyer's attention. His t-shirt, damp at the neck, hugs his torso in the most distracting way. I warm at the memory of his toned shoulders and biceps pinning me down as he drove me to the maddening brink of ecstasy last night.

His face is inches from mine. When his tongue darts out to lick his lips again, I pounce without thinking. The nanosecond our lips meet, he takes over with a fierce hunger, thrusting his tongue into my mouth to dance with mine, spreading his rough hands over my body as if he can't decide where they should land, and letting out a satisfied groan deep in the back of his throat.

Then his sounds turn frustrated as his hands continue their search over my mountains of gear. He rolls us over, removes one glove with his teeth, tosses it to the side with a jerk of his head, and crushes his mouth to mine as he works on the zipper of my jacket.

"This okay?" he asks.

"God, *yes*." If he doesn't touch me in the next ten seconds, I might combust.

The zipper of the snow bib is next, and then his cool hand is inside the overalls, pushing up my other layers, coming to rest high on my stomach as his cool thumb flicks my nipple. I gasp into his mouth, and his lips pull in a smile, but never leave mine.

When his hand drags lower, it lights up every nerve it touches, leaving sizzling scorch marks in its wake. His fingers toy with the rolled waistband of the boxers.

He nips his way to my ear. "I wondered if you were wearing anything under that shirt of mine. Made me hard just wondering. I couldn't decide if I wanted you bare, but" —he does his signature move and tugs the boxers up, giving me delicious friction— "this is better. I love knowing you're getting my shorts all wet. So fucking hot."

I feel his voice travel to the deepest parts of me, igniting a furious need for more. But he doesn't give it to me, teasing me with shallow dips into the boxers, just short of where I want him. A whimper escapes my throat.

He chuckles against my neck. "You're so fun to tease."

"It's torture," I whine, ripping off my gloves and diving my hands beneath the hem of his shirt, fascinated by how his muscles tense as cold air meets hot skin.

When his fingers reach lower, barely brushing where I need him, I arch against him.

"Needy?"

"You have no idea." As his fingers dip just inside me, spreading my wetness to my clit, I'm already close to a fiery explosion.

"That's where you're wrong, honey. I've got some idea." He tugs my bottom lip between his teeth as the heel of his hand massages my clit in tandem with his fingers driving into me.

A ragged moan rips through me. I'm already right on the brink. The edge is so close, all I need is one faint push for me to tumble over it.

And then he does it. His rhythm, steady and sure, drives me higher and higher until I'm fisting his shirt, back bowed, and half-moaning, half-gasping his name as his eyes bore into mine, watching me with stormy, hungry wonder. My walls clamp tight around his fingers as he pushes me over the edge and a shudder wracks through me.

"Holy shit, Brie. You're coming for me already?" He doesn't stop, he doesn't slow down, seeing me through to the end.

I crash back on the snowy ground, coming down from

my orgasm but not nearly sated. He kisses me deeply, and I want so much more from him.

But the second I have his pants unbuttoned, he grabs my hand, stilling it.

He pulls back, watching me as his chest rises and falls in a quick, heavy rhythm.

"No."

That's it.

One word.

And I. Am. Mortified.

I shoot up, scrambling to my feet. "Oh! Yeah. No. I mean . . . I kind of . . . need another shower. Got sweaty in all this" —this is when I gesture down, drawing attention to my half-naked torso, and cringe— "while we were . . . running around."

Then I run inside and lock myself in the bathroom.

CHAPTER 30

SAWYER

"RESPECT THE RULE, I SAID."

Thunk.

"Don't engage, I said."

Thunk.

"Stay detached, I *fucking* said."

Crack!

My axe finally finds its way deep into the large log. I toss the axe aside and dig my hands into the fissure to rip it apart myself. I'm so full of adrenaline right now, it splinters almost immediately.

I can't do anything right. I wanted her hands on me more than anything, and it took all my strength to stop what was happening, but that was still the wrong move because, clearly, I embarrassed her. The problem was, I remembered her one-time rule, and I had to stop things from going further.

But *fuck*, here I am trying to make us something we aren't anyway. Playing games like we're a couple, kissing her like I'm allowed to, putting my hands on her body as if she's mine.

But she isn't.

She isn't mine, and she doesn't want to be mine.

Especially after what just happened. I'll be lucky if she'll still look at me.

Blistering rage boils me from the inside as I drive my axe into another log. I'm sweating despite the freezing temperature. I strip off my jacket, toss it onto the porch steps.

Crouching, I shove my hands into the opening of the log, and I don't let go until I feel it give under my pressure, slowly coming apart for me in one satisfying yawn before both halves tumble to the ground.

I pick up one of the halves, orienting it on its face, and do it all over again.

Chop.

Pull.

Toss.

Chop, pull, toss.

ChopPullToss.

When I have a haphazard tower of wood, I feel no better than before. Brie's pained face as she stumbled to her feet before running inside flashes into my mind.

She's probably in the bathroom right now—*oh shit.* I realize with a jolt I've been out here ruminating this whole time when she probably ran right in without grabbing any clothes for herself. I abandon the wood, and head inside.

The dryer dings at the same time I walk into the laundry room. I rake all the clothes into a basket, pulling out her pants, her sweater—I hesitate before reaching for her bra and adding it to the growing pile. Finally, her underwear. I sewed them back together, though she'll probably throw them out after this. The panties are innocent, pink with white polka dots, but handling them makes my dick swell in my pants because they belong to Brie. This piece of fabric has hugged her ass, rubbed her pussy, gotten soaked by her.

I close my eyes and give myself a stern talking-to.

Brie will never *want you the same way you want her. Get a fucking grip.*

Outside the bathroom, when I don't hear the shower running, I rap lightly on the door.

It opens a crack, and one wary brown eye peeks out.

"I brought your clothes." I hand her the pile, with a few things of mine on top. Not because I'm hoping she comes out in another one of my shirts, but for comfort.

And because I want to see her in another one of my shirts.

The door opens wider, and I drink in the sight. Her hair is damp. Bare legs and feet. The only thing she wears is a towel, held tight with one hand at her chest. A bead of water trickles down her neck, and I want to lick it.

She moves to the side, letting me in. "Thanks." She won't meet my eyes.

I step inside just enough to lay the heap on the counter, but I stop short when I take in a breath. I know all the products in here. Brie used what I use every day. But it's different somehow, and it smells so good.

Nope.

Turning stiffly, I tip my imaginary hat in her direction and exit the bathroom, closing the door behind me.

Then proceed to tug at my hair when I realize I gave her a *hat tip.*

I have no chill when it comes to Brie Casey. I turn into a drooling idiot around her, and honestly? I'm not even ashamed.

But I do have to control myself. I know how this town

operates, and there's no way the roads'll be drivable even by tomorrow. I've got to keep my hands to myself from now on. It's the respectful thing to do, and it'll keep me from being completely destroyed when this is all over and Brie remembers who she was stuck with.

Defeated, I go back outside to bring in my jacket and some wood for the fireplace. I busy myself with building a fire, only looking up when the door to the bathroom opens again.

CHAPTER 31

BRIE

I PACE in front of the windows while Sawyer's in the shower. How do I know he's in the shower? Did he *tell me* he was going to take a shower? No. Did he *look at me* before he walked into the bathroom? No.

Did he walk into the bathroom without even a glance, shut the door, then *audibly locked it*? Yes. Yes, he did.

What am I even doing here? I'm not that same teenage girl. I don't have to take his shit. When I ran and hid (yes, I'm big enough to admit it: I hid) in the bathroom earlier? That's the last time I act like that little girl.

I look out the back windows, past the covered porch. It can't be more than six miles to Gia's house. It's barely snowing anymore. Surely businesses have salted the sidewalks by now. Maybe the streets in town are even cleared.

In a split second, I make the decision. I hurry to where I deposited Sawyer's jacket by the door, and pull it on. I take his gloves for good measure, and his stupid hat we used as a blindfold for that stupid game. Then I shove my feet into my shoes and walk out the door into the cloudy haze of the late-afternoon. In my seething ire, the door shuts behind me with a bang.

I storm off with enraged confidence, not bothering to look back or give myself time to second-guess. This is the right decision—I can sleep in my bed at Gia's tonight and never see Sawyer's stupid face again.

I'm not even halfway down his salted walkway when the door behind me opens and slams shut again.

"Brie!"

No. Refusing to let my guard down, I keep my gaze ahead and storm off *harder*. I will not be deterred. I will not be persuaded. I will not be coerced.

I hear the quick slapping of sandals, and in no time he's in front of me.

Naked.

Well, not totally. A towel is slung low on his hips, and he wears those slides I wore for the tour of his house. But his hair is dripping and his incredible torso glistens. His defined pecs and abs tense and goosebumps erupt as flurries melt on his skin. His large shoulders lean toward me just a fraction as he runs those long fingers through his damp hair.

"Where're you going?" he asks.

"Thought I'd try living with the forest animals, what do you think? I'm going back to my sister's."

His eyes narrow. "Gia's?"

I jut out my chin. "Exactly."

His expression turns hard. "You want to walk almost seven miles to Gia's house." He moves closer to block my path and looks down at me head-on, face twisting in outrage. "What're you trying to prove? That you're insane? No."

The fucking *audacity*. I stare up at him, heart pounding.

"No? You don't get to tell me *no*. You have no bearing on what I do."

He huffs out a breath. "I'm sorry if I embarrassed you back there, but I won't let you walk in the snow and ice, down the mountain and through town for almost seven miles dressed like that. Your feet would freeze before you make it a half-mile."

The fact he isn't wrong sends another bolt of irritation through me. And there it is again, louder this time: that nagging sense I'm missing something. Nothing about this situation makes sense. Why is Sawyer making me come one minute, rejecting me the next, and worried for my safety now? Hot, cold, hot, cold. Why has this been his game for years?

And why are we stuck up here in the first place? I can't think clearly when his throat pulses like that, his eyes boring into me as snow kisses his naked torso. But Sawyer living in a half-built cabin on *this* mountain feels like an elaborate ruse to trick me. It doesn't fit the Sawyer I know.

"Why're you even here anyway?" I snap. "Why don't you live where you belong?"

If he lived in Belmont like he should, I never would've been stuck with him in the first place.

"And where's that?"

"Town! The north side of town! Northwest, if you want me to be specific. That's where your kingdom is."

He practically sneers, "Town isn't for me."

That doesn't make any sense. It is *exactly* for Sawyer. The Strongs, collectively, are a paragon of Belmont. The most affluent neighborhood in town.

Unable to swallow the question down, I ask, "But, why?"

His eyes darken, and I can see him weighing his answers

in his head. The muscles in his torso are strung tight, but he gives me an airy shrug. "It's where all the hoity-toity folks live."

"But you're the hoitiest of the toities," I insist, as if it isn't the most ridiculous sentence to come out of my mouth.

He gives me a flat look, like there's something I'm *so obviously* missing here. And clearly, I am. Clearly, I just *don't get it.* Yet he's done nothing to help me get there, given me no hints or clues to any of the questions slithering in the back of my mind.

If he doesn't want to talk about town, that's fine, I have plenty of other things to ask instead.

I roll my shoulders, readying myself for the next stage of our verbal battle. "What happened to your old truck?" It sounds like a challenge. I dare him to tell me.

Both hands tighten into fists. "Got rid of it before leaving for the Navy."

"Why didn't you get something better when you came back?"

Now he's grinding his teeth. Now *he's* aggravated. It's in every flex of his muscle, every protruding vein in his neck.

"Define *better.*" He starts back toward the house.

Is he walking away from me? Shutting down on me? *Again?*

I am so tired of dancing around the meaning of things. He's being intentionally evasive. He is *impossible* to talk to. But I'm not letting him off this time. He has nowhere to go and, apparently, neither do I.

Stomping up the steps behind him, I say, "Why did you decide to become a principal? How come you're not outsourcing all this hard manual labor?" I gesture to his house as we enter it.

He grinds his molars as he takes a pair of boxer briefs from a dresser and pulls them up underneath his towel. My eyes involuntarily follow his every movement. He dries his hair with it before tossing it over a chair.

My brain glitches as I take him in, clad only in his black underwear before he throws on a pair of jeans that sit low on his hips. The horny part of my brain protests when he puts on a Navy t-shirt, and it's all I can do to internally tell the slut to shut up.

"Why'd you go into the army?" I ask, intentionally trying to get a rise out of him.

He points to his chest. "Navy."

"Are you going to answer any of my questions or just stand there? I'll even give you some easy ones. How do you know I don't like peppers? How'd you—"

"I paid attention," he interrupts.

Paid attention. He's talking about before, when we were younger.

I let out a humorless laugh. "That much is obvious. You knew just how to push my buttons." I shove my fingers into the air at imaginary buttons. "Just which ones to push for maximum humiliation."

His eyes harden on me. "And you think I don't regret that? You think it didn't keep me up at night, even then? That it didn't keep me up at night for *years*?"

For a moment, I stand still, shocked, but I recover just as quickly. "What, I'm supposed to feel sorry for you? *Poor Sawyer!* He felt bad for intentionally humiliating me for *years*! Oh! And laughing about it with his friends!"

All the pain of those moments hits me like a tsunami, except I'm not sad about it anymore. I'm furious. Sawyer robbed me of a happy school life. The one place I should have been able to forget about my problems at home, about my dad, the bills, the rundown house I was behind on maintaining, and Sawyer made it a different kind of hell without a second's thought.

Between clenched teeth, he says, "I'm not asking you to feel sorry for me. There's no excuse for what I did. None."

He averts his gaze, watching the floor. His body is strung tight, jaw clenched.

I snort. "Is that seriously all you have to say to me? Is that your version of an apology?"

His eyes cut to me. "There is no apology big enough to encompass everything I did. Any words would be meaningless."

Like a bull, my breath blows out through my nose, my head dips as I glare at him through slitted eyelids. I'm practically pawing at the ground, ready to charge at him.

"*Try*," I snarl. "Or, better yet, tell me why. Why did you do it? Day in, day out, for years. Did you just hate me that much?"

His laugh is hollow, and his voice rises a little. "I *didn't* hate you. That was the problem!"

I'm *so close* to actually strangling him. "I'm sick of your riddles, Sawyer. Just say what you mean!"

Tugging on his hair, he lets out a loud huff and turns away from me. After a few steps, he circles back around, huffing again. I recognize his expression. It's the same one I just wore. He's about to explode.

He stops a few feet away, hands in his hair. "You really want to know?"

I shout, "Yes, I want to know!"

Turning, he paces away and back again. "Fine!"

"Just tell me!"

"I was obsessed with you, Brie! Ever since we were little kids, I was fucking *obsessed*."

My mouth drops and I swear my heart literally stops in my chest. Surely he can't mean what it sounds like.

"You were shy, but sure of yourself," he says. "You barely ever spoke, but when you did it was *honest*, none of the usual bullshit that comes out of people's mouths. You were clumsy, but determined. Even when you were down, *even* when something awful happened, you'd brush yourself off and just keep going."

Anger replaces my shock as I take in his words. "What was I supposed to do?" I spit out. "Curl up in the fetal position and cry? Beg you to stop? Fight you?"

"No! Maybe. I don't know."

"Sawyer, you *only* made fun of me. You made my life a living hell. Constantly."

He blinks rapidly. "I know." He shuts his eyes and presses his lips tight, shaking his head. "I know."

"So you see why I can't believe you," I say more quietly. "I can't believe you were 'obsessed' with me and still treated me like shit."

When he opens his eyes, they're red. It barely makes a dent in my fury.

"Nothing excuses the way I treated you, so it doesn't matter."

"It matters to me!"

There's a moment of silence in which he watches me with pained eyes.

"Tell me," I hiss. "I want to know. I *deserve* to know why my entire childhood was reduced to a steaming pile of shit because of you."

His eyes meet mine, glassy and devoid of any spark. "I was scared."

Scared? What did Sawyer Strong have to be scared of?

He shakes his head again and then, evenly, he says, "I

was scared of people finding out how I really felt about you. I was sure it was obvious to anyone who looked that I only wanted to be around *you*." He lets out another hollow laugh. "I can't believe you didn't know. It only got worse as we got older. By high school, I was desperate for you. And I knew I couldn't have you. You never even guessed that night I drove you home? Or when we danced at prom?" His voice cracks on the last word.

My jaw drops, and I'm positive shock is written all over my face. I'd felt something in those moments, too. On the drive. At prom. Those months in between when my crush blossomed into something untenable. It was something I only ever admitted to myself late at night, when the whispers in my head were loudest. I thought I might have even been a little crazy to have feelings for him, after everything he'd done. I even acted a little crazy—keeping his jacket after the drive in the rain and pulling it out some nights just to prove it really happened, sleeping with it.

Even though the deepest parts of me wished he returned my feelings, I never believed he ever could. Because you don't treat someone the way Sawyer treated me if you like them.

Suddenly, I understand. Sawyer was ashamed to have feelings for me. Sawyer was the Prince of Blue Ridge, and I was vermin by comparison. And that's why he was a jerk.

Anger sparks to life again as I realize exactly what he's saying. "So you didn't want the town to know you were interested in the girl from the wrong side of the tracks." It isn't a question.

Pain flashes in his eyes.

I don't care. Why should I care about his pain right now?

"It wasn't that simple," he says.

"Then spell it out for me. Why were you so scared—so *ashamed*—of your feelings that you had to be cruel to me instead?"

He presses the heels of his hands into his eyes before meeting my gaze. "Take your pick. The town. My friends. My dad." He lets out a long sigh. "My dad's such an asshole. He was trying to raise me to be like him. Even as a little fucking kid, he made it clear it was heresy for me to play with anyone whose name wasn't Whitaker or Darvish, or any of the other families he deemed *good* because of their income bracket or what they could do for him. It was a lot of pressure." He looks far away now. "Sometimes I wonder if the difference between Will and me is how much more time he got with our mom, if that's why he didn't cave into it like I did."

Sawyer's mom died when he was young, like mine. And I only knew of Sawyer's dad as the mayor, but he was disliked in my neighborhood. Labeled an untrustworthy classist snake.

"There was no questioning my dad," Sawyer goes on. "No standing up to him. His word was canon." He rubs the back of his neck. "I knew from the first time I saw you that I liked you. I wanted to be your friend immediately. When my dad discovered my interest in 'a Casey'" —he uses air quotes— "he made it clear it was unacceptable." His voice turns into a dark growl. "I should've told him to go to hell from the start."

I let out a disbelieving sound. "You should've told him to go to hell when you were in kindergarten?"

"Even then I knew it was wrong. When I finally did tell him off, it was too late."

"What does that mean?" As far as I can tell, Sawyer is still very much the Prince of Blue Ridge he always was.

He scrubs his hands down his face. "After prom, everything I did to you fully sank in. I was disgusted with myself. A mess for a while. All I wanted was to escape. I enlisted in the Navy just to do something that was completely my own choice. I've never seen my dad so angry." He shakes his head and meets my eyes. "He had plans for me, you know? And enlisting wasn't it. He threatened to cut me off if I didn't undo it."

I'm stunned. Sawyer became a SEAL. I know that. Even so, I can't help asking, "What'd you do?"

"I handed over the keys to my truck. Left that night with one bag."

I draw in a deep breath. It feels like the first in a while. In my wildest dreams, I never considered Sawyer might have carried the weight of what happened between us. I'd always assumed he was unaffected. Proud, maybe, but remorseful? Never.

My voice comes out small when I ask, "You defied your dad and left . . . because of me?" Something inside me begins to thaw. Something I didn't even know was there. My hands start to shake, and I clench them tight.

His eyes hold mine. "Because of what I did to you. I wanted to be different. Someone who'd never hurt someone else just to save myself, especially not the woman I care about. Even though I never had you, I needed to learn to be the kind of man who could stand up for you no matter what. Not tear you down." He swallows hard. "Like at prom."

That memory is the most raw. It stings, and I can't hold back my choked sound as it surfaces. The giddy anticipation as I slid my hand into Sawyer's, the ignorant bliss of dancing with him. Then, the way he pushed me away, the eyes on me at the gym. His words.

I thought I'd give her a taste of the good life. It's all downhill from here for trash like her.

It was the moment I knew I'd never truly belong in Blue Ridge.

"You might not believe this, Brie, but that was the worst night of my life. I went to the dance alone, determined to ignore you. But the second I saw you, I knew I couldn't. You were so beautiful. I couldn't stop myself from going to you and asking you to dance."

The perfect memory of him standing in front of me that night, hand outstretched, causes my stomach to drop. I'd been so shocked, couldn't believe it was real, but dancing with Sawyer felt so good.

"It was everything," he says. "Getting to hold you was . . . everything. I finally got exactly what I wanted after years of fighting it."

"Sawyer, I'm still not getting it. If it was so fantastic like you say, why did it turn out the way it did?" Because that night I lived out the best moments of my young life, and the worst.

He looks up at the ceiling and shakes his head faintly. "God, it sounds so juvenile. We were dancing, and I got hard."

"You . . . got hard." Did I hear that right?

"I was embarrassed and I didn't want you to feel it, so I pushed you away. Then, I heard my friends behind me laughing, and I was terrified they saw right through me. Knew exactly how much I wanted you. All I could do was picture my father's face, red and angry, the words he always spat at me when he was mad." His expression hardens. "So I saved face. Said those disgusting words that've haunted me for years."

"You humiliated me . . . because you got a boner?" I

know I'm simplifying here, I know there's more at play, but . . . come on.

He swallows. "I'd give anything to take it back. I'm so ashamed of my behavior."

Since coming back to Blue Ridge, I've been cautious around Sawyer, certain he's playing some kind of game that'll result in a *gotcha* moment where I'll end up mortified.

But this is no game. His face is drawn, haggard almost. Like this has been weighing on him for a lifetime.

I believe him.

"Brie, I was lost back then. It wasn't just my dad, but the whole town expected me to worship the ground my dad walked on, then follow in his footsteps. They expected certain things of me, tried to fit me into their preconceived box of who I should be."

My breath hitches because I know exactly what that's like. The town expecting me to be—no, *telling me* I was— something I wasn't. The fact Sawyer felt the same pressure never occurred to me because . . . he was the prince.

Looking back, every awful interaction back then only ever happened when his friends were there, watching. Most of the time, it wasn't even him *doing* the thing, but looking on, stony-faced, as Rich acted like a jerk. His loud mouth, his evil smirk, they were a mask he wore for them.

"Look, Brie, I don't expect you to forgive me. I know better than that. But I'm glad you know. Words are worthless, but if it helps, I'm so sorry." He winces. "Fuck, that's so weak. But I am. So fucking sorry, Brie."

I swallow thickly. I used to *know* Sawyer had the perfect life growing up. I *knew* he was always in charge, always the lauded one, always sure of himself.

Just like everyone else, I put him in a box he didn't belong in.

But I can see it now. He's laid it open for me, the pain clear on his face.

Back then, Sawyer was larger than life. He never seemed like a kid even when he was one. But it's clear from his sadness now he regrets each and every one of his actions. Maybe that pain has been there all along, but it's only now that I can see past the man in front of me to the child he was.

My heart breaks for that little kid.

Sawyer was a *child*. The child to a hard, loathsome man, who fed him his personal brand of bigotry. Subjecting him to years of indoctrination.

And he's right, it wasn't just his dad. Back then, the town itself was a mirror of the mayor. I felt it in their stares, their whispers behind my back. And Sawyer would've been under the most pressure to join them, to ridicule me.

In one blinding moment, I see it: Sawyer and I are the same. Both of our dads were shitty role models, if for different reasons. Both of us had reputations in the town to live up to. And both of us suffered because of it.

I don't know why it never occurred to me before. I teach kids every day. I see them do stupid, thoughtless, sometimes cruel things to one another. And I never hold it against them, instead giving them grace to learn and grow.

It took the students in my class at Everett Academy mere *days* to begin calling me names when my back was turned. They never questioned whether any of what they heard about me was true because they trusted their parents implicitly. But I still don't blame them, even if I wasn't strong enough to stay and help them be better.

I was never able to give Sawyer the same grace—of

course I wasn't, I was a kid too. But he was never encouraged to learn or grow from his actions either. He was encouraged to keep at it.

Yet Sawyer was still able to claw his way out of his inculcation. He didn't just run away from Blue Ridge like I did. He questioned all that was drilled into him, and he came back to help build a better town, the next generation. That makes him stronger than I ever was.

I step toward him. He's sitting on the edge of the bed, head in his hands, looking miserable. There's still so much more to talk about—we've barely scratched the surface. But in this moment, all I want is for him to know I get it now. His actions since I've been back, the hot and the cold, the saving and the retreating. It all fits now.

I bury my fingers in his hair. "Okay."

He looks up, brows furrowed in confusion. "Okay?"

Abruptly, there's a thunderous crack. Our eyes widen as the floor shakes. Sawyer lunges, grabs me, and runs.

Another loud bang pierces the air as my back hits the far wall.

Breaking glass.

Crunching wood.

Sawyer covers my body with his, and I huddle into him as the sounds settle. Then, everything stills.

CHAPTER 32
SAWYER

I HAVEN'T FELT this kind of adrenaline in years. My heart crashes against my ribcage at a sprint, I can barely catch my slippery breath, and my skin is vibrating with the need to make sure Brie is alright.

I'm pressed up against her, my body folded over hers against the wall, shielding her. I feel her rapid breaths as her chest rises and falls in quick succession against mine. Her entire body trembles from the rush, teeth chattering.

My hands cup her face, and I press a kiss onto her forehead. "You're okay." My voice is rough.

I'm pretty sure a tree just took out part of my cabin. One look over my shoulder confirms it.

"Everything's fine," I tell her. "We didn't even need to move, we would've been fine."

"You saved me." Her big brown eyes look up at me, shock, fear, and . . . wonder? "You keep saving me."

Don't, I tell myself. *Don't do it.*

For one heavy moment, we stare at each other, my eyes bouncing between hers.

Don't fucking do it.

Her chin tips up the slightest bit.

"Fuck it." I cover her lips with mine.

My hands cover her perfect rear, lifting while she snakes her legs around my hips. Her hands are in my hair as she grinds into me, meeting my hungry thrusts. I bring one hand between us and slip it under her sweater, palming her breast as I knead her ass with my other hand. She lets out a soft little sigh that has my cock hard in my jeans. I rock it against her.

"Mm-hm," she hums urgently as she kisses my throat.

"There?" I ask, rubbing against the same spot.

She hums again, and I keep with it, hungry for her breathy sounds.

"Brie." I say, and she looks at me beneath hooded lids. Then I say it again, just because I can. "Brie. Fuck, look at the sight of you." Her lips are plump from kissing, cheeks flushed, eyes ablaze with need.

When we find a rhythm, her head begins to loll back. I catch it before it knocks against the wall. Watching her eyes roll to the back of her head is like a drug. I love watching her like this, knowing I'm the one doing it to her. I dive for the sensitive spot on her neck, grazing my teeth along the curve.

"I want to feel you," I pant into her neck. "I want to taste you." I suck the spot right beneath her ear, and she moans. "But you're too close for that already, aren't you?"

She lets out an unintelligible grunt, clutching me tightly. My hand tightens around her hair, and her eyes flick open. She nods, her movements frantic against me now. Her eyes glaze over, and her body tightens around mine. She's going to come for me. *Because* of me.

"Jesus, Brie. You're going to make me spill in my pants. You're too pretty."

Her mouth opens in a silent gasp, and her entire body

shudders in my arms. Knowing I'm the source of her plea-sure is enough. I pump against her once, twice, and on the third time, I jerk hard against her, coming in my pants for the second time in twenty-four hours. My face is buried in her neck, and we're both breathing hard, but not from fight-or-flight anymore.

My knees are weak, so I lean into the wall, flattening her to me. I nuzzle my face into her neck, taking a deep breath. She's so warm and perfect.

A hard wind blows snow against my back. It takes a few seconds for reality to wink back into existence.

Right. A tree fell on my cabin, destroying some of my hard work.

Keeping my forehead pressed into Brie's shoulder, I roll my head enough to look back at the damage. All in all, it could have been so much worse. At least two of the floor-to-ceiling windows are partially shattered at the back of the house, tree branches sticking through them like welcoming arms letting in the snow. Through the intact windows, I can see the huge oak sitting precisely where the brand new covered porch was about half an hour ago. In the back of my mind, I wonder about damage to the cabin roof, but I'm not sure I really care right now with Brie still clutching to me.

"Nuh-uh," I grunt when she starts to unwrap her legs. I hold tight, keeping her where she is for as long as she'll let me. It could be the last time. I don't know what she was going to say before the tree fell. All she said was *okay.* That could mean anything. *Okay,* but I never want to see you again. *Okay,* but your sorry excuses make me hate you more. Or *okay,* but I'm leaving town when the roads are cleared.

She tightens her hold on me, squeezing me back, and I breathe her in. It's enough to make a grown man cry. With happiness. With hope. With desperation.

Another whistle, another cold gust against my back, and I know we can't stay like this. I step back, and she gingerly drops her feet to the ground. We still have unfinished business to discuss, but there's a gaping hole in my cabin and temperatures are only going to plummet.

Aaaand the evidence of my climax is trapped in my underwear, sticking uncomfortably as I move. This is . . . kind of gross.

"Listen," I say. "You're not going to try and walk out on me again, are you?"

She drags her teeth over her pillowy bottom lip, her cheekbones high. "Not tonight."

I let out a relieved breath. "Okay. I—I just need a minute in the bathroom. But I've gotta take care of this." I point my thumb at the giant hole in my house. "It's going to be dark soon."

"Got it. No problem. Go."

After a quick clean-up, I come out to Brie sweeping up the glass, and my heart squeezes tight. It's so domestic, like she's right where she belongs. With me.

This is a fucking emergency, Sawyer, don't read too much into it.

She turns to me. "What do we do?"

"Keep doing that while I use a chainsaw to cut down the closest branches. Then I'll cover the windows with plywood." She nods dutifully, and my heart squeezes again. "Thanks."

It takes thirty minutes to get the worst branches out of the way. I have to do it at awkward angles, holding the chainsaw over my head at times, being extra careful of kickback and where the branches fall. Sawdust and mulch rain down on me, splattering against my safety glasses, but I'm in too much of a hurry to be tidy about it.

When I have enough of a clearing, I take a ladder to assess any damage to the roof over the main cabin. Luckily, it's in decent shape.

"Alright," I call to Brie through the opening.

She's nearly done sweeping up the extra mess I caused.

"I'm going to cover this up," I tell her.

It's fortunate that I've been lazy about returning extra materials, wanting to do it all at once rather than stand at customer service multiple times at the big box hardware store in Ridgedale.

I'm hefting a sheet of plywood onto the ruined porch when Brie appears. Without a word, she takes one side and helps me angle it over the window frame. She holds up one side while I hold my end with one hand and screw the corners in with the other, making quicker work than if I were alone.

She watches as I take my nailgun to secure the edges— a quick fix for an emergency. I haven't installed the flood-lights out here yet, and it's getting too dark to see well. The town's streetlights are distant winks from where we stand.

I keep my eyes on the gun, heart in my throat, and say, "You were going to say something before the tree inter-rupted us . . ." *and I dry humped you to completion.*

Out of the corner of my eye, I see her shift.

"I'd like to know what you were going to say," I press.

She sucks in a breath. "I'm not going to get over every-thing that happened between us from one conversation."

My heart plummets. It's what I should have expected.

"But I think" —she seems to be weighing her words— "maybe we could, like, work through it."

I force myself to temper my reaction even as my heart soars to heights I didn't know existed.

She goes on. "It's going to be hard for me. Especially right away. My instinct is to not trust you."

My heart is on a brutal rollercoaster.

"We can go slow," I say, voice gruff, and I'm not sure what I even mean by it. The truth is, I mean whatever she'll give me.

Going slow toward friendship? I'd be happy to have it, even if I'll always want more.

Going slow toward a relationship? I'm already hers.

Going slow toward forgiveness? The dream.

I pick up the second sheet of plywood. She's there in an instant, helping me place it just right, then holding it steady.

She picks up where we left off. "Going slow sounds like it could work."

Clearing my throat, I say, "It's okay if you want to be just friends, but . . ."

I don't have to look over to know her attention is fully on me. But that's great. I want her to hear this. No more beating around the bush. Direct communication.

"I want to date you," I say. "If you'll let me, I want to take you out. It doesn't have to be now, or next week. Just, when you're ready." Now that she's in Blue Ridge, I have nothing but time.

I finish the last screw and chance looking at her, but it's too dark to see her expression. I can't read her silence out here, and I start to panic, thinking I already blew my promise to go slow just by asking.

"I might let you," she says finally, and I think I detect a small smile in her voice.

My shoulders relax. *Thank fuck.* Then I'm grateful for the dark, because it means she can't see the goofy grin on my face.

She picks up the nailgun. "Can I try?"

"Definitely."

I show her how to use it and tell her about the kickback. She goes crazy with it, nailing along the edge with glee. I hold the ladder for her to reach higher.

"All this time," she says, "I was impressed with your craftsmanship. But, really, it's just a ton of fun."

A laugh booms out of me. "It can get monotonous and tedious. But yeah, it's fun, too."

When we're done, I send her inside while I put away the tools. Then head in as high as I've ever been. Brie might let me take her out on a date. That's good enough for now.

Stepping into the cabin, I realize it is *really* fucking cold in here. I start a fire, trying not to imagine all the ways Brie and I could keep each other warm tonight.

We're going slow, I chastise as I go to take my third shower of the day.

CHAPTER 33

BRIE

SITTING ON THE FLOOR, curled up by the fire, the familiar buzz of being around Sawyer is still there. I used to blame this feeling on annoyance, frustration, or even trepidation over how he might be setting me up. Now? I feel none of those things. There's a lightness in my chest just from being here, like I might float right up to the ceiling if it weren't for this blanket over my shoulders.

The fire crackles beside me like a chatty friend. Sawyer, fresh from the shower, is in the kitchen, moving around so fast I can hardly see what he's up to. When I asked if I could help, he gave stern instructions to just keep warm. For once, I didn't question his kindness as I changed into a flannel and boxers and settled by the hearth under a blanket.

He brings a cast iron pan over, carefully placing it in the fireplace to cook the chicken and vegetables nestled inside. He doesn't have to do this on the fire, but I like that he is. There's something intimate about it.

My stomach grumbles.

"I heard that," he says. The firelight casts his face in

reds and golds as he shoots me a teasing smile that cranks my pulse up. "Be right back."

A minute later, he's back with a plate of meats and cheeses, a bottle of wine, and a couple mugs. He's dressed in gray sweats and a waffle-knit henley. It's like a cozy second skin to his muscled body, and I can't help tracing my eyes over him. My nipples bead tight and heat pools low in my belly.

We agreed to take things slow. But what does that even mean when he's already seen me naked and had me writhing multiple times?

There's that ever-present buzzing electricity between us that has me clenching my thighs together.

The smart thing is to take things slow.

I spent nearly my entire life thinking the worst of Sawyer. Being suspicious of him at every turn. Even though he isn't that same kid, all it does is prove how little I actually know the true Sawyer.

He gives me a bashful smile as he pours, sending another little thrill through me. "Sorry I don't have proper wine glasses. Never needed them before."

"Why do you have wine if you don't drink it?"

"I didn't say I don't drink wine." He sits down on the floor in front of the hearth with me, elbows resting on his knees. "I'm just not fancy about it." He raises his glass. "I drink the cheap stuff, remember?"

"Right, because the Ikea wine glasses I own are the epitome of class."

He clinks his mug to mine. "Cheers to there not being an Ikea within two hours of here."

I smile, but I kind of love Ikea. I spent many a Saturday morning walking through the showrooms and buying seasonal items. Blue Ridge lacks other things I love, too. Target. Trader Joe's. An Ethiopian restaurant.

Sawyer interrupts my thoughts on small-town hell. "And cheers to the tree missing the main cabin."

"Cheers. You're taking the absolute destruction of your back porch pretty well."

"Best case scenario if the tree had to hit something."

He rolls a square of cheese into some prosciutto and, before I can do the same, he offers it to me. It could be a book of handwritten poems for the way my body reacts. A fizziness erupts in my belly, floating up to my chest and expanding. I bite my lip to keep from smiling, but it's no use. He sees it, and shoots me a devastating grin I feel between my legs.

"To be fair," he continues, "I wasn't crazy about the porch. I threw it together without much thought while waiting on materials for the back of the house to come in. I think I should've made it bigger."

He threw an entire porch together without much thought? Images of him chopping wood earlier today—was that just today?—come to mind. The thump of an axe on wood echoed to the bathroom where I was hiding. When I looked out, I saw him throw his axe down and rip a log in half with his bare hands. It was the most unhinged, sexy thing I've ever seen. If I wasn't so mortified from already trying to get in his pants, I would have gone outside and tried all over again.

"Silver lining," I say, shaking the image. "What else would you change about the porch?"

He pops a slice of salami into his mouth. "Besides the huge oak lying across it? Not sure. What would you?"

"Oh, I don't know," I say into my mug.

What's wrong with me? I'm suddenly shy with butterflies in my stomach. This is what it felt like those months after Sawyer drove me home in the rain. I noticed every look in my direction, keenly aware of him in every room.

And now, it's the same. Every look feels like a caress, making me as nervous as a schoolgirl.

Oh my gosh.

I have a crush on Sawyer.

Like a teenager.

Just like before.

But it's different this time. Sawyer's different.

His knee bumps mine. "You have something in mind, I can tell. What is it?"

For one panicked second, I stare at him, wondering if he can read my mind. *This is stupid.* We've more or less admitted we like each other, so why am I hesitating to tell him how I feel?

"Come on," he presses. "Tell me what you think would make it better."

I let out a shaky laugh. *Right.* He's asking about the porch.

"It's not my place," I say. And I don't know if I mean *It's not my cabin* or *We aren't even dating so I'm in no position to give you opinions on your home.*

"If it were yours," he cajoles, "what would you do differently? It's just a hypothetical."

I roll my neck. It's not like I didn't spend hours imagining a cabin of my own just like this once upon a time, before leaving Blue Ridge seemed possible. And even after, as I fantasized about my ideal home, Mr. Collins's cabin—*this* cabin—would flash to the forefront of my mind, taking me completely by surprise.

"A fireplace and skylights," I say as casually as I can. "So I could use it in the wintertime. Sip coffee and watch the creek on a chilly morning. I love the idea of feeling the bite of cold air for a second before getting warm by the fire. Or, if it was screened in, I could sit out on summer nights and hear the crickets and watch the fireflies dance in the woods. I'd need a fan for summer."

I look up and he's watching me intently. Then, because it's too embarrassing for him to know I've given real thought to this, I add, "And maybe a butler."

After a moment, he plays along. "Yeah, a butler'd be good. How about a portal that leads straight to the kitchen for snacks?"

"So, a door."

He moves his head from side to side, pretending to consider. "A door's too pedestrian. A portal really makes a *statement*."

I laugh, and Sawyer watches me as he takes a sip of wine from his mug. Honestly, the idea of having a butler is laughable to me, I was never rich enough for that to be a reality. But a nagging thought arises. Sawyer is. Or, he was.

"Uh-oh," he says. "What's that look?"

I don't want to bring the mood down, but when else am I going to get the chance to really talk to Sawyer like this? If we're going to "work through" our past, we have to actually work through it.

"I want to ask about your dad." He watches me steadily, and I continue. "How come I didn't know you guys had a falling out? Seems like big news."

He takes in a deep breath. "It would be," he agrees, and for a second, I think that's all I'll get, that he's back to his riddles. But he goes on. "Dear old Dad would never let the town in on his dirty secrets. As far as they know, me going into the Navy was his idea."

With a hollow laugh, I shake my head. "Right." It's so

obvious I can't believe I had to ask. And that's why Sawyer is still the Prince of Blue Ridge. No one knows otherwise.

"My turn to ask a question," he says.

I snap my gaze to him. "O-*kay* . . ."

Voice low, he asks, "How upset were you when Dev showed up with a date that night?"

Groaning, I slap my hands over my face. Of *course* he'd bring that up. But when I peek at him through my fingers, his eyes are flighty like . . . like he's *nervous*.

Grudgingly, I admit, "I was mortified I drunkenly invited myself on his date." A flush rises on my cheeks even now. "And I was furious you witnessed it, and even more furious because I should've known better."

He looks away before asking, "But you weren't, like, upset you weren't on a date with Dev?"

I shake my head. "I kind of hoped I'd have feelings for him after years apart, he's so great, but we're as platonic as they come." I look over. "Stop smiling!"

"Am I smiling?"

"Yes! You're gloating." I shove his shoulder, and he deftly captures my wrist, towing me closer.

"I'm not gloating." His fire-lit face is an inch away. "I'm just . . . happy. Dev's a nice, good looking guy."

My eyes widen. "You're jealous!"

Before, I would have assumed Sawyer asking about that night was a way to embarrass me. But he just wants to know whether I have a thing for Dev. Laughter bubbles out of me before I can stop it.

He heaves a sigh and shifts us so I'm nestled between his legs, back against his front, arms wrapped tightly around me, pinning me to him. A zing of arousal pulses through me. And then I feel his erection against my lower back, and the zing turns into a throbbing ache. I let out a trembling breath, trying to wrest control over my base desires.

"I was always jealous of Dev," he rasps against my ear. "He had everything I wanted."

"What?" I let out a shaky laugh.

Dev, who grew up blocks from me in a house almost as rundown as mine, sharing a bedroom with two siblings, had everything *Sawyer* wanted? Impossible.

"He got your secrets and your smiles." He says it quietly, a secret of his own.

Affection for the little boy Sawyer used to be, with untold desires and crushing pressure, seeps into me.

I lean my head back and brush my lips against his throat, smiling when I feel him shudder behind me. "Because you were 'obsessed' with me?" I tease, still unable to fully believe it.

"Mm-hm." He nuzzles into my neck.

Something between a moan and a gasp escapes. "I want to touch you." I try to tug my arms free, but he holds fast.

"Nuh-uh," he hums into the nape of my neck even as his cock presses hard against me, a reminder he's as affected by this as I am.

"Why?" I whine.

"If I let you go, and you touch me, I won't be able to hold back."

"That's f-*ine*." The word turns into a whimper as he sucks on my shoulder.

Goosebumps chase his hot breath on my skin. "It's not fine. I shouldn't even be holding you like this."

My stomach does a somersault. If everything Sawyer's told me is true, then whatever happens between us means a lot to him. It means a lot to me, too. As turned on as I am right now, the minuscule part of my brain that still holds rational thought says to listen to him.

Rewinding the conversation, I try to pick up where we left off. "When did your so-called obsession start?"

He waits until I look back at him. "Brie, I'm telling you it started the moment I laid eyes on you. First day of kindergarten, and it only got worse. Why do you think I always showed up to the first day of class after you, only to sit next to you? Or picked you to be on my team at gym? Or had all the same electives in high school?"

The back of my nose starts to sting and I'm forced to blink back unshed tears as I take in his earnest face. I always imagined he did those things to torment me. It turned into that for his own self-preservation, but it wasn't why he did it. He just wanted to be close to me.

The sound of the chicken sizzling in the pan has us both looking into the fire. Sawyer kneels to adjust it and add another log. When he sits back down behind me, my pulse races. I can feel the warmth emanating off him. Smell his clean scent. The air is thick between us, the room is silent around us, and in this moment, we're the only two people on the planet.

I clear my throat in the most unnatural way possible. "It's lucky you're prepared to feed an extra person."

His fingers are in my hair, massaging my scalp in a way that makes me want to purr. My hands trace up and down his calves on either side of me. I force them to stay below his knee despite the insistent press of his hardness beckoning me.

"Oh, that was by design," he says. "I was cruising around town, looking for scantily-clad, injured women to wait out the blizzard with."

"How many did you come across before me?"

"At least four."

I snort. "I'm flattered."

He leans over and kisses my temple. It happens so fast. My insides turn to mush and I can't stop the smile from spreading.

"Sawyer?"

I might be imagining the way his breathing kicks up when I say his name, but I get a little burst of satisfaction from it anyway.

"Hm?"

Without thinking too hard about it, I turn in his arms and straddle his lap. He takes in a sharp breath when I lower myself onto him.

"Did you really come in your pants over there?" With a tilt of my head, I indicate where he pinned me against the wall when the tree fell over.

He nods. "And over there." He jerks his head at the couch. "You tasted too good."

Need pulses between my legs. "It's not fair," I whisper. "I haven't even seen you yet."

His hands grip my waist. "You've got to stop rocking like that or I'll come. Again."

"Good. I want it in my mouth this time."

Lusty Brie is loose, admitting to things I've never wanted before, but I think he likes her based on the intensity in his eyes, the way he holds his breath, his bruising fingers tight on my waist, keeping a precise distance between my crotch and his.

I press my mouth against his ear and breathe, "Wanna try it? I'm aching for you."

When I pull back, his eyes are shut tight. He pulls in deep, deliberate breaths.

Voice gravelly, he says, "No."

A smile splits my face despite my body screaming for him. Hours ago, his response would have been a mortifying rejection. It *was* the mortifying rejection that had me running to hide in the bathroom. Now? It multiplies the butterflies in my belly. He wants to make it special between us, and he's hanging on by a thread.

I take pity on him and slip off his lap.

"Soon," he says.

When the chicken is cooked, it's one of the better things I've eaten, the succulent juice coating the vegetables in a rich broth warms me from the inside. But it's the easy conversation and stolen glances that has my cheeks hurting. If this were a date, I wouldn't want it to end. I'm suddenly very grateful for the blizzard.

After we've cleared the meal, I go to the bathroom to get ready for bed. The water is ice-cold as I brush my teeth, the tile frigid beneath my feet.

When I come out, Sawyer swaps places with me and I run to where he's piled blankets and pillows near the hearth. After a few minutes, he stands over me.

He rubs the back of his neck. "Is this okay?"

"Oh my gosh, yes, it's freezing over by the bed." Even with a mountain of blankets, it wouldn't be as warm as here by the fire.

"Yeah, plywood doesn't provide much insulation. But I mean . . ." he makes a back and forth gesture

Oh. *Oh.* He's asking if I'm comfortable sharing a blanket with him, now that we're in this vague "going slow" territory. It's a little ludicrous, considering everything else we've done and the situation we're in, but the sweetness of it has my stomach bottoming out.

I snap the blanket back for him. He grins as he clicks off the light and gets in next to me.

He exaggerates a shiver and pulls me into his body. "Warm me up, it's cold out there." He says his words directly into my neck, tickling me and forcing giggles out, which only encourages him to do it again. "What?" His words are muffled and drowned out by my laughter as his chin digs into the sensitive spot in my shoulder. "It's bedtime, calm down."

I wrest my arm free and tug his hair until his satisfied grin is revealed.

"Mean," I say.

His expression changes. In the light of the fire, his eyes grow darker.

"Can I kiss you goodnight?"

There it is again. That heady feeling that has my skin buzzing with anticipation.

"Yes," I breathe.

He tightens his arms around me, hands flattening against my back. His hard body is wrapped around my softer one, keeping me safe. His eyes, dark like the ocean at night, are attentive on my face as he slowly rolls us until I'm on my back looking up at him. He smells so good, like masculine soap and toothpaste.

"You're so pretty, Brie."

My stomach clenches tight. His nose rubs against mine. Our mouths are an inch away, breathing the same air.

"So fucking pretty." As he says the words, his lips feather over mine, and I bow under him until our mouths touch.

Somehow, this light kiss is more intense than any of the others. Those were spur-of-the-moment now-or-never moments. This is slow and thoughtful and deliberate, like he's trying to memorize me. When he lifts his head, I cup his jaw and bring him back to me. His lips meet mine softly with sweet, suctioning kisses. His tongue teases the seam of my lips, and I'm all too eager to let him in. We taste each other with unhurried strokes. If this is what he meant by going slow, I'm all in.

Eventually, we roll onto our sides. Our bodies are as close as they can be, his erection a hard rod against my stomach. It sends scorching desire through me. I caress his face, rough with fresh stubble as his hands rub circles over my back. And we kiss languorously until we fall asleep in each other's arms.

It isn't long before I wake up with pins and needles shooting through both arms, still posed at awkward angles. I run to the bathroom to pee, and by the time I get back, I'm a popsicle. A half-asleep Sawyer opens his body to me as I return, and he folds me in his warmth, planting lazy kisses on me as he drifts off again.

The last thought I have is: *This is what it feels like to be home.*

IT'S FRIDAY, and I wake up in exactly the same position as yesterday, to Brie's scent in my nose and her ass in my crotch. My arm is wrapped tightly around her, hand cupping one perfect breast. And, because I have a near-medical condition at this point, my cock is throbbing, ready to bust at the slightest touch. But this time, I stay right here, basking in the feeling.

I woke up on the verge of coming multiple times last night, replaying Brie's words in my dreams.

I want it in my mouth this time . . . I'm aching for you.

Just the memory has my cock twitching.

I roll onto my back and scrub my free hand down my face before reaching for my phone, looking for a distraction. Another snow day has been announced. Relief and anxiety braid through me. There's nothing I want more than to spend more uninterrupted time with Brie. But being stuck here together isn't reality. Reality is going slow, giving her space, letting her come to me when she's ready. Here, we're forced together and drowning in sexual tension.

I'm going to have a hell of a time keeping my hands off

her. Last night was hard enough—in every sense. Between the dim fire-lit cabin, Brie's lust-filled eyes, and her cock-throbbing words, I was only barely able to maintain my control.

I push my phone away and turn my body into her, spooning her again. The fire has died down from when I last added logs to it a couple hours ago. Sunlight moves slowly across the living room floor. Her breathing deepens and she shifts, rubbing herself against me. I flatten my hand over her stomach and nuzzle her hair, breathing in her scent. When she arches her back in a stretch, I can't help kissing along her neck, relishing in the throaty sounds she makes.

She rolls onto her back, smiling sleepily, and my chest inflates. This is how I want to wake up every day.

"Good morning."

"Hi," she yawns.

"What do you want to do today?"

She curls into me. "I want to stay here all day. With you."

My fucking heart. This woman wants to stay here all day. *With me.*

"Yeah? And do what?" I ask, knowing full well inciting things further is a bad idea, but unable to help myself. I roll onto her, covering her body with mine as I kiss her deeply. She sucks my tongue into her mouth and I rock into her.

"This," she says, tilting her hips to meet mine. "I want my turn with you."

Groaning, I say, "We're supposed to go slow."

"I can go slow," she say innocently. "It's part of my plan. Tease you with slow licks."

I drop my forehead onto hers, letting out a frustrated laugh. "I never guessed you were so evil."

She grinds into me from below. I can feel the heat of her

through the boxers she wears, and it takes every ounce of will power not to reach down, feel her wet heat and see how fast I can make her come.

It occurs to me, we've already done that. Going slow doesn't have to mean starting over.

My hand drops down to her bare thigh, and I trail my fingertips up and down her warm skin. Goosebumps chase my touch all the way to the bottom of her shorts.

Her own hand winds its way between our bodies, but as it inches its way to my dick, I stop it in its tracks even as my hips angle to meet it.

"What, you can touch me but I can't touch you?" she says.

"Exactly."

That grin reappears. "No way." She stills my hand on her thigh. "You're not allowed to touch me if I can't touch you."

I heave a sigh. Looks like we're at a stalemate. Because there's no way I'm fucking this up.

"Let's make breakfast," I say, needing a diversion for us both.

"On the fire again?" she asks, like it's the most exciting thing.

"Sure."

And then we make out for another twenty minutes—hands above the waist but not without some heavy rocking—before getting ourselves out of our warm cocoon.

She hops to the bathroom like she's dodging hot coals and shrieks at the water temperature when she splashes water on her face. Still in my clothes she slept in, hair messy from sleep, she looks so right. She belongs here in this cabin with me.

The thought stays with me as I get ingredients for

breakfast and stoke the fire. As Brie settles onto the blanket by the roaring fire, she rolls up her sleeves and unbuttons the top buttons of her shirt. I catch glimpses of soft skin, the swell of the top of her breast. My eyes drop to her bare legs, the boxers loose enough to slide both hands into from the bottom.

I've got to find something for us to do before I go caveman on her.

After breakfast, I practically shoved Brie into my snow bib and jacket, hoping to get away from temptation before I did something I shouldn't. I figured if I had any chance with her, then we need to spend time together in the present without the past looming over us like a dark cloud. So I suggested we build a snowman.

We step back and look at our creation. It's huge, nearly as tall as me with buttons for eyes and a smile.

"It looks good," I say.

"It?"

"Him? Her? They?"

She makes a face. "Not sure. We need to give it something else."

"Want me to go get a scarf or hat?"

"No, no," she says, casting around for something on the streaks of barren ground the snow for the spheres came from. Her face lights up when she finds what she's looking for and sticks something into the space between the middle and bottom sections. I come around to see a twig, barely the length of my pinky finger sticking out, with a perfectly round end. She adds two acorns beneath it.

Genitals for our snowman.

"There," she says, looking altogether too pleased with herself. "Perfect."

I rub my jaw. "What a stud. That's gotta be at least, what, eight inches?"

A laugh explodes out of her as she squints at the wooden stub. "You might need to get your eyes checked."

"*Ten?!*"

Another laugh, and I could live on the sound alone. Her cheeks and the tip of her nose are pink from the cold, brown hair framing her face beneath the beanie. My jeans are soaked at the knee from kneeling, and my shirt is wet from hefting sections onto the snowman. Brie's feet are probably wet and freezing.

"You ready to go inside?"

"Yes, please."

I help her shuck her gear before stripping out of my clothes. As I head to my dresser in my boxer briefs, her muffled voice comes from inside the blankets by the hearth.

"What?" I ask.

More urgent muffling.

My brows knit and I walk over without putting my pants on. Only her eyes peek out from beneath the covers.

I tug the blanket down to her chin. "What was that?"

"The fire's almost out." She lolls her head back dramatically. "Is this what it feels like to get hypothermia?"

My mouth quirks. "Poor baby," I tease.

It takes enormous effort not to climb in next to her and use my body heat to warm her. Instead, I reach for the logs I brought inside earlier.

"It'd be easier if you moved," I tell her.

She's lying so close to the hearth, I have no choice but to straddle her blanket-swathed body. I drop to my knees to blow on the red embers, keeping my focus firmly on stoking the fire as Brie ruffles around between my legs. My entire body jerks when I feel Brie's fingernails on my bare thighs. The logs catch, flaming to life.

I look down and hold my breath. The blanket's been tossed off Brie's upper half. The buttons of the flannel shirt she wears are undone, exposing the inner globes of her breasts to me. Her fingers trace the bottom of my boxer briefs, along my inner thighs. My cock swells.

"Brie." My voice is so hoarse, I hardly recognize it. "What're you doing?"

She sits up, and the sides of the shirt open, exposing more of her. I never thought of myself as a weak man, but as I watch my hand drift up to her collarbone and trail down her chest between her breasts, I know I'm feeble and defenseless when it comes to this woman. This woman who's protective of children, and caring of new friends. Who's stubborn and independent. Who always says what she means, and means what she says.

"Exactly what I want," she says.

Her fingers feather over my length from root to tip through the thin fabric of my underwear. My legs nearly give out. I trail my thumb over the pulse point on her throat, relishing in how fast her heart beats in this moment.

This is too soon. I don't want to mess this up with her.

"You do that again, and any chance of going slow flies out the window." I won't be able to hold myself back. I've barely got a grip on myself as it is.

She pulls back and shrugs the shirt off her shoulders. Her breasts, perky little nipples beaded into perfect peaks, are on full display. I'm so focused on how beautiful she is, the desire on her face, that her tugging on the waistband of my underwear barely registers until my cock springs free, heavy and hard, tip wet with precum.

"Brie." It's a stern warning.

But then, eyes holding mine, she leans forward and places one prim kiss on my slit before leaning back on her hands. Every muscle in my body pulls taut. She has a look of challenge on her face as she licks her lips, and I don't know how I don't come right here and now.

"Are you sure about this?" I ask, voice shaking with the effort it takes to maintain my control.

Her face sobers. "Yes. Everything I said last night is true, I'm not suddenly past our history. That's going to take time. But this?" She leans forward, and reaches her hand out slowly, eyes on mine as if she's asking for permission. When I nod infinitesimally, she drops her gaze and trails a finger lightly over me, root to glistening tip. "I'm ready for it now."

The last thread of my control snaps. "Lie down."

She does what I ask. I shove my boxer briefs off and yank the blanket off her the rest of the way. Dropping to the floor, I nudge her legs open with my shoulders and bury my face between her legs, breathing her in.

"I love your smell," I say against her.

She squirms, ticklish, and I nip her over her shorts in warning before I rise and palm her mound. *Fuck*, she's wet. She grinds into my hand.

"You soaked another pair of my boxers. When did that happen?"

"God, I've been horny since I woke up." Her hand scratches lightly at my scalp, sending a shiver down my spine.

"I know the feeling."

I replace my hand with my bare cock, only the thin fabric of the boxers separating me from where she's warm and wet and silky. My mouth covers hers, and she eagerly accepts my tongue. She tastes so good. I thrust shallow pulses against her clit. I swallow her sounds, hungry for every one.

"Sawyer," she begs.

A shudder rolls through me. I lean on my elbow and look down into her eyes, so big and trusting and needy. *For me.* I've wanted her to look at me like this my entire life.

"Fuck me," she says, and my brain short-circuits. "I need —I need you inside me. Just, please."

"Condom," I manage in a strangled voice and with herculean effort, I push myself off her and head toward the bathroom.

"I'm clean, by the way," I say a moment later. She got rid of the boxers. I fold my body over hers and toss the strip of condoms next to the pillow as I kiss the corner of her mouth.

Without warning, she rolls us over until she's on top, straddling me.

My muscles are tight, my dick is as hard as it's ever been, and I have the most gorgeous woman on the planet on top of me. She moves, and my cock flexes against her. Her eyes darken, and her cheekbones rise on an evil, fiendish smile.

She pins my hands by my head and draws my earlobe into her hot mouth. "I'll be right back."

I groan. Brie's touches, her kisses, her licks are all light and teasing as she moves down my body. It's exquisite torture.

Then her warm tongue is wet on my tip, laving at it like a melting ice cream cone. My stomach clenches.

Brie. Her tongue. My cock.

She looks up. "It's been a while since I've done this." She's almost apologetic.

"It's already the best," I breathe.

"Tell me what you want." She brushes her knuckles up and down the underside of my shaft.

"Oh." It's basically a moan. "Everything. Anything."

Her expression is almost sarcastic, and I would laugh if she doesn't right at that moment open her mouth and suck on my crown.

"That's good," I wheeze.

She rewards me by doing it again. Wet, sloppy, noisy sucks, then her tongue lapping at the sensitive spot at the bottom of my head.

"Yeah," I choke.

Her hands stroke my inner thighs, cup my balls, squeeze my ass. She smiles around my cock like she's having the time of her life, and *holy hell*, it's good.

"Amazing."

She looks at me, eyes boring into my skull, and in one, slow pull, swallows my entire cock. When I hit her throat, she swallows, taking more of me in until her lips circle the root, all while her tongue continues to stroke me.

I'm unable to form words.

She gags, and I try to pull back, but she swats my hands away and bobs her head up and down. Saliva runs down my cock, and her hand comes up to massage it into my balls as her swollen mouth works me higher.

This is better than all my fantasies. Louder, sloppier, wetter. Her enthusiasm is palpable. It's the hottest, dirtiest thing I've ever experienced as her eyes lock on mine.

Without notice, my balls draw tight. I dive my hands into her hair, tugging her off me.

"What's wrong?" She wipes her mouth with the back of her hand

"Too good," I rasp. "Too hot. Almost came."

She looks down at my cock, still throbbing, licks her lips, then back up at me. "I don't want to stop, I'm having too much fun."

My heart squeezes. I struggle for breath. *Everything*. Her words mean everything to me.

"You're killing me."

She lowers her head back down and sucks at my tip. The pleasure verges on pain. This is *so* not how I intended for this to go. I was going to turn *her* into the begging puddle of need.

"If you come in my mouth" —*lick*— "will you still be able to fuck me after?"

I fist my hand in her hair to pull her up, and do a crunch until our faces are an inch apart. "Where did that dirty mouth come from, Brie?" I kiss her, licking the inside of her mouth. Normally, I'm a one-and-done kind of guy. But lately, I've gone multiple rounds just to the thought of Brie. When we break apart, her lips are swollen and wet. "Yeah. I'll be able to fuck you how you need."

She shoves me back.

"It'll be fast," I warn.

"Not too fast." She grins. "I want to enjoy myself."

She licks me, nice and wet, swallowing me.

"So good," I grunt. "Perfect."

She releases me, licks up the shaft, then swallows me again.

"Yes," I hiss.

Release. Lick. Swallow.

"Brie."

She repeats as I ooze precum, moaning, muscles seizing.

When I can take no more, I grit, "Almost there. K-keep me inside."

She obeys with a hum.

"*Yesss.*"

With confidence, she drives her face up and down now. I watch her move her hand to between her legs and touch herself, having a good time, moaning on my cock and sending vibrations through me. *She really is enjoying herself.* The base of my spine tingles. My balls draw up. Pressure builds.

"Brie," I heave.

Her eyes snap up. I can read every emotion in them. Enjoyment, eagerness, need. I want to give it to her, show her what she does to me. The pressure erupts furiously.

"*Coming.*"

I explode in her hot mouth, feeling her swallow every drop, watching her do so with gusto like it's her favorite meal, rubbing herself and getting off to my taste. It's downright filthy in the best way possible.

She slows as I come down. When I can take no more, I reach for her and pull her up to me. My heart races, breaths coming short. I rub her back, squeeze her ass, kiss her temple.

"Nothing," I finally say, "nothing has ever come close to that."

Turning her head, she rests her chin on my chest. "I agree."

She squirms over me, and despite having the most intense, satisfying sexual experience of my life, my craving for Brie rises. As does my need to make her feel so good she can never leave.

"You didn't come while you were down there, did you?" I ask.

She faux-pouts. "No."

I roll us over. "Don't worry, honey. I'll remedy that."

SINCE RETURNING TO BLUE RIDGE, I've been fighting my attraction to Sawyer. But in the less-than-twenty-four hours since he confessed his feelings to me, my own feelings for him have risen exponentially. I can finally look at the way he's behaved these last couple months as genuine, not an act. He's competent and caring, he's quick on his feet, he's *funny*. He's a good guy.

My attraction to him now is almost unbearable. I'm absolutely quivering with need, and I am *so* not this girl. I've always *liked* sex, but I've never *needed* sex. Going down on a man was something I did as a courtesy, not because I craved him. Not because I needed to make him squirm like I needed my next breath.

I angle my body to press myself against Sawyer's thigh, seeking more friction.

"You wanna hear a secret?" His deep voice shoots tremors through me as he massages my ass. "In my entire life, I've never come harder than I just did in your mouth." He takes my bottom lip between his teeth, and I whimper.

"I want to make you feel that good." His hand comes

around from behind. I might be embarrassed by how wet I am, but when his fingers brush over me, his eyes glaze over, and he whispers, "So hot."

Against my stomach, his cock is already hard again, which I didn't realize was possible so soon. His mouth trails down my neck, and he sinks his teeth into me, making me draw in a breath. He pushes me to lie back and runs teasing fingers over my body.

"I have some questions." He looks at me like I have all the answers.

"Oh?"

"Do you ever come from penetration alone?"

I shake my head. "Just my clit."

"Penetration feels good, though?"

"I don't know, *try it*," I huff.

His chuckle is rough as he drops his hand between my legs and inserts two fingers into my slick heat. I moan and buck into him.

He tears open a condom with his teeth and sheaths himself with one hand.

"Last question," he says into my neck as he removes his fingers and positions his body between my legs, teasing me with the head of his dick. "Have you ever been this worked up before?"

"Nev-*er*—" my answer ends on a gasp as he slides into me.

I'm so wet, all I feel is the immediate, satisfying relief of being full.

"*Fuck*." His breath is hot on my shoulder, and we lie there for a few moments as we get used to each other. He rocks his hips into me, shallow thrusts at first.

"You feel so good," I moan.

"Good doesn't cover it, Brie." His voice is strained and

he leans on his forearms, hands cradling the back of my head as he looks me in the eye. "Talk to me. What's your favorite position? I want to make this good for you." With the way his neck muscles protrude, it's clear he's holding back, trying to keep himself in check.

I meet him thrust for thrust. "It's good."

With effort, he nods, wresting control to maintain his steady rocking. "What gets you off? I want to know." Something like a whimper exits my mouth at *I want to know*, and he raises an eyebrow. "Is *this* it? You like me asking?"

I don't know why I'm embarrassed to admit what I like, maybe because I've never had sex like this before. I'm not just physically naked, but the way Sawyer watches me has me exposed in other ways too. He's asking things no one's ever bothered to ask before, daring me to be vulnerable. I shut my eyes, protecting myself from his probing gaze. Then his mouth is on mine, giving me sweet kisses all the way to my ear.

"This gets me off, too." He whispers. "Learning what turns you on. Why do you think I'm barely moving? I'm already close again. When I finally let go, I'm going to come so hard inside you."

That pulls a moan from me. I scrape my fingernails down his sides, and he shudders.

"You like that? Knowing you turn me on so much I can barely last?"

"Yeah," I breathe.

"It's never been like this with anyone else. I've never wanted to do this with anyone. Brie, I want to be in your head, I want to know every one of your dirty thoughts."

Something's happening in the spot where we're joined. A buildup I've never experienced before. It's deeper inside me.

"No one's ever made me lose control like you do," he goes on.

Is he for real? I turn my head to look at him. His face is coated in a sheen of sweat, and his hair falls over his forehead. Every visible muscle is pulled taut, expression vulnerable as he continues to expose new pieces of himself to me. It's the most erotic thing I've ever seen, this way that he wants me. I whimper as I clench tight around him, digging my fingers into his sculpted ass.

He mutters a swear, arms shaking. "You see what you do to me?"

"*Sawyer.*" I don't understand what's happening in my body. I don't get how I can be thirty-two years old, with what I thought was a respectable sexual history, and suddenly feel virginal again, facing all these new sensations, body and mind.

"Fuck, I love my name on your tongue." He pulls out almost all the way before slowly bringing himself home again. "Oooh fuck." His eyes clamp shut for a second, then open just as quickly like he can't bear to miss a thing. "You're so wet. Do you hear it? Feel it between us?"

I do, and he sounds reverent. *He really likes it.* I decide right now to lean into whatever's happening here. If he's brave, I can be brave. My fingers rake into his hair, and I pull his mouth to me, relishing the groan in the back of his throat that has my stomach feeling like it's at the top of a rollercoaster, ready to drop.

"Ask me again," I say.

His eyes, dark with lust, gleam. "What gets you off, Brie?"

"You. This."

The grin he gives me has my belly clenching, ready to

free-fall. "That's sweet. What else." His hips shift, angling himself up as he continues his shallow thrusting.

"I like—" It's hard to talk now, the heat in my core is coiled so tight. "I like when you talk—keeps me in the moment, out of my head. And I—I like knowing what I do to you."

With a heave, he presses himself up, kneeling. It changes the angle, hitting a pressure point that has my mouth open on a silent gasp. Mouth quirking, he grips my hips tight careful of my cut, but he still isn't fucking me. It's more of a grind. I'm a pot set over a low flame. Eventually, I could boil over, but no sooner than Sawyer intends.

"You like knowing what you do to me? I'll tell you what you do to me." He hoists my legs up over the crooks of his elbows, and this angle is even better. "You make me hard again seconds after giving me the best blowjob I've ever had."

His words hook into my core, adding to the mounting pressure.

"You drive me so crazy, Brie." He thrusts into me harder.

"Oh *god*." My walls spasm around him, begging for more.

He winces, and shifts me to one arm so he can wrap his hand around the base of his cock, squeezing. And even though he's stopped thrusting for a few seconds, that's hot too, knowing he needs a break, knowing I did this to him. He gives me a sheepish smile then grips my hips with both hands again. This time he doesn't hold back, fucking me in earnest with deep, punishing drives.

"I'm going . . . to try my hardest . . . to make you come. Just like this." His words are jagged, like broken glass as his bruising fingers keep me in place. "If it doesn't . . . happen . . . that's okay. I love to eat you."

His words vibrate through me. Bafflingly, permission to *not* come is what has my hands searching for purchase. I grasp the edge of the hearth as my other hand grips the blanket. Pressure builds, internal and deep like I've never felt. But I don't know how to do this. I've never come without clitoral stimulation.

It dawns on me this has been his plan the whole time. His singular goal as he winds me tighter and tighter, to give me something he knows I've never experienced.

He's spoiling me for anyone else.

I will never recover from this.

The need to come corkscrews through me. His eyes flash like he knows. He doubles his efforts.

"Let go for me," he says in a strangled voice.

That coil snaps in half. The rollercoaster finally drops from the apex and I'm free-falling as an orgasm from somewhere deep inside floods through my writhing body. I make loud, helpless sounds as he sees me through my climax, pumping into me.

A heavy, animalistic grunt vibrates through him, and then I *feel* the moment he spills. It's so erotic, so *hot*, another tremor shoots through me, eliciting another grunt from him. My orgasm lasts a lifetime as I clench and unclench around him, gently continuing to grind against him from below to extend the sensations.

Finally, after eons have passed in which entire worlds have blinked in and out of existence in the universe, he flattens himself over me, his softening cock still inside. We're both breathing hard, unable to speak for a long time.

Sawyer lifts up to kiss my forehead. "What the hell was that?"

Sleepy and sated, I smile against his chest. "Literally the best sex anyone has ever had." Also, the most honest. I've never let go the way I did today with Sawyer. I don't just mean sex, either. I've never been unrestrained, completely open like this before, showing all of me to someone. No one's ever before made me feel like I could.

His chest rumbles beneath me. "Pretty sure the earth moved."

Gently, he removes himself out of me and heads to the bathroom. I want to protest, but I'm still too fucking satisfied to muster the energy. After a moment he's back. Then, I feel it. He's delicately cleaning me with a warm, wet cloth.

When he's satisfied, he adds logs to the fire, then lies down beneath the blanket, curling his body around mine, making me feel safe and cared for.

CHAPTER 36

BRIE

SAWYER HASN'T STOPPED SMILING, and he doesn't seem to know how to keep his hands to himself. Not that I've asked. There hasn't been one moment this entire weekend when he's stopped touching me, biting me, crudely *inhaling* me.

After we showered and made some food, he set blankets up against the couch to read together in front of the fire. It was all so innocent and sweet. But then he put on his thick-rimmed reading glasses, and I felt that familiar tug of desire. My gaze kept darting back to the sexy man in glasses next to me, so I angled myself away and lay my head onto his shoulder in an effort to focus on my book.

It became our downfall. I felt as much as heard him take in a deep breath, then watched as his pants tented. It was like espresso directly into my libido. The next second, we were making out like our lives depended on it, and a minute after that he was hooking my leg over his shoulder, yanking my shorts to the side, and eating me out like the weight of the world rested on me coming against his mouth.

Saturday, as I hulled strawberries for a snack in the

kitchen, dipping one in his homemade whipped cream and popping it in my mouth every so often, he looped his arms around me from behind and began nibbling my neck. Before long, he was inside me, thrusting from behind. I dipped my finger in the cream, fed it to him, then sucked his tongue into my mouth, the taste of strawberries and cream mingling between us as he pulled two orgasms from me with expert efficiency.

The rest of Saturday and all of yesterday continued on like that, with us unable to keep our hands off each other. And last night, the sky was clear, so he brought out the only outdoor chair he owns and set it in the clearing of his yard. We sat watching the stars, wrapped in a blanket, my legs strewn over his lap, utterly content as our breaths fogged in front of us. As stars winked, comets soared, and the moon arced closer to the horizon, he caressed my face, giving me deep, gentle kisses until he carried me inside and lay me down.

Now, we bump along the gravel drive and, just before he turns onto the mountain road, he stops and lets go of my hand to engage the brake.

I angle my body toward him.

Before I can ask a question, his hands cradle my jaw, lips on mine as his tongue coaxes my mouth open. I make a small sound in the back of my throat. One of his hands moves to my still-damp hair, tugging to angle my face upward. Heat flutters through me as if this is the first time we've kissed, as if we didn't just spend days holed up in a sex-fueled bubble where nothing else mattered.

After a minute, our lips separate, and he leans his forehead against mine. We watch each other, panting.

"I like you," he says. "So much."

I take both his hands in both of mine, kissing each of his

knuckles, then lean over the center console to kiss his smooth jaw, the corner of his mouth, his eyebrow. Because telling him "I like you too" doesn't feel like enough, I kiss him everywhere I think I might have neglected over the weekend, infusing all the feelings I'm not ready to speak yet into each gesture.

As he drives us over the ridge, the taste of him still on my lips, I suck in a sharp breath at the scene below.

"Wow." It's all I have the capacity to say.

Sawyer rests his large hand on my thigh. "Blue Ridge has its faults, but aesthetics isn't one of them."

The town is blanketed in white, which happened a few times in my youth, but this is the first time I've seen it from this angle. We're closer than at his cabin, details starker. It's so different. In the fourteen years I've been away from Blue Ridge, my memory of it was small and dingy. Dirty, even. Now, the snowy little town looks idyllic: white, pristine, and peaceful.

It's breathtaking.

Sawyer reaches over and laces our fingers together. I smile over at him.

Maybe this could work.

But as the mountain road flattens out and makes its seamless transition into United Avenue, an anxious flutter forms in my stomach, like I've just swallowed a small hive full of bees.

We have officially reentered the real world.

The brick box that is the school comes into view, and Christopher crashes into my mind. The bees, panicking now, form a bottleneck at my throat trying to escape.

What have I done?

Christopher was just a colleague. Sawyer is the *principal* of this school and, in the eyes of the town, he's still the Prince of Blue Ridge. I'm a *substitute* for shit's sake, one no one asked for. It would take zero paperwork to get rid of me if this thing with Sawyer goes up in flames. Because isn't it bound to?

This thing is fragile and new, everything that happened between us was isolated from the rest of the world. How could it possibly stand up under the weight of scrutinizing eyes and whispered words? And when it crumples, the entire town will probably chase me out themselves, appalled I attempted to sully the good name of their prince.

And unlike Christopher, I actually like Sawyer. A lot. When I leave, it'll be with a broken heart.

When. Not if. Because Blue Ridge isn't home.

Completely unaware I've been sitting in Sawyer's car spiraling, my car door opens. His wide grin only churns my anxiety more as he dips his head to catch my eye. Guilt worms its way through me. Since my first day here, Sawyer hasn't asked why I left my old school in such a hurry even though he's had every right to.

I should tell him.

The embarrassment at my own naiveté at letting Christopher manipulate me and the ensuing meeting with the Everett Academy administration is like a lead weight in my stomach.

He'll understand. I can trust him.

Heart pounding, I get out of the car. He moves closer, resting his hand on my hip and kisses me deeply. It unfocuses my mind for a second, and I sigh into him. My back hits the truck and his hips are flush against mine as my hands curl around his neck.

The rusty creak of the external school door pierces the air. As if I haven't already experienced every emotion this morning in flashing technicolor, adrenaline rushes through my blood stream. My hands come up and with one forceful shove, Sawyer is off me, and we're both breathing hard enough that it's painfully audible.

"Professional," I huff. "I want to be professional."

His hand goes to the back of his neck and he nods, eyes dimming. "Whatever you want."

He thinks this is about him. My stomach churns.

There are two choices: I can keep on like this, tell him I want to be professional without giving him any context. Or, I can tell him about Christopher, every mortifying, humiliating detail.

An image of Sawyer in his cabin solidifies in my mind, red eyes blinking rapidly as he relived the ghosts of his past in an effort to be honest with me, apologized for actions provoked by pressure too complicated for a child to parse on his own.

I don't know what it took to do that. The thought of revealing my own deeply-buried traumas, even to Sawyer, is like injecting ice straight into my veins.

Telling him about Christopher is cake by comparison.

I swallow.

Be brave.

Stepping forward, I say, "Sawyer?"

His eyes search mine. "Yeah?"

I open my mouth when Tess's voice cuts in. "Hey, guys!"

Her grin is wide as her sparkling eyes travel from my face to Sawyer's.

Licking my lips, I open my mouth again, but this time Señora Martinez's tinny voice comes through the loud speaker by the alcove to the door. "Principal Strong, you're needed in the main office. Principal Strong, you're needed in the main office." Then, "Sawyer, you're three minutes late."

"We'll talk later?" Sawyer asks, concern painted over his face.

I inhale, and when I let it out, I put on my teacher-smile. "Yes. I will talk to you later."

Tess is already at the teachers' lounge when I arrive for lunch. The tornado that ensues after a long unplanned break made it impossible for us to have a conversation this morning, which is why I spent the last few hours spiraling about what, exactly, to tell her.

When she notices me at the door, she prances toward me.

"*What* did I witness this morning?" she asks. "Because I'm pretty sure it looked like you and Sawyer were . . . *touching*. Like, in a kissing sort of way."

"What?!" My voice is three octaves too high.

She shrugs. "Before you pushed him away."

I wish there was a shark tank somewhere in Blue Ridge that I could throw myself into, it would be less painful than this. This isn't how the rumors about me started at Everett Academy, but it's close enough.

But Tess wouldn't betray me like that, would she? As far as I can tell, no one's heard about me making out with Funny Bunny in my classroom.

Knowing this, and how Tess shared with me about her ex, I sense a connection with her I'm not used to. It's enough to consider telling her everything. About my history with Sawyer, his confession at his cabin, my worries that I'm repeating history.

I almost do it. I open my mouth, the words in my throat.

But I quickly swallow them down, the enormity of what happened at the cabin comes crashing down on me like an avalanche for the hundredth time today.

I, Brie Casey, social pariah and generally deplored citizen, slept with Sawyer Strong, beloved principal and town treasure. Sure, *he* may have paved his own path in the eyes of his dad, but the town doesn't know that. They all still adore him.

Tess watches me expectantly.

"Um," I blather as I walk to the microwave.

I pull out my lunch, leftovers Sawyer and I cooked together yesterday, and an errant thought hits me: *I wonder if he's eating his right now.* An ache forms in my chest, and it takes me a second to realize what it is. I miss him.

Focus, I tell myself. This is how I've operated all morning, and it's driving me insane. If I'm not anxious over him then I'm missing him.

Tess tips her head up and shows me her palms. "Look, if you don't want to tell me, that's really okay."

I'm simultaneously touched and guilt-ridden. Tess understands better than most my desire to keep parts of myself under lock and key.

"But," she goes on, "I'm not dumb. It seems like you and Sawyer are a thing now even though you swore it'd never happen."

I press my lips together because, as much as I hate to admit it, this is different than when she caught us in the classroom. I still hated him then. Now, my chest inflates at how it felt just this morning to wake up with his body wrapped around mine and his lips on my hair.

She pulls me to the table. I automatically sit down.

"This is Blue Ridge," she says, not unkindly. "People are

going to know about it. Heck, people probably *already* know about it if you drove past a single soul on your way in together."

Once again, the magnitude of it all weighs down on me. I didn't see the thing with Christopher coming *at all*. I was naive and got caught out. The smart thing for me to do here is to cut things off with Sawyer completely. Say, *That was fun while it lasted,* and be done with it. But I can't do that. Just the thought of it has my heart writhing in discomfort, my gut twisting. I've never experienced with anyone else what I experienced with Sawyer these past few days, and I want more. More of it, more of him, more of us.

How do I do that *and* maintain some modicum of professionalism?

Even though I haven't said a word, Tess keeps talking as if she can read my mind. "I'm not trying to burst your bubble. I just want to reset your expectations if you think you can keep something secret in this town."

I drop my head to the table, already imagining the phone tree alight with news of Sawyer shacking up with the likes of me.

I have to tell him about Christopher. It's the only way he'll understand why I need to remain professional at school. Even if we can't hide it.

Tess prods the top of my head. "It's alright," she soothes. "Sawyer really is a good guy."

"Ms. Casey?"

I lift my head to find a fifth grader I recognize as one of the front office helpers.

Putting on a smile, I say, "Hi, Jorge."

"I have this for you." He hands me a folded note, then waves and leaves.

Holding my breath, I unfold the note. In Sawyer's sharp handwriting, there are four words.

My office. After pickup.

I look up, sure Tess can hear my heart's deafening thumps.

Her overly nonchalant face tells me she read the note.

And that's how I spend the next few hours spiraling. Again.

CHAPTER 37

SAWYER

I STOP my pacing to glance at the clock. Another ten minutes go by before I decide she isn't coming.

I trudge over to my desk and sit down, head bowed into my hands.

What did she mean by wanting to be professional? What are the parameters? These are the things I should've asked her this morning, ignoring the call to the front office that turned out to be a petty argument over parking spots between the music and gym teachers. Consequently, I spent a large portion of my day driving myself up the wall.

There's a swift rap on my door, and Brie's voice floats in. "Sawyer?"

I stand so fast I knock my knee on my desk drawer. "Yeah," I say in a strained voice, rubbing at the pain.

Brie comes in, pink cheeked and looking frazzled, and I don't know how I was able to stand not seeing her the whole day. Every instinct shouts at me to go to her, press her body against the door, and show her how much I missed her, but I force my feet to stay put.

"Henry Kim's grandma wasn't on the approved pickup list. It was a whole thing," she says, waving her hand.

Her eyes meet mine, and they change. I feel the moment she puts up an invisible forcefield around herself.

The important thing, I tell myself, *is that she's here.*

"We need to talk," I say at the same time she says, "I have something to say."

My stomach roils, but I force myself to wait for her to speak.

She swallows as she looks at the ground. "I want to tell you why I came here mid-year."

My jaw drops. That's . . . not what I expected. A lightness takes over me. She wants to tell me something I suspect she hasn't told anyone. I've been waiting for her to open up to me. I laid myself bare, told her every shameful detail of my past. And it was all worth it because now she's going to open up too, let me in.

I lean forward, gesturing to the chairs across from my desk. "I want to hear it."

She glances at me before dropping her gaze to her hands. "I was at Everett Academy for a few years. Even though it was stuffy, full of traditions and stuck in their ways, I liked it there. I think they liked me. It was a private school, so the pay was great, I always had materials for the classroom, there were more school holidays than usual. I even taught at the summer camps."

I nod. Most of this isn't news to me, Everett Academy is one of the best private schools in the country, right alongside Groton and Exeter.

Her lips press together. "There was this teacher. He

was about ten years older than me, and he'd been there from the start of his career, almost twenty years. He was respected and had Everett's version of tenure. Christopher."

Christopher. Already, I hate him. My heart clenches at the turn this is taking, but I stay utterly silent, not daring to move a muscle.

Brie tells me how it started innocuously. They went out barely more than a month when she decided she didn't really like him.

"What I didn't know," she continues, "is he wasn't actually getting divorced."

My gut corkscrews.

Her voice wavers. "He was in the process of moving back in with his wife the whole time we dated." She laughs humorlessly. "They were trying to reconcile. It finally made sense why he kept hearing of these great new restaurants that just happened to be across the city."

How could anyone want to hide Brie? This cheating piece of shit Christopher, that's who.

"Well," she goes on. "I didn't know this, I always stayed out of the politics of the school, but his wife turned out to be this really powerful board member. And she was *not* nice."

Her eyes grow shiny as she tells me about the ugly aftermath of him twisting the truth to his wife. The rumors that spread about not just Brie and the scumbag, but falsities about her and other teachers, dads of students. Her persecution, thinly veiled as a meeting.

She avoids eye contact as if she's ashamed. "I was told I could stay for the rest of the school year, but my contract wouldn't be renewed. I applied for jobs over winter break, but I figured the break would mellow everyone out, that I'd finish out the year at Everett. But things got way worse on the first day back." Her voice lowers to a whisper. "I was a pariah."

I'm grinding my molars now.

She finally meets my eyes. "After school that first day, I had a missed call offering me to sub the third grade class here in Blue Ridge. I didn't think twice, just put in my notice and started packing. It wasn't professional, but I had to get out of there."

I want to break something. Of course she had to leave for her own sanity. Nasty rumors? Whispers literally behind her back? An entire community utterly against her? It must have been deja vu, the exact same shit that happened to her when she last lived here. Except this time, Brie was completely alone.

She hugs her arms tight around herself, her words hanging in the air between us.

White hot fury thrums through my veins. I stand and pace in front of her.

I hate it.

I hate what she went through, I hate the weasel who caused her pain, and I absolutely hate she's making herself smaller because of it. My anger boils over again at *Christopher*. I even hate his name.

Brie wrings her hands again, eyes shifty, and I realize I haven't said a word since she started talking. I resist the urge to touch her and stuff my hands in my pockets.

"Brie." My voice is unintentionally dark and gruff. I stop pacing and brace myself on the arms of her chair. "I'll ruin him."

Her eyes cut to me and she laughs, a wet sound between relief and amusement. "While I'd pay any amount of money to see him 'ruined,' he's not worth your energy."

My fingers twitch, but I keep my mouth glued shut as I count to three in my head.

This isn't about how I feel.

"Okay," I say, tabling my rage for the moment. "What do you need?"

She nods, like she's gearing herself up to say something she rehearsed. "I need us to be professional at school. I don't want to give anyone a reason to accuse me of . . . anything."

I eye her for a moment before standing upright. If that's all, I'm happy to give it to her. But does this mean she thinks I might betray her like Christopher did? My chest tightens and I want to throw up. *I'd never.*

Then I remember how I acted when she first arrived. Unpredictable. She didn't know I was fighting my own feelings for her. It probably messed with her mind, made her wary. Not to mention our twisted history.

And that son of a bitch did such a number on Brie, I can't believe she ever gave me a chance. She might not have if it wasn't for the blizzard.

A cold fear chills me to my bones. *I could've lost her before this even started.*

I can't ruin this. I'll do anything to make her feel safe with me. *But how?* How do I have Brie feeling safe after everything she's been through?

"Okay," I say. "I know it might be hard to believe, given" —I let out a frustrated sigh at my younger self— "given who I used to be. But I'll never hurt you."

"I do believe that," she says quickly. And even though she says it without hesitation, I can't help feeling like she's holding herself back just a little. Even though she's fully justified in it, it still sends a pang of helplessness through me.

I fight the urge to pull her to me and hold her, kiss her

until she knows how much she means to me, that I would never, *could* never, hurt her.

But that would prove the exact opposite after everything she just revealed. She asked for one thing, so I keep myself planted firmly against my desk, maintaining the distance between us. All I want right now is to prove she can trust me.

"Good," I say hoarsely. "Because it's true. I will never hurt you."

The air shifts between us, and she sighs. "I believe you."

I quirk a smile, peering at her. "You could tell me right now how disgusting you find me, and I swear it'll never affect your job."

She exhales on a laugh, and something like mirth dances in her eyes. "Oh, I could never insult my boss."

"Please," I tease back, "I'll even reward you for it." For the first time all day, my muscles start to relax.

She lets out a loud mock-sigh of relief. "Good, because just the sight of you makes me want to throw up."

"Full marks on your performance review."

"Also," she continues, "the sound of your voice makes me gag."

"Let me find my checkbook," I say, "I need to write you a bonus."

"Don't get me started on how you smell," she says, holding her nose with exaggerated revulsion.

"Here," I hand her the nameplate on my desk, "take my job. I insist."

"And that cabin of yours," she says. "So *gauche*."

"That's too far. You're fired."

She rewards me with the best sound in the world, her laughter.

CHAPTER 38

BRIE

WE WEAVE through the crowd at the Persian New Year festival to find someplace to eat the food we just bought. Every inch of free space is occupied—benches, grass, the large steps surrounding the clocktower. It's the first time Sawyer and I have spent time together outside school since the blizzard.

At school we've been the paragon of professionalism, everything more or less the same, if friendlier. But here, our hands brush as we walk, his hand hovers over my back as we navigate past people, we lean into each other to be heard. I know I should feel nervous about people seeing us like this, but my happiness over spending time with him eclipses everything else.

"This is the best festival," he says. "A great one to start the year with. Excellent food, rich culture, beautiful flowers." Sawyer bends over to smell one of the billions of hyacinths that adorn the booths. The whole square is painted with them, every shade of pink and purple, yellow and white. "What's your favorite festival?"

"I really loved the fall festival in Indy," I say. "The

pumpkins and turning leaves, the smell of spices, the chill in the air."

He smiles. "I mean, what's your favorite festival here?"

"In Blue Ridge?" I'm not sure why it takes me by surprise.

He nods and I look around, like maybe the answer will be written on the clock tower. This is the first time I've willingly come to a Blue Ridge festival, and only because Sawyer asked so sweetly. He was almost shy about it. I typically avoided public gatherings like the plague, hating the weight of people's stares like a bright spotlight shining wherever I went, only ever going if Mara begged. And even then, only when we were at the age when roaming a festival without an adult wouldn't have raised questions.

I lick my lips. "I don't know."

His head tilts. "Like, you can't decide?"

Exhaling, I say, "I mean, I don't know. I didn't go to a lot, but Mara liked the Christmas market."

His gaze is heavy, and I force mine to the booths we pass, giving the police station a wide berth out of habit. Each table has the same collection of items at one corner: hyacinths, vinegar, garlic, apple, coins, what looks like wheatgrass. It's what I saw every year on Dev's side table as spring approached, but the scale is magnified. Also, Mrs. Shah used to put Goldfish crackers on the table, which I always thought were for snacking, but every booth here has a fishbowl with one or two real goldfish swimming around.

"What do the goldfish mean?"

Sawyer whistles, and I look over to see he's taken a seat at the bottom of the empty steps leading up to the station. Because *of course* he has. He didn't spend his youth being called here by the police at odd hours. He never knew the humiliation of officers averting their eyes when he arrived to retrieve his still-drunk dad with money that was supposed to go to bills.

With a jolt I realize it extends beyond the police station, this difference between Sawyer and me. It applies to the whole town. Sawyer's childhood memories include him stomping around town, good times to balance the bad at home. Whereas the bad at my home followed wherever I went. I ventured out only when I had to. School, work, bailing out Dad. I have happy memories too, belly laughs with Dev, telling Mara I had enough saved for her to attend the eighth grade class trip, Gia spending her entire Saturday getting me ready for prom. But these all happened in private, behind closed doors.

What's it like to have Sawyer's confidence? To know you belong wherever you go, to not have this town mired by the past?

After a moment's hesitation, I walk over and sit down next to him in front of the police station.

A SWAT team does not descend upon me.

He hands me a plate piled high with herbed rice, buttery fish, golden chicken kabobs, and two types of stew. "The goldfish are a symbol of life, movement, and the passage of time. Pretty much everything here signifies rebirth and renewal."

I nod, remembering Mrs. Shah telling me something similar. "Why do you know so much about Persian New Year?"

"Ethan," he answers simply. "His parents used to have a big Nowruz gathering on the first day of spring every year, whether it was a weekend or not, and insisted everyone wear brand new clothes."

"Is that why I was recently compelled to buy new underwear?" I half-whisper.

He chokes on some rice. "Jesus."

His eyes darken. They rove over me, as if he might be able to see my underwear through my clothes. It feels like warm honey dripping through my body. He braces a hand against the step behind us and leans over. His face is inches from mine, and I can't help darting my eyes around, looking for onlookers.

His hoarse voice pulls my gaze back to him. "I want to kiss you."

I expect alarm bells, but they don't come.

"Okay," I whisper.

Slowly, like I'm an easily-startled deer, he raises his hand to cup my neck. His eyes drop to my mouth before rising to meet mine again. He gives me plenty of time to stop him. When I don't, he kisses me.

An illicit sort of giddiness jolts through me. Sawyer is kissing me. In public. He did it. *He* kissed *me*. If anyone's reputation is at stake from this, it's his, and he doesn't care because he's kissing me, and I don't care because *he's kissing me*. The sensation travels through my body, landing in a puddle of molten liquid right between my thighs.

His lips are soft, his hand commanding, his tongue teasing.

We break apart, smiling. A woman on the sidewalk staggers, catching my attention. Even through the hazy high of our kiss, she looks vaguely familiar. The parent of one of my old classmates maybe. She openly stares, literally clutching the pearls around her neck. Definitely from the north side of town.

It sobers me right up, nearly causing me heart palpitations. I'm suddenly fourteen again, wanting to crawl under a car and hide from the glaring spotlight.

"Mrs. Beaufort," Sawyer says by way of greeting because he *does* belong here.

And in that instant I know who she is. She's the wife of Garrett Beaufort, a now-prominent judge who, decades ago, dealt with misdemeanors. The kinds of cases my lowlife dad was always going to court for. They were good friends of the mayor, Sawyer's dad. I only know her because of the community outreach program my dad forced Mara and me to attend to garner sympathy. Judge Beaufort was always there, along with his Stepford wife and greasy son.

Her eyes flicker between us, and the familiar urge to crumple into myself rises.

Sawyer sets our plates down before pulling me up to stand with him, and tucking me close. He towers over her, making her look small despite being a pit bull in disguise.

"Mrs. Beaufort," he says again, this time in the same tone he uses on the youngest children at school. "Have you met my beautiful girlfriend, Brie Casey?"

Ears tip in our direction. My breath catches at the word *girlfriend*, and a torrent of emotions washes over me. *Yes!* I want to scream, *I am his girlfriend.* At the same time, panic rises. With that word comes a longevity, an intention to one day make things permanent. It's too soon for that. Too unrealistic.

Pushing all of it aside, I focus on Mrs. Beaufort. She's watching us with a sharp expression that, oddly, has me leaning into Sawyer. For the first time, I'm not alone in an interaction like this. She tracks my movement and her lips pucker like she's just sucked on a lemon.

"Hi." I wave, trying for some semblance of normalcy.

She straightens up, lifting her chin. "I am familiar with her . . . *family.*"

She speaks as if I'm not even here, and I wish I could

dissolve into the sidewalk, disappear from the shame that comes with that word, *family*. I know she really means that other f-word, *father*. I used to expect treatment like this, hide from it. But I can't hide now, so I lean into Sawyer more, making myself smaller, hating myself for it. *This isn't how I want to be.*

"Oh, but not Brie personally?" Sawyer says, innocently unfazed, though his arm squeezes me tightly in place, not letting me shrink away. "She's one of the best teachers the elementary school's ever had."

She practically gawks. It's the same kind of expression that had me counting the days until I could leave Blue Ridge my senior year, the kind I trained myself to never outwardly react to.

"I wasn't aware she was a *teacher* to the *youth*." She's basically a caricature of herself, but it doesn't make her words sting any less.

"Substitute," I say. It's almost an apology, and I have no idea why I'm giving her the ammo, but I'm unable to keep my mouth shut.

Another shoulder squeeze.

"We're hoping to make it permanent." Sawyer smiles earnestly.

Don't freak out. Mrs. Beaufort is the perfect reminder why *permanent* is impossible for me where Blue Ridge is concerned. I have no happy memories from town because there are none to be had for me. As much as Sawyer belongs here, I do not.

Her scrutinizing eyes widen, then narrow. "I see. Well," she turns to speak specifically to Sawyer, "give your father my best."

Then, she makes to continue in the direction she was heading.

"Mrs. Beaufort." Sawyer's voice is authoritative.

I want to shout *let her go!*

She pauses mid-step and very deliberately whirls to face us again, her shapely eyebrows shooting up.

His voice is casual, but it carries an icy undercurrent. "My girlfriend said hi. I'm sure you didn't mean to ignore her. Not with your impeccable manners."

I hold my breath. *Not with your impeccable manners?* Now, something like exhilaration blooms in my chest. I wind my arm around Sawyer's back, securing myself to his sturdy confidence, no longer shrinking but feeding off it and standing slightly taller.

I lift my hand and say, "Hi, Mrs. Beaufort."

She looks uncertainly between me and Sawyer, who wears an expectant expression, then, looking down her nose not *at* me but *toward* me, she says, "Hello."

She turns to leave.

I look up at Sawyer and burst into laughter, muffled by the back of my hand.

"That was *amazing*," I whisper at the same time he says, "That was awful."

It makes me laugh harder because he has no idea. I've dealt with so much worse than a pearl-clutching platinum blond with drawn-on eyebrows and lipstick on her teeth.

He gives me a bemused smile. "Are you broken?"

We sit down on the steps again, and I catch my breath. "I didn't know 'bless your heart' had a bougie sister." He cocks his head. I lower my voice to an imitation of him, saying, "'Not with your impeccable manners'!"

He grins. "She used to be a rotating member of the school committee, otherwise I would've used it on her a lot sooner."

"I hope to bring it into the modern lexicon." I say

around a hearty bite of stew. "Like when your date eats with his mouth open and talks about crypto the entire time."

"Sounds like a real example," he says.

"Oh, it is."

"How about when someone brings a tuna salad sandwich to a staff meeting?" he asks dryly. "Because that, too, is a real example."

"Or, and I'm just spitballing here, when your younger-by-only-four-years sister says you're too old for TikTok."

Sawyer mock-gasps. "With *her* impeccable manners Mara said that to you?"

CHAPTER 39

BRIE

IT'S MONDAY. I spent most of yesterday updating my spreadsheet as I frantically submitted more job applications, a little panicked that April's already around the corner. Most schools start their hiring process for next school year around now.

Today after school pickup, Sawyer approached me, leaving a respectable three feet between us. He looked around, which prompted me to look around. Some parents were huddled near the fence while their children ravaged the playground, but no one was within earshot.

"I can't stop thinking about you." He kept his voice quiet. "Have dinner with me?"

A giddy smile spread across my face even as the thought of going out on the town again churned my stomach because with him, I can't hide. The spotlight only shines brighter. "Okay, tonight?"

"Now."

I couldn't help smiling. "It's, like, three-thirty in the afternoon."

His lips quirked, and he shrugged. "I just want to spend time with you."

My stomach flipped, and that's how we came to stand outside Valley View Provisions at four in the afternoon. Sawyer opens the door, and I step inside. It's a large, open space with clean lines and modern accents. Tables and chairs taking up most of the interior. Toward the back, comfy seating is arranged around a see-through fireplace, which separates a smaller dining area that overlooks Orme-wood Mountain through the wall of windows. To one side of the counter are displays of artisanal meats and cheese, and against the wall are freezers with prepared meals and fridges full of fancy beverages. There's a counter that, by the looks of it, offers coffee, deli meats, and fresh-to-order food.

"Is this place new?" I ask, picking up a small wheel of brie to get a whiff of its pungent tangy scent.

"A few years old," he says, then points at the cheese in my hand and winks. "My favorite."

I grin and shake my head as I put it back. Sawyer walks to the array of drinks in the fridge and picks up two cans before leading me to the counter.

"I'm surprised a place like this can survive in Blue Ridge," I whisper.

He lowers his voice to match mine. "It's no Jiffy's, that's for sure."

Jiffy—known colloquially as *Jiffy's*—was the one general store we had in Blue Ridge when we were younger. At some point, the *J* had fallen off the sign and for several years it simply read *iffy*, which was apt in every way.

"Man," I say, "that place was great. Where else could you shop for groceries, a camo sundress, *and* bait?"

"You still can," he tells me. "Except now, it's a bar after

five. They call it Old Bard's because Brad Crenshaw couldn't spell his name right on the form."

My hand goes to my mouth. "Oh my god, I thought Mara was joking when she told me that. Does it smell like fish?"

He tilts his hand side to side. "Not like it used to. Speaking of fish, today is the weekly fish fry here."

"Is that what I should get?"

"If you like fried fish, it's the best you'll ever have. We're the only ones here now, but you'll see, it'll start getting really busy as dinnertime nears. When they run out, it'll get rowdy."

"Dinner and a show? You're spoiling me," I tease. His eyes darken not with sexual heat, but with some other unspoken desire.

When we get to the counter, an older Black woman approaches from the other side and plants her hands on her hips as she smiles broadly at Sawyer. I wonder if he knows how special it is that people are happy to see him wherever he goes.

"Well if it isn't his royal highness himself," the woman says with mock-scolding.

Color crawls up the back of his neck, and I have the sudden urge to rub his back. He hates this. Being called royalty isn't a compliment to him, and I understand why now. He doesn't want to be lumped in the same box as his dad, yet all people of this town see is the happy Strong family that the ex-mayor has carefully cultivated.

Sawyer smiles at her in a way I used to consider cocky, and this tugs at my heart, too. He'd rather endure this woman's teasing than hold it against her.

"Hi, Ms. Clarke. What's good?"

"Is that Sawyer?" A voice from the back bellows. A

Black man trudges up to the counter, his meaty arms folded as he looks down his nose at Sawyer.

My heart drops into my stomach because I recognize him. He's older, but it's definitely him. Justin Clarke. He used to be an EMT for the fire department.

Memories crash into my brain. Waking up to find my dad not home *again*. Getting Mara ready for school and on the bus. Walking the familiar path to Dad's favorite dive only to find him passed out on someone's lawn or on a bench, not sure if I should hope he's okay or hope this one did him in for good.

Mr. Clarke was the one who'd usually come. His deep brown eyes full of pity as he told me Dad would be okay.

Unconsciously, I move so that Sawyer blocks me.

Mr. Clarke tips his head at his wife. "You know, she has me slaving away making those little cornbread bites all because 'Sawyer said he loves them'?" He raises his voice to imitate his wife.

Sawyer's body stiffens as more color tints his neck.

Slapping her husband's arm, Ms. Clarke says, "Leave him alone, I *asked*." Then, with a wink, she adds, "But we can't have our Sawyer going hungry."

"Great! We'll take two orders with our fish fry." Sawyer's voice is casual, almost playful, but I notice a tension beneath his words.

"We?" Ms. Clarke says, and both of them crane their necks until their eyes find me.

I cringe internally.

Sawyer turns, a look of dismay when he sees me standing behind him. He drops his hand to the small of my back and draws me in front of him.

"Is that Brie Casey?" Mr. Clarke asks.

I wish the floor beneath me was made of quicksand.

Sawyer's arms snake around me, his chin resting on the top of my head.

"It is Brie Casey," he confirms. "She's been back for a few months now. One of the best teachers I've ever seen, and definitely my favorite. I'm trying to keep her."

My breath hitches at the compliment.

Ms. Clarke reaches over the counter to put a hand on mine. "Well, then. Welcome back to Blue Ridge, sweetheart. We are so glad you're here."

Her smile is like stepping into the sun. Warmth seeps from my skin directly into my pores and dispels throughout my body. To my immense embarrassment, my eyes dampen.

"Thanks," I manage.

"Cornbread on us," Mr. Clarke says, massaging his wife's shoulders, "as much as you want."

As if he knows the effect their kindness has on me, Sawyer speaks up, mock-offended. "I never got free cornbread."

"Yeah, but we're trying to keep her," Mr. Clarke says. "Besides, you aren't as pretty."

"That's true," Sawyer agrees, tugging me closer.

I smile up at him, but that unease in my subconscious grows. This is better than the nosy crowds at the festival or Mrs. Beaufort's pearl-clutching, but even this effusive attention is more than I want.

After Sawyer orders for us, we sit at a table in front of the windows. Main Street is right outside, but the peak of Ormewood Mountain is visible from behind the buildings across the street, a deep blue in the waning sunlight.

Sawyer pops the cans he bought and slides them both to

the middle of the table. "Are you a blueberry girl or a black cherry girl?"

I look at the two cans. "I've never had blueberry soda, so I'm not sure."

"Well, yeah, they only started canning it in the last five years or so, and they only distribute locally. But it's the same one they always had at the picnics." He turns the can so I can see the name on the label, Brume Bubbles.

Of course. Chateau Brume, the largest local winery, used to sponsor annual end-of-summer family picnics. They had finger foods, bounce houses, and water games within view of a wine-tasting tent the parents would congregate under. The winery made special kid-friendly sodas just for that weekend, often introducing a new experimental flavor alongside the regulars.

I know this because it was all anyone could ever talk about for days before and after.

I do *not* know this from experience.

As an elementary schooler, I'd listen enviously when someone mentioned anything as exotic as the peach and blackberry sodas. But as I became more self-aware, it was a relief not to attend. I could just picture Dad slipping into inebriation in front of the parents of kids I had to go to school with.

"Which flavor is your favorite?" I hedge.

Sawyer's eyes are sharp, studying me. "I always liked the black cherry best," he answers, "but the blueberry was a close second."

I push the black cherry toward him.

Sawyer opens his mouth to speak, but Ms. Clarke's voice calls out from the counter, "Order's ready!" and Sawyer gets up to retrieve our food.

I take a sip of the blueberry soda. The flavor explodes in

my mouth, and I can one-hundred-percent see why kids went apeshit for this stuff. It's addictive. I take one more quick sip before pushing it away.

When Sawyer returns, he places baskets of fried fish, cornbread bites with honey butter, coleslaw, and potato salad on the table between us.

"Thanks, it smells amazing," I say.

"It tastes amazing too." He rips a piece of fish off and pops it into his mouth.

It's borderline obscene the way his eyes close and he makes a satisfied sound. Maybe it's the lentil soups and salads I've seen him bring for lunch, or the chicken and vegetables we made at his cabin, but his reaction surprises me.

"What?" he asks when I still haven't tucked in. "Not a fan of fried food?"

"Of course I'm a fan of fried food," I say. "I just didn't expect you to be."

He laughs. "I suggested it."

"But you just moaned," I argue.

"*And?*" He lowers his voice and waggles his eyebrows ridiculously. "Did you feel it in your loins?"

"Ew," I laugh. "Don't say *loins*."

Grinning, he pushes a basket toward me. "Try it."

I do. It's salty and nutty from the peanut oil and savory from the spices, with just a hint of pepper, before the buttery fish melts in my mouth. Before I realize it, I'm moaning with my eyes half-closed.

"See?"

"I didn't doubt it," I argue around another bite.

"You're right, though," he says with a smile. "Fried food isn't my favorite."

I point at him with my fork. "I knew it."

"Don't get me wrong," he says. "While on deployment, I'd miss this sort of food if I was on the ship, but when we got to go ashore for port calls and eat real food? I never did."

"Where'd you go?" I ask.

"A bunch of places in Southeast Asia. My favorite was Vietnam, but Thailand and Indonesia were great, too. The food just bursts with flavor out there. Sweet and tangy with a good amount of spice. The first time I tasted papaya salad in Thailand, my brain chemistry changed. I would've been happy to eat that for the rest of my life."

"And yet you live in a town with basically three restaurants," I point out.

"I cook a lot," he shrugs.

"You wouldn't have to if you lived somewhere else," I say. After a hesitation, I add, "Would you? Live somewhere else? Or, I guess what I want to know is: why did you come back?"

He places his elbows on the table and rests his chin on his steepled fingers.

"When I left," he says after a while, "it was for one specific reason." His father. I know that much. "But that reason was loaded. I didn't just want to get away from my dad, but to find my path in life, away from what anyone else wanted for me, including the town. I needed to get away from all the scrutiny to figure it out."

I get that.

"After leaving," he continues, "any time I pictured my future, it was in Blue Ridge. It bothered me because I hated who I was when I lived here, how could I want to come back? It took finding a therapist to realize this town doesn't define me. It's understandable that I was swayed when I was a kid, but I'd changed. I wasn't that same scared boy anymore, and I knew myself enough by that point to be at peace with returning."

My heart squeezes for the tormented young man he was.

His smile is contemplative. "Same same but different."

"Same same but different?" I ask.

"I heard that phrase everywhere in Southeast Asia, but it applied perfectly to me. I was the same in so many ways, but I was fundamentally different, too. And when I came back home, I could see Blue Ridge more objectively. There's a lot that's special here. Traveling all over the world helped me see that this really was home."

I swallow. *Could I ever see Blue Ridge that way?* It's doubtful. Even when this was home, I longed for a different one.

But I can't deny the good here. My sisters. Lizzie. Tess and Dev. Sawyer.

"It's a unique place," he says. "Do you know any other small towns like this? That have festivals for Lunar New Year, Nowruz, and Holi? I mean, yeah, for some reason we only have three restaurants downtown, but there are some on the outskirts, and popups happen frequently. The farmers market usually sates any of my cravings for Asian food, and it doesn't take long to get to Ridgedale."

"True," I say. What used to only harbor the drive-in and hospital has been hugely developed. I saw it in passing last week when I joined Gia and Lizzie on errands. "There's even a Target now. When we were young, we just had Jiffy's."

He beams. "Exactly."

There is more to Blue Ridge than I previously imagined, but people here have always loved Sawyer. It's different for me, I could never live here permanently. Not with them either clutching their pearls or offering me pity gifts like Mr. Clarke and the cornbread bites.

He pops one of them in his mouth before taking a sip of his soda, smacking his lips after. "Man, that's good. It takes me right back, you know?"

I don't.

"Wait, you didn't tell me what your favorite flavor was. Let me guess, it isn't even one they have here, is it? Probably one of the experimental ones they only ever had once."

With every word my heart plummets more and more. I'm sad for the girl who didn't get to try the exciting sodas. I'm sad for myself for not being able to taste the nostalgia in my can. And I'm sad for Sawyer for being here with someone who can't relate to this thing that's obviously exciting to him.

He looks at me expectantly.

Swallowing a lump down my throat, I say, "I always liked the idea of peach or blackberry."

His smile freezes in place. "But they always had peach and blackberry."

Oh god. Why did I say anything at all? He doesn't get it. He wouldn't get it.

My pulse races like I'm about to dive off a cliff.

"I didn't go to the picnic," I say.

"Which year?"

Abruptly, I stand. "I'm going to get a box. Need one?" I leave before he can answer.

When I get the courage to head back to the table, Neil Ford from our year is standing there, talking to Sawyer. Not wanting yet another unwanted interaction, I hang back until he goes to the counter to order.

The thing is, Neil Ford wouldn't even look my way if I were alone. Mr. Clarke would have never noticed me if not for Sawyer. Or, more likely, I never would have come here.

I peer around the market. It's almost empty, but the spotlight is as bright as ever this afternoon because now there are two. Mine and Sawyer's.

I'm glad Sawyer found his peace in returning to Blue Ridge, but I never could.

I have to get more applications out.

CHAPTER 40
BRIE

THE FOLLOWING WEEK, Sawyer backs into a parking spot and hops out of his truck. "Stay here."

I've never been inside the gates of the drive-in theater, and I don't know what's better: that I'm here for the first time, or that we're away from peering eyes.

When Sawyer and I are at school, it's like our own little world. We eat lunch with Tess most days, and while it's professional, I've had fun developing our friendship.

But as soon as we're in the community, my anxiety climbs. The town's attention makes me sweat, but then there's the mortification every time Sawyer's forced to defend me.

He'll be relieved when I'm finally gone and he no longer has to.

I slam the door on it all because it's irrelevant tonight.

My gaze is drawn to the hill outside the gates. I would've never spend my hard-earned pennies to enter the grounds properly. Besides, neither Dev nor I had a car to *drive in*. The experience was a luxury I couldn't afford in multiple ways. But on those rare occasions I wasn't working,

Dev and I would sit up on that hill, a radio tuned to the movie between us.

I rarely paid attention to what was on the screen, watching the people below instead. Sawyer's big red truck was there every time I went, backed in just like now. Even then, I wished I was down there with him. I hated him, but would have accepted an invitation. Not from Ethan, not from Rich. Not from anyone else. But if Sawyer had asked, I would have gone. After some arguing.

Several minutes later, my door opens, and he leads me to the back of the truck. He's laid down blankets and placed pillows against the cab. To the side are a couple sodas and a huge tub of popcorn from concessions.

He grins as he helps me onto the bed, the skirt of my dress billowing as he pulls me up like I weigh nothing.

We settle against the pillows and stretch our legs out in front of us. I lean back against his chest. He threads his fingers through mine and I feel his lips on the top of my head. My pulse leaps in my throat, just like a teenager with a crush.

"You know," he says, as if reading my mind, "when I used to come here, I always wished it was with you."

"You looked like you were having enough fun," I blab.

It was meant to be teasing, but my heart jumps to my throat when I realize what I just admitted.

He leans to look at me. "I don't remember ever seeing you here."

I shake my head, heat climbing up my spine. "That's because you didn't." I swallow. As casually as I can, I say, "Dev and I sat up there. Just a few times."

"Too cool for the rest of us, huh?" Sawyer smiles as he offers me a soda and plops the popcorn between us.

I make a sound I hope he mistakes for a laugh. "Yeah."

He looks at me for a long moment before leaning against the pillows again. He knows better than anyone how untrue that is. Even though it was years ago, there's still a little twist in my stomach at the reminder. The same feeling I had about not having tasted those Chateau Brume sodas before. A wistfulness for something I never had.

If this were just about differences in our upbringing, I could move past it, meet him where we are. But it's broader than that, extending to the here and now. Maybe because, as much as Sawyer and I have both changed, this town hasn't. It forces us to travel back in time whenever the spotlight catches us.

Why couldn't I have met you anywhere else? I want to ask.

I ignore the painful pangs. No need to dwell on the reasons Sawyer and I don't make sense. I already have a job offer, and another interview scheduled. At the end of the school year, I'm doing what I couldn't as a kid: leaving. Escaping Blue Ridge for the last time. I'm allowed to enjoy this while it lasts.

A light breeze blows, tenting my dress and sending goosebumps down my legs as the opening credits play on the screen.

"Cold?" he asks, moving the popcorn and covering us with the blanket.

"Thanks," I say, resting my hand on his thigh. It's hard and unyielding.

We watch the movie for a few minutes like this. Or, in my case, pretend to. I'm so aware of him. The way his chest rises and falls. His thigh muscle tensing as he shifts to make us both more comfortable. His scent overwhelms me, even outside, even with the nutty smell of popped popcorn permeating the air.

Hand flexing on my thigh, he says, "I like this dress." His breath is warm on my neck.

Goosebumps rise from my exposed skin just below my clavicle.

He raises his free hand and skims them with one delicate finger. "Still cold?"

I shake my head, heart galloping beneath his touch.

Beneath the blanket, his other hand begins tracing circles over my dress. With each one, the hem draws up. Heat scorches a trail up to the apex between my thighs.

With me living at Gia's, and him in an active construction zone that has him shacking up with his brother at the moment, we haven't had more than a couple steamy make-out sessions since the Nowruz festival a couple weeks ago, and I'm famished.

I suppress the urge to nudge him closer with a slight tilt of my hips. We are, after all, in public. I glance around. It's a Tuesday. Despite the mid-week promotions, there are only a few other cars scattered around the lot, and almost all of them are sedans, too low to see over the side of the truck anyway.

Sawyer cups my chin, tilting my mouth to his as he leans over me. His lips taste like salt from the popcorn, but his tongue is sweet from the soda. I break the kiss before I'm tempted to climb onto his lap. *That*, I'm sure, people would be noticed.

I rest my head on his shoulder again, trying to catch my breath. My nipples bead when his tongue slides along the shell of my ear. I dig my nails into his leg.

"What's your favorite part of the movie so far?" he whispers in a hoarse voice that grates the most sensitive parts of me.

His hand creeps up my bare thigh, no fabric between us.

"I liked the dancing hotdog," I sigh.

The rough sound of his chuckle ripples through me. "You mean the dancing hotdog that warned us to keep our radios on the right station?"

"Yeah. Great performance."

The pad of his finger brushes against the damp cotton of my panties, and I jerk against him, a small sound ripping through me.

"Shh," he soothes, holding me firmly against him. "If you do that again, I'll have to stop. I don't want to stop." He slides his finger along the edge of my panties. "And judging by how wet you are," he slips a finger just inside, "you don't want me to either."

"I don't," I breathe.

He removes his finger and sweeps his hand up and down my thigh, driving me crazy with want. "You know what my favorite part of this dress is?"

I shake my head.

With a smile in his voice, he gravels, "I like this part."

He raises his free hand to my chest and hooks one finger into the front. I look down. You can *almost* see my nipples, but not quite. Just a shadow of an outline. My hand moves up to where he's hard beneath his jeans, and he immediately releases my dress and threads our fingers together.

"If you touch me" —his fingers slowly move toward the bundle of nerves already eager to explode— "this whole place will know when I come."

At that last word, *come*, Sawyer presses on my clit. I shudder.

"But I have to touch you," he grits out, gently moving my panties to the side, "I'm desperate for it."

He slides in, barely to the knuckle, but it feels like coming home. I release a shaky, shallow breath.

"Your little sounds drive me crazy." He inserts a second finger, and when he hits the spot he knows I love, I clamp my mouth shut, trying my damnedest to be quiet.

His lips skim down my neck. "You like that?"

"Mm-hm."

He bites my shoulder and I'm dimly aware of the way his hips pulse up and down.

"I wish" —it's hard to talk with his fingers inside me, but I swallow and force the sounds out— "you'd let me touch you."

"I'd get us arrested." He circles my clit insistently now. Tingles blaze up my spine. "When we can be together in private again, I won't say no."

His fingers drive into me. A keening sound starts to climb out of my throat but he molds his lips to mine just in time to hold it between us.

He brings his mouth back to my ear, talking low as he goes back to rubbing my clit, more urgently now. "God, Brie, I love this" —he licks the shell of my ear— "love being the reason you feel good."

There's no hope for me anymore. My chest heaves like a Victorian harlot as concentrated pleasure winds me tighter and tighter. His arm anchors me to him as my body bucks against him. I grip his free hand, dig my nails into his other forearm.

"I've got you." Sawyer's breath is hot on my neck. "Come for me right here. Let go."

And then I do. Just as the deep pulse of pleasure blasts through me, Sawyer's mouth is on mine, swallowing my moans. He holds me to him, steady and strong. When I start clenching around nothing, I urge his hand down. He gets the message and drives two fingers into me, chasing my orgasm, extending it to the last drop.

Then, when I'm a satisfied lump resting against him, he eases his fingers out, brings them to his mouth, and licks them clean. The sight sends another rippling shudder through me.

After a few minutes of satisfied bliss, I turn to kiss him, tasting myself on his tongue. He releases my hand, and I automatically reach for him. His thick erection has my need blooming all over again.

"Let's leave," I whisper.

"The movie's not living up to your expectations?" he asks, voice ragged.

"What movie?"

I TOSS the blankets and pillows into the back of the cab while Brie throws away the popcorn and sodas. Then I hightail it out of there . . . at the posted speed limit of five miles per hour.

"Woah, tiger," Brie deadpans. "Take it easy."

"I'm scared of the security here," I say, matching her tone and nodding my head at the geriatric guard dozing off in a chair by the concessions booth.

"You get in trouble for changing the radio station one too many times?" she teases.

"I wish. Rich smuggled beer in once, and I got the blame since we were in my truck. Got banned" —I look over and widen my eyes exaggeratedly— "for life."

She snorts. "Is that the real reason you got a new truck? Hiding from the fuzz?"

Smiling, I say, "Worth it so I could bring you."

I can't stop thinking about it. She used to come all the way here just to sit outside the fence. I have so many questions, most of them trivial just to paint a picture. I want to ask how she got here in the first place, a good twenty minutes outside of town. What movies she saw. If she brought snacks.

But just like every time Brie drops a breadcrumb, I get the feeling it was accidental. If I push for more—and god, I want so much more—it'll end like it did at Valley View Provisions when she hid by the to go boxes for ten minutes. I'm not sure how Brie went from telling me to go fuck myself as she walks home in the freezing rain to hiding behind my back, but I hate it. If my goal was to make Brie feel safe with me, I'm failing.

I thought when she told me why she left Everett, that she was opening up to me. But the more time I spend with her, the more it feels like she's retreating into herself.

It's killing me, trying to rack my brain for ways to make things better. I would *ask*, except she won't let me in. The most mundane questions—what's more mundane than soda flavors?—has her changing the subject or shutting down.

Is this because of how I tormented her when we were kids? I'd get it if it were, but then why be with me at all?

Maybe she'll never be happy with me.

I grip the steering wheel with both hands, knuckles turning white. I won't believe it. I won't let myself assume she can't be happy with me. Not until she says so herself. One word from her, and I'll leave her alone, but until then I'm going to keep trying.

Before I turn onto the main stretch of highway that'll lead back to Blue Ridge, Brie leans over the center console, bracing herself with one hand on my thigh. The action sweeps away all my thoughts, and my cock roars to life when her lips skate up my neck.

"We can't go to your house." She nips at my ear.

I inhale. "No." Sheetrock dust somehow made its way

everywhere, and I'm staying at Will's until the drywall is all done.

"And you can't come home with me." She kisses along my jaw.

I'm rock hard.

"Right," I croak.

Her mouth feathers over mine as she says, "Is there somewhere we could go and . . . park?"

She squeezes my dick through my pants. I cradle the back of her neck and crush my mouth to hers, thrusting my tongue into her mouth.

"Yeah," I heave, "let's go park somewhere."

I frantically try to think of an empty lot between here and Blue Ridge as I turn onto the road.

"Where're we going?" Brie asks.

She's retreated back to her side of the car, but her hand is still distractingly on my leg.

I glance over and squeeze her knee. "I'm not sure yet."

"You don't have, like, a spot?"

Her skin is so soft. That's distracting too.

"A spot?" I ask.

"Yeah, a spot. Somewhere you used to go . . . *do stuff* with girls."

I look at her out of the corner of my eye. She has that same shifty look I've come to understand means she's uncomfortable.

"No, I don't have *a spot*," I tell her, keeping my tone light.

She angles herself so she's facing me in her seat. "You say that, but I know you took Melanie Crowe to homecoming once. Anna Ludwig another year. And there were rumors you had sex with Linda Flowers when she was a senior and we were sophomores."

Suddenly, this feels like an ambush. "That's all true," I say carefully.

"So?" she prods.

I rub the back of my neck, but she takes my hand and puts it back on her knee. It's a small relief that she wants it there in spite of the turn the conversation's taken. It centers me.

"So," I say, "they were all really nice, pretty girls. But I went out with them because . . ." I search for the right words. I won't do what Brie's been doing, I won't hide parts of myself from her. I did that for far too long already. "I went out with them because I was a horny teenager and I couldn't have you," I blurt.

Her hand freezes on my leg. After a moment I look over, not sure what I'll find.

She's looking at me with a thoughtful expression, brows furrowed, mouth bunched to one side.

"What?" I ask.

"Nothing, I—"

I don't say a word, silently urging her to keep talking.

She does. "I just— It's hard for me to believe you liked me even while you were having sex with Linda Flowers."

One side of my mouth pulls up. "It's true, though. I liked you *especially* while Linda Flowers de-flowered me."

When I sneak a glance at her, she still looks dubious.

"You wanna know when?" I say.

"What do you mean?"

"For a couple months, Linda made it abundantly clear if I wanted her, I could have her. Do you remember our field day toward the end of school?"

She visibly winces. "The year I slipped in the kiddie pool during the obstacle course and got absolutely drenched?"

I smile at the memory and lift an eyebrow at her. "Yup. And you'd chosen the *white* field day shirt."

Her hand goes up to her forehead. "Don't remind me!"

"I must have jerked off to that image thousands of times after that," I admit. "But I didn't have to that day because that's when I finally took Linda up on her offer. Eyes closed, thinking of you the whole time."

She punches me on the bicep. "That's awful," she cries.

"I know!" I'm laughing, but I mean it. "If it makes you feel any better, she was using me to get back at her on-again-off-again boyfriend, Steve Martinez."

Brie laughs. "So you deserved each other."

"That's one way to put it," I say.

"Who did you lose your V-card to?" I ask, taking a risk. "And if you say Steve Martinez . . ."

"Linda Flowers," she says, and I laugh.

Her fingers idly rub my thigh.

After a moment, she says, "A guy named Allen Ow. We were both freshmen, living in the same dorm. We dated for about a year, and he was sweet, but," she shrugs, "we were eighteen. We both got bored, I guess."

I'm immediately jealous of Allen Ow. He must've been an idiot to get bored of her.

Her fingers trail higher up my leg, distracting me enough to almost miss the next turn.

Brie chuckles. "Did you really jerk off to me looking like a wet rat?"

Even after all these years, the image still stirs up the deep yearning and gratitude teenage-me felt at the time.

Voice a bit deeper, I say, "You did *not* look like a wet rat. And yes. I jerked off to you in that wet t-shirt. I jerked off to you in your tiny gym shorts. Hell, I jerked off to you in your winter jacket."

She snorts, and I look over to find her cheeks darkening, a sly smile curling her lips upward. "Did you have any particular fantasies?"

I blow out a long breath. "Tons. I mean, as a horny teenager, basically anything's fair game. I fantasized about taking you in the locker room, in an empty classroom, in the gym. On desks, in chairs, against bookshelves. Literally anywhere and everywhere."

I slow to a stop at the three-way intersection. She caresses my thigh.

Her hand delicately trails up, avoiding my groin, to my waistband. Her nails scrape across my stomach as she pops the button of my jeans. My hips nearly come off the seat, thrusting against nothing.

"Any other fantasies?" she asks innocently.

Precum leaches out of my dick as she gives me a sultry look and slowly lowers my zipper.

My throat is dry. She raises her eyebrows.

"Yeah," I rasp. "This one."

She leans over, giving me a tortuously quick view down the front of her dress, and kisses me. Headlights reflect in my rearview mirror, and I take the turn as Brie snakes her hand into my underwear to free my cock.

"Oh fucking fuck," I curse under my breath.

"Eyes on the road," She flicks the buttons on my flannel. When it falls open, she takes in a sharp breath. "*Oh my god.*"

A bubble of pride expands in my chest that I can inspire such reverence in her voice, but I keep my voice even, borderline dry. "You've seen me fully naked before, Brie."

"Not in weeks," she says. "You're perfect."

My breath hitches. She reaches for me, but I circle her wrist with my fingers.

"Not while I'm driving," I tell her in as stern a voice as I can muster. "Eyes on the road, remember?"

"What do you expect me to do, then?" she pouts.

"Whatever you need to, but I'm not getting in a wreck with my dick out."

"Okay," she says, and a prickle of suspicion climbs up my spine as I approach the first stoplight into Blue Ridge. That was too easy.

The instant I pull stop at the red light, she twists her body over the center console.

"You aren't driving right this second," she says.

Her lips brush my slit with a kiss. She twirls her tongue around the head of my cock before taking it into her mouth and sucking gently.

"Brie—"

I put my hand on her back, but can't speak. She hums around my crown and folds her knees beneath her on the seat. I mold my hand over her perfect ass.

The light turns green. As before, a car approaches from behind. I lift her off me, kiss her, sucking her lower lip into my mouth, then drive.

Before we get to the next light, the car behind us makes a turn. My cock twitches in anticipation of her warm mouth.

I stop at the red. She leans over and takes my entire length into her mouth until I hit the back of her throat. I groan loud, reaching for her ass again, giving her a playful spank before sliding my hand down to dip into her heat.

"So wet." It's a growl.

Not wanting to waste any time, I move her panties to

the side and pet her clit. I watch as her head bobs. I wrap her hair around my free hand to catch a glimpse of her pretty face.

"Beautiful," I grunt. "You're beautiful."

I slip two fingers into her entrance, caressing her sweet spot, matching her rhythm. Her moans vibrate through me.

There are no other cars on the street. The light washes over her, cycling from green to yellow to red again. As with everything related to Brie, reality puts my fantasies to shame. Her fervor, the little sounds she makes, the feel of her.

"I can't take it anymore," I bellow, and with a wet *pop*, I pull her off me.

The streetlights shine on her wet mouth, her gleaming eyes, highlighting her darkened cheeks. The light turns green. I drive.

"Take off your panties." Even to my own ears, I sound like a man possessed.

Next to me, Brie follows my instructions beautifully. She gets extra credit for pulling up the skirt of her dress.

"I wish I could take my time with you," I rumble.

I smack my hand onto her leg, relishing her gasp of pleasure, and tug it toward me, opening her wide. At some point, her scent diffused into the inside of the truck, overwhelming me in the best way.

My hand covers her, and she begins grinding into me. Her arousal is the hottest fucking thing.

"So fucking hot," I heave. "Tell me what you need from me."

"You," she pants. "Inside me."

I drive two more blocks, reaching for my wallet and tossing it at her. "Condom."

A dark lot is up ahead. I hear her tear the foil packet.

Then, against the rules, she leans over for a long, sloppy suck before rolling the condom on. I make a sharp right turn, put the car in park, and unbuckle both our seatbelts. Then my hands are on her hips, lifting and dragging her. I hold her over me just long enough to look into those drugged, needy eyes. Then I impale her. We both make tortured sounds of relief.

My hands rise to the top of her dress, and I tug, exposing her perfect tits to me. I cover one hard nipple with my mouth as I pinch the other. My free hand kneads her ass. Anywhere I can touch her, kiss her, I do. I'm a man starved.

She grinds against me, making sweet whimpering sounds that inflate my ego. After I've given both breasts their due attention, I lick my way up her sternum, suck on her throat, bite the curve of her neck. She fills my truck with gasps and moans, whimpers and sobs.

"Come for me," she says.

The words alone almost make me spill, but I can't. Not until she's come first.

"You," I huff.

She shakes her head. "Not going to happen. Angle's all wrong."

I lift her off me, and she gasps a protest.

"Why didn't you tell me?" I growl as I turn her around so she's facing forward on my lap. I guide my cock into her again.

This time, her moan is guttural. It's the same sound she makes when I hit the right spot. My eyes roll to the back of my head, she feels even better this way.

I force myself to focus. "Is this it?"

"Ye-esss," she moans, head falling against my shoulder.

Nipping at her neck, I bring my hand around to find her clit, rubbing her breast with my other hand.

"You gonna—" *fuck*, her walls quiver around me, and I nearly black out. "You gonna come?" I wrench the words out.

She makes an incoherent sound as she grabs my forearm. I grit my teeth and keep a steady rhythm.

Her thighs begin to shake. A sound from deep inside her chest rises. I stay with her, stroking her, coaxing the orgasm out of her. She slaps the top of the truck, body arching. Then her walls clamp around me in shuddering convulsions. Her cry of pleasure is loud as she comes undone in my arms, giving me permission to take what I need.

I work her harder and faster from below, holding her firm in my arms. It only takes a few more pumps before I'm undone, my seizing breaths hot against her bare shoulder as she slumps against me.

My movements slow, and we sit like this, sweaty and heaving for several moments. Then I reach into the door pocket, where I keep some wipes. I draw myself out and shift her to sit sideways on my lap. Even with a condom, wetness glistens on her thighs.

"You don't have to," she says.

I look into her eyes. "I want to, Brie. This is part of it for me."

She doesn't protest after that. When I've taken care of her, I pull her closer, holding her tight, wishing this moment would last forever. This, the physical part, is easy, we're so good together. But I want her to understand she can open herself up to me. I love her independence and stubbornness, but I want to be the person she can be vulnerable with, too. Trust.

I give her a final kiss and reach across the cab for her panties. As they catch the moonlight, we both freeze.

"What in the Bob Ross . . ."

Her laugh is muffled as she hides her face in my neck. "I —didn't—know." She can't speak for laughing. I take the time to look at the sky blue panties covered in Bob Ross's face. On the crotch, the sides, both butt cheeks. Everywhere, Bob Ross smiles back at me.

After she's collected herself, she says, "I didn't know tonight would end up like this. I would've worn something sexier."

"Not sure you can get sexier than Bob Ross," I say. "I just wish I'd seen them earlier. *Meow.*"

She laughs harder. "They were a gift from Mara."

"Think if I hint hard enough she'll get some for me next Christmas?"

Abruptly, all the levity in the air gets sucked out. Brie ignores my joke and tugs the top of her dress over her chest. When she moves to her seat, a hollowness forms in my chest.

I don't get it or know how to stop her from pulling away. With her, it's always one step forward, two steps back.

Part of me wants to beg her forgiveness all over again, do anything I can because I want a future with Brie. Family time and holidays and sitting on the porch at night, all of it.

Just give her time. She's still working through our past. I had years to do that.

But something in my gut makes me wonder if time will help.

"Should I take you back to Gia's?" I ask.

"Yeah, sounds good." She's looking out the window, voice far away.

THIS WAS *Brie's Saturday night idea*, I remind myself as we drive to the bowling alley in silence so thick that, for the first time in my life, I feel like I'm drowning. The worst part is I have no idea what the problem is. If I knew, we could work through it. I keep telling myself all she needs is time, but as time goes on she gets farther away.

I've tried coming up with new activities for us, thinking maybe the problem is my undivided attention, I was putting pressure on her without realizing it. I thought if I could just get her out, she'd loosen up. I've taken her to Moo Crew for ice cream, the April's Fool festival, the farmers market, but it's like I'm using the wrong playbook. She only grows more distant.

"We have a few minutes," I say after I park at the bowling alley.

We're meeting Dev and Tess. Even though I'm mere days away from a finished cabin, I jumped at the opportunity to spend tonight with Brie. The cabin's stifling. Every time I enter the living room, glance at the kitchen, look out the damn window, I think of Brie, laughing and beautiful and happy. Although she's anything but those things right now, I'd rather be here trying than there wishing. Even if my determination is wearing thin.

"We can go ahead and find a lane, order some appetizers," I say.

She nods.

Neither of us moves. I look straight ahead, racking my brain for how to bring some lightness to the evening. Nothing comes to mind. The tone is all wrong, anything I'd try would seem forced. Because it would be.

I look at her one more time. She's staring out the window. My gut twists. I open the door and step out.

As we cross the parking lot of Soup'o'Bowl, the doors open to an outburst of families with younger children, heading home for a reasonable bedtime.

"Ms. Casey!"

Maeve Dragan, a student in Brie's class, runs across the pavement, her two burly, leather-clad dads plodding after her. It's a testament to Brie that Maeve, one of the shyer kids in third grade, is comfortable enough to barrel into her and wrap her arms around her waist.

"Hi, Maeve," she says, squeezing back. Brie's smile is warmer than I've seen it in weeks, but even now there's something wistful about the way she looks down at the girl.

"Wow," Bosko says, "*the* Ms. Casey." He's the larger of Maeve's two grownups. A scraggly beard covers most of his tan face, eyes bright with energy.

"Brie, this is Bosko," I say.

Bosko shakes her hand. "You're famous. And not just at home" —he winks at me— "but around town, too."

I grin, knowing the parents have spread the word about how great the third grade substitute is. But when I look at Brie, she's ashen and wide-eyed.

"I'm Maeve's father," Bosko adds unnecessarily.

"*One of,*" Stan interjects. He's clean-shaven with short-cropped salt and pepper hair.

Bosko rolls his eyes.

"This is Stan," I say.

Brie smiles politely. "Let me guess." She eyes them both, pointing first at Stan. "You're *daddy*." She transfers her point to Bosko. "And you're *papa*."

Maeve jumps up and down and yells, "How'd you know?!"

"Because I pay attention." She boops Maeve's nose like I've seen her do to Lizzie, and Maeve giggles.

Stan says, "Maeve loves your class."

"And I love having her," Brie says. "She always has something insightful to contribute."

"Maeve's gained a lot of confidence these past couple months," Bosko says to me, quietly so his daughter can't hear. Then, as he tips his head toward Brie, he loudly adds, "Y'better keep this one."

That's what I'm trying to do. He has no idea how hard I'm trying.

I look meaningfully at Brie. "I intend to. She's a shoo-in for the full-time position we need to fill next year." I put my arm over her shoulders.

Brie stiffens beneath my touch. I immediately take my arm back.

Fuck.

FUCK!

Brie coughs out a goodbye to Maeve and her dads, and we head inside. It's busy. Every stool at the bar is taken, a steaming bowl in front of each diner, and half the lanes are in use. I get all my waving and *Hey how you doing*s out of the way. With every one, I can tell Brie's annoyance with me grows. I imagine my voice like nails on a chalkboard for her. I knew it would take time for her to open up, but she's going in the wrong direction. I don't get it, why spend time with me if she can't stand me?

When we put on our rental shoes, I don't know what to say. I'm growing impatient. It's clear we need to have a real conversation and she's not going to start it, so I will. But Soup'o'Bowl with her friends is not the place or the time.

On cue, Dev and Tess walk in together, chatting like old pals—a direct contrast to me and the woman I've spilled my heart to and had in my bed.

They bring their own rentals to a narrow bench across from us. Dev spreads out in the middle, and Tess body checks him to make room. Dev being Dev, I can't tell if there's something to his doting smile or not. Blue Ridge is small enough I'm not surprised they would know *of* each other, but Tess never overlapped with us in school.

"How do you two know each other?" I ask after we've greeted one another. Or, rather, after I've greeted both of them. Brie stands off to the side pretending to peruse the menu, which I can attest is not that interesting. The three laminated pages are almost exclusively soup. There's one stew and a chowder, but they're watery, almost like they're embarrassed for being off-theme.

Brie lifts her hand in a poor imitation of a wave, then furrows her eyebrows as if she's concentrating on whether to order the broccoli cheddar or the French onion.

"Dev's sister was one of my best friends in school." Tess smiles affectionately up at him.

"Sana, my youngest sister," Dev adds with his trademark smile, and I remember Dev's the oldest of five or six kids.

"We were roommates in college, and Dev helped us move *every* year."

"I was always pack mule and chauffeur for those two anyway. Moving was just another version of that."

He squeezes her shoulder, and pink tinges Tess's cheeks. I look away, feeling as if I've intruded on an intimate moment. My gaze finds Brie, who's missed the whole thing, concentrating on a spreadsheet on her phone.

Deflated, I go to the counter for something to do, opting to order the bar food I know is off menu.

"No soup for you?" Lois asks.

"Not today, thanks."

I join the others at our lane, dropping a round of drinks on the table. With another glance at Brie, I make a show of stretching my arms.

"I'm already embarrassed for all of you," I deadpan. "I don't wanna brag, but I think it's important you know I've bowled exactly twice" —I hold up two fingers— "in the last decade. So, I'm pretty good."

Tess laughs, but it's Brie I'm focused on. I don't know if she even heard me as she busies herself with picking out a ball.

I rub the back of my neck, trying to come up with some way to bring her out of whatever funk she's in. But if it's me that's upsetting her, anything I do will only exacerbate things.

"Step aside, old man," Tess jokes back. "I wouldn't want you to pull a muscle."

"Look at the man," Dev says, "the only thing he's pulling with those guns is the *ladies*."

Man, Dev really is that nice of a guy. But the only lady I want is Brie, who might as well not be here.

Tess walks up to the lane with her ball, hingeing at the

waist. Dev's eyes immediately go to the ceiling, but they drop again at the sound of the ball hitting pins. A strike. Tess shimmies in celebration.

"Nice one!" he tells her with a broad smile, and I whistle cheerfully.

The hair on the back of my neck stands up. My gaze cuts to Brie. She's already looking at me. The second I catch her, her eyes widen then dart away. My intestines are in knots now.

When I reach for my beer, I grip the plastic cup so tight it cracks, and I have to pour its contents into a fresh cup before it seeps out everywhere. Brie stands and walks to the ball return. She bowls a split. I pull my lips upward into what I hope is a casual smile as I walk toward her for my turn.

"Not bad," I say, holding my hand up for a high-five.

She eyes it as we get closer. Her palm feathers over mine in the slightest of touches. It's enough to almost make me wish we were back to before my confession in the cabin. At least she *felt* something for me, even if it was sheer loathing. But this? She's shutting down completely. Building an impenetrable wall.

Why?

All at once, my frustration at Brie overwhelms me. I pick up a ball, weighing it in my hands, wanting to hurl it across the lane just to see what it feels like. Just to see if she'll notice.

But I force myself to take a deep breath in, then a long breath out, and I bowl a spare.

Then, as Tess takes her turn, Dev says something that nearly floors me. "How's your job search coming along, B?"

Tess gasps, guttering her ball. "Wait, what?! What job search? Brie, you're staying here, right?"

The knot in my gut tightens. *It's April.* The feeling of an impending doom scatters through me.

No. She can't leave yet.

How could I have been so stupid? Here I've been, thinking I have all the time in the world for her to open up, to grow to love me, when there's been a ticking clock all along.

How do I show her this is where she belongs? She's so loved here. By her students and their parents, her friends, her family. Me.

I stand and walk to where she's sitting, two seats over. "Brie, I need to talk to you."

"We're bowling," she says, looking anywhere but me.

"Brie," I say again, more insistent this time.

She looks up, and she's completely indifferent. That wall is firmly in place, the last brick laid. I see no way through.

And I've had enough.

"Why did you even invite me tonight?" I grit out.

There! A small break in her facade. Her mask slips for just a second, but it's enough.

"Why did *you* come tonight?" I press. "You clearly don't want to be here."

She looks down at her hands. "I don't know."

Talk to me.

"If this is about a job, I told you, the district is in charge here. It's all very small-town and informal." I can't stop myself from rambling. "The members on the committee rotate, there aren't any set meeting times, it's casual. I'm sure they just haven't gotten around to the hiring process yet. I wasn't named principal until a week and a half before school started."

She holds her hands up and shuts her eyes. "You're right."

For a split second, I think we're getting somewhere.

"I don't want to be here." Her voice has a tinge of helplessness in it, but when she looks up, it's with her flawless mask and impervious wall.

That knot in my stomach? It's burning in a pool of acid now. But I can only watch as she walks past me, exchanges her shoes, and leaves.

I'M numb as I walk back to Gia's beneath the streetlights.

It was Tess's idea to go bowling, part of her self-exploration now that she's out of her ex's clutches. I invited Dev and Sawyer because it sounded like fun at the time.

So what was the trigger? The thing that made it suddenly not such a good idea?

Fucking Bob Ross.

This afternoon, I was folding laundry with trashy TV in the background like normal. But then I glanced down. One eye peeked out at me. I yanked the garment out of the pile of clean clothes. Happy little Bobs everywhere.

Acid pooled in my stomach as I recalled Sawyer's reply when I said Mara gave them to me. *Think if I hint hard enough she'll get some for me next Christmas?*

It was so quick and casual, like he didn't even think about it. Just assumed I'd still be here then. Assumed we'd still be together.

Christmas is seven months away. I'll have a real job by then, at a different school. In a different town.

I swallow, picturing what that'll look like.

After I leave, I'll keep in touch with Mara and Gia like I always have. Dev and I will text on occasion, but hopefully exchange more than memes. I'll talk to Tess every once in a while. And next Christmas, I'll FaceTime Lizzie as she opens the presents I send, as usual.

I blink tears away.

Blue Ridge is charming over the holidays. Even as a kid, I recognized the beauty in the holiday lights, decorated houses, the festive cheer.

But this way is better. I'm used to spending the holidays alone. It's cozy.

It'll be fine.

Better than fine because of how close I've gotten to everyone since coming back home.

Not home. Blue Ridge.

And that's the crux of the problem. That's what Sawyer doesn't get. To him, Blue Ridge has always been, and will always be, home. He doesn't mind the spotlight that follows wherever he goes. He doesn't mind when people look his way. But I'm different. I can't possibly stay here.

Right?

My heart lurches in my chest. Suddenly, the weight of my end-date in this town, the one that's always been the light at the end of the tunnel, feels like it might be an oncoming train.

Even if I stuck around, even if I continued to ignore the job offers I've already gotten from schools hours away—one from two states away—there's so much Sawyer can't possibly understand about me. About my past here.

Because you haven't told him. I physically flinch as that thought enters my brain.

Telling Sawyer about Christopher was a feat for me.

Revealing to Tess what Sawyer did to Squeakers was a breakthrough.

But I could never share with anyone, least of all Sawyer, how unhappy my childhood was, the things I had to keep hidden from the world to ensure Mara's safety and mine. I can't believe he would ever understand, not when he grew up the golden boy—the *prince*. Even if he had his trials, they weren't the same as mine, didn't threaten broader consequences. Back then, people averted their eyes, even as the spotlight followed me. If someone looked close enough, there's a real chance Mara and I would have been removed from our house. Separated.

Even now, the thought is painful to my bone. I shove it away.

This is why I have to leave. Go to an actual city. Somewhere I can blend into a crowd, knowing no one's looking my way. Not because they're avoiding me, but because they simply don't care. That's my happy place, and I'm only out of sorts now because I've been stuck here for far too long.

I increase my pace.

Gia's house is less than a mile's walk, but I'm still surprised how fast I arrive. My steps stutter when I see Mara's car parked in the driveway—she'd come over for a movie night with Gia and Lizzie. A quick glance at my watch tells me Lizzie's been asleep for at least half an hour.

I'm suddenly embarrassed at being back so early. Probably, Gia didn't expect me home at all tonight.

Maybe I could enter through the back? I quickly reject the idea. Gia's open floor plan wouldn't give me any cover anyway.

Listen to yourself. I sound like a paranoid lunatic. What's happening to me? Why am I trying to hide from my sisters now, too?

Determinedly, I march up to the front door and let myself in.

The chatter in the kitchen stops as I step into view. My sisters are standing on opposite sides of the island. Mara, taller than I am with soft curves and sweet features, smiles and waves over her glass of wine. Gia, shorter than me with sharp elbows and a sharper jawline, tilts her head, eyes darting to the clock then back at me.

"Hey, Sis," Mara says. "How was bowling?"

"It was good," I say. "I'm going to bed."

Hurt flashes across my little sister's features, and it echoes in my entire body. My feet automatically take me to her. Old habits die hard.

"I'll hang for a bit," I hear myself say as I sidle up beside her. "What movie did you watch?"

Gia folds her arms, wine glass hanging from one hand. A glint of emerald flashes on the shell of her ear, and I notice it's inflamed.

"Is that new?"

When our older sister continues to, not exactly glare, but watch me with quiet intensity, Mara cuts in. "Lizzie finally decided she wanted her ears pierced. Gia got one too! Sweet, huh?"

"Yeah, super sweet—"

Gia silences me with one arch of her eyebrow.

This is worse than when my fourth grade teacher sent home a note saying I wasn't turning in my homework.

My mouth opens, then closes, then opens again. "What?"

She takes a sip of her wine. "You know what."

A flush crawls up my chest.

Her other eyebrow joins the first.

Instantly, I feel prickles in the back of my nose. "I don't really know," I say, voice lilting up. "I just walked out tonight. I just had to get out of there."

Mara puts her hand on mine, but it's Gia we're both looking at.

"What happened before you walked out?" Gia asks.

Hesitating, I shake my head and say, "You know what? It doesn't matter." I pull in a deep breath and give them a wan smile. "I think I'm just tired. Lots going on, you know?"

Something changes in Gia's eyes. They turn piercing, the way I've seen her do when a kid under her care steps out of line.

"Oh, shit," Mara mutters under her breath, and I couldn't agree more.

It's a Mom Look, but I've never had one directed at me before. Ever. The full force of it has my skin crawling. I turn my head, trying to avoid it, but my eyes stay locked on hers. There's definite witchcraft happening here.

My chest is too small for my pounding heart, and my limbs turn to jelly. Explaining things with Sawyer would mean opening up about *everything*.

The thought makes me nauseous. Neither of my sisters knows the half of what really happened all those years ago. Not with Sawyer, and not what was going on at home. I'd done everything I could to shield Mara from it, and I'd done everything I could to hide it from Gia, ensure she wouldn't abandon the life she was building to come take care of us.

Telling them now will only induce guilt. But not telling them means holding on to all these secrets that have been simmering since I got back to Blue Ridge.

I probably already lost Sawyer tonight, I can't stand to lose my sisters, too.

"Fine," I cry.

My eyes start to sting with unshed tears. Mara pulls out a stool and guides me onto it before pouring a glass of wine and sliding it toward me.

I start from the beginning. The *very* beginning. I tell them about Sawyer's relentless teasing, Squeakers, being taunted during presentations and at lunch, the night he drove me home in the freezing rain, those following few months when my crush blossomed, and prom.

I tell them what it was like at home, Gia's face growing tenser with every word. Bailing Dad out, trying to keep the bills paid, struggling to keep Mara well-fed. How I could barely keep my head above water with all that and school.

Both my sisters look murderous when I move on to Christopher—the clandestine dates across town, the ensuing scandal at Everett Academy, why I moved here mid-year.

Voice shaky with emotion, I skip over to when Sawyer found me in the parking lot during the blizzard. His confession.

Mara belly laughs when I explain how I freaked out at the drive-in because he asked if she'd get him a matching pair of Bob Ross undies.

"It's not funny!"

She bites her lip. "Sorry."

"And tonight," I say, "Dev and Tess were having such a good time. Sawyer was trying so hard to bring me into the fold. But I just couldn't stop thinking how I didn't belong." Sniffling, I add, "I guess it's a good thing I'll be gone in a couple months."

I'm a sponge, wrung out to the last drop, with nothing left to give.

"Bullshit," Gia says.

I nearly spit out the sip of wine I just took. It's the first time she's spoken since I started talking. Mara interrupted with questions, but Gia just listened.

"This is about more than Sawyer." Gia sighs and shakes her head. "I really failed you, didn't I? I never should've left. At the time, I thought I was doing what was best for all of us, but I was thinking about the money. I had no idea about this other shit." Her jaw tenses. "And now I see you haven't moved past any of it."

Her words pinch. "Yes, I have." It was hard, but I pushed past the hurt of childhood.

"Clearly," she says in a flat tone. "Before you came back to Blue Ridge, Mara and I would get some Christmas presents and the occasional phone call. I thought maybe you just didn't want much to do with us." My heart fractures, I never meant for them to think that. "But it's not us. It's *you*."

I make a face. "Isn't it, 'It's not you, it's me'?"

"I said what I said. Just from the short time you've lived with me, I've seen you push everyone away. You don't let people in."

I don't know what to say. Gia's blunt words are razor-sharp.

She gives me an *Am I wrong?* look. "How many friends do you have, Brie? *Real* friends, not acquaintances, people you know, or women you saw regularly at yoga while you were in Indy. *True* friends."

My eyes shoot up to the ceiling to count my innumerable friendships, but she interrupts me.

"It's a rhetorical question, Sis. The answer is zero."

"You don't know that." It comes out petulant and childish.

"What are Dev's hobbies?" It's barely a question.

"Um—"

"How many men has Mara slept with?" Gia interrupts.

"Hey!" Mara says, and Gia gives her a Look that has her slumping sheepishly in her seat. "I guess maybe I could be more open, too."

"Where am I taking Lizzie for spring break?" Gia asks.

My shoulders rise to my ears, both annoyed and embarrassed at the truth of it all. So I'm an introvert, what's the big deal? We're all entitled to our own solitude if we want it. It's not like Gia's any better.

"I'm not done," Gia says. "These are all things *you* haven't asked others. But it's a two-way street. Whenever someone asks you a personal question, your instinct is to deflect at best, run away at worst."

I want to argue, but it would be a lot easier if I hadn't literally run away tonight.

"You don't open up to anyone, you don't let anyone in. We've all just learned to not ask questions of you. But Mara has me, she has Tucker, she has Layla," Gia says, referring to Mara's boyfriend and her friend-slash-boss. "And I have my own people I can rely on. People I trust who I'm open with. Can you say the same?"

This, by far, is the most interesting revelation, and I get a twinge of jealousy. *Who is Gia close to?* If anything, I assumed she was more of a loner than I am.

Before I can ask, Gia plods on. "This instinct to keep to yourself is a bad habit you *must* break if you ever want a relationship. I don't just mean with a partner, but with anyone, including Mara and me. Lizzie. Dev. Tess. Or," she adds slowly, "anyone in the new city you move to."

"Are you really leaving?" Mara asks.

I've already been offered jobs at three schools, and I have more video interviews scheduled.

"It's the plan," I say helplessly.

"Why?" Gia asks. "So you can keep running from the people who love you? So you can have an excuse to never open up?"

I wince.

"If it'll make you happy, we won't stop you," Mara murmurs. "But we just got you back."

"Blue Ridge isn't my home," I tell her. "It never really was."

"That's a choice, Brie," Gia insists. "If you want to make a home here, you fucking do it. Whatever you say, I think you never really left this place. It follows you wherever you go, and you pulling away from everyone shows that." She sighs, face softening. "A lot of people here love you. If you do go, then own it. Don't leave because you're running away."

I think about all the questions I've skirted from Tess. About Sawyer's confession, raw and honest, about his past that I didn't match.

About how I considered sneaking in through the back to avoid my sisters and this exact conversation.

I've been running away since I got here. Since long before that.

Gia drains the last of her wine. "You belong wherever the hell you want." Her tone is fierce, uncompromising.

The truth is, I never felt like I belong anywhere. Growing up in this town wasn't easy. My deepest desire back then was to go unnoticed. By Sawyer, by this town. So I learned to close myself off from everyone.

Mara shifts, and I look at her. She clears her throat,

pushes her wine glass away, then pulls it toward her. Then gazes up at the ceiling.

Before I can say anything, Gia uses her Big Sister Voice. "Mara."

She bites her lip. "Just to, uhm, add to all that . . ."

"Yeah?" I prod.

"I kind of forgot about this, it happened right around when Tucker and I got together. Actually, Tucker and I got together kind of *because* of it, and—"

"What?" I interrupt, impatient.

She inhales. "I ran into Sawyer before you came back into town. Like, a week before."

I make a *move it along* gesture.

"He was in a rare mood, chatty almost. He asked about you, said he thinks about you a lot, that his therapist basically has tomes about you. And he even jokingly, but not jokingly, asked me to pass an apology to you. But then he told me not to bother you, then he asked me about helping out with the school computers."

That explains why Sawyer and Mara were acting strange my first day at the school.

"This was before I came back into town?" I ask, voice breaking.

Mara nods. "Gia's right, Brie. A lot of people here love you, and I think that includes Sawyer. Based on what you told us, I think he always loved you. And I know Blue Ridge was a hard place for you to grow up in, harder than either of us had it" —she gestures between herself and Gia— "but if you want to belong here, there's room for you. We'll *make* room for you. Especially Sawyer."

Something in my brain clicks into place. Christopher tried to hide me, and I never thought twice about it, preferring the anonymity.

But Sawyer is nothing like Christopher. It never crossed Sawyer's mind to hide me. Partly because he simply *can't* hide in this town—it's a given that he'll garner attention wherever he goes—but mostly because he's only had honorable intentions since I got here. He's a genuine, good man.

Tenderness spreads through me, followed swiftly by shame at how I behaved tonight.

Don't all my problems with Sawyer boil down to the publicity of being with him? The itch to slither into the shadows every time we're out together?

That's not what went wrong tonight.

I think back to a couple hours ago. To earlier this afternoon, and Bob Ross. To Sawyer's comment about Christmas. The itchiness I feel every time I think to the future.

At once, it dawns on me: *I don't want to leave.* Something that's been coiled tight in the deepest parts of me begins to unknot.

I've taken it for granted that I *have* to leave. But the discomfort of living in this town is eclipsed by the overwhelming desire to stay with the people I love.

When did that happen?

Cold fear penetrates my bloodstream. What if I *can't* stay? The hiring process isn't up to Sawyer, it's done differently here.

It would break not just my heart, but maybe Sawyer's if I'm forced to leave after confessing I want to stay. I've already caused him too much grief as it is.

I've got to make sure I know what I want before I talk to him. He deserves that much.

"Now," Gia says, pushing herself off the counter. "I belong in bed."

Mara and I watch as she puts her empty wine glass in the sink, recycles the wine bottle, and wipes down the counter with practiced efficiency. Then, she walks around the island to where Mara and I sit.

We swivel on our stools to face her.

Her arms come around the two of us. Simultaneously, we stand, wrapping one another in a tight hug.

"I love the two of you so much," she says into my hair. "And I'm so profoundly proud of you both. You deserve happiness."

Mara sniffles. "I love you both, too." Her voice is a restrained wail. "Thank you for taking care of me."

"I love you too," I ugly-cry into their shoulders.

"THIS THING IS the weight of a thousand suns," Will grunts.

"You're the one who wanted to move it with the drawers in," I heave.

"Because I'm *efficient*." He wheezes the last word as we lower the dresser onto the floor of my bedroom.

"Pretty sure it was because you didn't want to make multiple trips *down the hall*." It comes out testier than I intend.

He shoots me a flat look, and I'm instantly aware of how much time my brother's put into this place with me, and how much my bad mood is not Will's problem.

This whole week, I've stayed away from the teachers' lounge and ignored the urge to text Brie. And you know what that means? It means we've had zero contact.

Because she hasn't sought me out.

She hasn't come to me to explain why she left me at the bowling alley with her friends.

She hasn't come to me to break things off.

And she sure as hell hasn't come to see how *I* feel about any of it.

I've made it all too easy for her to ghost me, and she's, apparently, perfectly happy with that. It's clear now: not only will she never love me the way I love her, but this was never about feelings for her. Probably just convenient sex.

But none of that is Will's problem.

Clearing my throat, I say, "I take it back. Thank you, Mr. Mayor, for your generosity." Despite the title, which I'm required to throw in as his little brother, I mean every word.

He rolls his eyes and heads back to the living room. "I'm just glad you're not out with that Casey girl right now."

I reel. Even with my complicated feelings about Brie, the way he calls her *that Casey girl* rankles. "Her name is Brie."

Will huffs as we lift my headboard and walk it down the hall. "What I mean is, I was starting to worry you were getting attached to *Brie*. I'm glad you're here, doing something that really matters."

I do a double take at Will, shocked by his words. Yeah, this cabin's important to me, but we're talking about a *person*. Maybe I don't matter to her, but she really mattered to me.

Mattered. I roll my shoulders and shake my head. As much as I keep trying to put whatever we had in past tense, it isn't.

Brie still matters to me. One week can't change that.

Voice hard, I say, "I'd like to know what you have against Brie because you sound a little too much like Dad right now."

Will cracks his knuckles, a sure sign he's mincing his words. "I don't have anything against her."

I sense a *but* coming. For the first time, I get the brotherly urge to pummel him right in that pretty-boy face of his, see if I can't knock some of that perfectly-styled hair out of place for once.

He inhales. "But" —I fold my arms and he catches the gesture— "how well do you really know her?"

"Pretty damn well," I sneer.

But it isn't true. She never let me in deep enough to *really* know her, constantly keeping a wall between us.

Fuck. One week is all it took to show how little she cares about me. I've been chasing her this whole time, initiating every interaction between us. But without me prompting it, it's like I don't exist. She'll never be the one to come to me.

Will seems to see right through me. "How well do you know any of the Caseys?"

I frown. What the hell do Brie's sisters have to do with this? "Mara helped with the computers at school. She can be shy, but she's really polite and sweet."

Will levels me with a blunt look like I'm an idiot. "Not the youngest one. The rest of them."

And that's when I know Will's grasping at straws. Without answering, I head back toward the living room to move the rest of the bed frame.

"You know their dad was the town drunk, right?" he calls as he follows me. "Blue Ridge was an eden until he went off the rails, disrupting order, picking fights, making the whole town stink like cheap bourbon."

I whirl around. "What does this have to do with Brie?"

"The apple doesn't fall far from the tree," he says dismissively as he squats to pick up the rest of the bed frame.

I don't move. "You *do* sound like Dad. This is exactly the kind of classist bullshit I thought you were above."

He stands to his full height. I'm bigger than he is by a lot of pounds, but he's taller. He points a stern finger at me. "I'm not Dad, and it's a valid question. You're too young to know it, but he was a hustler and a scammer. Cost the town hundreds of thousands of dollars we never got back. And here's his oldest daughter, a college drop-out living in the most affluent neighborhood, as a single mother? Doesn't add up. Then the middle one's back in town all of a sudden, and has you wrapped around her finger? Does she even know you don't have an inheritance coming your way? Because if not, you might tell her, see how quick she disappears." He sighs. "That youngest one seems honest enough, but I wouldn't trust the others one iota."

Almost all of this is news to me, but it doesn't matter. Protectiveness creeps through me, and not just for Brie. "They have names." It's almost a growl. "And *Gia* is a damn good mother." My voice rises. "She's always the first to volunteer her time. She's the approved pick-up parent to at least five kids who don't belong to her so they have some-place to go when their parents do a double."

This seems to stun him, but only for a second. He scoffs. "Don't start with me on her. You don't see her at the city council meetings. She doesn't exactly support what's good for the community."

"There it is." I squat for the frame, and Will automati-cally does the same. "You don't like that she makes your job harder."

As we heft it back to the bedroom, he says, "That's not it. I don't trust her" —I drop the wood before he's ready, making his next words strained— "and I don't think she came by that house honestly. I mean, do *you* know what she does for a living? And how anyone can entrust their child to her is beyond me. I saw her coming out of the tattoo parlor with her daughter last week."

A burst of anger shoots through me. "You can't seriously think she let Lizzie get a tattoo." God, the insanity of it. "And you can't seriously hold their piece of shit father against those women." I look pointedly at him, willing him to draw the parallels here.

His jaw clenches. "That's different. You and I are nothing like Dad. Gia is basically a tiny version of hers, but sharper in every way. I've seen her hustle, and not that long ago. I know what I'm talking about here. And Brie—"

"Brie's important to me," I interrupt with a rasp. "I don't know if I'm the one for her, but she's the one for me" —my heart stops for an instant. *The one for me*— "and if that's a problem because of some grudge you had against their father, or a crazy conspiracy you have against Gia, then you've got two options: you can keep it to yourself, or I'll see you at the monthly dinners with Dad, and only then."

And I mean it. Regardless of where Brie and I stand, I won't put up with Will's bigotry.

He scrubs a hand over his jaw. "Okay," he grits out. "Where's your screwdriver."

I'm suddenly aware of how fast I'm breathing, that my hands have tightened into fists, that I'm grinding my molars in irritation. Except it's not just irritation at my brother.

What I said is true. Brie is the one. And, what? I'm going to let her ghost me?

No. I love her, but if she can never love me back, if she's willing to just leave, then she needs to say it to my face. There's a limit to my patience, and I'm there. I'm done.

And if she won't come to me, then I'm going to her one last time.

"You know what?" I tell Will, "I've gotta go."

With determination, I stride across the room for my wallet and keys. Next to the front door is the old shoebox I scrounged up while putting the cabin back to sorts. When I found it, I worried what would happen if I gave it to her. It could make or break our relationship.

But now, I'm past the point of worrying.

Will holds his hands up. "Hey, I mean it. I'm sorry."

I turn. "We're fine. But, really, I've gotta go. I have to talk to Brie."

His brow furrows and he uses his thumb to crack the knuckles on the same hand. "All good?"

Rubbing the back of my neck, I say, "I don't know. The silver lining is: if it isn't, I won't force you to get along with Gia."

One eyebrow ticks up. "I don't know what to wish for, then."

"Wish for a close personal relationship with Gia. For my sake."

Will flashes that million-dollar smile everyone seems to love. "I could wish for it all my days, it'll never happen. But good luck anyway."

I'M in the kitchen when I hear a sudden, impatient knock at Gia's front door. She and Lizzie already left for their spring break trip, and it's too late for packages.

My heart starts to pound when I see the outline of a man distorted through the glass of the door. I know just by the way he's standing who it is.

Sawyer.

I haven't spoken to him all week. I should've called, should've sought him out, but I needed time to figure out what I want.

Gia's words got through to me. I do push people away, and I'm scared. I'm scared of wanting him as much as I do, and I'm scared of having to leave before this even begins. I've had two more job offers this week, from prestigious private schools on the opposite end of the country. Nothing from Blue Ridge.

With a deep, fortifying breath, I open the door.

Sawyer isn't smiling, mouth tight, eyes hard. My heart squeezes in my chest. Now I'm scared I missed my chance.

He steps inside, and I'm vaguely aware of him holding an old box, frayed at the edges. I lead him to the living room, neither of us speaking. There's a heavy tension in the air.

"Sawyer." I turn to face him.

But his face startles me. It's ice cold.

My pleas and explanations die in my throat. "Do—do you want something to drink?"

His face grows hard, and I instantly know that was the wrong thing to say.

"I'm done."

I blanch at his words. My heart lurches, and I don't know what to say, how I can fix this.

"I'm done trying to get you to open up to me. I'm done trying to earn your trust."

My breath stutters out as I squeeze my eyes shut, trying like hell to prevent the tears from falling, and wishing like crazy this is just a bad dream. Then I feel his warm hand cup my face. I open my eyes, and all the ice thaws.

He caresses my cheek, holding my gaze. "I'm in love with you, Brie. I love you so much."

His confession steals my breath. I lean into his touch, tell myself there's nothing to be scared of now. But when I open my mouth, everything I have to say bottlenecks at my throat. Where do I begin? And how?

His hand drops, and the ice is back. "Yeah. I'm done."

With that, he shoves the shoebox he was holding at me, and walks out of the room. His footsteps thud as he heads to the front door.

Move, you idiot, he's getting away!

I toss the shoebox, so light it could be empty, onto the coffee table and rush after him, heart in my throat.

He throws open the front door, and we both freeze.

Tess stands there. Her blond locks are out of place, cheeks splotchy from crying. She has raccoon eyes, and her clothes are dirty and ripped in some places.

"Two Emerson Ave," she says.

CHAPTER 46

BRIE

WHEN I HAVE Tess sitting on the living room sofa, exactly where Sawyer ripped my heart in two just minutes ago, I grab the tissues from a side table and put them in front of her. My hand shakes, and I don't know if it's from seeing my friend like this or from the adrenaline of hearing Sawyer's words.

Yeah. I'm done.

He's in love with me.

But he doesn't want me.

I turn around, and Sawyer's gone. Cold panic floods my body.

Then I hear the refrigerator door open. *He didn't leave.*
Yet.

I try to focus on Tess, but all I want to do is follow Sawyer. What would I say to him? My mind races, unable to process everything that happened and is happening. All I know is I don't want him to leave, not like this.

I spent the entire last week processing the conversation I had with my sisters, everything I had to hide growing up. Mara's come over almost every night so she and Gia could help me through it. My relationship with my sisters is better because of it, but there's still so much I need to work on. A week isn't enough to undo lifelong habits.

They've helped me process my reactions to Sawyer, to this *town*. Never in my wildest dreams did I expect any relationship, let alone *this* one. When I returned to Blue Ridge, it was temporary. When I arrived, I hated Sawyer.

Before tonight, I thought I figured out what I wanted. To stay here, with him.

But now? Even when we were younger, at least he showed *feelings* toward me, even if they were the wrong ones. Tonight was different. Sawyer's never been that cold.

Because I hurt him.

My chest pulls tight. I don't want to lose him.

I already have.

I shove the invasive thought away. It can't be true. Not that quickly, not without a fight.

Turning to Tess, I sit next to her and put my arm over her shoulders. Sawyer comes back with a glass of water and the first aid kit Gia keeps under the kitchen sink. He kneels in front of her.

"Tell us what happened," he says, voice so warm for her.

He begins tending to cuts I hadn't noticed on her bare arms and legs, reminding me of the way he cared for me during the blizzard. I blink and focus.

Tess sniffles. "It was CJ. He showed up completely wasted. I opened the door without looking—I was so stupid."

"No," I say vehemently. "This isn't your fault."

Tess hiccups. "He shoved his way in and broke my phone." She lets out a humorless laugh and looks at me. "I was talking to my brother."

Sawyer stands, phone already in hand and shoving it toward Tess. "Dial Nash's number."

She does, and Sawyer steps away, phone to his ear. Even though he's only ten feet away, I want to go to him, stay close.

"What happened?" I whisper.

Tess's eyelashes flutter. "I couldn't get out, so I ran inside. He followed. I made it to my bathroom, and locked the door. He was banging and shouting, then it was quiet for a long time. At least an hour, maybe more." Her voice starts to wobble as Sawyer comes back. "I knew he hadn't left, so I stayed in the bathroom. Then, he started talking to me through the door. Really sweet-like. When I didn't give him the answers he wanted, I swear he was going to break down the door, he was so mad."

I pull in a deep, shaky breath. "How'd you get away?"

"Broke the bathroom window." She laughs, an incredulous, almost prideful laugh. "I just jumped out!" Her voice is high-pitched, maniacal. Then she turns serious again. "I'm so sorry to involve you. I remembered what you said last—last time this happened. I remembered Gia's address. Two Emerson Ave. I didn't know what else to do."

"This was exactly the right thing to do," I tell her.

The doorbell rings again, and Tess lets out a startled shriek.

"It's your brother," Sawyer says.

Tess's eyes go wide. "Oh no, he's too busy to deal with my mess."

What?

As Sawyer leaves to answer the door, I take her by the hand and make her meet my eyes. "Tess, listen to yourself. You've got to let Nash in."

She shakes her head. "But I'm fine." She tries for a smile, and it's nothing short of horrific.

Something weighty falls into place in my brain with a satisfying *click*. Tess has kept a part of herself hidden. Not for the same reasons I've done, but the end result is the same: she's isolated herself from someone who cares about her.

I put a gentle hand on her shoulder. "Tess, listen to me. Nash cares about you. We all care about you. You aren't a burden to the ones who love you. Let him in. He deserves that much. "

My heart lurches as Sawyer's words come back to me in full force. *I love you so much.*

He deserves more, too.

When Sawyer walks back in, Nash Brooks is with him, looking devastatingly handsome in a suit, and like he's out for blood.

Tess flings herself into her brother's arms, and he holds her tight.

"It's going to be okay, Tess." Sawyer's voice holds a certain note to it that sends a shiver down my spine. It's not the same coldness he spoke to me with. It's threatening.

Nash releases his sister. The two men exchange a nod, and turn toward the door.

"We'll be back."

Tess and I run after Sawyer and Nash as they head for the front door, adrenaline coursing through my veins like a bullet.

"What're you going to do?" Tess asks at the same time I say, "Let's call the police!"

The men turn. Sawyer won't look at me, but he answers me. "The restraining order hasn't deterred him."

"We need to have a little chat with him," Nash finishes, looking at his little sister. He gives me a once-over, an acknowledgment of sorts. "We'll be back." His voice brokers no room for argument.

They turn, and pull the door closed behind them with a definite *click*.

I look at Tess. Her expression is a mirror to how I feel. Totally and completely terrified.

"Is your ex dangerous?" I ask.

She shakes her head, voice oddly monotonous at first. "I —I don't know. He's turned into something else over the years, and I really don't know what he's capable of anymore." Her voice grows more frantic. "The people he hangs out with, they aren't good people."

My stomach seizes, and I nearly throw up. What is Sawyer running toward right now?

And will he come back?

That's the question pumping through me, over and over again. Will he come back *to me*?

My nose stings as tears spring to my eyes. I can't believe less than an hour ago he told me he loved me, and I kept my mouth shut, paralyzed.

He left without knowing how I feel.

I want him. Every day, all the time. I want his loving warmth, and his smiles, and his teasing. I want his scent in my nose and his taste on my tongue.

But I can't tell him any of that because he's gone. I clutch the doorframe to hold me up.

It's too late.

I messed up. All because I couldn't bear to show him all of me.

My sob echoes in the entryway.

I would even take his icy tone back, his coldness, if he just makes it safely out of whatever danger he's going into. *Just let him be safe, and I'll tell him everything.*

I only now realize Tess and I are clinging onto each other. As one, we turn and trudge back to the living room. My breaths stutter as I spot the shoebox.

RELEASING MY HOLD ON TESS, I pick up the battered box Sawyer thrusted at me earlier, needing any connection to him.

I blink my tears away to examine it. It's old and badly worn, more tape than cardboard at this point. The faded label says it's a kids' size seven. Carefully, I lift the lid just an inch.

Faded pink peeks back.

I gasp.

It can't be.

I nearly rip the lid off to get at the bulbous mouse.

Squeakers.

She's flatter than she used to be, definitely seen better days. Something like a sob tumbles out of me as I squeeze her to my chest. I drop my head, nuzzling her with my face the way I used to.

Except Squeakers doesn't smell how she used to.

Chlorine and boy smell.

My eyes well with new tears.

Sawyer.

He had to have held Squeakers more than once for his smell to be embedded in her softness. I take in another big whiff, and it centers me. He really did love me. This entire time, Sawyer loved me.

Even when I thought he hated me, he loved me.

And my feelings were always deeper, too. It's why I kept his jacket, snuggled it close to me on nights I couldn't sleep, breathing in his smell when I needed comfort. Even when I hated him, I cared about him.

And now, I love him.

The realization explodes into me like colorful confetti, finding its way into all the nooks and crannies of my being, filling every open space with the words: I love Sawyer.

And I might never get the chance to tell him.

If he comes back to me, I'll tell him everything. All the words I've wanted to say deep down, but couldn't. I'll never hide from him again.

Then what? I move away for a real job?

I squeeze the stuffy to me. Squeakers is the epitome of why I detested Blue Ridge. I *hated* living here. Coming back for a temp job was a last resort to something even worse, and I couldn't wait to leave.

But now, I'm determined to stay.

Tess, whom I'd all but forgotten about, joins me in the living room with two steaming cups of tea, our roles reversed from earlier. Because we're friends. And not just from these awful events that keep pushing us together. I look forward to laughing with her every day at lunch. We've grown to know each other, delicately dancing around the pieces of each other that've been closed off to the world, but finding ways to connect anyway.

"Thanks." I give her a watery smile.

"You looked like you could use it." She sits next to me, warming her hands around her mug. "They'll be okay."

Desperation shoots through me again. "How do you know?" A second ago, she was as devastated as I was, but now she seems so certain.

She nods to Squeakers, still smushed against my chest. "Because you and Sawyer have unfinished business. There's nothing in this world that'll keep him from you."

My lips pull wide like an ugly toad as I wail, "He's done with me."

Tess sets her mug aside and pulls me into a hug. "He's not. He's just upset you're leaving and afraid of losing you. And so am I."

I look at her. "You are?"

She nods. "You're the first friend I've had in forever. And you're leaving us."

I open my mouth to tell her that's always been the plan, but nothing comes out. Gia's words come back to me. *You belong wherever the hell you want.*

For what feels like the millionth time tonight, another piece of me clicks into place. I *do* want to belong in Blue Ridge. I've been here four months, and already I have more of a life here than I ever did anywhere else. Those other cities feel sterile and cold to me now. Blue Ridge has Jolly Jalapeno and festivals and the drive-in and so much I haven't explored yet. I want to eat the apple cider donuts at Maddy's Bakery, go to Tattoo, Brute? to get commemorative ear piercings with my sisters, surprise Gia with the newest romance novel from the Book Nook.

Suddenly, I realize Blue Ridge truly feels like home. I might not like the spotlight, but I've gained more friends than enemies since I've been back. I feel grounded here in a way I don't anywhere else. Here, I have Tess. Lizzie and

Gia and Mara. Even Dev, with his paradoxical amiable detachment.

And most of all, Sawyer. I won't leave him. I just hope he'll still have me.

And I love him, I repeat to myself, so desperate to say those words to him.

CHAPTER 48

BRIE

TESS, Squeakers, and I are curled up under a blanket together, a romcom on TV in the background that was supposed to distract us. Instead, all I can think about is Sawyer and how worried I am. It feels like days have gone by. In reality it's barely been more than an hour. But every minute, every *second* has been an opportunity for me to catastrophize.

A car door slams outside, and we both jump. My heart races me to the door. I don't know what to expect. Ripped clothes? Bloody noses? Black eyes?

But when I yank open the door, they look . . . almost exactly the same as when they left. Not a hair on Sawyer's head is out of place, his flannel sleeves are rolled up to his elbows, and his jeans look as good as ever. Nash's tie is loose around his neck, but I can't remember if it was like that already.

For a long moment, Tess and I stand frozen, staring at them. I'm sure she was expecting the worst right along with me.

Then, at the same time, we jump into their arms. Me in

Sawyer's, her in her brother's. I nuzzle my face into the crook of his neck, guzzling down his perfect scent.

"I'm so glad you're okay," I whisper.

And that's when I realize his entire body is stiff. A two-by-four would be more snuggly. He pats my back once, and I untwine myself from around him, hurt.

His eyes flick down to my hand, where I'm still holding Squeakers. Expression inscrutable, he very intentionally looks away, and a fist squeezes my heart tight.

A hopeless kind of desperation takes hold of me. I need to tell him I love him. I want to shout it at him, but now isn't the time. This isn't about us. My entire body tenses at the effort to hold back the words, to have patience. But I have to tell him tonight. I won't let him leave until I do.

Tess, who knows enough, ushers Sawyer and Nash inside, and I close the door behind them.

Once we're all sitting around the kitchen table with a round of drinks, I can't keep my eyes off Sawyer, willing him to meet my gaze. If he'd just look at me, he'd know how I feel, but he keeps his eyes firmly on Tess.

Tess says, "So?!"

"He won't bother you again." Nash's voice is scratchy, and he takes a sip of his whiskey.

His sandy hair is darker than her bright blond, his square jaw more masculine than his sister's delicate features. But they both have the same full lips, the same blue eyes.

"What—what did you do?" Tess asks.

Sawyer clears his throat. "We made him understand you're not alone, gave him some much-needed rules to abide by. And if he breaks them, he'll regret it."

"It was easy," Nash says, disgust heavy in his voice.

"The little shit doesn't have much fight unless you're small and helpless."

"I'm not small," she pouts, which is true. She has a good half-foot on me.

Nash ignores his little sister and points his finger at her. "If he *ever* bothers you again, contacts you in any way—and I'm talking him or someone on his behalf—you tell us."

In his words, his demeanor, I see the successful lawyer he is. But more than that, I can see how hard he loves. Nash is the kind of man who'd burn the world down to protect the lucky people he cares for. He turns to Sawyer, who nods in agreement.

Nash drains his glass and turns to me. "Brie, thank you for being there for my sister." He stands, and so does Sawyer. "Sawyer. Anything you need, brother. I'm there. Anytime."

Their bro-hug has Tess and I reaching for each other, hugging too, Squeakers still clutched in one hand.

"Alright, I'm ready to get all this behind us," Nash says to Tess. "I know it's spring break. Let's go fill a couple bags with your stuff. I'm bringing you to my place for the week."

I let out a relieved breath, glad she's going to be okay.

Tess nods at her brother then hops to her feet and gives me a giant hug. "Thank you."

I squeeze her back. "I'll be here when you get back."

She rounds the table to Sawyer. He hugs her warmly, lifting her off her feet.

"I'll see you after break," he murmurs. "Be safe."

As we walk to the front door, I duck my head, trying to get Sawyer's attention, to communicate with him that I want to talk, but he dutifully averts his gaze. That desperation from earlier winds its way through me. In a shameless effort to trap him here, I wedge myself in front of him, opening the door for Nash and Tess and blocking his way out with my back squarely to him.

"Bye!" I say, a little too loudly.

"Brie." His voice abrades the back of my neck.

My nose stings as I swing the door closed.

He catches it from behind me, keeping it ajar.

I push harder, trying to shut it.

"*Brie.*"

"No!"

Turning around, my face inches from his, I say it again. "No. Please, you got to say something to me. Please hear me, too." I'm speaking too quickly, breathing too fast. I hold Squeakers up between us. "*Please.*"

MY BRAIN IS CHAOS, a jumbled mess of words, as I lead a reluctant Sawyer up to my bedroom, hugging Squeakers to me. Now that I have his full attention, I want to tell him *everything*. So that when I say those three words, he feels the weight of them. I need him to understand why I've been holding back.

I lead him to the bed, and it takes two tugs of his hand before he sighs and sits down next to me. His body is tight and I can tell, one wrong word and he'll be gone.

My mind scrambles for how to start. How do I tell someone all my deepest secrets? All my fears?

Swallowing, I reach under my bed and pull out my old JanSport. I lay it between us.

He runs a frustrated hand through his hair. "Brie, if this is a walk down Memory Lane, I'm not interested."

When he starts to stand, I reach for his hand. "Please!"

He sits, but he takes his hand back. My chest caves in at the pain of the rejection.

I look down at Squeakers, still in my tight grip. "My mom used to call me her Brie Cheese." My chest fills with love and grief at the nickname. "Everything I had was second-hand from Gia. *Everything*. Except this mouse, and I had her for as long as I could remember."

Sawyer is silent beside me, and I can't look over at him. If I do, I might lose my nerve, and I *have* to be brave. I need to get this out.

"Squeakers was the only thing I had from her when she died. One night, in a drunken rage, my dad threw out *everything* that reminded him of Mom." I still remember the way his eyes landed on Squeakers. The way he stomped toward me. "Gia stopped him before he could take her away from me, and I never let her out of my sight after that. She was always in my backpack, even at school."

Sawyer's indrawn breath is loud, but I keep my gaze firmly on the mouse in my lap.

"Dad wasn't just a stain on the town." I laugh humorlessly. "I mean, to even call him 'Dad' is more than he deserved. He spiraled worse and worse, especially after Gia left. I was trying to take care of everything, basically raising Mara on my own."

Sawyer's big body grows more tense. He shifts, and suddenly he's closer, elbow brushing mine. I shiver at the contact.

"It was all on me. I had to keep everything together without drawing attention because if I didn't, they'd take Mara away. Me too, probably. We'd both go into foster care, get split up." My voice hardens. "There was no way I was going to let that happen. I worked every spare second. I tried to keep up with school. With what Gia sent home, we had just enough to pay the bills and for food."

It's not until Sawyer's hand covers mine that I realize I'm shaking.

"Brie," he chokes out, "I had no idea it was that bad."

I swallow the lump in my throat. "I was always so scared someone would find out. Every time I couldn't pay a bill, every time I had to bail out our dad, I worried someone would figure it out."

Sawyer's thumb traces over my knuckles, but I ignore the sensation, focusing on the words.

"I had to hide everything from everyone, all the time."

This was something Gia, Mara, and I discussed over and over again this past week. I cut myself off from everyone because it was how I operated for so long. It was a survival skill drummed into me at an early age that I'd never let go of. Except now, it was doing damage, hurting relationships with people I love, people I want to let in.

"My dad, our rundown house, my second-hand clothes —I was ashamed of all of it."

"You were a *kid*, Brie." Sawyer's voice holds so much anger that I can't help looking up. His eyes are dark, jaw clenched. "You had nothing to be ashamed of. *Nothing*."

This time, it's easier to hold his gaze. Something about his words take away some of my fear, makes it easier to admit the next part. "I'm still ashamed. It's like when you talked about those sodas at the Chateau Brume picnics. I was embarrassed to tell you I never tasted them because I'd never been to one. My dad would never take a day off drinking to take us to one, and I wouldn't have wanted him to anyway because he would've made a fool out of all of us."

"Christ, Brie. I wish I'd known."

I give him a faint smile. "What would you have done? Nothing. At least not back then, you had your own problems to deal with."

"Fuck that," he spits. "I could've made your life easier, rather than harder. I could've helped you. Instead, I tortured you, made it so even school wasn't a safe place for you." His mouth is a tight slash on his face as he surges to his feet. "I even took the last connection you had to your mom." He jabs a finger toward Squeakers as he starts pacing.

"But you kept her," I say, shoving Squeakers toward him. "You didn't do what your friends wanted because you were too good for that."

He's shaking his head, barely listening. "How the fuck can you even stand to look at me?"

"Because you were going through a lot back then too. We both know that. And . . ." I take a deep breath. "Because I love you."

He stops dead in his tracks, his back to me, shoulders tense. "What did you just say?"

"I love you."

When he turns, I see the hope on his face beneath the outrage. "You shouldn't . . ."

"Doesn't matter," I tell him. "It's done. You showed me who you are, and I love you for it. My whole life, I was afraid of letting someone get too close. I was afraid of needing someone. But, Sawyer, I'm not afraid anymore." The second the words come out, I know it's true. I'm not afraid of this.

He hesitates for the briefest of moments before stomping to me and dropping to his knees, bowing his head so his forehead rests on my lap. I lay Squeakers on the bed and bury my fingers in his hair. He shudders.

After a moment, he looks up, eyes rimmed red. "I love you, too. You have no idea how much. I will spend the rest of my life showing you every day just how much I love you." His eyes dim. "And how sorry I am."

My fingers flex, tugging his hair. "Don't. Let it lie. The truth is, I always knew who you were deep down. I always had feelings for you. A part of me always loved you."

He shakes his head. "Don't say that," he whispers. "You don't have to say that, Brie."

"It's true." I reach for the JanSport. "Let me show you."

CHAPTER 50
SAWYER

AS SHE UNZIPS THE BAG, the one I recognize as hers from school, gray fabric appears from inside. It's so familiar.

But it's impossible.

She reaches in and pulls the garment out all the way. My mouth drops open.

My letterman jacket. I was sure she trashed it years ago.

I can't breathe as I watch her bring it to her nose and visibly inhale. "It doesn't smell like you anymore," she says. "But it did for a long time. I kept it under my bed, and on the worst nights, I'd reach for it. It helped me sleep. It's the only thing I kept with me from my life in Blue Ridge."

My heart stutters in my chest, a dull ache forming there.

What she said before was true. This is the evidence. She really did have feelings for me, even back then. Even when I was my worst.

"Why?" I croak.

"Like I said," she says, voice breaking, "I always knew there was more to you, that it was all an act, that you were going through something, too. Maybe because I could see the signs, because of what I was going through." She clutches the jacket tighter. "And this helped me through it all. It was a reminder of the real you."

I shake my head. "What I went through was nothing like what you did." I look at the mouse—Squeakers—laying on her bed. "But I get it. Squeakers helped me through stuff too."

When I look back on my behavior, it makes me sick. I can't believe she could have seen any good in me, even now, let alone back then. I don't deserve her. I don't deserve her forgiveness.

But I'm going to take it because I won't be without her anymore. I'll just make damn sure she's taken care of from now on. I want her to always feel loved and secure, even when she distances from me again, closes off because of some trigger. Now that I understand the reason, I'll be prepared to get us through it, I won't lose my patience.

I'm going to keep her.

As if she can read my thoughts, she presses her palm to my heart. "You're too hard on yourself. You can't punish yourself for not suffering the same way." She pauses. "That night in the rain, when it was just the two of us, I saw the real you, the one I *knew* existed before I even had proof. The you that I had feelings for. It's the same you as now, and I love you."

My whole body quakes at those words.

"Say it again," I rasp, stepping into her touch.

She looks up, biting back a smile. "I love you."

Finally, I let myself touch her. Cupping the back of her neck, I bring her toward me until my lips almost graze hers. "I love you, Brie."

My lips brush hers, and an electric current moves through me.

CHAPTER 51

SAWYER

SHE LOVES ME.

The jacket falls to the floor, and her hands dive into my hair, scratching lightly at my scalp. I pull her tighter to me, one hand splayed on the small of her back, the other cupping her neck, angling her so I can take her mouth deeper. When she moans, I feel it in my soul. Her pleasure is my pleasure. All I want is to give her more.

I graze my nose along her throat, up to her ear, breathing her in.

A shiver runs through her, goosebumps forming on her neck. I nip at them. Her pleased little whimper is like a dopamine hit straight to my veins.

I bring my mouth to her ear. "I love your sounds."

She pulls back, rich brown eyes searching mine. "I love *you.*"

My heart is too big for my chest. I'll never tire of hearing that. I drop my hands to cup her ass and lift her. She wraps her legs around me like they belong there. When we pull apart, our eyes meet. Her mouth widens into a smile, happy and sweet.

I can't help my own grin. "I'm so fucking happy, Brie."

"Me, too." She threads her fingers through my hair.

We're still smiling when we draw together. Our teeth clack, making her laugh. Warm honey isn't sweeter.

I turn and lay her gently on her bed, planting wet, sucking kisses down her neck, her collarbone, where her shirt cuts into her cleavage. She rewards me with more moans, more whimpers, her body quivering at every touch— *my* every touch. I move down to her belly, lifting her shirt, making her squirm and gasp as I tickle her with my lips, teeth, tongue, the stubble on my cheeks.

Before I can move lower, she tugs me up, circling her legs around my waist again.

I try frowning, but I can't wipe my smile completely. "I have important work to attend to."

"You have important work up here," she says against my jaw. "Stay with me."

She rocks her hips beneath mine, eyelids fluttering when she gets the friction she needs. I trace my fingertips lightly up and down her side, tracing her bra, teasing her nipples, watching heat and need and satisfaction flow over her features. I'd be happy to just do this the rest of the night, watch her take pleasure from me however she chooses, but I know she's going to want more.

I try rolling off, give my hand room between us, but her legs are like a vise.

"I don't have any condoms," I say.

She bites her lip, a wicked gleam in her eye. "You told me you're clean . . ."

Time stops. During the blizzard, I told her I was clean, an off-hand comment to give her peace of mind.

"That's true," I say.

Her nails scrape down my neck. "I'm clean, too. And I'm on birth control."

But blood surges to my cock at her implication. "I'm going to need you to be more explicit, honey."

She rocks her hips, shudders, and pulls my face down to hers. "I want you to come inside me, Sawyer. No barriers."

My hips jerk involuntarily, making her laugh.

I press my forehead against hers. "I love when you talk dirty."

But it's more than that. It's the meaning behind her words, the trust.

Her cheeks turn pink, and I love that too.

We're in no hurry. We undress each other slowly. I take my time caressing, teasing, kissing, drinking in her reactions, savoring every sound. When the duvet's thrown off the bed and we're naked, lying side-by-side tangled in each other's warmth, it feels like it did during the snowstorm. Like we're the only two people on Earth. I could gaze into her eyes for an eternity, memorizing every detail, and it still wouldn't be enough. We've been naked before, but not like this, armor set aside. Brie isn't holding anything back. Just when I thought I couldn't love her any more, my love for her grows.

I grip her thigh, pulling it up to my hip. "You're so soft."

She drags her hand over my chest, a corner of her mouth tilting up. "You're so hard."

My hand trails toward her warm center. I cup her gently, groaning at the feel of her. "You're so wet."

Her fingers blaze a path downward, finding my cock with her silky palm. She grips me loosely and pumps upward before focusing on the head and spreading my precum over the crown. She gets a goofy grin and says, "You're so wet."

A laugh bursts out of me, and I crush my mouth to her

smiling one. It only takes a second before she's kissing back in earnest. She tightens her hold on my cock and gives me shallow strokes, making my laugh die in my throat, replaced by a low, animalistic groan.

I never dreamed I could have all of Brie like this, where she's sweet and funny and sexy all at the same time. Her complete self.

This is what it means to make love, to be with the right person.

As if she can read my mind, Brie says, "It's real. This is love."

I shake my head and begin rubbing tight, slow circles over her clit. "I can't believe how lucky I am right now."

"I'm the lucky—*ooh*." Her sentence is interrupted by her own moan when I slide a finger inside, hitting her G-spot. There's no resistance.

"Jesus, I love that you're ready for me."

"Always," she breathes.

"This is new for me," I say. "I've never gone without a condom before."

"Same," she says.

Wonder courses through me, that she wants this with *me*. It hits me all over again, how incredible and rare a love like this is, how we almost missed it.

I ease my finger out and line myself up at her entrance. "Good?"

"*Yes*." She's impatient now, and affection burns in my chest. I rub the head of my cock over her, teasing her clit. "*Sawyer.*"

I shudder at the way she says my name, throaty and needy, like I'm the only one who can give her what she needs. Gently, I push her onto her back and in one steady move, press into her wet heat. I groan, and her eyes roll to the back of her head.

When I've buried myself to the hilt, I grind myself into her, watching her face as I give her clit friction. Her hands come up to clutch my biceps, looking small.

"I feel you," she sighs. "I feel *everything*."

"Me too," I mutter. I've never been this close with someone, able to feel every ridge, every tremor so perfectly. Knowing the same is true for her weaves arousal and desire through me.

I pull out almost all the way before coming home again.

"It's *never* been like this," I rasp.

Her mouth opens on a silent gasp, only single, unintelligible syllables escaping. A moment later, her walls squeeze, threatening my early release. Every muscle in my body tenses in an effort to hang on, give her what she needs, before I lose my mind completely.

It takes only a few more pumps. She quakes around my cock, body shivering beneath me as her fingernails dig into my arms. Her eyes are locked on mine. I cup her face and drag kisses along her jaw as she comes harder than any before.

When she stops shaking, she fists a hand into my hair, tugging until I meet her eyes. My thrusts grow erratic and jerky, control slipping as I give myself over to pleasure.

"I" —it's a whimper, and she tries again— "I love you."

Those three words from her mouth make it impossible for me to hold back anymore. I drive myself into her again, basking in the way her walls continue to squeeze me tight. I spill into her with a shudder, groaning into her mouth. She moans my name. Another shiver runs through her, walls clenching tight as a second release washes over her.

"I love you," I exhale into her neck as my hips slow to a gentle rock. "I love you."

We're both breathing heavily as I lie on top of her. I'm still inside her, and even though we're both sated, it feels so good. Neither of us moves for a long time.

"Did you swim today?" she asks after a while, kissing my neck.

"First thing this morning, why?"

"I love the way you smell."

Huffing into her neck, I say, "I love the way you smell. Pear and citrus." I nuzzle into her more and inhale. "And sweat."

A trickle of our mingled arousal drips out between us.

"The sheets are getting wet," she says.

"Let's run a load of laundry before we leave in the morning," I say, still not moving.

"Where are we going in the morning?"

"Home."

A FEW WEEKS LATER, my cheeks hurt from smiling as I drive to my job interview for . . . my job. It's the full-time position for the third grade class I've been subbing for at Blue Ridge Elementary.

Almost everything has fallen into place since that night with Squeakers and the letterman jacket.

After spring break, Tess came back from Nash's happy and confident. Gia insisted Tess stay at her house for now because "I have the room, and there's no need for you to rush your apartment hunt and end up somewhere you aren't happy."

Lizzie loves having her former teacher as a roommate.

Sawyer and I had a do-over bowling night with Tess and Dev, who surprised us all by winning.

And, I've spent almost every spare second with Sawyer since spring break, kissing, laughing, and making plans for our future together. He asks me to officially move in with him at least twice a day, just because he likes hearing me say yes.

My job status is the only question mark on my life right now, but this interview is going to solve that.

I'm still grinning wide as I park my car and enter the quiet building where the offices are for the higher ups in the district.

Even as the receptionist doesn't smile back.

Even as the air pressure drops when I walk into the meeting room.

And even as I take in the five rigid faces frowning down at me. Two of them I don't recognize, but the ones I do turn my blood to ice.

They sit behind a long table on the dais, raised just high enough that I have to tilt my head back to meet their stern eyes. There's a single metal folding chair in the middle of the room, facing them.

Suddenly, I'm back at Everett Academy, called in to speak to the board after rumors started spreading.

How could I have been so stupid? I was so sure, so absolutely certain, this was just a formality. Even right now, a shadow of that grin lingers, though my brain screams, *ABORT! ABORT!*

I want to cringe at how I practically skipped into the building, so confident, just a minute ago. This is no interview. Did the woman on the phone yesterday even use that word? My mind races, trying to remember.

No one speaks. The only sound in the room is the second-hand ticking on the clock to my right. Heart thudding, I take in all the faces. A rock sinks into my stomach when I realize who three of them are.

Mrs. Beaufort.

Judge Beaufort.

Ted Strong, the ex-mayor and Sawyer's dad.

I know from Sawyer this county operates differently

than anywhere I've worked before. The schools here are run under the oversight of a small committee, a rotating group of so-called "pillars of the community." I hoped for volunteers like Sadge Brown, the former principal, and Justin Clarke, an ex-EMT. General do-gooders who want what's best for the town. But this? This is my worst nightmare coming to life.

Mr. Strong doesn't deign to look at me when he says, "Do you know why we called you here, Ms. Casey?"

What did Geri say when she called? I skim the contents of my memory.

I wipe my palms on my skirt, swallowing the tight knot in my throat. "I'm here regarding my employment status."

Mrs. Beaufort puckers her lips in distaste.

"Very good," Mr. Strong says indulgently, like I'm a very slow, very dumb child.

The woman I don't recognize, Geri Belinger probably, speaks next. "I called you in today for a formal . . . review. Take a seat."

Itchy, burning shame rises, like I've just been caught cheating on a test. This is exactly how it felt at Everett Academy.

I step forward and do what I'm told, just like I did last time.

The metal is cold through the fabric of my suit.

"Ms. Casey," Judge Beaufort begins. I crane my neck to meet his eyes. "I see you applied for this position back at the end of December, and have filled the role as substitute for the same class since January. How long have you been a teacher?"

Okay. So far so good. I can answer this.

I open my mouth, but Mrs. Beaufort cuts in before I can speak.

"This seems to be a pattern for you, does it not, Ms. Casey?"

"A pattern?" I squeak.

"Entangling professional responsibilities with personal . . . desires." She hisses the last word like it's dirty.

I blanch. She might as well have asked, "How long have you been whoring?"

This is *exactly* like what happened at Everett. And I'm all alone, just like I was then.

When I don't answer, Mr. Strong finally looks at me expectantly, as if Mrs. Beaufort's question was perfectly reasonable.

I lick my lips. "What is this, exactly?"

Mr. Strong laughs, like I'm just too funny. "Assessing your fit as a teacher here, of course."

The man I don't recognize says, "Someone has been pushing very hard for your full-time hire."

Looking at me over his glasses, Mr. Strong adds, "We, however, have several concerns. Indeed, this committee has reservations over your fitness as a substitute."

A black hole forms in my chest, eating at me from the inside. I'm not here to get a job for next year. I'm here to get fired from the one I have now, the temporary position that doesn't even require a teaching license.

What am I going to tell Sawyer? My sisters? Lizzie?

"Are the rumblings true, Ms. Casey?" Judge Beaufort asks. "That you had an affair at your previous school, and the same is occurring here?"

Like an excited child, Mrs. Beaufort says, "It's true! I saw it myself, in public in front of everyone. Absolutely disgraceful."

How could I have been so reckless? I can't believe I thought Sawyer was protecting me by making a show of us together that day at the festival. Of course that wouldn't matter, I was always going to be the bad guy here.

They were never going to give me a chance.

While Mr. Strong gives a dissertation about professionalism, my guilt and shame morph into anger, indignation, and the pure euphoria that comes with no longer giving a fuck what these people think of me.

They have no bearing on the way I live my life anymore. I have no one to keep safe except myself now, and this right here is the worst they can do to me.

No teaching job? Fine, I'll work at the damn diner again if I have to.

Slut shaming? No problem. If I had a scarlet *A*, I'd pin it on myself.

I won't run away again, not because of them. I found where I belong, and I'm staying right here. With Sawyer. With my friends and family. All the people who love me. And I can't wait for these jerks to see how happy I am.

". . . completely against community standards," Mr. Strong continues. "You can understand why we'd be concerned about someone from your family teaching the impressionable youth here."

Mrs. Beaufort eagerly chimes in, "We really should have known better from the beginning. I did warn that committee it was a bad idea to take a chance on a Casey."

Mr. Strong nods gravely. "It's a shame none of us were on it at that time." His eyes cut to me. "We aren't finished. Sit down."

"Why?" I half-laugh. "Clearly, you've already made up your minds about me. Why even invite me here in the first place?"

"No need to be aggressive," Mr. Strong says.

"No need for the misogyny," I lob back. "You said it

yourself, Mrs. Beaufort, you knew from the beginning you didn't want me here. Was there anything I could have done to impress you?" I scoff. "Doubt it. I want this job. I'm damn good at it. But you have this weird vendetta against me, a bias that I don't deserve and that you'll never be able to look past." I point up at the committee. "You are doing the youth of this community a disservice. *You.*"

I take in Mrs. Beaufort's stunned, puckered face, and Mr. Strong's look of disapproval. Then spin around and walk out.

CHAPTER 53

SAWYER

TODAY IS THE BRES JAMBOREE, and the petting zoo I secured for it is a hit. There are bunnies, pygmy goats, chicks, ducklings, and a baby pig. I promised Brie to get extra cuddles from all of them for her while she's at her interview. I had Señora Martinez get video evidence as proof.

"Remember not to get too close to the animals' behinds," I tell the new group of kids as they walk into the pen.

"Because of poop!" Tori, a kindergartener, yells, delighted at herself.

"That's right," I sigh, "because of poop."

"Hi, Mr. Mayor!" kids shout.

Will said he'd make his appearance later this afternoon. I turn around to rib him for not resisting the baby animals, but the words die in my throat. He's red, something close to distress on his face, as he strides swiftly over.

"You aren't answering your phone," he huffs, ushering me away from tiny ears.

I sweep my hand at the Jamboree. "We've been here. What's going on?"

He cups my shoulder. "I'm not Dad."

"You having a stroke? What's going on?" I repeat.

"I don't hate your girlfriend," he says.

I poke his face. "Do you feel any numbness?"

He swats my hand away. "I just found out the school district, they're having a special committee meeting right now."

Even with Will's agitation, my chest inflates at the mention of Brie's interview. "I know."

He shakes his head. "You don't understand. Dad's on it. *Both* Beauforts. I don't know how they managed it, but they—"

Brie. She's all alone with those vultures.

I don't wait to hear another word as cold panic propels me in the direction of the parking lot.

"Cover for me," I shout over my shoulder.

"Here!" Will shouts. "My car's faster!"

He doesn't have to add that no one pulls over the mayor's car.

I turn around in time to catch his keys, and spot his Audi on the curb just ahead.

It's a thirty minute drive to the building.

I get there in seventeen.

I SHOVE into the ladies room, throw open a stall, and promptly vomit. The retching sounds echo off the tiles.

How do I keep surprising myself? Every time I think I've learned a lesson, I prove myself naive all over again. It's like I learned nothing from what happened at Everett.

Then again, pride thrums deep in my chest at the way I stood up for myself back there. I never would've said those things six months ago.

When my body has calmed down, I flush and go to the sink to rinse my mouth. I glance at the mirror, startling at my appearance. Smudged eyes, clammy, pale skin, hair sticking to my forehead.

"What a mess," I mutter, tying my hair back and splashing cold water on my face.

What am I going to do? I don't regret telling the committee off, but now that my adrenaline's faded, the stark reality of the situation hits me. I have student loans. A car payment. *Hunger.* Working at the diner is not a viable option. I need a real job, one with benefits and vacation days.

It's an equation with no solution. I'm not qualified to do anything except teach. The committee won't let me teach here in Blue Ridge. And I won't leave Blue Ridge.

I swipe all these worries into a drawer in my mind and lock it. One obstacle at a time.

With a paper towel, I dry my face and take another look in the mirror. At least I resemble a human being again. Buttoning my jacket, I square my shoulders, lift my chin, and walk out of the bathroom, determined to stride straight for exit. I have to pass the meeting room to get there, and I refuse to let those bloodsuckers see me upset.

Halfway down the corridor, I stop short at a familiar, deep voice.

Sawyer.

He's come for me.

I can't hear what he's saying, but his tone is serious and urgent. With quick steps, I ease closer, careful my heels don't click.

Someone else speaks, Mr. Strong, I think.

"Granted," Sawyer's words are audible now, "that makes it impossible for me to recommend Ms. Casey for a permanent position . . ."

What?

My heart stops, and a roaring in my ears blocks out everything else. A stinging sensation starts at my chest, spreading through my limbs. Did I think being on trial in front of the likes of Mr. Strong and Mrs. Beaufort was my worst nightmare? I was wrong. *This* is. Sawyer taking me in, letting me fall for him, only to blast me like this.

He let me believe I was worth loving, that Blue Ridge was somewhere I could belong. But here he is, doing it all over again, saving face by putting me down.

Tears fill my eyes as I hurry for the door. I'm taking the

steps two at a time when a shock of understanding, overwhelming in its intensity, forces me to stop, nearly doubling over.

This instinct to flee has controlled me my entire life.

It had me dashing down those big, marble steps of Everett Academy.

It had me leaving Blue Ridge behind all those years ago.

It had me running away from prom.

It kept me from relationships, and love, and happiness.

And I'm doing it all over gain, reverting to the same instinct.

Not anymore.

I *know* Sawyer. He wouldn't do that to me, not again. Instead of assuming the worst from the tiny snippet I heard, I need to talk to him.

Whirling around, I stomp up the steps and into the building.

Sawyer's coming out of the meeting room. When he spots me, emotion spills over his face in waves. Relief, concern, love.

His arms open to me, and I fill them without hesitation.

"I didn't know," he says. "I wouldn't have let you come alone if I knew what this was."

"It was bad," I tell him.

His brows pinch. "I know. I was just in there."

I can't help asking, "What'd you tell them?" Heart pounding, I add, "I heard you say you couldn't recommend me."

He nods. "I told them that as principal, I couldn't recommend you. I was up front about our relationship, which is a conflict of interest."

Warmth spreads in my chest. Of course he was, because he's never tried to hide me.

His arms circle my waist. "I also told them they'd be foolish not to do everything in their power to keep you. That you're one of the most passionate teachers I've ever seen. You're great at what you do, and the parents and students love you."

I give him a sad smile. "I'm still not getting the job."

He rubs the back of his neck. "It's that busybody, Beaufort. She saw us that day and got to my dad. But we can figure this out. This isn't how public schools should be run. We can fight it."

I look up at him. "You sound confident."

He grins down at me. "I'm the Prince of Blue Ridge. Might as well wield that power for good."

Laughing into his chest, I notice his tie for the first time, red with adorable mice and cheese. How could I have ever doubted him?

The door to the meeting room creaks open, and we turn to see his dad walking out. "Sawyer, I'm not done with you."

With his arm slung over my shoulders, Sawyer turns us away without a word.

"Sawyer," his dad says, warning in his tone.

My boyfriend guides us to the door, and we step into the sunshine together.

"Why do you have Will's car?" I ask.

Mr. Strong's voice bellows Sawyer's name from behind us.

Sawyer says, "I'll tell you at home, honey."

CHAPTER 55

EPILOGUE

"YOU'RE GOING to have to get along with her after all," I tell Will when I catch him sneering at Gia from across my cabin.

For her part, she seems oblivious to Will as she acts like a Party Mom, gathering used napkins and discarded plates.

It's officially summer break. This semester was such a whirlwind, and we have so much to celebrate, it felt right to throw a party.

The day after the special committee meeting, Brie got a call from Geri Belinger offering her the full-time position. Mrs. Beaufort and my dad were alone in voting against Brie. Geri was appalled by the way she was treated and liked the way Brie stood up for herself. Walter Lemons, the fifth on the committee, was persuaded by what I had to say about her. And Judge Beaufort, judicious as he is, wanted evidence our relationship was affecting her job, since that was the basis for his wife's vote. He had his court clerk call every single family with a student in Brie's class. The raving reviews convinced him she's an asset.

"Leave it, Gia," I call. "Go get yourself a drink."

She lifts a challenging eyebrow at me as she reaches for another plate, and I chuckle.

"Pretty sure she's not used to being told what to do," I mutter to Will.

"Sounds right," he mumbles into his drink.

Normally, I'd push him on this, but this isn't the time or the place. Besides, he gets points for finding me at the Jamboree that day.

I leave him to stew and look for my girlfriend. My cabin's packed. Lizzie and Finn Santos, another rising third-grader whose parents work at the school, tuck and roll around furniture, spying on adults. Teachers and staff from school mingle. Ethan walked in with Abbi not that long ago, and I saw Tess's blond ponytail bobbing over the crowd at some point. Nearly everyone Brie and I care about is here.

The front door opens, and in comes Mara, Brie's younger sister, with Tucker, her firefighter boyfriend. She smiles like I'm just who she wanted to see.

"Hey," I say.

I give her a friendly hug. Tucker and I shake hands as he's immediately drawn into conversation with Señora Martinez behind us. He keeps his pinkie linked to Mara's.

"I have something for you," she says, holding up a gift bag.

"You didn't have to," I say. "This isn't a house warming party."

She thrusts it toward me. "This isn't a house warming gift."

I eye her suspiciously before reaching in. My hand closes on something soft and rolled up. I pull it out. A pair of boxers unfurl, Bob Ross smiling proudly at me from every inch.

"Welcome to the family," she grins. "I'm not sure Gia wears hers, but we all have a pair."

Her words hit me hard. We *are* family. Because even though Brie and I have only been together a short while, we're forever. There's no doubt about that anymore.

"Thank you," I laugh, giving her another hug, the kind a brother might give a little sister. "I was hoping for these at Christmas."

She beams. "I couldn't wait that long." She lowers her voice to a stage whisper. "But I have another idea for Christmas."

"Oh, yeah?"

"I hope everyone likes Fred Rogers as much as Bob Ross." She winks just as Tucker tugs at her pinkie, folding her into whatever he's talking about with Senora Martinez.

"Thanks, Mara, I love them," I holler, and drop the bag off in my room before hunting for Brie again.

"Seen Brie?" I ask Ethan quietly as Abbi and Nash chat politely. Tess's brother is in the process of moving to Blue Ridge this weekend, so I appreciate him making an appearance.

Ethan shakes his head.

"Do you have lots of friends here from school?" Abbi asks Nash.

He tips his head toward me and Ethan. "I'd call these guys friends, but not really, no. I only lived in Blue Ridge for part of high school. What about you?" he asks her. "If you were away for ten years, was it hard to come back?"

Abbi smiles warmly at Ethan. "Easiest thing I ever did. Besides, Ethan's sisters, my two best friends, live here still. And more people than I thought stuck around or came back."

Ethan frowns down at his wife. "Like who?"

"Like Roxy. Kira."

Nash shudders.

"What was that?" Abbi laughs.

"Just a pavlovian response to that name," Nash says.

"What, Kira?" I ask, and he does it again, making us all laugh.

"There was a Kira at law school with me," he explains. "People talk about the devil like it's a man, but it's not. Satan is a woman, and her name is Kira."

Abbi's in stitches. "Not this Kira, she can be intense and competitive, but she's also the sweetest. You'd like her."

Nash shakes his head. "Better to just keep a safe distance from anyone with that name."

Ethan rolls his eyes. "Wuss."

"What is this, seventh grade?" Nash says.

"If the shoe fits," Ethan shrugs.

"No pressure," Abbi says to Nash. "But once you're settled, we'll have a night out, you can meet some people, make some friends. And if one of those new friends happens to be named Kira Mehr, then"—her eyes widen—"What? What's wrong?"

"Kira . . . Mehr?" Nash says. "Kira *Mehr*?"

"Yeah," Abbi says, drawing out the word.

"Fuck me," he mutters.

I shake my head and walk away, searching for Brie again. Dev walks through the front door, and we nod our hellos from across the house. Lizzie barrels into me, wide-eyed.

"I was never here," she whispers, before throwing herself over the couch.

Finn, her classmate, comes out from behind the kitchen island, Nerf gun at the ready as he searches for, presumably, Lizzie.

There's only one other place Brie could be.

It's only the start of June, but the heat and humidity is oppressive when I walk out onto the expansive back porch. Brie stands beneath the ceiling fan, across from the still-unused fireplace. The sun shines on her through the skylight, and I'm struck again by how beautiful my girl-friend is, and how lucky I am.

"I was looking for you," she says accusingly.

Stepping toward her, I say, "I was looking for you."

She looks up at me, unamused. "How come when I wanted nothing to do with you, we ran into each other constantly—"

"But now that we're together, we lose each other in our own house?"

Her cheeks color just like they always do when I call this cabin *ours*. "Yeah."

I wrap my arms around her, kiss her on the head, inhaling her pear and citrus. "It doesn't matter," I say.

"No?"

"Nope. I found you, didn't I? I'll always find you."

"I believe that."

She kisses me, then turns in my arms so we can look in at the party, her back to my front.

"I can't believe I was planning to be gone by now," Brie sighs.

"Me neither," I whisper, squeezing her close. "You belong here."

We watch our family, friends, and colleagues glow with the jubilee only summer seems to bring about. There's a distinct feel to summer in Blue Ridge. The town is lighter, the streets more alive, hiking trails and creeks and Shady Lake are busy with familiar faces.

"What do you say we host this party every year?" I ask her.

"Love that idea," she says.

I squeeze her to me. "The first of many traditions for us."

"Speaking of which," she says coyly, "I might have another new tradition for us tonight. In private."

Chuckling into her neck, I say, "Can't wait."

Later that night, when everyone's left and the house is clean, I find Brie on the back porch again. It's not as muggy as the sun sets. The buzz of crickets and katydids mingles with the gurgle of the creek. She's wearing one of my flannel shirts, hair in a messy bun.

I love being with her like this, comfortable and at home together.

Her eyebrow ticks up when I walk out, holding two glasses of chilled white wine.

She bites back a laugh. "Since when do you wear a bathrobe?"

I put the glasses on the table in front of her. "Since now." I untie the belt, and the sides of the robe fall open, revealing my new boxers.

Her head tips back on a laugh. She stands and begins to unbutton the flannel. It's not the reaction I expected, but with Brie, I can be ready to go in seconds.

She flicks the last button open.

And Bob looks up at me from her crotch.

This is the Brie Casey I always wanted to get to know. The one who's unabashedly, unapologetically herself. Who will stand here, on our back porch, naked except for the sleeves of a flannel and a pair of gag panties. Who makes me want to laugh and tackle her onto the furniture at the same time.

I close the distance between us, cup her face with both hands. "I still can't believe how lucky I am. After all the mistakes I made with you."

She shakes her head. "Sometimes I think we needed the bad to make the good so great. Besides," she adds, pulling back and pointing to my crotch, "there are no mistakes. Just happy accidents. I think the picture we're painting together is beautiful."

The End

If you enjoyed *The Principal Problem*, I'd love if you'd leave me a review on Amazon! Reviews help other readers find books they'll love.

Want a steamy Brie and Sawyer bonus scene?
Visit:
https://books.siennamillsromance.com/briebonus
or scan the QR code below:

Want Mara and Tucker's short story (which includes her conversation with Sawyer before Brie came back to town)?
Visit:
https://books.siennamillsromance.com/betterlate
or scan the QR code below:

THE BLUE RIDGE SERIES CONTINUES

My old law school rival just moved to my small town... and now he's my fake fiancé. But ***For the Record, We're Faking It***.

Nash's book is next!

Coming Summer 2026

ACKNOWLEDGMENTS

Matt. There is no one more kind and caring, no one more thoughtful and considerate, no one more fun and hilarious. I have stomach muscles because of all the times you've made me laugh in our nearly two decades together. I live my best life because you do everything in your power to make sure of it. I'm the luckiest person on Earth to have ended up with you; there's no one better. I couldn't do any of this without you, thank you. I love you.

E & M. I'm so proud of each of you. Mama loves you.

Ava Pine & Jackie.

Ava for insisting I "push the scene," "let things breathe," and "make you *feel* it."

Jackie, for our monthly croissant-fueled talk-throughs and your frogs, which were the encouragement I needed to keep going.

Thank you both for reading Every. Single. Draft. Including the deleted ones. All of them.

Thank you also for all the comments, discussions, hype-ups, talk-downs, and hours and *hours* of tolerating me. This book wouldn't be what it is without the two of you or your unwavering belief in it (and me). Not to make every other writer jealous, but this is the *best* writing group ever to exist. I'm honored to be included. (And you can never leave me.) I look forward to each of your debuts.

Ana Kirk Shaw, thank you for being my unwitting mentor, reading my completed manuscript, and for writing the most swoon-worthy MMCs.

Cindy, it's always a pleasure to discuss books with you, but it was an honor for you to be the first to read this completed one. Thank you for your insightful thoughts, and thank you for your trademark geniality every time I complained.

Lois, I can't say I know a lot of septuagenarians who read sexy romance as voraciously as you, but I'm glad we found each other. Your feedback is invaluable.

Scott, thanks for always being available, always providing great advice, and always obliging me with your knowledge of Comedy, Good Game, and Attraction. Some of my favorite memories of writing are from the endless hours of talking through that would-be romcom with you. It'll be published someday...

Jen W, thank you for answering my very urgent queer-sensitive question. I consider you an expert on snowperson anatomy now, and will be referring all relevant inquiries to you.

To my Sirens: Thank you for making this launch so special and fun! I'm overwhelmed by your support and appreciate each and every one of you.

There are people in my real life who do not know my pen name, but who are supportive and excited for me all the same. One day, I will let my two selves merge, but until then, I remain grateful for your love and support. Thank you for taking me seriously when I talked about writing like it's my job, even before it officially was.

My family: Mom, Dad, Parents-In-Law, Brothers, Sisters, Nieces.

My friends, especially Eileen and Arielle. But also: Abany, Bill, Carly, Cheyenne, Gabby, Gabi, Heather, Jenn, Joey, JT, Jimmy, Krystle, Matt, Melissa, Naz, Roman, Sara, Sarah, Sarah, Susan, Teresa.

And everyone at the climbing gym. Special thanks to this group for ~~letting me dub myself~~ naming me the "best up-and-coming climber of a certain age," and openly acknowledging that *everyone* knows which parking spot is mine.

ABOUT SIENNA

Sienna Mills lives in Atlanta, Georgia, where she spends most of her time dreaming up her next book boyfriend and the woman he's obsessed with.

If she isn't writing, she's with her family.

siennamillsromance.com
sienna@siennamillsromance.com
@siennamillsromance

Charming Player

♡ Best friend's older brother

♡ Inexperienced heroine

♡ Childhood crush

♡ Good girl

Charming Casanova

♡ Brother's best friend

♡ Frenemies to lovers

♡ Reformed player

♡ **Spicy** banter

♡ Good girl

Charming Wanderer

♡ Brother's best friend

♡ Opposites attract

♡ Pining

♡ Reading **spicy book** aloud